PRAISE FOR THE

D0372343

"*The Voiceover Artist* connects a community of disparate ~~~~~~~~ ~~~~~ .ng stars and fading elderly, drunks and dreamers, performers and mutes—who yearn to find their voices and prove their value to the world. In a chain of intimate, first-person narratives, each character takes a turn at the microphone, confessing to the reader the secrets that separate them from the people they love. *The Voiceover Artist* is a compelling and unforgettable exploration of the power of the human voice and the human heart."

— *Valerie Laken*, AUTHOR OF DREAM HOUSE
AND SEPARATE KINGDOMS

"With this voice-driven (literally) novel about a young man (literally) finding his voice, Dave Reidy moves into the front ranks of Chicago writers, Catholic writers, writers about stuttering, and writers about sibling rivalry: a list that will give you some idea of his range and literary ranginess. *The Voiceover Artist* is winning, smart, and generous."

— *David Leavitt*, TWO-TIME PEN/FAULKNER AWARD FINALIST AND
AUTHOR OF THE TWO HOTEL FRANCFORTS: A NOVEL

"I often wonder what happens in a person's life to change him from a boy to a man. But brothers don't change from a brother into something else. They remain brothers. As a man, being and having a brother might start to feel claustrophobic. No way out. Dave Reidy's *The Voiceover Artist* examines this from every angle. This novel is brotherhood, is boyhood, is manhood. How poignant that these characters are searching for their voices while attempting to use these voices to make a living. There is family, life, raw realness to be found in their father's stutter, in their jealousy and love for each other, in every word of Reidy's book."

— *Lindsay Hunter*, AUTHOR OF UGLY GIRLS

"*The Voiceover Artist* is tender and beguiling. It is a wonderful story, told with artful directness about family, faith, forgiveness, and the large human struggle we all face to find our true voice."

—*Scott Turow*, AUTHOR OF TEN BEST-SELLING WORKS OF FICTION, INCLUDING *PRESUMED INNOCENT* AND *IDENTICAL*

"My first thought picking this book up was what if Binx Bolling [of Walker Percy's *The Moviegoer*] were really Catholic and winds up not glib in New Orleans but stuttering in Chicago? This is a completely errant, if not arrant, idea. *The Voiceover Artist* is a broad, ambitious, multifaceted, exacting set of portraits of some very twisted folk. They are their own analysts, viciously jockeying to win. Mr. Reidy can be frightening."

—*Padgett Powell*, WHITING AWARD WINNER AND AUTHOR OF SIX NOVELS, INCLUDING *YOU & ME*

"Woven into the middle of this captivating story is the most accurate depiction of the Chicago improv world that I've ever read. When you open *The Voiceover Artist*, you can smell the stale beer and hear the clever quips."

—*Keegan-Michael Key*, CO-CREATOR AND CO-STAR OF THE COMEDY CENTRAL SERIES *KEY & PEELE*

"Rich and varied . . . an energetic parade of characters and voices . . ."

—*Kirkus Reviews*

"Moving and honest. [. . .] The love-hate relationship between Simon and Connor is a stirring depiction of a troubled sibling bond."

—*Booklist*

THE VOICE OVER ARTIST

DAVE REIDY

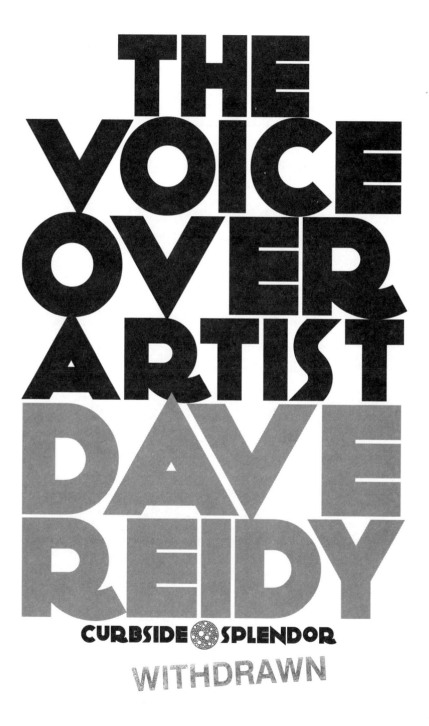

CURBSIDE ⬤ SPLENDOR

Curbside Splendor Publishing

Published by Curbside Splendor Publishing, Inc., Chicago, Illinois in 2015.

First Edition
Copyright © 2015 by Dave Reidy
Library of Congress Control Number: 2015939312

ISBN 978-1-94-043055-3
Edited by Gretchen Kalwinski
Designed by Alban Fischer

Manufactured in the United States of America.

 WWW.CURBSIDESPLENDOR.COM

" . . . what true intimacy entails: supreme attunement alternating with bewildered estrangement."

–*Judith Thurman*

IN *THE NEW YORKER*, SEPTEMBER 13, 2010

Simon Davies

BEHIND A DOOR I'd closed against a father who wasn't home yet and the wintry draft seeping through the living room window, I sat on my bed—my childhood bed, though I was twenty-four years old by then—listening to a clock radio, waiting to hear the right word. What I heard first was the voice of Larry Sellers, a man I considered a better friend to me than my brother ever would be.

From the age of thirteen, I'd devoured Larry's masterful renditions of the bargains to be found in my grocer's freezer—a twenty-count box of Van de Kamp's fish sticks on sale for three ninety-nine, or Dole Fruit and Juice bars for eighty-nine cents a piece—but his run as the voice of Jewel Foods had ended two years ago, and I hadn't heard much of Larry on the radio since then. As he called my attention to the Winter 2007 Sales Event at Peoria's Prairie State Chevrolet, I heard the excess weight in his jowls and detected some shortness of breath, but Larry's voice was still a flawless instrument. I closed my eyes, immersing myself in the warmth of Larry's sonorous performance and floating over the waves of its subtly rhythmic rising and falling.

And then Larry Sellers said the right word: "Financing."

I wasn't in the market for a car loan, so the tingling that climbed the back of my neck had nothing to do with zero-percent rates. The rightness of "financing" lay in its linguistics. "F" was a fricative. A fricative would do the trick.

I slid a greasy fingernail into a ridge on the volume dial and spun it toward me until it clicked. Radio off. I sat in the silence I'd made, a silence that was mine to break.

I pulled in my lower lip. The chapped skin adhered to the ridge of my upper teeth. I drew a breath through my nostrils. Then I forced air against the lip and the teeth, and at the mere thought of voicing the word's first vowel, my esophagus clenched in a wrenching seizure. What air I could snatch was quickly released in frantic nasal snorts. I could have strummed the tendons in my neck like the strings of a lyre. It went on, this strangulation from the inside, for more than two minutes.

When it was over, I triggered it again.

So commenced the process—who could have known how long it would take?—of using the convulsive power of my stutter to jolt my vocal folds from the atrophy that set in seven months after I went silent as a seven-year-old boy. Once the heavy chain that choked and tethered me, my stutter had become the key to my finding a place in the world—outside of this child's room, far from this motherless, brotherless house, and maybe, incomprehensibly, on the radio, among the voices who'd kept me company throughout eighteen years of speechlessness.

Even then, I understood that my stutter and I would not go on exploiting one another so productively. Long after outliving its utility to anything other than itself, the stutter would be at my throat, awaiting any opportunity to take its sadistic pleasure at the expense of everything that mattered to me.

1

Simon

I HAD NEVER done a studio session. I didn't have an agent. I'd started speaking again only three years before. But I already thought of myself as a voiceover artist. Five months after croaking the word that broke my lengthy silence, I decided that telling myself I am something more—and then working to make a truth of that lie—gave me my only hope of ever pulling even with my brother.

In an attempt to nudge my self-conception closer to reality, I volunteered, a couple of weeks after moving (alone) to Chicago in early June 2010, to serve as a lector at St. Asella's, a church a few blocks from my apartment. I supposed that reading scripture aloud before strangers, with no opportunity for a re-take and no engineer to touch up my mistakes, would help to prepare me for the first time I'd step into a sound booth in a professional studio. And St. Asella's, in its summertime desperation for able-voiced volunteers, required no audition, only a stand-here-sit-there training session with a weary liturgical minister and a signed (though unenforceable) commitment to lector weekly through Christmas. So it was that I first found myself lifting a Book of Gospels above my head of straight, dull brown hair and following two altar servers down a church's center aisle to provoke in public the stutter that had prolonged, by many years, the silence I'd chosen as a seven-year-old boy.

The enormous pipe organ boomed in the church's choir loft, which was empty except for the organist. Sunday mass at a thriving parish might have featured a cantor, who would lead the assembled in song. It seemed that someone at St. Asella's had decided to drown out the few singing voices in its anemic congregation. As I walked, I took a waggle: four noiseless, almost imperceptible, lateral shakes of the head where it meets the neck. While rebuilding my voice three years before, I'd discovered that a waggle could ward off the tension that incessantly besieged my vocal folds. In large part because I took waggles whenever I needed them, hiding them, when I could, in a glance at a clock or behind the thoughtful expression of a person solving an equation in his head, I had not suffered a stuttering fit since May 25, 2008—two years, one month and two days before this first attempt at lectoring. I marked the time from my most recent fit as a recovering alcoholic counted the days from her last drink. Why shouldn't I? Stuttering, like alcoholism, is a disease—my father suffered from both conditions—and neither has a sure-fire cure. And just as the urge to drink might clamor a little louder in a stressful situation, so my stutter's grip tightens when I become even a little anxious. As I marched toward the front of that church, the prospect of reading aloud in front of people was only the second most upsetting thing on my mind, so my stutter was giving my waggles all they could handle.

The day before—the last Saturday in June—a pale yellow envelope with a Brooklyn return address had arrived in the mail. Enclosed with a note on heavy, artisanal card stock was a check for $748, the amount I had loaned to Brittany, my (former) girlfriend, to pay for the emergency extraction of her wisdom teeth.

Brittany and I had made plans to move to Chicago together after we left Southern Illinois University as undistinguished members of the 2010 graduating class. Then, at the end of April, just a month before graduation, Brittany told me that she had changed her mind: she would not be moving with me.

I had not seen this coming.

My career prospects—a voiceover artist with a stutter: it doesn't look promising—were one of about thirty potential reasons Brittany would not join me in relocating from downstate Carbondale to Chicago. But the reasons she gave me that day were about Chicago itself: the cold winters, the city's distance from her mother's home in Delaware, and the limited market for rare books, the treasures it was her dream to buy and sell for a living. When I asked where she wanted to go instead, she said she didn't know. Eventually, I understood that wherever Brittany Case was going, I was not welcome.

For the better part of a month, I'd been holding out hope that Brittany would find her new city of residence, Brooklyn, as lonely as I'd found

Chicago and change her mind again. Unless she'd found a job or sold a very rare book, the check suggested that Brittany had decided it was worth the financial and emotional cost of dipping further into her trust fund—the same fund her father was doing time in a federal penitentiary for having nearly emptied—to sever the final tie between us.

The note said only, "Hope you're doing well, Simon. Britt."

I had never called her Britt. Not once. The note's signature hurt more than the check did.

As I relived this moment from the day before—the moment I realized Brittany was never moving to Chicago—just minutes before I was to read Bible stories to the parishioners of St. Asella's, I felt the slipknot around my vocal folds drawing tighter.

At the edge of the sanctuary, I bowed from the waist before the altar, sneaking a waggle on the way down. Then I walked around to the altar's congregation-facing side and placed the tall, red Book of Gospels on the wooden table. I stepped back to accommodate the heft of Fr. James Dunne, the parish's pastor and only priest. As he leaned forward to kiss the altar, I passed through the sanctuary and took the seat reserved for the lector, in the front pew on the left-hand side of the center aisle.

The organist held the final chord of the opening song for several measures and cut it abruptly. Fr. Dunne blessed and greeted the assembled. With my body angled toward the center of the altar, I stole glances at the people around and behind me. Near the front of the dimly lit nave, but not sitting together, were two African-American women dressed in skirt suits and broad-rimmed summer hats. In the front two rows of the narrower pews on the far right side stood six Filipina women of middle age. One of the women held her hands to her chin, the beaded string of a rosary interlaced with her fingers. There were a few older couples whose wealth was visible in their health-club vigor and the quality of their casual weekend clothes. A handful of younger adults, most of them women, sat further back, no closer than the middle rows. I counted five people who looked to be homeless in the last few pews, far behind the Filipinas. Despite the summer heat, one of the homeless women wore a heavy overcoat, and a navy stocking cap pulled low over her eyes. Her cheeks had baked to a deep, brick red in the sun.

The cover of the weekly bulletin I had scanned at the back of the church noted, alongside a faded illustration of a porcelain-complected, heaven-gazing girl I assumed to be St. Asella, that the parish had been founded in 1907 by a small group of nuns dedicated to serving the local Italian immigrants. If the people of St. Asella's had once had everything in common, from homeland to employment prospects to holiday traditions, they did not seem to have much in common anymore.

As Fr. Dunne continued the opening prayer, an aged woman walked slowly up the right side aisle with a four-footed cane in her left hand. At first, I assumed that her gentle, close-lipped smile was a mask intended to conceal the aching pain in her hip or knee, or both. But I understood almost immediately after having it that my first impression was wrong. The woman's smile, I remember thinking, seemed to emanate from within her, an authentic expression of a grace and self-possession I had never possessed. Her husband—they both wore thin wedding bands of dull gold—trailed her. Taking short, unsteady steps, he careened more than he walked, but covered ground no faster than his wife did. He held her elbow with his right hand until they reached the third-row pew. I guessed that this habit had been modified as age took its toll on the man's independence. He was still escorting his wife, but she was leading him.

Also among the assembled were the wraiths that had haunted almost every mass I had ever attended: solitary older men whose loneliness was visible in their wispy, unkempt hair, ill-fitting eyeglasses and ratty windbreakers. I wondered if the men had any family to visit or friends to meet at a diner or corner bar, or if the walk to Sunday mass was their only regular foray out of tiny, dirty apartments. Either way, I wished they had stayed home. They were what I would have been if I had never reclaimed my voice, and they reminded me that a person without relationships is alone, no matter how many people stand around him, no matter how trusty the radio in his bedroom. But forging a friendship with any of the strangers at St. Asella's seemed a remote and distasteful possibility. Only my belief that lectoring would prepare me to make the most of my first voiceover session compelled me to spend an hour in their presence.

At least they were strangers, though. There's something horrible in facing, when you're suffering, someone who really knows you. For a few moments a day, you might fool strangers and yourself that you're feeling better than you are—maybe even doing well, considering the circumstances—until you speak with someone who knows you and you hear the truth of your condition in their voice or see it in their eyes: you are not doing well. Not at all. What I wanted that Sunday was the comfort of being around someone who really knew me, without the aching pain of seeing myself as I was. I wanted the impossible. So it was just as well that my brother Connor, younger than me by two years and more charming and self-assured than I would ever be, had not returned the voice message I'd left more than a week before to tell him that I had made the move to Chicago but Brittany had not. Nothing he could have said or done would have helped much, anyway.

"Lord have mercy," Fr. Dunne said.

The order of the liturgy—somehow, I still knew it by heart from years of attending mass with my family—called for communal repetition of the invocation, but the people of St. Asella's managed only an inarticulate murmur. I made no response at all.

"Christ have mercy," said Fr. Dunne.

Without waiting for a reply he must have known would not come, Fr. Dunne finished the petition—"Lord have mercy," he said—and moved on.

"Glory to God in the Highest."

In response to the priest's prompt, a few voices rose above the congregation's murmuring, but each recited the *Gloria* at its own pace, creating the effect of a tuneless song performed in an arrhythmic round.

I, too, said the words of the *Gloria*, but I wasn't praying. I was preparing—tightly controlling the rate of my exhalation, using just enough breath to power my voice at what I guessed was the ideal volume for amplified public speaking, making it halfway through the prayer before inhaling again and waggling as I did so. Left unchecked by my waggles, the tension creeping around my vocal folds would paralyze them. But the paralysis would not become a full-blown fit unless I acted on the powerful but self-defeating instinct to force the folds open. If I did, my eyelids would flutter, and my chin would nod as if I were emphatically agreeing with something. These histrionics would pull my vocal folds apart for just a moment—long enough to let out one gagging syllable—before the offending tension, fed by the stress and vigor of my effort, slammed them shut again.

Once a fit had started, no combination of mental and corporeal strength could budge the folds. They would remain fused together, despite my nodding and straining, until the tension receded of its own accord or the muscles of my esophagus were exhausted. Managing my stutter was a struggle not only with its symptoms, but against the fit-inducing quack cure I reflexively wanted to provide. The waggles, for their part, were merely an as-needed preventative regimen—generally efficacious, but unpredictably impotent. I lived with the awareness that every word I uttered had the potential to bring me to a sudden, humiliating halt.

At the conclusion of the *Gloria*, Fr. Dunne read a prayer with his palms turned up to a painted ceiling discolored by a century of incense and candle smoke, an image of Jesus being raised bodily to heaven while his disciples, emboldened by their awe, dared to look on. When the prayer was over, the focus of the mass would shift from the priest to me. I swallowed hard, a habit born of my childhood assumption that my stutter was triggered by mucus stuck in my windpipe.

"We ask this through Christ our Lord," Fr. Dunne said.

"Amen."

As everyone else sat down on the hard, lacquered pews, I stepped into the center aisle and approached the altar. I stopped in front of it and bowed my head, as the liturgical coordinator had instructed, then entered the sanctuary and climbed three steps to the ambo. I found the lectionary as I'd left it twenty minutes before: open to the first passage, a red ribbon draped across the page as a bulwark against the movement of machine-chilled air. Lifting the ribbon and laying it on the facing page, I tried once more to repel the encroaching tension with a waggle. Then, taking in a breath, I began.

• • •

DURING THE EIGHTEEN years I was unable to speak, I was certain that I'd need a voice to make myself understood. My mother had tried to get me to learn sign language along with her, but I wasn't having it. No one I knew spoke sign language. What good is it to speak a language that no one you know understands? I had gestures, of course—furrowed brows and puppy-dog eyes, headshakes and nods—but these were blunt instruments. I would need a voice, and the colors and tones my voiceover heroes gave to their words, to show the world who I really was and find my place in it.

My mother died one month after my twenty-third birthday, and Connor moved out of the house and three hours away to Chicago less than a year later. These events—and the horrifying prospect of a life that was little more than an unspeaking stalemate with my father—led to my enrollment in my hometown's junior college, Leyton Community, and to my tortured daily attempts to revive the atrophied tissue of my vocal folds with stutter-induced spasms. Six months of provoking my stutter gave me the strength to gasp a few syllables, but it was seven more months of learning to tame the stutter before I could voice a complete sentence—"My name is Simon"—without shattering it into jagged shards.

With an associate's degree and tenuous control of my stutter, I left the father I blamed for my long silence and moved four hours south to Carbondale to attend Southern Illinois University. That's where I found Brittany. She was beautiful. She was smart. She wasn't much for chit-chat, and my quiet way appealed to her. She was also contrary by nature, and I knew that at least part of the reason she chose me was because I was the last guy on earth her born-rich, smooth-talking father would have chosen for her.

Brittany and I were walking back to my place from a coffee shop, having just broached, for the first time, the subject of life after graduation—where we might live, what we might do for a living. Just the *idea* of making plans like these with Brittany was making me heady, but some part of me must have sensed Brittany's hesitation to envision a time when the credit hours we needed, the school calendar that dictated our time off, and the college-town boredom we'd endured were no longer pushing us together. Because, after all the forward-looking talk that had put such a charge into me, what I told her—what I really believed—was this: "Just because we graduate doesn't mean we have to leave. We *know* we're happy here. We can stay here and be happy."

Brittany looked at me and, in the weak light thrown by a streetlamp half a block in front of us, she smirked and shook her head.

"What?" I asked.

"That's bullshit," she said.

"What is?"

"What you just said."

It was as if Brittany had waved away a smokescreen of my own making. The truth was, I wanted things that Carbondale couldn't give me. To become a voiceover artist, I'd have to live in some version of Radioland, the big city I'd imagined as a boy, home to the Great Voices and the powerful antennas—like birthday candles, their red flames pulsing atop skyscraper cakes—that beamed their sixty-second masterworks to my radio. My line about being happy in Carbondale revealed little more than a safe-seeming untruth I'd sold myself and wanted Brittany to buy, too.

Brittany had understood me beyond my power to make myself understood. My mother had, too. And Connor still did, whether he wanted to or not. Whether I wanted him to or not.

When we were together, Brittany discussed the details of her father's crime only once. He had stolen from her and lied to her, she said. He'd looted a trust that Brittany's grandfather, the last good son of an old Carolinian family, had funded for her. When Brittany came to him as a seventeen-year-old with statements in hand to ask about the plummeting balance, he assured her it was the stock market fluctuating, that she had nothing to worry about, that time and the free market would right the whole thing. Eventually, she might have allowed her father's circumstances to mitigate her anger over the theft. By the time he stole from Brittany, he'd lost almost all of the money he'd misappropriated from investors, the Feds had started sniffing around, and he owed his lawyer three years of back pay. But the lies, Brittany said, she'd never forgive. During her freshman year, Brittany's father was convicted of twenty-seven counts of interstate securities fraud. And the verdict suited Brittany just fine.

In the midst of the same monologue about her father, Brittany told me that she'd rebuked her mother for marrying a man who would defraud his own daughter, for not seeing through her husband's lies, for seeing him, for so long, as something other than what he was. But she also blamed herself.

"Why didn't I see it happening?" she asked. "How could *I* have missed all this?"

I understood at that moment that part of the reason Brittany was with me was because I was incapable of deceiving her as her father had. I wasn't a practiced liar who always had the right word at the ready with a wink and a smile. Just seven months before, I'd spoken my first full sentence in eighteen years. Brittany's need to never again be less cunning and cruel than the people she loved should have worried me, but I buried any worry beneath the pleasure I took in listening to Brittany reveal her innermost self. My voice had delivered me to that moment, but as Brittany made herself understood, I kept my eyes on hers, I nodded at the right times, and I didn't say a word.

I wished I could go back and tell the boy I'd been, the kid who'd yearned for the kind of human connection made impossible by his refusal—and then inability—to speak, that he'd been right about needing a voice, but wrong about connection. How could I have known—alone in my room, daring to believe I might speak again one day—that I'd experience my life's most exhilarating moment of closeness in silence?

• • •

ON A SUNDAY morning in the August before our senior year, Brittany and I lay in bed, relishing the languor of half-sleep.

Brittany broke the silence by saying, "When we first met, I thought you had Asperger's."

I'd heard of Asperger's syndrome, but I didn't know exactly what it was. Even so, my face reddened with new embarrassment at whatever I'd done when I met Brittany to make her think I was strange.

"You're offended now," she said.

"I'm not offended."

Staring at the ceiling, I replayed our first meeting in my mind. We were sitting in our adjacent, assigned seats in the back row of a nearly empty lecture hall, a few minutes before the second class session of a course, "Mathematics 139: Finite Math," we were both taking to fulfill a requirement, when I felt a mobile phone's rhythmic, intermittent vibration in my feet. The vibration came from Brittany's bag, which lay on the floor between us.

Brittany made no move to answer or silence the phone. As the heels of her sandaled feet were tucked up onto the front edge of her chair, making a platform of her bare knees as she examined her nails, I thought it was at least possible that she could not feel the vibration.

So I waggled, leaned toward her, and said, "Your phone is ringing."

The look she gave me communicated, in not so many words, that no one had ever told her anything more obvious and less helpful.

"Thanks," she said, leaving her phone where it was.

The sting of the exchange stayed with me throughout the hour-long lecture. By the time the professor dismissed us, I'd decided I could either say something to this woman before she left, or sit next to her in uncomfortable silence, twice a week, for the next fifteen weeks. So I hid a waggle in a glance at the floor and said, "See you next week, then."

Brittany, already heading for the exit, responded with only one word: "Yep."

But all-importantly, she smiled just a little as she said it.

Looking back, I could see that I'd been awkward, but I couldn't recall that I'd done anything pathological, or even strange, which made me feel worse. Maybe *everything* I did was strange, and I just couldn't see it.

I waited another moment before I said, "What made you think I had Asperger's?"

"Well, I thought your little headshakes were a tic or something."

That was reasonable. I couldn't conceal every waggle I needed, and most people needed no waggles at all.

"And I thought you were, you know, missing social cues," she said.

I groaned at the thought that I was giving this impression to everyone I met. "It's not that I *miss* them," I said. "It's just that, sometimes, I don't know what to say when I *see* them."

"I get that now."

"I know what *other* people might say," I said, "but I didn't speak for almost two decades. I haven't had enough conversations to know what *I* should say."

"I know."

"Or I know what I *should* say, but I really want to say something else, and I'm trying to figure out if what I want to say will make trouble."

"Simon," she said. "I know."

I waggled and tried again. "It's like, I get the cues, but I'm still learning my lines."

I turned my head to look at Brittany. She rolled her eyes and threw off the covers.

"What?" I asked.

"Your metaphor melted down, Simon," she said, getting out of bed.

"Where are you going?"

"To the bathroom," she said. "You should've come on to me a half hour ago. You missed that cue."

● ● ●

THE FOLLOWING APRIL, on the night before Connor made his only visit to Carbondale, Brittany was watching television on the couch in my apartment, a one-bedroom on the first floor of an old home long since divided into rental units. Her bare legs were hugged to her chest and swaddled in a thin fleece blanket. I was sitting alongside her, but only the hem of her blanket touched me. Brittany didn't like to be touched while she watched television. "I can't concentrate if there's touching," she'd say.

On the old Panasonic box I'd purchased at a Carbondale garage sale, a woman in an orange jumpsuit was bemoaning her imprisonment for a capital crime—the murder of her former lover—that she swore she hadn't committed. The frizzy ends of the woman's ponytail whipped back and forth, punctuating her denial. Brittany leaned her head over her knees, hanging on the woman's every word.

I had decided in the show's first five minutes that I agreed with its producers: this woman had killed her boyfriend. But I kept watching and kept my seat. Near the end of a dinner of spaghetti and jarred tomato sauce, I'd agreed to put off until after the show a conversation about Connor's visit to Carbondale the next day. I knew that Brittany's doing what I planned to ask of her became less likely with each passing minute, so I wanted to be with her when the credits rolled. And even without touching her, sitting close to her made me excited for what lay ahead for us in Chicago.

After some difficult conversations on the matter, Brittany had finally decided to move to Chicago with me. We would share an apartment and try to turn our longtime professional dreams into careers. I'd look for representation as a voiceover artist, and Brittany would scour estate sales and auctions to build her stock of the rare books she hoped to buy and sell for a living.

We had money saved, though Brittany had much less than she'd expected. By the time her father was indicted, the balance in her trust, once more than four hundred thousand dollars, had been reduced to nine thousand. To preserve what capital remained for her entry into the rare-books business, she'd forsaken the heavy financial burden of a private-college education for the low tuition and renowned rare-volumes collection of Southern Illinois University.

Both of us blamed our fathers for the fact that our lives were less than what they might have been. But Brittany had started out at a higher station than I and fallen further—if her father hadn't defrauded her, Brittany and I never would have met.

My radio-ready voice and years of experience as a busboy had helped me land a job as a server at The Nile, Carbondale's finest restaurant, a white-tablecloth establishment frequented by local professionals and visiting university trustees. For almost two years, I'd worked five dinner shifts per week and, with scholarships and grants covering most of my tuition and fees, had saved almost $11,000. I offered my savings for our living expenses so that Brittany could use what remained of her inheritance to buy the right rare books. I wanted her to have her dream job, despite the damage her father had done. I wanted the same for myself.

As the woman on TV attempted to express to the unseen television interviewer how much her murdered lover meant to her, and convince the audience she never could have harmed him, she sucked her lips into her mouth and shook her head, trembling.

"Oh, Jesus," Brittany said, sitting back. "She had me until the fake crying."

"She did it," I said.

"Yeah," Brittany said over a sigh. "She did."

As the prisoner pinched the bridge of her nose in tearful silence, Brittany found the remote in a blanket fold and turned off the television. She leaned against me and pressed her lips to mine as consolation for the touching we'd forgone while the prisoner told her lies.

Then Brittany laid her head on the far arm of the couch and stretched out her long legs, putting her feet in my lap.

"So why did your brother wait until a month before graduation to visit you?" she asked.

"He doesn't have many free nights," I said. "He's always doing some kind of show."

"He's not doing a show tomorrow night?"

I waggled. "I guess he's taking a night off."

I understood that Brittany, in her way, had given me a chance to tell her something meaningful about my relationship with my brother. I could have confessed that our longstanding refusal to apologize to each other for anything made things between us difficult. I could have admitted that I hadn't invited Connor to visit me in Carbondale until a week before, that I'd withheld the invitation until I was certain that Brittany and I were moving to Chicago and that my brother's one-night stay would give me every occasion to unveil to him a life that was already better—and more promising—than either of us had imagined my life could ever be. I could have told Brittany I loved my brother but was plagued every day by my fear that his dazzling talent for improvisation and comedy, and the success his gifts stood to bring him, would put him beyond the reach of my ambition and my love. But I didn't say any of these things. I answered Brittany's question as if what she really wanted to understand were the scheduling challenges of the working comic actor, and she didn't push me for more.

"So what's he like?" Brittany asked, sliding her hand under the blanket and scratching her bare thigh with the crescent-moon whites of her fingernails.

At that question, my mind generated a cloud of adjectives that described my brother: talented, charismatic, dedicated, pained, ambitious, impatient, selfish, determined, unflappable, amazing. Getting a little uncomfortable with my silence, I waggled and picked one.

"He's amazing."

Brittany laughed at me. "He's *amazing*?"

I shrugged again. "He is."

"How is he amazing?"

"Well, for one thing, he creates characters and they're real. Like, believable."

"What else?"

She was daring me to make her care about Connor's visit.

"He can make almost anyone laugh," I said.

"Amazing!" Brittany said, mocking me with her smile, which was somehow made even sexier by her sarcasm. "What else?"

"He knows me better than anyone."

The wide, brown eyes Brittany had inherited from her Laotian mother narrowed and darkened.

I waggled again and made a weak attempt to undo my mistake. "But not as well as you know me."

Pulling her feet away, Brittany rolled onto her side and wrapped the blanket tightly around her. I recognized a pattern it had taken me months to identify and understand: when she was hurt even a little, Brittany became furious with herself, incredulous that after all she had been through and how little she expected of anyone, she could still be negatively affected by another person's words or actions. The pain surprised her every time. I'd stopped wondering why Brittany couldn't see that her vulnerability, like my stutter, could be chased away but never banished. This was another lesson about personal connections that I'd learned the hard way: that my seeing Brittany as she was—and loving her—could never guarantee that she'd see and accept herself.

I put my hand on the bump in the blanket that was her ankle.

"Don't," she said, kicking me.

I sat in purposeful silence, letting her anger burn off. To scatter the tension surrounding my vocal folds, I took one waggle, and another, and then a third.

Then I said, "Connor knew me when I couldn't talk."

This was where I should have started. Connor had seen me struggle and stew in my long silence. He had witnessed my constant, soundless screaming match with our father. No one, except our mother, had known the silent me—for eighteen years, the *only* me—better than Connor had.

"He knew me then, and you know me *now*," I continued. "Now, nobody knows me better than you do."

It was true. Insofar as my being able to speak had changed me, Connor hardly knew me anymore.

Brittany's body seemed to soften a little, but she said nothing. Her eyes were pointed somewhere beneath the dark television set, her lower jaw thrust out. There was no talking her out of her inward-aimed fury. She would take it to bed with her.

Because of my gaffe, the last reasonable moment I had to ask Brittany to change her plans for the following afternoon, so that we could make the most of Connor's brief visit, was also the least favorable. But I tried anyway.

"Connor gets here around four tomorrow," I said, softly.

"I'm at the hospital then."

I knew this, of course. Brittany volunteered every Tuesday afternoon in the neo-natal intensive care unit of the university hospital—in the two years I had known her, she had missed one shift, on account of stomach flu. Her job was to hold and feed incompatible-with-life newborns whose parents were gone, already mourning an imminent death that simply hadn't happened yet. It was an unlikely fit for a woman who sought daily refuge from human interaction in the windowless, climate-controlled rooms that housed the leather-bound books she studied. Brittany did not stop to coo over babies in strollers and, outside of my apartment, did not so much as stroke my head or hold my hand. I'd always wanted to watch Brittany cradling the infants, to see that soft part of her even through glass, but she would not allow it—the hospital would not allow it, she said—so I was left with imagined glimpses of her standing stiff-legged, holding other people's dying children, loving them as she loved me: as much and as little as she could.

"As it stands, we'll be asleep about half the time Connor is here." Feeling my throat tighten, I waggled twice. "So could you find a substitute for your shift tomorrow?"

She shook her head. "No."

"It's still almost a full day's notice. I can make the calls for you."

Brittany met my eyes. "No."

"We can say you're sick."

"No, Simon!"

She stared at me, driving home her refusal with her cold gaze, then turned her face toward the television again. I said nothing more.

She had never admitted as much to me, but Brittany seemed to bear the burden of a responsibility to me that was similar to her sense of responsibility to them, as if she was certain that I—like the babies—would have no one if not for her. As I sat silently beside her, I reminded myself that even if Brittany were to leave me—and the thought of her leaving made me sick to my stomach—I would still have someone the other motherless children did not: I would have Connor.

● ● ●

WHEN CONNOR CALLED from the road and said he'd be later than expected, I was relieved that Brittany hadn't missed her shift at the hospital just to wait around for my brother. My relief evaporated when she returned home crying.

"What's wrong?" I asked.

There were pouches beneath her eyes, and her cheeks were bright red. She stalked past me without a word and shut herself in the bedroom.

I walked slowly to the bedroom door and cracked it. Brittany was in bed, everything but the crown of her head buried under the covers.

"What is it?" I whispered.

Her only reply was a sniffle. But I couldn't bring myself to leave her alone—not without knowing why she was crying.

"What happened?"

Brittany made a guttural sound from beneath the blankets and rolled over to face the far wall.

Taking a waggle, I pushed the door and let the heavy brass handle hit the wall. "I'm trying to help!"

Brittany threw the covers down to her waist and yelled, "You can't help!"

She waited another minute for me to leave. I didn't. *I couldn't.* I still had no idea why she was crying.

With her back to me, Brittany wiped her eyes with her palms. Then she closed a nostril with her wrist and sniffed. "I was holding a baby girl today," she said.

I waggled again and whispered, "Yeah."

"And she died."

So far as I knew, this was the first time, in the hundreds of hours Brittany had spent holding doomed infants, that a child had died in her arms.

I wanted to crawl into the bed and hold her but knew it was the wrong thing to do.

"I'm so sorry," I said.

I watched her, trying to come up with some comfort apart from the loving words she would not accept. I waited another moment in the hopes that she would roll toward me and wave me into the bed beside her. But Brittany's only movements were the still irregular swelling and shrinking of her rib cage.

So I backed out of the bedroom and pulled the door closed, watching her for any last-second change of heart even as I admitted to myself that the most helpful thing I could do for Brittany was leave her alone.

● ● ●

SHE WAS ASLEEP—or still in bed, anyway—when Connor arrived that day.

I met my brother at the back door with an index finger over my lips, led him out the French doors that opened from the living room onto my unit's section of the wraparound porch and asked him to wait there. I returned to the kitchen to pour my brother his drink of choice, bourbon neat, and opened a bottle of light beer for myself. Drinking, like high emotion, hindered my management of my stutter, so I was determined to drink slowly that night. I wasn't about to risk having a fit in front of Connor.

I handed the glass of bourbon to Connor and closed the French doors.

"Should I come back later?" Connor whispered.

"No, you're fine," I said. "Brittany is sleeping. She volunteers at the hospital in the neo-natal intensive care unit, and a baby died while she was holding it."

"Today?"

"Yeah."

"Jesus," Connor said. "Is she in trouble?"

"No, no. None of the babies she works with have more than a few weeks to live."

"Oh," Connor said, seeming baffled. "Okay."

"She'll be up soon," I said. "If she isn't, you'll meet her in the morning."

I unfolded an aluminum lawn chair for him, not so much hiding the little waggle I took as drawing attention away from it, like a magician showing an empty palm during a card trick.

"How was the drive?"

"Long," Connor said. "Longer than it had to be. I got a late start."

"Did you have an audition or something?"

Connor shook his head and swallowed a mouthful of my cheap bourbon without wincing. "I went on for a friend of mine in a late show last night. The pay was free drinks, and I was very well paid."

I smiled and took a sip of my beer.

"Then I overslept and got caught in some rush-hour traffic south of Chicago," he said.

"How long were you driving?"

"What is it? Ten?"

"Almost."

"Six and a half hours."

"Ouch."

"Yeah."

I waggled. "If you want to stay another night to make it worth the drive, you're welcome to."

Connor shook his head and sat up in his seat. "Nah. I want to be back onstage tomorrow night."

He took a deep sip of his bourbon and swallowed, and I poured more beer between my lips.

"So you're moving to Chicago," Connor said.

"Yeah."

"And your girlfriend is coming with you?"

"Yes."

"And you're living together?"

"Yes."

Connor nodded, the edges of his lips curled downward and his eyes smiling.

"You think that's a bad idea."

"No, no," Connor said. "It sounds fantastic."

By which he meant it sounded terrible. Though Brittany's agreeing to join me in Chicago was the signature success of my life to date, for Connor, sharing a small apartment with one woman, day after day, would have been unbearable. Onstage, he could make an audience believe he was a caring husband or an attentive boyfriend. Offstage, Connor wanted no part of intimacy. Even the questions he asked me were electrified prods he waved to keep me from getting too close.

"What'll you do for work?" Connor asked.

I settled into the fabric straps of my folding chair and waggled. "Voiceover."

Connor laughed.

"What."

"What do you mean, 'what?' It's at least a little funny, Simon. If I played a character who spent eighteen years in a hospital bed and decided to try out for the Olympic team after a jog in the park, I'd get laughs. Even on an off night. Fuck, that's a good idea. I'd write it down except that improvisers don't write anything down."

I let a barking dog in the neighbor's yard fill the space where Connor was expecting a laugh. You don't go two speechless decades without learning to use silence the way Connor used humor: as a weapon.

"Look," Connor said, "you should definitely try it. You've got a great voice—you've got my voice, actually."

Connor wasn't wrong. He and I had both been surprised to find, after my eighteen-year silence, that my voice sounded just like his.

"But, so you know, it's tough to break into voiceover," he said. "My agent said it's easier to get on-camera work in a national TV spot than to get a local radio commercial in Chicago. Most of that work goes to the old guys who've been doing it for years."

Part of me was warmed by the thought of the radio voices of my youth—especially my hero, Larry Sellers—holding their ground.

"Everything is harder than you think it'll be," Connor said.

"Breaking into voiceover can't be much harder than rebuilding my voice," I said.

Connor chuckled, holding his glass in front of his lips. "It might take about as long." He took a sip of bourbon and shook his head as he swallowed. "But if anybody can do it—"

Connor drained the rest of the whiskey from his glass, leaving his halfhearted encouragement half-finished.

"And if I ever do voiceover," Connor continued, "I won't use my normal voice. You can have it."

So there it was. Connor was not impressed with my life or prospects. As my determination rose on a tide of anger, I wondered if this was the reaction I had *really* wanted from Connor, if I'd known that his disdain would motivate me more than his encouragement ever could.

I took two more swallows of beer. "So how are things for you?"

"Good," Connor said, playing with his empty glass.

"You're doing shows?"

"Every night," Connor said. "Tonight is my first night off in—" He squinted, calculating. "Three months?"

"Wow."

"Trying to get as many reps as I can. That's how you get better."

I nodded coolly at what I took to be more unsolicited, condescending advice. Then I asked, "Who are you on with tomorrow?"

"Just some guys I know."

"A group?"

"Yeah."

"What's the name?"

My brother stared at me for a moment through slightly narrowed eyes. "You did this last time I saw you."

"What?"

"You asked me the name of the group."

"I like hearing the names."

"They're never funny."

I waggled and said, "That's why I like hearing them."

Connor shook his head. "I'm not saying."

"That's fine," I said. "You don't have to."

I watched Connor try to decide if telling me the name was victory or surrender in the face of the little trap I'd set for him.

"The point is, these guys are really good. They've had a show running at this bar for two years. One of them was a finalist for a correspondent slot on *The Daily Show*."

"So he didn't get it."

"No."

"Are you playing with them full time?"

"No," Connor said. "One of their guys is on an audition in L.A. and they asked me to fill in for him."

"Oh."

"They said they might want to make me a permanent member, though." Connor glanced down at his empty glass, and then raised his eyes to mine again. "So, yeah. Things are pretty good."

But things were not good for Connor. Sure, he was still handsome. A mess of curly brown hair spilled over his forehead, accentuating by contrast the pale green of his eyes, and a day's beard growth darkened his strong, cleft chin. Even so, he looked worn from the inside out in a way that a good night's sleep wouldn't fix. And in the rundown of his life in comedy, he hadn't mentioned New York even once. That told me everything I needed to know about how things were going for my brother.

New York was the place where Connor saw himself when he'd made it in comedy. His fixation had started with *Saturday Night Live* but, at some point, the lights of 30 Rockefeller Plaza glowed so intensely in Connor's mind that they illumined the entire city. For the past four years, Connor had been working in Chicago to win the attention of New York, and New York had paid him no mind. The pleasure I took in my brother's struggles was fleeting—it meant nothing for me to catch up with Connor if our evenness was measured in unhappiness—but I was secretly pleased that he'd claimed things were going well for him when they were not. It was the first time I could remember that my brother had deemed me peer enough—or threat enough—to tell me such a lie.

"Another drink?" I asked him.

"Sure."

Connor held up his glass by the base. I grabbed it around the middle, accidentally covering his thumb with one of my fingers for just an instant. At this glancing contact, I realized that Connor and I had not so much as shaken hands when he arrived, and it seemed too late by then to do anything of the kind.

I pitched my empty beer bottle into the plastic garbage can in the kitchen. Pouring Connor's whiskey, I took two waggles and vowed to drink my next beer more slowly. Going drink for drink with Connor was certain to bring the evening—or my participation in it—to a stuttering, premature, and potentially mortifying end.

Carrying a full bottle of beer and a glass of bourbon, I reached the open porch doors and stopped. Brittany and Connor were standing next to one another, smiling. It looked as if they had just shaken hands.

"You're up," I said.

Brittany turned to me, opened her eyes wide, and let her smile fall. "You sound *exactly* like him," she said. "Exactly."

I handed Connor his whiskey, feeling hurt and a little indignant that my girlfriend had said that *I* sound like *my brother*, instead of the other way around.

She turned back to Connor. "How did that happen?"

"Well," Connor said, "I like to think that when Simon was teaching himself to talk, he had his pick of any voice he wanted and chose mine."

Brittany laughed.

It seemed that her nap had lifted her out of the horror of her afternoon, at least for the moment. She had ironed her hair flat, except at the ends, which curved in and brushed against her jawbone. Her small, high-set breasts stretched the vertical ribbing of her pale green tank top, the tail of which hung over the waistband of her favorite pair of short nylon shorts. An open black hoodie hung loosely over her arms. I knew her well enough to know she had applied a little makeup to her eyes and considered each piece of clothing she was wearing, but Brittany always gave the impression that her beauty was effortless, which made her all the more beautiful.

For his part, with a second whiskey in hand and an attractive, one-woman audience to win over—with someone besides *me* around—Connor seemed more comfortable already.

I touched Brittany's elbow and, as she turned to face me, she pulled it out of my fingertips.

"Drink?" I asked.

She looked over the edge of Connor's glass. "Bourbon, please."

A waggle delayed my reply. "Bourbon it is."

"Thank you, baby."

I set my beer bottle on the warped wood planks of the porch, sending a warm rush to my head. Then I went inside, pulled a second glass from a cabinet, and poured another bourbon, feeling buzzed and buoyed that Brittany was awake and feeling social, and that she and Connor were hitting it off. He was even flirting a little, which I took to be a harmless expression of our brotherly rivalry. Despite his tardiness and Brittany's grief, my brother's visit was beginning to take the shape that I had hoped it would.

I returned to the porch to find Connor seated and Brittany standing over him. I handed Brittany her glass and picked up my beer.

"This is easily three shots, Simon," Brittany said, holding up her glass and smiling.

I waggled. "I figured I'd save myself a trip."

"Next time in, you'll have to carry *her*," Connor said.

Brittany flashed Connor a hard look that softened when she read the hint of a smile on his face. "We'll see who's carrying who."

She took a swig of bourbon, held it in her mouth for a moment, swallowed and coughed. Connor laughed, letting his head fall back against the aluminum frame of his chair.

I held my beer bottle in the air. "I'd like to make a toast."

Connor stared at me. Then, with an amused look on his face, he stood up and raised his glass.

I waggled, suddenly embarrassed by the formality of my gesture. I had never given a toast before. I stood there between the two people who knew me best, awash in feelings that were too predictable, too revealing, or too sentimental to be given words and voice. As Brittany and Connor waited and tension mounted in my neck, I waggled again and said, "To the Windy City!"

Connor laughed. "He sounds like a radio commercial already."

I angled my bottle toward Connor's tumbler and made contact with it just as Brittany's did. Then I chased Brittany's retreating hand hungrily, as if the tapping of my bottleneck against her glass would somehow make binding our spoken plans and promises. The bottle caught only her knuckle, a flesh-muted tap that made no sound. I would have tried again, but Brittany was already drinking the toast, so I put the mouth of the bottle to my lips, tipped it back, and gulped.

● ● ●

THE MONDAY AFTER my debut as a lector at St. Asella's, I started pursuing the part of my Chicago dream that still stood a chance: the part that had nothing to do with Brittany.

I plugged a gently used microphone into my computer and recorded the radio commercials I had been rehearsing for weeks: one for the Chicago Blackhawks, another for Arc Home Electronics, and a spot for the Ulysses S. Grant Museum in Galena, Illinois. Then I cut together a one-minute medley that demonstrated high-quality performance across my wide range of energies, tempos, volumes and tones. My deliveries extended from whispered to stentorian and from gentle to aggressive, but I did only one voice—my own—and played only one role: myself. The kind of voiceover work I wanted to do was the kind I'd always appreciated most, the kind Larry Sellers did: straight announcement, which relied upon the artist's virtuosic vocal ability and won the listener's attention with a subconscious appeal to her innate desire for perfection. In a commercial that called for straight announcement, the meaning of the words mattered less than how the words were said. And characters didn't matter at all.

If the voiceover agents want someone who creates characters, I thought, *they'll have to find Connor.*

Early Tuesday morning, I burned my demo onto seven CDs and

scrawled my name and phone number on their non-writable sides in permanent marker. I stuffed the CDs into envelopes along with folded copies of my cover letter, the characters of which bore the white striations left behind by a nearly empty ink cartridge. With the envelopes in my otherwise empty messenger bag, I headed out on foot.

The first agency I visited was Skyline Talent, the organization that had represented Larry Sellers for much of his long career. Sellers had grown up in Sampere, a small, Central Illinois township near my hometown of Leyton. Since coming to Chicago in the 1970s, he'd done national radio commercials and had been, for almost two decades, the voice of Jewel Food Stores. I'd studied Larry Sellers' work since I was thirteen years old, and it was while listening to one of Larry's performances that I selected the word I'd use to induce the seizures, spasms and fits that brought back my vocal muscles from atrophy. *"Financing."* Because of the agency's connection to Larry Sellers, and the inseparability, in my own mind, of the sound of his voice from the existence of mine, the four-block walk from my apartment to the offices of Skyline Talent was more pilgrimage than errand.

I walked through the front door and left my demo in the hands of the receptionist. Then I turned around and walked out. I didn't introduce myself or ask to speak to any agents—not at Skyline, not at any agency. I wasn't interested in, or good at, making small talk. Besides, I saw no reason to put a face to my voice. My demo was my good side, and I wanted the agents to see it before they knew anything else about me.

By noon on Tuesday, back at my apartment, all the momentum I'd felt while making and delivering my demo was gone. In its place was a gloomy understanding that simply *seeing* myself as a voiceover artist did not make me one. I hadn't considered, until just then, the sheer number of things that had to happen before an agent would call with an offer to represent me. A receptionist would have to put my demo in the hands of an agent. That agent would have to decide the demo was worth listening to, with nothing more to go on than a cover letter. Any agent who *did* decide, against her better judgment, to give my demo a chance would have to find the time and attention to listen to it. And even if she found the time, there was no telling if she'd like my work. If having talent wasn't enough to ensure Connor's success, how could it guarantee my own? I began to see each of my morning deliveries as a missed opportunity. With a chance to do any of them again, I would have gladly initiated and endured small talk to increase, by even a fraction of a percentage, the likelihood that an agent would give my demo a fair listen.

Whenever I find myself waiting, I look for a way to prepare for what I'm waiting for. That's how I now understand all the hours I spent as a kid sitting on my bed with a radio in my lap, listening to commercials: I was preparing, even when I could not speak, to be a voiceover artist. I picked up my lector's workbook and turned to the scripture readings I was scheduled to deliver this coming Sunday in my second outing as a lector at St. Asella's. Maybe, I thought, it is preparation that will separate me, in a way that talent alone cannot, from other voiceover artists with a range and timbre like mine.

So I dug into the text. Over more than ten recitations, I sought out the natural rhythm of each passage and gave voice to it. I practiced the multi-syllabic Hebrew and Canaanite names in the first reading until they sounded as natural on my lips as my mother's name, and repeated the Greek names of the cities mentioned in the second reading until their pronunciations were as familiar to me as those of Leyton and Peoria. When I'd honed my delivery of each reading, I closed the workbook. Part of preparing effectively, it seemed to me, was knowing when you were doing more harm than good to your voice and performance. All told, my preparation for Sunday had eaten up only ninety minutes. It was still Tuesday, and only two in the afternoon.

Connor still hadn't called me back. The prospect of calling him again, conceding my need of him even as I waited helplessly for some share of success that might rival his, seemed doubly debasing. I held my phone, waiting another minute for it to come to life in my hand and for Connor's name to appear on the pale blue screen. Then I opened the phone's address book, arrowed down to my brother's name, and selected it. Connor did not answer. I imagined him in active pursuit of his own dream, at work without waiting, his phone ringing silently in the small pocket of a backpack he'd thrown in the corner of a rehearsal space somewhere on Chicago's North Side. I listened to his voice—my voice, but steeped in confidence—in the outgoing message and hung up.

I lay down on the dusty upholstery of my couch, trying to persuade myself that an afternoon with good work already done and nothing left to do was a luxury I should enjoy. I could take a nap. I could read a book. I could get out and explore my new neighborhood. But what I did instead was think of Brittany. With equal parts imagining and recollection, I felt her breath on my neck as she rubbed herself against me, acting out the closeness we'd made with our voices and our attentiveness. Alone in my apartment, I acted out my present deprivation with a hand down the front of pants still buttoned, as if I might finish before I realized what I was doing.

2

Young Simon

SIMON WATCHED THROUGH his open bedroom door as his mother, May, tried to roust his father from an easy chair.

"I— I— I'll s— stay h— home with C— Connor," Frank said, keeping his eyes on the television. "He— he's s— still f— f— feverish."

"Connor is coming with us," May said.

Simon's father looked up at his wife. "He's s— s— still sick, m— May!"

"He's fine, actually. His fever broke last night."

"H— he should be h— here!" he said. "R— r— resting!"

"Frank," she said, calmly. "Please."

Out in the yard, Simon climbed up and into the back seat of the pickup truck and scooted to its far side. He pulled a seatbelt across his lap and buckled it at his right hip. Connor hoisted himself up on the truck step, squealed as he fell forward into the cab, and took the seat next to the near window. May leaned in and drew Connor's seat belt from its sheath.

"I don't need the seat belt, mommy," Connor said.

"Everyone needs a seat belt," May said.

"Not me, mommy. I can hold on. See?"

"I see," she said, and clicked the tongue of the buckle into its clasp. May looked up at her older son and found that he was already strapped in safely. "Oh!" she said. "Thank you for buckling yourself, Simon."

Simon did not reply.

"Next time I'll buckle myself, mommy," Connor said.

"Okay," May said.

Frank covered the three-and-a-half miles to St. Paul's, the only Catholic parish in Leyton, in less than five minutes, delivering himself and his family to church ten minutes before mass would start. Having unbuckled himself and announced his achievement, Connor was lifted out of the back seat by his mother.

"Whoa!" Connor said. "You're strong, mommy!"

May laughed. "Well, thank you!"

She extended a hand to Simon, but he ignored it and jumped down to the asphalt. Cloaked in the solitude of his newly adopted silence, Simon felt rugged and brave. No one could make him say how his father had failed him. No one could make Simon say a word.

As they neared the church doors, Frank said, "I— I— I'm having a cigarette."

"Okay," May said. "We'll see you inside."

"See you inside, daddy," Connor said, turning his head to smile at his unsmiling father.

On another day, Simon would have gladly followed his father to the patch of grass beside the church doors and pulled needles off the evergreen shrubs while Frank smoked. But today, Simon followed his mother into the flowers-and-old-people smell of the church, hoping that his father felt very much alone.

● ● ●

FEVER AND SORE throat had kept Simon out of second grade the previous Friday and put him in bed early Friday night. Before sunrise on Saturday morning, he walked into the dark living room to find an empty pizza box on the folding tray next to his father's recliner and, on the couch, a plate with the crusts—Connor never ate the crusts—of three pieces of pizza. Standing with one bare foot on top of the other, Simon fretted that he had missed out on some fun with his father, fun that could neither be recreated nor recouped. Later that morning, Simon heard his mother telling his father that Connor woke up with a throat so sore he wouldn't talk, and that she'd be taking Connor to see the doctor. Simon was not happy that his brother's throat was sore, but he was not sad, either. Simon had been sick; now, it was Connor's turn to be.

When his father went out to rake the leaves in the yard, Simon returned to his bedroom, sat on the bed with his radio in his lap, and listened to the voices. They spoke of football and test drives and lawn tractors. Simon repeated after the voices, the way that Connor repeated after the television characters, and counted how many words he could speak before his stutter caught one in his throat and clutched it tight. Simon's all-time record was six consecutive, cleanly repeated words. That Saturday morning, his best was three in a row.

When Frank opened Simon's bedroom door, Simon's first thought was that he was in trouble.

Frank's flannel shirtsleeves were cuffed to the elbow and he smelled of wet leaves.

"W— we're going into t— town," Frank said.

The moment his father finished speaking, Simon turned off the radio and returned it to the top of his wooden bedside table. Then he hopped down off of his bed and followed Frank out of the house. The leaves from the two big oaks were gone from the front lawn but still littered the larger sideyard, covering most of the orange and yellow blooms of the marigolds in his mother's garden. A black mound of leaves smoldered, sending wisps of gray smoke into the wind. It seemed strange to Simon that his father was leaving a chore half done, but he didn't mention it.

Most of the four-mile drive between the Davies residence and Leyton town square was two-lane highway. Simon sat in the front seat, fighting the urge to smile as his mind made a flipbook of the rows of tall, dying corn stalks on either side of the road. It's not that a trip into town was a rare event. Frank would bring Simon and Connor into town whenever their mother spent the better part of a Saturday at a baby or bridal shower. What made today different was that Connor was not along for the ride, which meant that Simon now had what Connor had enjoyed the night before while Simon lay in bed breaking a fever: their father all to himself.

At the western boundary of incorporated Leyton, Frank slowed at a stop sign and rolled through an empty intersection. To Simon, whose closest neighbor lived an eighth of a mile away, the modest one-story homes that lined both sides of the street seemed to be just inches away from each other. Simon wondered if any of his classmates lived in these houses. He had never been invited to a classmate's home, and Simon's own home was, as he'd heard his mother say before, seldom presentable, even if the visitors were just kids.

"Kids have parents," May would say.

The streets surrounding Leyton's town square were paved in red brick. As the truck's worn tires rumbled over the masonry, Simon stared out the windshield, and then his father's window, at the obelisk at the center of the square. The pointed column reminded Simon of the big monument in Washington, D.C., a picture of which hung above the blackboard in his classroom. Simon figured the smaller version commemorated something, but what was a mystery to him. The idea that he and his father might solve that mystery together made Simon want to smile again.

Frank parked the pickup two storefronts down from the confectioner's. Simon unlatched the passenger-side door and kicked it open with his right foot. He shoved the door closed, then ran around the front of the truck to the window of the candy store, pressing his nose to the glass and cupping his hands at the side of his head to better see the jars and boxes filled with sweets.

"T— t—"

Take your face off the glass.

Simon knew what his father was trying to say, but he knew better than to do what his father said before he had finished saying it. He kept his face and hands where they were.

"T— take your f— face off that glass."

Simon stepped back as soon as his father had finished speaking. He eyed the smudges he'd left on the window and felt bad, but figured that trying to wipe them off with the sleeve of his shirt would only make his father angry.

Frank pulled open the candy store's door, ringing the rusty bells that hung down its interior side. Simon rushed in ahead of him and stood over the central display: clear plastic boxes, four across and six rows high, tiered up and back like stadium seating, each box protecting a different treat from the open air. Simon ogled loose chocolate-covered raisins, chocolate-covered almonds, and malted-milk balls as densely packed and plentiful as the multi-colored plastic balls in the nets at the Chuck E. Cheese in Peoria. There were also individually wrapped hard candies: root-beer barrels, peppermint swirls and butterscotch disks. Beneath one of the scratched plastic box lids were several pounds of cashews, a favorite of Simon's father.

"C— candy," Simon remembered his father telling him, "is k— kids' s— stuff."

Sensing that his father's patience for browsing was running short, Simon hurried to the shelves lined with cardboard boxes of wrapped candies he had never seen anywhere outside this store. They had names like Necco and Beemans and Zotz. Something about the names and the letterforms on the wrappers told Simon that these were the kind of candies his father might have enjoyed when he was a kid.

"A— a— all right, ch— choose something," Frank said.

Simon walked straight to the store's front counter, no longer a browser but a serious buyer. Suckers were his candy of choice. They were sweet from start to finish, and each had a clean, white paper stick that kept his hands from getting sticky. But what Simon liked best about suckers was his recent discovery that, when he was actively working a sucker, melting its layers of hard sugar with his tongue, people were more likely to ask him yes-or-no questions that he could answer with a nod or a shrug instead of a stuttered word. Only Connor's presence did more than a sucker to ensure that no one asked Simon to speak. Connor could make himself sound like the cartoon characters on TV and mimic the announcers who narrated his father's ballgames. Even when Connor spoke in his regular voice, people listened to him, and they laughed right when Connor wanted them to.

Simon stood on his toes and reached into a fish bowl filled with Dum Dums. When he pulled his hand out, he was holding two suckers—one butterscotch-flavored, the other cherry soda. He looked up at his father.

"O— Okay, get 'em both."

Simon set both Dum Dums on the glass top of the counter while the bespectacled man behind it rang them up on his mechanical register.

"Fifty cents."

Frank handed the man two quarters.

"Do you need a bag?" the man asked Simon.

Simon shook his head and grabbed his suckers off the counter.

"Y— you mean, n— no— no thank you."

Simon turned back toward the man, but did not look up at him. "N—
no th— th— tha— thank you."

"Okay," the man said. "See you soon."

Simon followed his father to the door, unwrapping the butterscotch
sucker as he walked. Outside, lost in the task of scraping away a piece
of waxed paper from the sucker's upper hemisphere, Simon headed for
the truck.

"Th— this way," Frank said.

Simon's father was still standing in front of the candy store, jerking
his thumb in the other direction. Simon eyed the obelisk and considered asking his father if they could have a look at the inscriptions on
its base.

"C— come on, now."

Walking slowly toward his father, Simon picked the last bit of paper
from the sucker and popped the tiny yellow planet into his mouth.

Lately, Simon had been thinking about going silent permanently,
whether he had a sucker or not. He recognized that, at first, when he
stopped speaking, his parents and teachers and schoolmates would try,
with commands and demands and unkind words, to make him talk. Simon also knew that they could not make him speak, that to speak or not
was his decision. Simon felt powerful in silence, but he also felt alone.
And he worried that Frank would take his silence as an insinuation that
he, too, would be better off shutting up than stuttering. Silence was
something fun to imagine, something to enjoy with the sweetness of a
sucker, but Simon understood that he could not allow himself to go silent forever unless his father went first.

Simon kept his head down, milking the sucker for a slow, steady
stream of flavor and watching the backs of his father's boots. The boots
stopped in front of a single cement step.

"Pit—pit stop," Frank said.

He held open a green door and waved Simon through it. The sign
above the door read, The Four Corners.

Simon had been to the Four Corners before. It was dark inside, he
remembered, and smelled clean and dirty all at once. He didn't like this

place, but Frank's hand clamped down on his shoulder, and they were inside before he knew it.

"Hey, Frank," someone said.

The voice came from one of the three silhouettes at a table toward the back, to the left of the bar. As their faces became visible in the low neon light thrown around them by the beer signs, Simon did not recognize the men from church or school or anywhere. He figured that they worked with his father at the factory, as many parents of his classmates did.

Frank raised one hand to the men and pushed Simon away from them, toward the bar, with the other. "F—fellas," he said.

Frank lifted Simon up, set him on a barstool directly in front of the television, and took the stool to his son's left. Peering behind his father's back, Simon spied on the men at the table. He wished that they would ask his father and him to join them. He wished that the men were his father's friends. So far as Simon knew, his father didn't have any friends. Simon imagined that his father felt the same way about men his own age that Simon felt about the kids at school: that they knew too much about him without understanding him at all.

Afraid that his father would somehow read his thoughts, Simon turned away from the men at the back table and followed Frank's eyes to the small television. Two gray-haired men holding microphones and wearing jackets and ties stared out from the screen, a wide expanse of green spread out behind and beneath them. The bartender stepped over and stood in front of Frank. "What can I get you?"

"W— whiskey. Double."

The bartender looked at Simon. "How about you, little guy? Want a pop or something?"

Simon locked his lips around his sucker and shook his head.

"No? Okay."

The bartender poured Simon's father a double whiskey and served it neat in a cloudy glass.

"Thanks," Frank said.

"No problem."

Frank drank down the whiskey and stared up at the television while Simon worked the sucker. When it was roughly half its original size, Simon stashed the head of the candy scepter between his molars and his cheek, hoping to make it last a little longer.

The bartender moved toward Simon's father, smiling. "Another whiskey?"

"Y— Y— Y—Yeah. And a p— pack of p—Pall Malls."

Simon stared at his father. *Whatever whiskey is,* Simon thought, *it's worse for his stutter than beer is.*

One of the three men, the one sitting with his back to the wall, spoke to Simon's father.

"So how you been, Frank?"

Frank turned a few degrees to the left and looked at the men over his shoulder. "N—n— not bad."

"No?" the man said. "Everything's good?"

Frank shrugged. "C— c— c— can't c— c— complain."

"Sure you can," the man said. "It just takes you a little longer."

One of the other men laughed.

Simon felt his father summon all the eloquence he could with a deep, quiet inhalation.

"W— we're good. Th— thanks."

The bartender poured another whiskey into Frank's glass and laid a pack of cigarettes and a green Four Corners matchbook in front of him. Keeping his eyes on the television, Frank unwrapped the cellophane on the pack, flipped open its cardboard lid, and fished out a cigarette. He held the cigarette between his lips, struck a match, and bowed his head to the licking orange flame. His hand was shaking as he waved out the match with more vigor than was necessary, nearly catching Simon's ear with his elbow.

The men at the table laughed again as one of them poured liquid from a brown bottle into their glasses. Then one of the men, the first one to speak, stared hard at Simon. That's when Simon realized he had been eyeballing the men again. He looked away as quickly as he could.

"Is that your son, Frank?"

Too late.

Frank exhaled the smoke in his lungs. "Y— y— yes."

"What's his name?"

Frank threw his hand up toward the television and yelled, "Oh, c— come on!" at someone or something on the screen.

"What's your boy's name, Frank?"

Simon's father smiled and took another drag from his cigarette. Though the words themselves weren't mean, Simon heard something unkind in the man's questions, and neither the football nor the whiskey nor the cigarette had stopped the man from asking them. Frank was finally trying what Simon would have tried first: silence.

"I don't think his mother would like him being in a bar, would she, Frank?"

Listening to the men laugh, Simon wished that Connor were there. Connor would know what to say. He would answer all the questions and make the men laugh with him, not at him.

With a start, Simon remembered the second sucker—maybe the sucker would stop the questions. Simon pulled the sucker out of his pocket, unwrapped it, and held it in front of his father's face.

Frank took the Dum Dum and dipped it, bulb first, into his whiskey glass. He stirred the whiskey twice before pinning the paper stick to the side of the glass with his finger and taking another deep sip.

"What's your name, son?"

Frank stared at the television. Simon tried to read his father's face for some direction—*Answer the question,* or *Don't answer the question,* or *Get up, we're getting out of here*—but he couldn't tell what his father wanted him to do.

Maybe it's up to me, Simon thought. *Maybe my answering will make them stop.*

So Simon pulled the sucker stick out of his mouth and, throwing unhelpful force behind it, started his answer.

"S— S— S—"

"Whaddya know, Frank! He's part snake!"

The men laughed. Simon's father didn't move.

"—S— S— Simon."

As soon as he had said his name, Simon put the saliva-soaked sucker stick back into his mouth.

"Glad to meet you, Simon," the man said. "You're a chip off the old block."

"Jesus, Artie," the bartender said, shaking his head but smiling.

Shame rose from Simon's neck as a kind of heat that warmed his face and ears. He knew the men were making fun of him. Worse, Simon knew that his answering had done no good. The men were not through with him yet.

Simon looked at his father and begged him with his eyes: *Say anything that will make it stop.*

But Frank stayed silent, right when Simon needed him most, and Simon embraced his own silence as the punishment his father deserved.

● ● ●

THE DAY AFTER Frank took Simon to the Four Corners, May led Connor and Simon into the narthex of St. Paul's Catholic Church. Two women much older than May, widows who had appointed themselves the parish's greeters and observers, were standing just inside the door.

"Oh, look, it's May," the shorter woman said.

"Hello May!"

"Hi there, Agnes," May said. "Hello, Bea. How are you?"

"I'm fine, thank you," said Bea, the shorter one. "Hello, boys."

"Hello to you!" Connor said.

He arched his back to display his smiling, squinting face to the ladies, who put their hands to their chests and opened their eyes wide.

"Oh my!" Bea said, laughing.

"And how are you today, young man?" Agnes asked.

"*This* young man," Connor said, thrusting his thumb against his chest, "is pretty good."

Again the ladies pressed their fingers to their bony bosoms and laughed.

Simon was used to seeing his brother hold the rapt attention of strangers. Connor's pronunciation was so exact that he sounded more like a high-voiced adult than a kid. In his head, Simon again paid his younger brother the highest compliment he knew: *Connor could be on the radio.*

"And how about your brother?" Bea asked, keeping her eyes on Connor. "How is he doing?"

Simon's mother looked down at him. "How are you, Simon?" she asked, quietly offering Simon the respectful but distressing opportunity to answer the question himself.

As he stood there in silence, wishing he still had the sucker he had wasted on his father the day before, Simon felt Connor's eyes on him and met them.

"He's been better," Connor said.

Though Simon could hear that Connor wasn't trying to be funny, the ladies laughed again, delighted.

Simon caught sight of his father pacing past one of the anteroom's windows with his head down and a lit cigarette cupped in his hand. In that moment, Simon wished that he were out on the church lawn with his father. It wasn't that Simon had forgiven Frank for what happened at the Four Corners—he had not—but Simon was disturbed that even a cloak of silence could not hide his true feelings from his little brother. He wanted a brick wall between himself and Connor's see-through powers.

"Do you want to know something, ladies?" Connor asked.

"Tell us," Bea said.

"My mom is really strong."

"Is that right?"

"Yeah. She can carry me!"

"Really!"

"Yeah!" Connor said. He turned to May. "Show them, mommy!"

And before May could answer, Connor threw himself at his mother's torso. She caught him awkwardly and gathered him up into her arms with a groan.

Bea and Agnes applauded and said, "Well done!"

Connor, now seated on his mother's left arm, faced the ladies and beamed.

Bea took a halting step toward May to say, "You must be very proud."

May pulled Simon gently to her side with her free hand. "Oh, I am," she said.

When she squeezed his shoulder, Simon looked up at May, worried that she expected him to say something. But May smiled without expectation or condition, and Simon understood that his mother had intended for the ladies to see her do so.

"We'll see you after mass?" May said.

"Oh, of course, dear," Agnes said. "'Til then."

"Goodbye, ladies!" Connor said, still beaming.

"Goodbye!" the women said.

Simon's mother turned toward the sanctuary doors and lowered Connor to the ground with another groan. "Okay," she said. "Let's find our seats."

"But it's not starting yet," Connor said.

"It's starting soon."

Connor looked back at the dozen or so people—his audience—milling about the anteroom. "I don't want to go in early."

"Come on," May insisted calmly. "We need to say our prayers."

"I don't want to say my prayers."

Holding the interior door with her backside, May ushered Connor through the doorway with a hand between his shoulder blades, and Simon followed her.

Simon knew what praying was, but found it hard to pray at church. How could he be expected to talk to God with all of these strangers around, whispering and sneezing? Simon prayed only when he was alone in his bedroom, with the lights and the radio off. He articulated his wants, worries and thanks in his head only, putting each sentence beyond the reach of his stutter by leaving it unspoken. Kneeling beside May, his chin resting on the back of the pew in front of him, Simon decided that whenever he prayed next, he would start by thanking God for his mother. And when he heard his father coughing as he entered the church, Simon relished the thought that no one—not his father, not God himself—could make him break his silence.

3

May Davies

IN TWENTY-THREE years of motherhood, no moment frightened me more deeply than the moment I realized that Connor, still so young, was leaving his older brother behind.

Connor was not yet five when he began to dominate our family's dinner conversation. He dominated because he could, and because Frank and Simon were content to let the people without stutters do the talking. Connor would ask me questions about my day and try to make Frank laugh with jokes about baseball. And when Simon got stuck on a word, as he often did, Connor would finish his sentence for him, even though I told Connor, every time, not to do that. Once in a while, Simon would keep at his thought until he had spoken every syllable, but by the time Simon was finished, I would be the only one still listening to him.

The year Simon entered first grade, money was tight. Frank's hours at the plant had been cut to less than full-time, which hurt everything from our income to our deductibles. I got my mother to watch the kids and took a job at the dentist's office in Leyton, answering phones and doing bookkeeping. We needed my paycheck to make our mortgage payment. Any money left over at the end of the month was on account of my job or my Sunday afternoon coupon cutting. I kept my breadwinning in mind when I stood in front of the television on a Sunday evening in June and announced to Frank that I'd enrolled six-year-old Simon in piano lessons.

After a long moment, Frank said, "H— how muh— much does that c— cost?"

"Forty-five dollars a week."

"Ch— Christ, May! W— we don't even h— h— have a piano."

"He needs something structured to do this summer," I said.

"Wh— why don't w— we p— p— put him in tee-ball or s— something?"

"Why don't I handle the piano lessons," I said, "and you handle the tee-ball."

Frank waved me out of the way—something had happened in the ballgame he was watching—and I immediately understood two things: Simon would not be playing tee-ball, and Frank would not fight my spending forty-five dollars a week on Simon's piano lessons, which weren't piano lessons at all.

That summer, three days each week, I'd leave the dental office during my lunch hour and pick up Simon from home. The speech pathologist at Simon's school had agreed to work privately with him for what little we could pay. In every session, the speech teacher—her name was Janice—would draw Simon into conversation, patiently listening with her eyes until he'd said whatever he had intended to say. Then, gently, she'd ask him to repeat any words that had caused him to stutter. She'd give him a raw almond and ask a question, but insist he finish the almond before answering. And every night, I'd wrestle Simon's clock radio out of his hands and do the same exercises with him behind his closed bedroom door. I told myself that Simon was making improvements so small that an untrained person like me could not really see them, and that these tiny improvements were building toward the breakthrough I'd been hoping for.

After a session in mid-July, with Simon waiting in her living room, Janice sat me down for what she called a "progress report."

Sitting behind her oversized oak desk, Janice said, "I'm afraid I'm wasting your money."

My breath caught in my throat. I had been expecting her to run down a list of improvements. "What do you mean?"

Janice winced and crossed her legs. I think she'd been hoping that I'd be grateful she'd voiced a concern I'd been too polite to mention myself.

"Simon's speech is not improving," Janice said. "It may be getting worse."

Her pronunciation was so flawless—fussy, even—that I thought she might be rubbing it in.

"And when we reach the point at which it may be doing more harm than good," she continued, "we have to discontinue therapy."

I nodded and tried to smile, pretending too late that I agreed with her and was relieved that she'd spoken up. I kept pretending until I felt the tears running down my cheeks.

Janice picked up a white piece of paper, stood up, and walked around to my side of her desk. Handing me the paper, she said, "I'm referring you to an expert. His entire practice is children who stutter."

I looked at the address. "In Rockford?"

"Yes."

Rockford was three hours north. "Does he do weekend appointments?"

Janice shook her head. "No."

That left me with the choice of getting Simon to the speech expert or staying in the job we needed to keep a roof over our heads, which wasn't really a choice.

"I'm sorry I wasn't more help," Janice said.

She was still standing over me. I stood up to shake Janice's hand. And as I walked out of her office, I thought, *That's it. Simon will either stop stuttering on his own, or he will stutter his entire life, like his father has. And his little brother will talk circles around him at home, at school, everywhere they go together, until one or both of them decide they will not go anywhere together anymore.*

This stutter will cut Simon off from the whole world.

• • •

THAT SAME SUMMER, I enrolled Simon in real music lessons. My hope was that music was a kind of communication he might still master.

Frank had been right about one thing: we didn't have a piano, and we couldn't afford one. At the supermarket, I saw a posted ad for guitar lessons. I imagined Simon playing the guitar and smiled, but my face fell when I envisioned him trying to sing along with his playing and gagging on a song's first word. So I ruled out guitar. I wanted music to be Simon's refuge from any expectation he would use his voice. I wanted an instrument he would have to put in his mouth.

Mr. Shaughnessy, the band director at Leyton High, offered private clarinet lessons. For the same forty-five dollars per week I'd spent on speech lessons, I secured a rental clarinet and lunch-hour lessons twice a week, on Monday and Wednesday. Thumbing through a magazine in Mr. Shaughnessy's living room, I'd listen while Simon played airy, squeaky notes in the studio across the foyer. Every question Mr. Shaughnessy asked Simon could be answered with a nod or a headshake, and doing as the teacher instructed required no words, only music. Simon could not yet play the clarinet, but the lessons were achieving some of what I'd hoped they would.

At the end of every lesson, Mr. Shaughnessy would emerge from his studio smiling, but looking slightly exasperated. Simon was not a natural.

"He needs to practice every day," Mr. Shaughnessy would say.

"I'll make sure he does," I'd answer. "Thank you."

Then I'd take Simon home.

With the frame of our Ford four-door rattling as the engine idled in our side yard, I would remind Simon that he needed to practice his scales for at least an hour before I returned home from work.

"O— o— Okay," he would say.

He would practice both Saturday and Sunday—I know, because I'd sit with him in his room while he did. Weekdays were a different story. My mother's addiction to soap operas and game shows made it easy for her to watch television-obsessed Connor, but Simon was left to his own devices.

Upon arriving home, I'd go straight to Simon's room. Seeing me at his bedroom door, Simon would turn the volume of his radio down just slightly—not a meaningless courtesy, coming from a six-year-old.

"Did you do your scales?" I would ask.

Yes, Simon would nod.

"For a full hour?"

Simon would nod again.

"Good. And how did it go?"

"F— f— fine," he would say.

I believed him. What else could I do? Once, I asked my mother as she was leaving if Simon had practiced his clarinet.

"His what?"

"His clarinet."

"Oh," she said. "I'm sure he did."

That meant she had no idea if he had or not.

There was only one weekday I knew for certain that Simon had practiced. I had gone grocery shopping and had the oil changed in our car after work. By the time I got home, Frank was sitting at the kitchen table, watching Connor spoil his appetite with a plate of cookies.

"I th— th— thought S— Simon was t— taking p— p— piano lessons," Frank said to me.

"He didn't take to the piano," I said.

"H— he's not t— taking to th— this, either. S— s— sounds terrible."

Connor, chewing another cookie, laughed. "You're funny, Daddy."

Frank smiled with the kind of pride a grown man should never take in a compliment from a four-year-old.

"He's learning," I said. "You should be proud of him. He's trying to improve himself."

I hoped Frank heard my suggestion that *he'd* stopped trying to get better at anything a long time ago. I was thinking only about myself—what I had hoped for and stopped hoping for in married life—when I said that to Frank. If I'd been thinking about Simon, I might not have said anything. Telling a man that he doesn't stack up to his son does the son no favors.

It was after work on a Thursday in the middle of August, the day after one of Simon's lessons, when I got into my car after work and saw Simon's clarinet case sticking out from underneath the passenger seat. I pulled the case out from under the seat and opened it. Each piece of the instrument was nestled into the velveteen-lined mold that matched its shape.

When I got home, I knocked on Simon's bedroom door and opened it, keeping the clarinet case behind the wall, out of his sight.

He was sitting on the bed with his clock radio tuned to some commercial or other. He turned the volume down and stared at me.

"Hi, Simon," I said.

He waved.

"How are you?"

He nodded, which meant, *Good.*

I nodded back and raised my chin and eyebrows, asking him to say the word.

"G— g— good."

"I'm glad," I said. "Did you do your scales?"

Yes, he nodded.

"For a full hour?"

Simon nodded again.

I brought the clarinet case into the room. Simon only blinked. It seemed that lying to me about his practicing had become so routine that he had gotten used to the idea that he would be caught in the lie, eventually. And in that moment, I realized that all my suppositions about my son's diligence and willingness to better himself were wishful thinking. All I knew for certain was that I'd been wasting my Monday and Wednesday lunch hours and forty-five dollars a week, and that Simon, right then, looked very much like his father.

I pulled the radio out of his hands and turned it off. The look on Simon's face was one I might have expected to see if I strangled a rabbit before his eyes. He sat up on his knees and reached for the radio. I held it away from him, over the foot of the bed.

"You've been lying to me, Simon."

"M— Mom—" he said.

But I wasn't finished, and this time, I decided, Simon would wait for me to finish speaking.

"I've been driving you all over town on my lunch hour for weeks! Do you know how upsetting it is to find out you're not practicing? So you can listen to commercials?"

I held up the radio in front of him. Simon eyed it. I think he thought I was going to take it away from him. I let him believe that I would.

"You could have *music*, Simon!" I said. "Music! You could make music speak *for* you if you would practice!"

Then, like a hungry cottonmouth, Simon lunged toward the radio with his entire body. I pulled the radio away from him, and Simon's momentum carried him over the foot of the bed. I dropped the radio and grabbed for him, but only changed the angle of his fall for the worse. His shoulder and head hit the floor with a thud that made the room shudder, and his thin neck bent strangely to one side as it bore his weight for an agonizing instant. When he came to rest on his back, Simon looked up at the ceiling. By the time he let out his first cry, with his mouth and eyes wide open, I was on the floor, holding him in my arms. I stroked Simon's head and rocked him back and forth while he waited for the pain and fear to go away.

"Is he okay?"

Connor's question was barely audible over Simon's moans and my softly spoken comforts. Connor stood in the doorway, nervously poking the corner of his closed mouth with his finger. The sight of his big brother crying on the ground had robbed my four-year-old boy of his bold tongue.

"Simon fell off the bed," I said, reassuring the boys and myself. "He had a fright, but he's fine now."

Connor said nothing.

"Go back to the living room now and watch TV," I said. "We'll be out in a minute."

When he had stopped crying, Simon sat up and scooted out of my arms. Sitting on the floor, he looked at me, waiting for me to hand down some punishment or leave. When I did neither thing, he picked up his radio and turned it on. The plug had been pulled out of the wall in the commotion, but the batteries I'd loaded into the black plastic underbelly months ago, at Simon's request, powered the radio's single speaker. Simon drew the tuner past music and static until he found a speaking voice, a woman's. She told me how hard it is to be the working mother of an infant, and how much easier my life would be if I'd only use her same brand of formula. I pictured a woman shaking her head with a sympathy she didn't really feel, and her face breaking into an empty smile.

"M— M— Mom," Simon said.

"Yes," I whispered.

"Th— this is m— myoo— music."

The commercial was *not* music. It was chattering nonsense. But I buried this opinion deep inside me, alongside the very next thought I'd had: *If there is any music in this, Simon, it's a kind of music you'll never make.*

● ● ●

AFTER SIMON GAVE up on the clarinet, I focused my energy on something I could control. My boys would never be equal in every way that mattered, but I could do everything in my power to show them they were equal in my love.

For example: if, at dinner on Monday, I asked Simon about his day before asking Connor about his own, I made sure to ask Connor the same question first on Tuesday evening. If I read a book to Connor, I'd listen to the radio with Simon for the same number of minutes I'd spent reading. Chores were doled out in pairs—one for Simon, one for Connor—and if one boy's chore proved easier than the other's, he was made to help his brother finish his job.

"You start together," I'd say, "and you end together."

All of this came naturally because I loved my boys equally. But even my demonstrations of equal love would join speech therapy and clarinet lessons on my list of failures.

Connor's fifth birthday was August 25th, two weeks after Simon's seventh. That night, when the cake plates and empty milk glasses had been cleared away, I sat the boys down at the kitchen table to show them two receipts. The first was for the gift we'd just given to Connor, a year's subscription to *TV Guide*. The second was for the Matchbox cars Simon had received as his present—what do you get the boy who already has all he wants in a radio older than he is?

I pointed to the total on each thin, wrinkled piece of paper.

"Do you see these numbers?"

Connor and Simon knelt in their chairs and leaned in for a closer look.

"Connor's birthday gift cost fifteen dollars and thirty-two cents," I said. "Simon's birthday gift, including tax, cost fifteen dollars and thirty-four cents."

The boys looked up at me, seeming confused about what to make of the numbers.

"I want you to see that, although your gifts are different, your father and I spent the same on each of you for your birthdays. Neither gift was more expensive than the other."

That was good enough for Connor. "Okay!" he said, sliding off his chair. "Can I go watch TV now, Mommy?"

"Yes, you may," I said.

Having made my point, I went back to the sink, picked up the gray sponge, and dipped my hands into the dishwater, which was now lukewarm. It was another minute or so before I saw that Simon was still at the table, staring at the receipts.

"What's the matter, honey?" I asked.

Simon glanced in my direction without meeting my eye.

I dried my hands on the towel hanging over the oven-door handle and sat next to Simon, leaning forward until my head was on the same level as his. "Tell me."

With his eyes still on the receipts, Simon licked his lips. "W— w— w— we're n— not th— the same."

"Who isn't the same?"

"M— me and Connor."

I tilted my head and smiled. "Honey," I said over a laugh, "everyone is different from everyone else. And the ways that you and Connor are different don't matter to me."

It was this afterthought of a phrase—"to me"—that betrayed the truth about the differences between Simon and Connor, a truth that Simon seemed to confirm for himself as he stared right through me. The ways in which Simon and Connor were different would matter very much. They mattered already. And my attempt to minimize the truth had only proven to Simon that his mother's love—impartial though it was—had no power to change it.

• • •

THROUGH IT ALL, I tried to show Simon that he was loveable, even with his stutter. Part of the way I showed this was by trying to love Simon's father.

Frank responded by refusing the little courtesies I paid him in front of Simon, from the cream I offered to pour in his coffee to the kisses I tried to plant on his cheek before he left for work. And when he and I were alone, he ignored me. In short, Frank proved to me that his gut feeling had been right all along: he didn't deserve my love. Even so, I kept trying to love Frank. I refused to let Simon believe that inheriting his father's stutter meant that Simon, too, was unworthy of love and incapable of loving as he should.

I might have been able to do without Frank's love if he'd loved Simon as well as I wanted him to. But their shared stutter came between them. Frank saw too much of himself in Simon. When he stuttered, Simon could not help but hold up a mirror to his father. Because he had never really liked himself, Frank could not love Simon enough. He couldn't even see Simon's boyish adoration for the blessing it was.

Frank courted Connor's love in a way he had never courted mine. Connor was still four when I first understood how Frank saw him: as his belated chance to win over the fast-talking boys who'd teased Frank when we were at Leyton Elementary and Leyton High, boys who were now the kings and court jesters of the union hall and the bar in town and the break room at the Caterpillar plant. While I plotted to find speech therapy for Simon, Frank refashioned himself from a quiet, hard-working loner into a sitcom stereotype. He made a throne of his easy chair and sat Connor alongside him, drinking beer and barking his disapproval at the televised mistakes of men who were ten times the ballplayer he'd ever been. Frank made himself worthy of Connor's love, in his own mind, by ensuring that the man Connor loved was hardly recognizable, to himself or anyone else, as the Frank we knew. As his father transformed before his eyes, Simon was made to feel his love was not enough.

And because I had known Frank as the wounded, vulnerable stutterer he was, my love was discounted even as it died.

● ● ●

THE OCTOBER AFTER he turned seven, Simon went completely silent.

At first, I thought he might still have been recovering from a sore throat that had kept him out of school the past Friday. By Wednesday of the following week, I supposed that Simon was just tired of hearing his stuttered sentences finished by his little brother. But Wednesday night, at dinner, I noticed Simon staring across our Formica table at his father with wet, wide-open eyes. His food was untouched, but the muscles of Simon's jaw were flexed in front of his ears. Frank fixed his eyes on his plate, which he guarded with his elbows as if someone might try to stab his half-eaten slice of meatloaf and run off with it. While asking Connor various questions about his day at school, I glanced at Frank several more times. He never met Simon's glare.

I knew then that something had happened between Simon and his father, but I didn't know what, and I didn't believe that asking either Frank or Simon about it would do anyone any good. So I waited and listened. And Simon stayed silent.

On Thursday, I got a call from Simon's teacher, Ms. Wells.

"I'm sorry to bother you at work," she said, without sounding the least bit sorry.

Speaking to Ms. Wells, who was probably ten years older than me, I had to fight the feeling that I was seven again and speaking to my own teacher.

"Oh, not at all," I said. "Is anything wrong?"

"I'm calling about Simon," Ms. Wells said. "He hasn't been speaking all week."

"Well," I said, sighing, "I appreciate you telling me. Simon hasn't said a word at home, either."

"He hasn't," she said.

"No."

"Is he ill?"

"I don't think so, no."

"Well, Mrs. Davies, as you surely know, dealing with Simon's stutter requires patience from me and his classmates, and my patience is running out. This silence amounts to insubordination. It is disrupting my classroom."

My mouth hung open until I felt the heat rising in my face. "I'm sure this has been very hard for you."

"It has, yes," Ms. Wells said. "And I'm concerned for Simon, of course."

"Oh, your concern for Simon is coming through loud and clear."

"Well," she said, clipping the word. "I've said what I called to say."

"All right, then."

I wallowed in my irritation with that silly, self-important witch for the rest of the afternoon. By the time I arrived home, though, I worried only for Simon.

We sat down, the four of us, to a dinner of fish sticks and mashed potatoes. While Connor jabbered away about his playground adventures, Simon baited Frank with his eyes, and Frank ignored the baiting, looking only at Connor.

When the boys had gone to bed, I walked over to the television and turned the volume all the way down.

Reclining in his chair, the balls of his feet aimed up at me, Frank said, "W— w— w— what i— is it?"

His four attempts at "what" reminded me that Frank was smashed—his stutter got worse when he drank—but I couldn't wait for him to sober up.

"Simon isn't speaking," I said.

I'd been wondering if Frank would pretend not to notice—he didn't. But he tried dismissing my concern with a wave of his hand.

When he got uncomfortable with my standing there, staring at him, demanding an explanation, Frank said, "I— I— I— d— did the s— same th— th— thing w— when I was a kid. He— he— he'll s— s— snap out of it."

"The last time I remember hearing him speak was Friday night," I said.

Frank shrugged and brought a beer can to his lips.

"What happened?"

He put his beer down and pulled the wooden handle on the right side of his recliner, bringing the footrest down. "W— w— what do you m— mean w— w— what happened?"

"What happened on Saturday? When I put him to bed Friday night, Simon was speaking. When I got home from taking Connor to the doctor, Simon wouldn't say a word. And he's staring daggers at you!"

"He bet— bet— better not be," Frank said, shifting in his chair.

"What *happened* on Saturday, Francis?"

"N— nothing!" he said, leaning forward in his chair. "Nothing happened. N— now tur— turn up the v— v— volume and g— get out the way."

He stared past me to whatever was happening on the part of the screen I'd failed to block. I stalked off to the bedroom, slamming the door behind me and leaving the television's volume where it was. If he was content to let Simon stay silent, Frank could turn up the TV himself.

Clumsy with outrage, I struggled out of my clothes and caught my reflection in the mirror above my dresser. I pushed a strand of my thick, wavy hair out of my face. The bags beneath my eyes were dark, and deep wrinkles slashed across the skin of my long neck.

A ballerina's neck, Frank used to call it.

To hell with Frank.

I didn't need anyone to give me the particulars. It was enough to know that Simon remained silent because of something his father had done or failed to do.

●　●　●

SIMON'S SILENCE WENT up like a wall between us. His nods, head-shakes and gestures could not create the closeness I felt when Simon had risked speaking to me, and I'd made good on his risk by listening with my eyes and ears until he had finished. Even as Connor wowed me with his knack for the speed and rhythms of adult speech, I found myself wishing for a chance to sit next to Simon on his bed and show him, just by listening patiently as he started and restarted his words, that there was nothing he couldn't tell me. But Simon would not say anything to me or anyone else.

Every day or two, I'd try to draw him out. Once, when he was listening to his radio in the early evening, I knocked on his door and said, "Dinner is ready."

Simon nodded and gave me a flat, close-mouthed smile.

"Would you like something to drink?"

He nodded again.

"What would you like?"

I knew the answer was Sprite. Simon always picked Sprite if given a choice. But Simon wouldn't say the word. So he shrugged.

"You don't know what you want to drink?" I asked.

He raised his shoulders again, even higher, and let them fall.

"Why don't you tell me what you want to drink, and I'll pour it for you?"

I turned toward the kitchen, trying to suggest with body language that the Sprite was as good as poured if Simon would only say what he wanted.

Simon looked at me. He seemed to be asking me, with his eyes, to let him be. But I wouldn't.

"It's no trouble," I said.

Simon turned off his radio. He hopped off his bed and scooted past me in his stocking feet. By the time I reached the kitchen, he was hoisting himself onto the counter to retrieve a tall, green plastic cup from the cupboard. He lowered himself to the floor, opened the refrigerator, and pulled out a two-liter bottle of Sprite. Then Simon poured himself half a glass—the same limit I would have set—carried his drink to the table, and took his seat without a word.

With his obedient refusal, Simon sent me the unspoken message that there was nothing, big or small, I could do to help him out of his silence, and that I should save myself the trouble of trying.

But I didn't quit trying. I couldn't.

I sat Simon down and told him how much we valued what he had to say, no matter how long it took him to say it, whether he stuttered or not. Driving home from the grocery store with him, I praised the strength of Simon's will—his ability to make a decision and stick to it—in the hope that he might decide he had made his point. And when my birthday came, I asked Simon for only one gift.

I waited all evening for him to speak to me. After my birthday dinner—burgers from Wendy's, the best meal Frank could serve up on his own—I sent Frank and Connor into the living room to watch the ballgame so that Simon might feel safe enough, or generous enough, to say something. But when he had finished his piece of the birthday cake I had baked—yellow cake with chocolate frosting—Simon wiped the crumbs from his lips, slid off of his chair, and set his plate and fork in the sink. Then he kissed me on the cheek and disappeared into his bedroom.

The day after my birthday, when Simon had brushed his teeth and changed into his pajamas, I went into his room, closed the door, and sat down on his bed.

"I'm worried about you, Simon," I said, allowing myself to cry. "And I miss you." Simon would not look at me. His radio, muffled by the leg under which he had stashed it when I came in, mumbled commercial messages.

"I want to hear you again," I said. "Please. Say something to me."

When he was certain I was finished speaking, Simon raised his glistening eyes to mine.

At last! I thought. *He'll speak!*

Then Simon closed his eyes and shook his head. *No.*

My crying kept up for the rest of the evening. Frank must have heard me sniffling from the living room. I was folding a load of whites on our bed when he walked up behind me, laid his hand on the small of my back, and asked, "W— w— what's wrong?"

It was Frank's bad luck that this tender gesture—his first in months—hardened my sadness into something brittle.

"If you don't know," I said, "I'm not going to tell you."

With that, Frank pulled his hand away and stormed out of the bedroom, stuttering and muttering his curses.

• • •

IT WAS ONLY a few days later when, having spent the night chewing my nails down to the quick and nibbling my cuticles, I asked Frank for his help.

"Will you talk to him?" I asked.

Looking up from the game, he said, "W— w— what about?"

"Anything, Frank! He hasn't said a word in almost six months! Were you ever silent for six months?"

Connor, sitting on the couch, said, "What are you guys talking about?"

"Please," I said. "Just try to make him talk."

With his shoulders slumped forward even as he sat back in his chair, Frank looked defeated already.

"F— fine," he said. "Br— br— bring him in here."

I leapt into action before Frank could change his mind. "All right, Connor," I said. "Let's get you in your pajamas and you can watch the little TV in your room."

"Okay, Mommy!"

With Connor settled, I knocked on Simon's bedroom door, opened it, and asked him to come with me. I led him into the living room and stood him in front of his father.

"Your father would like to speak to you."

I stepped back to a spot just outside of Simon's peripheral vision.

Frank sighed and shook his head, as if he couldn't quite believe what he was about to say. "Wh— what's wrong w— with you, Simon?"

Simon said nothing.

"Wh— why d— don't you s— speak up?"

Simon made no reply.

"S— s— say s— something!"

I leaned forward just in time to see Simon's bottom lip slide over the top one. His eyes glowed with defiance. My heart leapt at the thought that Simon might scream.

But it was *I* who screamed when Frank stood up and raised his right hand to slap the scorn from his son's face. I put myself between the two of them and carried Simon away, cowering against a blow that didn't come.

When I had delivered him safely to his bedroom, Simon wriggled out of my arms. I had assumed he'd be visibly frightened, maybe even crying, but his expression, now directed at an empty corner of his room, was the same defiant one he'd shown his father. I understood then that Simon had become a mirror for more than his father's broken speech. In Simon's hateful gaze, Frank had glimpsed his own self-hatred.

I should never have left Simon unprotected in front of Frank. A man pretending he isn't wounded can only look in a mirror for so long before he tries to break it.

● ● ●

SIMON HAD BEEN silent for seven months when I got it in my head that I should try to scare a sound out of him.

I left work an hour early and parked my car down the road, off the route of the boys' school bus. I hid my purse in my bedroom, lay down on the far side of Simon's bed, and waited. The hiding itself was thrilling—I hadn't hidden from anyone since I was a little girl—but what really excited me was the idea that I could break my son's silence. I told myself that once it was broken, Simon would have no reason to start a new string of days and weeks and months without speaking. He'd outlasted the wishes of his mother and commands of his teacher and shown his father what he thought of him. What could possibly be left for him to prove? And to whom?

The airbrakes of the bus shrieked. The engine chugged as it idled and growled as the bus accelerated past the house. I put my feet under me and squatted in a crouch. Feeling a giggle rise, I buried my smiling face in the comforter hanging over the side of Simon's bed.

When the back door opened into the kitchen, the house seemed to exhale, as if it had been holding its breath until the boys returned home. Connor called for me from the kitchen, and called my name again in the living room. When he got no answer, he said, "Yippee!" and turned on the television.

I listened to two game-show hosts—the one actually on TV and the much younger one in my living room—for what seemed like several minutes.

Then the door to Simon's room opened.

Still smiling, I sprang into view. "Boo!" I screamed.

Simon jumped back and his mouth opened wide, but no sound came out. He stood with his back to the wall, clasping his windpipe between his thumb and his fingers. My first thought was that he'd inhaled a cookie. Then I heard the air coming in and out of his nose and understood: His stutter had seized him and would not let go.

Alarmed, I hurried around the foot of the bed. Before I could reach him, Simon ran at me and started pounding my hips with the heels of his open hands.

"Stop it!" I yelled, grabbing at him. "Simon! Stop!"

He hit me a few more times, and then ran out of the room.

I pushed my hair out of my eyes and let the tears come, crying not over the blows that my son had dealt me in his wordless rage, but at a possibility I hadn't considered: Simon's silence was not a matter of choice. His stutter, emboldened by his silence, had strangled his broken voice.

It was only in his withholding of them, in his unwillingness to meet my eye for the next thirteen days, that I came to understand just how much love my Simon had been showing me in his glances and gestures and heavy smiles.

● ● ●

KNOWING THAT SIMON was unable to speak changed everything for me. I no longer took his silence as a slight. I stopped pleading for him to speak and trying to trick him into speaking. I began to treat the silence as something I couldn't change, as if it were any other crippling injury a boy could suffer.

I signed us both up for a sign-language class, but Simon didn't want to sign any more than he wanted to play an instrument. For two half-hour sessions, he refused to take his hands out of his lap. I agreed to stop taking him but believed we'd go back, eventually. In the meantime, though, I asked Simon questions that he could answer with a nod or a shake of his head, and we developed our own pidgin signs for the niceties I couldn't let go: two open palms for *please*, palms together in prayer for *thank you*, and a fist to the breast, the same *mea culpa* I'd learned in church as a little girl, for *I'm sorry*. Simon never learned *I'm hungry* or *I'm thirsty* or anything else that would've helped me to meet his needs. He did things for himself. If he was hungry, he went to the kitchen and had a snack. If he was thirsty, he poured himself a Sprite. Soon, I was raising a highly independent little boy I was afraid to let out of my sight.

At the beginning of each school year, I informed Simon's teachers that he could not speak, and made them promise me that they would never, under any circumstances, demand that he do what he could not. And I gave Connor an assignment.

"You stay close to your brother before and after school," I told him. "And if you see anybody doing or saying anything mean to him, I want you to tell me."

"Okay," Connor said. Then, after a couple of nervous *um*s, he asked, "Do you want me to try and stop them?"

"No," I said. "Just tell me. If it's an emergency, go find a teacher and tell her."

I assumed that Connor talking Simon's way out of a schoolyard fight would only move the fight to my living room. The boys were fighting all the time, it seemed. If Connor spoke for Simon once too often, or hit a little too close to home with his teasing, or, God forbid, laid a hand on Simon's radio, Simon would tackle Connor and pound him in the shoulders. I pulled Simon off of Connor a few times a week, at least, and made him say *I'm sorry* with the same fist he'd been using to hit his brother.

But if, when the fighting began, I was outside hanging the washing or deafened to Connor's protests by my hair dryer, I would find Connor on top of Simon, giving the punches he'd been getting, and Simon under his smaller, younger brother, calmly taking blows he didn't have to take.

For months, I worried that Simon was taking pleasure in his own pain and humiliation, but I came to see the fights as something else entirely. Simon was acting out his longing to be Connor's equal, if only in a game he rigged himself.

There was one adjustment to his silence, though, that Simon would not allow me to make. When he handed me a permission slip to join the Boy Scouts or Little League or become an altar server, I'd ask Simon a question: "Will you let me come with you every time you go?"

Simon would wince at me, stomp his feet and shake his head emphatically.

"I'm sorry," I would say. "I can't let you go alone."

There would be more stomping then, until Frank had yelled for it to stop and Simon had shut himself in his room.

I understood that no boy wanted his mother watching over him, especially if his was the only mother around. But a boy who cannot speak is too tempting a target for a predatory coach or priest or scout leader—who is more likely than a mute child to keep a pedophile's secrets? Somehow, I managed to convince myself that Simon would be safe at school. But after school and on the weekends, I'd only leave him in the care of Frank or my mother.

From the time they were babies, I'd tried to raise boys brave enough to be more than their mother's sons, to be students and musicians and volunteers. To be themselves. But because of his silence, I couldn't allow Simon to take his independence into the world. Until he was older, I wouldn't let Simon go anywhere I couldn't protect him.

● ● ●

I KEPT OFFERING Simon music and sign-language lessons from any teacher who would let me sit outside an open door and listen, taking care not to suggest that Simon wasn't good enough as he was, only that he might like to make music or communicate. But Simon wouldn't take the lessons. I think they frightened him, actually, as if learning an instrument or sign language would guarantee he'd never, ever speak again. Whatever the reason, even after six years without speaking, Simon wouldn't give up listening to the radio for a chance to make music or sign language.

When he was thirteen years old and in eighth grade, I pulled Simon away from his radio to see Connor perform as part of the choir in the junior high's Happy Holidays Concert. Frank was still in front of the television in his undershirt fifteen minutes before the performance was to begin, so I left without him. He arrived late and spent the concert frowning and fidgeting uncomfortably in the folding chair I had saved for him. Simon endured the singing with his arms folded and his head down. He might have feared that I'd take his paying attention as some hint he finally wanted music lessons. But during "The Twelve Days of Christmas," Simon looked up to watch Connor get the night's only laughs by singing "five golden rings" eight different ways, each hammier than the one before.

After the concert, Connor rode home with Frank in his truck. Simon went with me. Whenever it was just the two of us in the car, Simon would sit in the front passenger seat and take control of the stereo, which must have had more powerful reception than his clock radio did, because Simon would bypass perfectly audible commercials to scan the AM dial for ads broadcast from far-off places. We were about a mile from home the night of the concert when a voice, calling out through a storm of static, told me to "come on down" to a restaurant in downtown Omaha for "eastern Nebraska's finest steaks" and one-dollar draft beers. Even in the December darkness on an unlit two-lane highway, I could see the open-mouthed amazement on Simon's face. At the beginning of a long day, I might have reminded myself that Simon didn't feel, as I did, that the radio voices were taunting him in his silence, and I might have wondered aloud at the modern miracle of invisible waves carrying speech across the prairie to our ears. But at the *end* of a long day, after twenty minutes of irritating electronic hisses and squeals had paid off only in a commercial for a restaurant four-hundred miles away, I said, "I've got to hand it to you, Simon. You've found a way to make radio even more boring."

Two days later, on Saturday, I was at the kitchen table reading the *Peoria Journal Star* when I came across a profile of Larry Sellers, a voiceover artist who was born and raised in Sampere, Illinois, not far from Leyton. According to the paper, Sellers had done national television commercials for Maalox, Hertz, and Wendy's, and for the past ten years, he'd been the radio voice of Jewel Food Stores. In the words of his long-time agent, Larry Sellers was "one of the very few voiceover artists who can take a mediocre script and make a great radio commercial without changing a word."

I read the entire profile, hoping to find the reason why my silent son listened to nothing but commercials. When I reached the end of the piece, though, I'd learned more than I wanted to know about Larry Sellers and nothing about Simon. Even so, I thought that Simon might find the article interesting. I hesitated to hand my silenced son a story about a man who had grown up nearby and made it on the radio, but I decided there was no more harm in Simon reading a profile of Larry Sellers than there was in a wheelchair-bound boy reading the sports page. So I folded the Lifestyle section into quarters, putting the Sellers profile in front, and walked to Simon's room.

He was lying on his bed with his clock radio, tuned to a commercial for a Monster Truck rally, in his lap.

I held up the newspaper and pointed to Sellers' photo. "This man is on the radio."

As I handed it over, I made the profile, in my own mind, a kind of peace offering, a sign that I would let Simon enjoy his simplest pleasure without any more criticism from me.

Later that same day, when I stepped into his room, Simon shut me up with a wave before I could say anything.

"Hey!" I said, sharply.

Then Simon gestured toward the radio in his lap and, more politely but just as urgently—with his eyes, this time—insisted I be silent.

I listened, indignant at the idea that anything short of an emergency Presidential address could justify Simon's shushing me this way. What I heard was a man telling me about a sale on bananas and a two-for-one deal on cans of Campbell's Soup. It was a commercial for Jewel Food Stores. The voice belonged to Larry Sellers.

I stayed silent until the commercial was over. Then I said, "Dinner's ready."

Simon nodded, turned off his radio, and rolled off the bed onto his feet. As he passed me in the doorway, he put his arm around my back and leaned his head against my arm, a kind of half hug that offered more affection than I'd gotten from Simon since he entered junior high.

As he walked away, I smiled at the possibility that, by introducing Simon to Larry Sellers, I'd done what few mothers who'd so poorly chosen a husband ever did: given my son a hero.

I began to listen to Larry Sellers' voice as closely as Simon did. I asked him questions about the voiceover artist's style and technique, and Simon answered them as best he could with headshakes and nods. But my questions weren't about Larry Sellers, really. They were about Simon. I came to treat the voice of Larry Sellers as a kind of surrogate for my son's, as if the much older man's speech—not what he said, but how he said it—could give me some idea of how Simon might sound if he could talk. The only voice I remembered as Simon's was that of a little boy. And as Simon grew into a young man with acne on his shoulders and hair sprouting out of his Adam's apple, my memory of that little voice faded until, when I lay awake in bed at night, with Frank snoring a few inches and a million miles away from me, I was no longer certain that the voice I heard so faintly in my mind's ear had ever belonged to Simon.

● ● ●

THE DAY AFTER Connor left for college, I left Frank.

I moved out of the house to a one-bedroom apartment on the town square in Sampere. I offered Simon, who was twenty by then, my pull-out couch and some space for his clothes, but he declined. The reason he gave me when I finally asked the right yes-no question was that he wanted to stay close to the Tippecanoe restaurant, in Leyton, where he'd worked for four years as a busboy. It's just as likely that Simon believed moving in with me would look too much like surrendering to his father, and more likely still that Simon had come to depend on having Frank around to hate. It gave him a kind of energy. I had seen Simon silently stoke his hatred to get himself out of the house and off to work on the coldest, wettest days. For my part, I was tired of spending my days and nights hating Frank. I hoped Simon would tire of it, too. If he didn't, his life would be a poorer version of his father's.

I sat in my Ford with the keys between my legs and my bulging suitcases in the back seats where my sons used to sit. As I steadied myself to leave Simon behind in the house where I'd raised him, I couldn't reconcile these two ideas: 1) that I hadn't failed Simon, and 2) that so many of my attempts to help Simon had failed.

● ● ●

I'D BEEN LIVING on my own in Sampere for nearly three years when I came down with what my doctor suspected was a case of walking pneumonia. She drew some blood just to be sure and sent me on my way. A few days after that appointment, she asked me to come in for follow-up tests, which led to more tests and evidence that my walking pneumonia, which turned out to be cancer, had spread from my lungs to my lymph nodes, liver and bones. It was not long before I wasn't walking at all anymore, but lying in a hospital bed in my apartment's tiny living room.

The morphine haze made me feel like I was dead already. The hospice nurse had given me a beige plastic cylinder with a button I could press to dose myself. To stave off the cloudy-headedness, I would wait as long as I could, pushing the limits of my endurance, before plunging the button and releasing the morphine into my blood. The first time I watched the clock, I lasted an hour before the pain became too much. Then, fifty minutes. Two days later, I could manage only twenty minutes. Fighting the tide, I tried, in the middle of the night, to go from twenty minutes back up to twenty-five by dropping the device over the edge of the bed, but at eighteen minutes, I was wailing, begging the nurse to return the cylinder to my trembling, outstretched hand.

The day I awoke to what I guessed would be ten minutes of barely tolerable clarity, I asked for my boys. I had a vague awareness that Connor was home from school and that he and Simon had been sleeping at my apartment. I had no memory of Frank coming to visit me and no desire to see him.

Connor appeared at my bedside. He covered the back of my free hand with his and smiled down on me, trying to give me some of the confidence he had in surplus. Simon hung back behind Connor. I could not see his face.

"Simon," I said. I'd tried to call him, but what came out was a hoarse whisper.

Connor turned his head to him and said, with some impatience, "Mom wants you over here."

When they were standing side by side, I said, in a voice I knew they'd one day forget, just as I'd forgotten Simon's, what I'd called them in to hear.

"It's impossible—" I said. I took a shallow, wheezing breath. "How much I love you—" Another breath. "Both."

"We love you, too, Mom," Connor said, answering for himself and Simon. "We love you tons."

A faulty wire crackled and a light flickered in the frosted light fixture above us. The heart-rate monitor beeped, counting up to some number I couldn't guess before the many short beeps were answered by a single long one. I tried to focus on my sons, to drink them in, as if they could do what morphine did, only better.

"How's your breathing, Mom?" Connor asked.

Something in my throat was clicking with each little inhalation.

"I'm going to go check in with the nurse, okay?" Connor said. "I'll be back in a minute."

I nodded once, slowly. Connor leaned over and kissed me gently on the forehead. Then he glanced at Simon and walked out of the room.

Simon didn't take Connor's place at the head of my bed. He stayed where he was, near my right leg, its femur close to bursting with tumors. Since the day a doctor told me I had only a few months to live, I'd been picturing my last moments with Simon. I'd imagined him wanting to say goodbye and hating that he could not.

Simon kept his eyes on mine as tears pooled in their bottom lids. He gave me three deep, slow nods, a gesture I imagined spoke as clearly to me as any voice could have: *I know you love me,* it said. *I love you, too.*

Then Simon stooped to lay his head on my bony breast, and he held my head in his hand, leaving nothing worth saying unsaid.

4

Frank Davies

CONNOR CAME HOME for his mother, not for me.

He stayed at her apartment until she passed. He called the funeral home. He met with the priest. He sent the death notice to the newspaper. He stood beside her casket throughout the seven-hour wake, accepting condolences from May's cousins and old friends and the church ladies who read the obituaries for something better to do than wait for their own funerals. Connor did everything May would have wanted— right down to seeing that her favorite prayer, the *Memorare*, was printed on the mass card—and he did it all himself. Neither Simon nor I were any help, for our own different reasons.

They buried May on a Thursday, in a plot within spitting distance of her parents' headstones. The priest flung holy water on the casket while Connor and Simon stood front and center on an electric-green carpet and May's friends wept and sniffed, their shoe heels sinking into ground still wet with rain. I stood off to the side, unsure where you're supposed to stand when the person being buried is only your wife in a legal sense. A few people shook my hand or smiled sadly at me. Others, the ones who imagined they had loved May better than anyone had—or, at least, better than I had—gave me the old Simon treatment: they avoided me except to claw at my eyes with the spite in their own.

The night of the funeral, I turned on the White Sox pre-game show and pulled three beers—two for me, one for Connor, who was taking a nap in his room—out of the refrigerator. I set one of the beers on the carpet, leaning it up against the couch in front of what had been Connor's usual spot for watching ballgames with me.

But when he came out of his bedroom just before the opening pitch, Connor had his jacket on and the straps of his packed duffel bag in his hand.

"Wh— wh— where y— you going?" I asked.

"Back to school."

"T— tomorrow's f— f— Friday, for Christ's s— sake."

"I've got class on Friday, Dad. And I've missed a week already."

I tried to act disgusted with him so that I wouldn't seem what I was: hurt, and embarrassed to be.

"Take y— your beer, at— at least," I said.

Connor glanced down and noticed the sweating beer can on the floor. He stared at it a moment. Then he walked over to it, bent over at the waist, lifting one foot off the floor for balance, and picked up the can with his free hand. He didn't crack it open, though.

The ballgame's first batter was in the box with a one-and-two count. Standing there with the unopened beer and his bag still in hand, Connor watched the next pitch. Ball two. The pitcher wiped the sweat from his forehead with his sleeve, got the sign, and threw again. Strike three. One down.

"Okay," Connor said, sighing as if he were sad to leave. "Take care of yourself, all right? I'm home again in a few weeks. Let's hope the Sox are in the playoffs."

I said nothing.

"See ya," he said, heading for the back door.

I reckon Connor was around eight when he realized that his staying up past his bedtime to watch the end of the ballgame wasn't me doing him a favor, but the other way around. Another father might have held Connor's interest into junior high, but I'm not sure any father could have kept him in Leyton. A boy with Connor's gifts leaves home. Period.

But Simon stayed.

● ● ●

MAY HAD ASKED me time and again if I knew why Simon wouldn't speak, and I'd put her off every time. Even the story's basics—that I'd had my young son in a bar on a Saturday morning, for one thing—would have made trouble for me. So I wagered that Simon would be speaking again soon enough, which would make telling the story behind his silence unnecessary. That turned out to be a bad bet, and when I lost it, Simon lost pretty much everything.

Only Simon and I knew that he had gone quiet because I'd sat silently by while Artie Schoen and his buddies made fun of him. But I knew something that Simon didn't: the cost of standing up to Artie Schoen.

Artie used to give me shit in high school. He'd see me in the Leyton High hallways and grip his arm tight around my neck. Then he'd say something like, "Hey, sing with me, Frankie! 'P—people try to p— p— put us d— down . . . .'"

His buddies would laugh and I'd force myself to smile, as if I were in on the joke instead of the butt of it. I never complained to anyone—if all Artie did was rib you and rough you up a little, you were getting off easy.

The autumn of my senior year, I missed a week and a half of school with the flu. On my first day back, I had to stay late after school to make up a test I'd missed. Greg Gibbons, a starter at tight end on the Leyton High football team, must have missed the test, too, because he was in the desk next to mine, waiting for the teacher to show.

Our seats, which were near the windows, gave Gibbons and me a clear view of the school's front steps with nothing better to do than watch the other kids leave for the day. Artie and his buddies, wearing their black leather jackets with every zipper and buckle undone, were in their usual spot, leaning up against the wall where the stairs met the sidewalk, trying to scandalize girls with catcalls and one-liners. Then, for what I'm sure was no good reason, Artie shoved some guy to the ground. Artie's buddies broke up laughing at the sight of the kid sprawled out on the concrete. The steady stream of students parted around the kid, but nobody stopped to help him. For his part, the kid collected his books and his glasses and hurried away without even a backward glance at Artie, checking his elbow for blood.

A minute later, when he was sure that nobody coming out the school doors had any idea what had happened and what was coming, Artie knocked another kid down the last few stairs.

I heard Gibbons snort and looked over at him. He was shaking his head.

"Some tough guy," he said.

"Y— yeah."

I finished the test before Gibbons did and left the classroom, walking the empty hallways to the school's front doors. When I went outside, Artie and his pals were still there. He was shouting at a white Chevy as a girl, hugging her books to her chest, got in on the passenger side.

"Looking good, mom!" Artie said.

The girl's mother started pulling away before her daughter had closed the door.

With my head bowed, I hustled down the far side of the steps, putting a steel railing between me and Artie's crew.

"Frankie!"

Artie sounded almost happy to see me, as if he couldn't believe his luck.

I waved to him without slowing down. Before I reached the bottom, Artie had swung his feet over the railing and corralled me against the stairway wall, blocking my escape in both directions with his arms. He needn't have bothered. Once Artie had you, there was no use trying to run away.

"Where ya headed, Frankie?"

"Ho— ho— home," I said.

"And a Merry Christmas to you, too!" he said.

His buddies laughed. I wondered if they really found Artie that funny or if this were simply their agreement: Artie tells a joke, and they laugh, whether they want to or not.

"Before you go," Artie said, "I want you to do me a favor."

I didn't agree, and I didn't refuse. I just waited.

"Say my name."

My eyes were glued to the flags in front of the gymnasium, three banners blown almost flat in a gust that whipped across the schoolyard.

"Look at me," Artie said.

So I did.

"Say my name before you go."

He opened his eyes wide and made the shape of an "a" sound with his mouth, as if I were a child who needed a hint.

I didn't want to say Artie's name. There was something about the request I didn't like—something sexual in it—but I didn't see that I had a choice. Even if I ducked away from Artie, his buddies would grab me. And then Artie would be pissed.

So I started in, fighting my stutter and the nervousness that egged it on. "Ar— ar— ar—"

"That's it."

"—ar— ar—"

"Articulate, Frankie."

"—ar— ar— Artie."

"There!" Artie said, his arms still keeping me prisoner. "That wasn't so hard, was it?"

Then a deep voice said, "Hey!"

All four of us looked up to the top of the stairs and saw Greg Gibbons standing there. Artie dropped his arms to his side. With Greg there, he forgot all about me.

I left the moment I was free, not running away, but walking pretty damn fast. I never looked back. I hadn't asked Gibbons to help me. I hadn't needed help, really—Artie had been about to let me go. And Gibbons had problems with Artie that had nothing at all to do with me. Anyway, those are the things I told myself when I heard that Greg Gibbons would miss the rest of his senior season, and his chances at a football scholarship, with a broken eye socket and shattered cheekbone.

There was a reason Artie forgot about me when Greg Gibbons showed up. Artie had little use for the people he was picking on. They were bait for guys who thought they were heroes. In Artie's world, there were no heroes—there were bad guys and the rest of us—and the bad guys, if they were smart like Artie was, always won. When he went after Simon that day, Artie taught my son a twist on what he'd already taught the rest of us: *There are no heroes, kid. Not even your old man is a hero.*

If there were any heroes, I already knew I wasn't one. I didn't want what had happened to Greg Gibbons to happen to me. Did it burn me up that Artie was teaching my kid the hard ways of the world, and making me look bad to do it? You're goddamn right it did. But what was I going to do? I could have gotten my ass kicked in front of my kid and been put out of work for weeks. But how would that have served Simon or Connor or May?

What I did was keep my seat. And that was brave enough. I could have led Simon right out of the bar when Artie started into us, and that might've been the end of it. But that lesson—that you leave when somebody starts poking fun at you—was one I couldn't allow Simon to learn. Simon was a stutterer. He was going to take shit worse than Artie was giving to him. So that day, I tried to show Simon that you go about your business—you do what you were planning to do. You don't let anybody's teasing stop you. We went into that bar to watch football, and that's what we were going to do.

Whether or not you give any of that shit-talk back or put up your fists is up to you, once you're full-grown. I gambled that Artie would get bored with us and lay off if I kept my mouth shut, and that Simon would just be glad when it was all over. I was dead right about Artie. He left after a while, popping me in the shoulder as he passed and tousling Simon's hair with his thick, greasy hand. But I guessed wrong about Simon. He wasn't glad when it was over. He was irate. And the lesson I'd tried to teach him—that you go about your business no matter what anybody has to say about it—wasn't what he took from that day. I gathered from Simon's going silent that, the way he saw it, his own father would not defend him, and if I wasn't going to love him all the way, he wasn't going to love me at all.

How do you explain to a seven-year-old that hanging him out to dry like that had been my attempt to teach him something he could use? I could have spit out the words to say so, but they wouldn't have done any good. Once Simon decided he'd been wrong about me all along, no explanation could have have changed his mind.

But as it turned out, Simon didn't want an explanation. He wanted an apology.

● ● ●

AFTER HE'D BEEN silent a good long while, May started harping on me to make Simon speak. I didn't blame her for asking. She was worried sick about him. But I knew it was useless, my telling Simon to talk. So far as Simon was concerned, I'd lost any right to boss him around when I didn't stand up to Artie.

When he'd been silent for six months, May put Simon in front of me for the kind of father-son chat that he and I were never much good at. It started with Simon wrinkling up his forehead and cussing me out with his eyes. Then I raised my hand to him, and May rushed him out of the room before I could bring the hand down.

So far as May ever knew, that was my only attempt to get Simon to speak up before his voice went dead. But two days later, I tried again.

He got scared when I came into his room—part of me was glad I could still scare him a little. I sat down on the edge of his bed and nodded in the direction of his radio.

"Tur— turn that off, p— please."

Simon stared at me, deciding whether or not to defy me from the get-go. Then he spun the dial toward him until it clicked, shutting up whatever goddamned gabbing huckster he'd been listening to.

I took a deep breath and rubbed my face with my palms, dragging the calluses over a three-day beard.

"I— I— think I m— might have t— taught you a l— lesson I n— never meant to."

I didn't look at him. I was afraid I'd see that look in his eyes, get as fired up as he seemed to be, and end this one-way chat the way I'd tried to end our first one.

"Y— you think that s— s— silence gives a st— st— stuttering m— man a fort to hi— hide in. Y— you think it m— makes you s— strong." I shook my head. "It doesn't. N— not f— for long."

I checked his face then. He must have felt my eyes on him, because he looked up and met them for just a second. For the first time in months, he didn't seem to hate me.

"I've tried s— silence," I said. "L— like y— you're trying it n— now. A— and I've l— learned two th— things. Woo— whether you sss— say a lot or a l— little, it— it's b— better to be able t— to talk, e— even how we— we do it. And si— si— silence is day—dangerous. You use y— your voice o— or you l— lose it." I shook my head and waved off that last part. "Y— your s— s— stutter t— takes it away."

I felt Simon stiffen in the spine, which told me he'd never considered losing his voice for good, and that now he was worried that maybe I knew what the hell I was talking about.

I turned my head to him, brushing my chin against the top of my shoulder, and when our eyes met that time, I was reminded of a truth Simon well understood, and I did my best to forget: Simon's stutter was my fault. He was how he was because I didn't have any better to give him. That's why Connor is such a miracle! He came from me, just like Simon did. Connor is proof that there's something in me that doesn't hack words to pieces.

"Y— you nee— need to s— s— start s— speaking again, Simon," I said. "Or— or your s— s— stutter w— w—"

I wrapped my hands around an invisible neck.

"—will throttle you and it w— won't let go."

When I looked at Simon again, he was calm. He pointed at me, and then tapped the flat part of his fist to his chest. I recognized the second gesture as one of the bastardized signs May had taught him, holding the line on Simon's manners even as he stayed silent. The gesture usually meant, *I'm sorry.* But Simon had pointed at me first. He wanted me to apologize.

I saw an opportunity there.

"T— tell me wha— what you w— want m— me to do."

I nodded at him slowly and even smiled a little. I wanted him to know that I was ready to make amends—and I was, whether I'd done wrong or not. All Simon had to do was open his mouth and tell me to.

But he just stared at me, insisting with those stubborn blue eyes of his: *Apologize.*

"S— say the wor— words," I said.

In my own mind, I'd already broken Simon's silence and delivered him to my tired but lovely wife. I was already the hero Artie had said I'd never be. I wanted this.

"Say the w— words, Simon."

He closed his eyes and shook his head.

No. And I think I also saw, *You first.*

Something snapped in me then. I swatted the radio out of Simon's hands, and he dove after it like a lifeguard after a sinking toddler. Without a word.

And less than a month later, when his mother tried to scare him into screaming only to find that the stutter had snuffed out his voice, just like I'd said it would, Simon blamed me. He couldn't say so, but I'm sure of it.

I've taken no joy in Simon's silence, but it has been the occasion of my only real achievement as his father: I have never once looked my son in his hateful eyes and said, *I told you so.*

● ● ●

CONNOR LIVES IN Chicago now. He's doing comedy every night, he says. In the past year, I've seen him once, for a Thanksgiving dinner that wasn't much of one: rotisserie chicken from the grocery and a carton of mashed potatoes Simon had brought home from the restaurant the night before. Connor did what May would have done during the meal— he asked Simon if his work at the restaurant was going well and if the commercials he'd been hearing lately were any good. Simon answered with head nods and shrugs. A little while later, I asked Connor how things were going for him with the comedy. He said they were fine, considering he hadn't been in Chicago long.

"W— what are y— your sh— shows like?"

Connor winced a little. "They're hard to explain," he said. "We improvise, so every show is different."

I got the idea I'd asked an ignorant question and felt my embarrassment as a pulsing pain.

"How's work for you?" he asked me.

"S— same."

We were all silent after that. We ate our food and missed May. When we were finished, Simon went to his room, and Connor and I went into the living room to watch a football game neither one of us could gin up much interest in.

Late in the third quarter, with the score tied at seventeen, Connor was slumped down on the couch, his eyes barely open. He was tired, I figured, from all those late nights, but he looked more bored than tired. Half-drunk by then, I started to worry that each minute Connor wasn't entertained pushed his next visit, which was already too far off for my liking if it wasn't next week, further into the future.

"A— anything you— you'd r— rather watch instead?"

He glanced at me—I think he might have thought I was being smart with him, but he must have seen I wasn't.

"It's Thanksgiving," he said over a yawn, as if it was nonsense that we'd let anything other than football bore us that day.

I would have watched anything he wanted. I just wanted him around.

As I followed Connor out to his car the next morning, I worked up the guts to say that I hoped to see more of him.

"What about coming up to the city, Dad?" Connor said. "You could stay at my place."

"I— I appre— appreciate the offer," I said, "but I— I've got n— no interest in d— driving in that city."

He laughed at me. "Most of the drive is highway."

"It's n— not a hi— highway if y— you're s— stuck in traffic." I shook my head. "N— no, thank you."

Connor nodded with his lower jaw jutted out, measuring my readiness for what he would say next.

"I've got to tell you, Dad. I don't think I'm going to be coming down here very often."

I knew this, of course, but hearing it still stung. "Be— because of your sh— shows," I said.

"That's part of it."

I felt myself getting sore. "W— well, what's the r— rest of it, then?"

"Being in this house with you and Simon—it's no vacation. Mom's funeral was more fun."

Walking back to the house as Connor's car pulled out of the yard, I had an idea: I would throw Simon out. He was a twenty-three-year-old man. He had a job. He wasn't paying any rent. I could have most of his stuff out of his bedroom and under a tarp in the yard by the time he got home from work. I wasn't about to let the son who hated me keep me from seeing the son who loved me as much as anyone could.

I stood in the living room, glancing at Simon's bedroom door, and imagined calling Connor to tell him the news: *Simon is out for good! Come on down whenever you can. We'll have the place to ourselves!*

Only then did I realize that Connor's line about being in the house with Simon and me—that wasn't an explanation for the long stretches between his visits. It was an excuse. Watching ballgames with me was what it had been for Connor since he was eight years old: an easy chore, made harder now by the travel it required. Standing in my living room, I felt like a fool for supposing that throwing Simon out of the house would bring Connor back more than a couple nights a year. Connor was gone—I don't know why I couldn't get that idea fixed in my head. He'd been on his way out since he was a boy.

And Simon was still here. I shit you not when I tell you that, just minutes after I'd planned to evict him, I took comfort in the fact that later that night, when he'd wiped the spots off of the glasses at the Tippecanoe restaurant, Simon would come home. There was a closeness in being the only two people who knew why he'd gone silent, the kind of closeness that might exist between two witnesses to a crime who agree, for their own selfish reasons, not to report it and never to speak to one another again. That closeness had left us with a photo negative of the relationship we might have pictured for ourselves. But it was better than nothing. No, I didn't want Simon out of the house for good. I didn't want to be alone.

So five or six nights a week, I leave for the Four Corners while Simon is still at work. I say hello to the fellas, but I sit by myself at the bar. My drinking buddies are the sports announcers on that little TV in the corner. When I yell at the screen, I yell to them, and if they see the same thing I saw, I let myself believe that they heard me. And some nights, when the game is over and the bar is quiet, I am back in the Four Corners as it was on the day Artie went after Simon. My blood is up. My stutter is closing its hand around my throat. And in my head, where memory and imagination and whiskey meet and mix, I do more than keep my seat. I stand up and, struggling my way through the words and ignoring his interruptions, I tell Artie that he can't talk to my son that way.

And Artie says, *Oh, no?*

And he gets up, and his buddies get up, and I get one good punch in, one solid right hand that I grind into the pulp and bone of his nose, before I'm knocked to the ground and they're stomping on my head. And then I wake up groggy in a white hospital room, and May is there, and Connor is there, and Simon is there, too, and I am certain, from my first blurry look at him, that I still have my older son's love and respect.

I usually leave the bar some time after midnight. When I pull the truck into the yard, the house is dark. I come in the back door, pull off my boots and walk across the kitchen floor in socks that won't stay up. And if his radio isn't on, I stand outside Simon's bedroom door and listen, like May and I would do when he was a baby. I stay there, sometimes for minutes at a time, teetering a little but otherwise keeping still, until I've heard something—a snore or a breath or the creak of a mattress spring—that reassures me that Simon has once again come home to what little we have left.

● ● ●

HE IS TRYING to speak.

The first time I noticed, a wind-spanked January night a little more than a month after Connor told me he wouldn't be coming home much anymore, I was standing outside Simon's bedroom door with the liquor still whirring in my head, listening but unsure what I was hearing. I thought he was dry heaving, maybe. But now I know that Simon is working a word—maybe just a syllable—over and over again. It was just a tortured, airy letter *F* for a few months, but now, every once in a while, he gets past the *F*, and I can hear a weary croak—a voice—for a split second before the stutter strangles it.

It's a goddamn miracle Simon has any voice at all. But to call it a miracle isn't fair to Simon. He is *working* for it. He picks fight after fight with his stutter, knowing full well he'll lose. It's the sound of him riding out a fit that kills me—the gagging and straining against a tightness that makes a man feel as if his own body is smothering him. And when Simon's fit is over, while my waterworks run and the snot drips over my lips so I don't reveal myself with a sniffle, Simon starts in on the word again.

Now, every night I go to bed knowing one thing for certain: Simon will leave this place. His trying to talk isn't the only reason I know so. I saw him walk out of the house the other morning, well before he was due at the restaurant, with a textbook and a notebook under his arm. Simon is going to school. He graduated high school, so far as I know, and the only college he could reach on foot is the two-year, community outfit a mile down the highway from our place, so I'm guessing that's where he's enrolled. A man content to keep sharing a house with a person he won't speak to doesn't bother with self-improvements. I never have.

If you'd told me a year ago that Simon would speak again, I'd have said you were full of shit. Simon is still a long way from saying even one word, and he'll always have his stutter to contend with, but I'm not fool enough to bet against the boy again. He stayed silent as a seven-year-old, despite people ordering and even begging him to speak. If Simon getting his voice back is a question of will, like giving it up was, how could *anyone* bet against him? The boy doesn't have Connor's gifts, but he's got his mother's determination in spades.

And when he can speak again, he'll leave me here, just like May and Connor did. I bet he leaves without telling me off. Simon decided a long time ago to stop talking to me, and he sticks to his guns. I admire that about him.

5

Elaine Vasner

A TALENT AGENCY as good as mine—and in Chicago in 2010, there is no agency better—might get two-dozen unsolicited voiceover demos every day. Unless there's an intern sitting around with nothing to do, or an agent as young and hungry as I was when I started, those demos usually get thrown away unheard. Not at Skyline Talent. I listen to every unsolicited demo sent to our office.

Nothing much comes of these private auditions. In more than thirty-five years in the business, I've signed only a handful of artists on the strength of a demo I didn't ask for. These days, once they've had a few minutes of my attention, almost all of the CDs—even demos from operators shrewd enough to direct their padded manila envelopes to "Elaine Vasner, President"—end up where they belong: in the trash.

Most of my day is spent chasing down the money my clients have earned. I talk tough with the ad-agency people until I'm sure they've heard my unspoken threat—I never dull its edge by saying the words—to cut them off from the finest stable of non-celebrity voiceover talent in the English-speaking world if they don't pay in full, and soon. I play the demos after hours, when I'm finally finished hearing and dismissing the excuses of the accounts-payable hacks I have to deal with. The ritual begins when I pull the bottle of vodka from the bottom drawer of my desk and pour four fingers into the lipstick-stained mug I've been using all day for coffee. I open my office window—just a crack in the winter—and light a cigarette. Then I load the first CD into the player I bought years ago at the Walgreen's on the corner, kick back, and listen.

Most of the demos are bad in mundane ways. They feature voices so weak I can hear them cracking after just thirty seconds, or so grating—the accompanying cover letters, usually written by housewives with a computer, a microphone, and too much time on their hands, tend to describe these voices as "unique" or "quirky"—that I have to sit on my hands to keep myself from pressing the stop button. But some of the demos I hear are spectacularly awful. There are the people who record commercials off the radio and try to shout over the professional performance. Some hopefuls write their own scripts, proving only that their chances as copywriters are as dim as their prospects in voiceover.

Other people break into jingles. I hate jingles.

Then there are the impressionists. Not a month goes by that somebody—usually an out-of-touch white guy—doesn't send in a Jell-O Pudding spot as performed by Bill Cosby. Has any woman who does Mae West ever seen a Mae West movie? Most of the impressions I hear make her sound more like Jimmy Cagney. And just how big is the market for fake celebrity endorsements by Christopher Walken? Do people think the *real* Walken is that hard to get? He's in fucking everything!

But the most tragic—and, therefore, the most hilarious—are the people who, God love them, have so completely suppressed their insecurity about a speech impediment that, apparently, they can't hear themselves anymore. How else would you explain a man with the wettest of lisps, and his pick of any brand name in the world, sending me his recording of a spot for Sears? Or the Asian guy, whose *L*'s came out as *R*'s, choosing a Cadillac commercial? The real gem arrived just a few months ago. A young woman submitted her performance of a sixty-second radio commercial that, the way she did it, took almost a minute and a half. Every third or fourth word took her five or six tries to spit out. This demo I did not throw away. Sometimes, if the delivery of new unsolicited demos is light, I return to the stutterer's demo and try to figure out what the hell I am listening to. It isn't a joke, that's for sure. The performance is earnest as all hell. One night, after one too many vodkas, I found myself getting a little weepy at the girl's determination, the same way you might tear up watching an amputee finish a marathon. There's something compelling about a person who makes a prize of doing what she's set out to do. And that might be what this demo is—a girl who battled a stutter her whole life proving something to herself and honoring the achievement by sending out the recording. I can tell you what it's not: any reason at all for me to sign the girl who made it.

You might think I listen to these demos for the same reason people watch *American Idol* auditions: to feel superior, to enjoy the thought that, as bad as I may be on my worst day, things could be worse—I could be *this* deluded asshole. But the real reason I hold these auditions night after night is more practical: my other options are going home to a man I've never loved, or calling Larry Sellers, and I don't want to do either thing.

● ● ●

I STARTED AT Skyline as an agent's assistant in 1974. I was right out of high school and only six months removed from telling my parents what my uncle had been doing to me every time he got me alone. The fearless part of me was born that day. Once you've worked up the nerve to tell your mother that her big brother has been putting his prick where it doesn't belong and that you want it to stop—now—no tough-talking ad man can scare you.

I was promoted to junior agent at twenty-one. Jesus, I was young. To build my client list, I went to theaters—everything from The Second City to storefront avant-garde. I would call ahead, drop the name of the agency to get on the list, and spend the show listening for a voice I could use. Most of the time, I heard no bankable voices, but if I did, I'd wait in the bar across the street after the show and, when the cast showed up, chat up the actor I'd taken an interest in. I would say I'd enjoyed the show, whether I had or not, and ask about voiceover representation. Many of the actors I asked already had agents but rarely had work. I would hand over my card no matter what, and my first clients were actors who called me back—months later, in some cases—having decided they'd be better off with me than with the agent they'd had when we met.

When things were slow at the office, I'd ask the receptionist if any tapes had come in over the transom that day. If she hadn't already thrown them away, I'd bring the tapes to the tiny studio in our office and play them. Unsolicited demos were no better then than they are now. In many ways, they were worse, because decent recording equipment was so expensive. I heard many demos that seemed to capture the sound of a person shouting across a large room. And many of the people with the means and good sense to buy an external microphone didn't know how to use one. No sound is more lethal to a voiceover audition than an amplified gust of heavy breathing from the nose.

Larry Sellers' demo tape was different—by which I mean better—than any other I'd heard. As I found out later, Larry had made the recording after hours in a studio, with an engineer pal working the knobs and faders. But the main thing was that voice. It was incredibly rich in its timbre—especially rare in the voice of someone so young—and it seemed to possess a persuasive quality that worked independently of his spoken words. As Larry described the beauty of the landscape of Illinois' Starved Rock, his voice persuaded me—it gently commanded me—to make a pilgrimage to a state park I'd never even considered visiting before.

Larry's letter, too, was different in how credibly it flattered me.

"Ms. Vasner," the letter said, "I asked a friend in the industry to give me the name of a talent agent who is a rising star. The name he gave me is yours.

"My audition tape is enclosed with this letter. For now, I've sent it only to you. I hope to hear from you soon. Sincerely, Larry Sellers."

He'd been my client for six years when, over drinks—after a while, anything we did we did over drinks—Larry came clean: there was no "friend in the industry." Larry had overheard me making my pitch to a member of the Goodman Theatre's cast of Mamet's *A Life in the Theatre*.

"I didn't know who you were," Larry told me, "but I'd had my eye on you since you walked in."

"I bet," I said, pretending not to believe—and not to be a little excited—that Larry had wanted to pick me up the first time he saw me. I'd liked the look of him from the start. He wore his beard closely cropped beneath a thick head of dark brown hair, and he was beefy without being fat. There just seemed to be *plenty* of him. I felt the urge to take him by his massive upper arms and *squeeze* until my hands were exhausted. I've always preferred big men. My uncle was a skinny shit.

"I'd moved over to the bar," Larry said, "and was about to buy you a drink when the thespians arrived and you sprang on that string bean of a man."

I laughed. "You mean Charles Garnett. A wonderful actor."

"He took himself too seriously."

"Larry, it was business. Did you want him to slip on a banana peel?"

"What I mean is, he took himself too seriously, and didn't take you seriously enough."

I hadn't felt that way as I made my pitch to Charles Garnett, but as I recalled the exchange now, I could see him looking down his nose at me and holding my card by one corner, as if it might be contaminated with some disease.

"And when you were done with Garnett," Larry said, "you left. I hadn't said a word to you. So I figured the only thing I could do was get in a studio, make a tape, and send it to you."

"So this whole voiceover thing was a ploy to get my attention."

With that, the greatest voiceover artist of his generation lifted his cocktail glass, held it in front of his lips, and said, "Here's hoping it works."

And I laughed again. Larry was always a flirt, but his flirting wasn't the funny part. What had me laughing was the idea that anything was more important to Larry than his work. So far as I knew, doing voiceover—what Larry described as the wine-like feel of the words in his mouth as he whispered or crooned or bellowed into the microphone— was all he'd ever loved.

But the story he told about our near meeting worked. It got my attention. I decided I didn't want that night to end with a sloppy, drunken kiss on the street after one round too many. I didn't feel right inviting Larry to my place, and he didn't ask me to his, so I suggested we get a room at the Hilton and Towers. As we rode the elevator up to the tenth floor, standing at the back of the car behind two fat, middle-aged conventioneers, Larry put his hand on my ass and gently goosed it. I let my hand drift over his thigh, brushing the head of his cock through his pants with the back of my painted fingernails. If not for the two conventioneers, I would've fucked him right then and there.

Up in the room, I lit a cigarette and let it dangle from my lips as I undressed for him. Larry lay on the bed in his boxer shorts and purred. I came quickly and put all the energy I had left into pleasing Larry. When we'd finished, I wrapped my arms around him and put my ear to his chest, listening to the workings of his incredible voice and delighting in the feel and the sound of him.

After that, we slept together when we were both between dates and when big residual checks came in. We each had little relationships, but our own seemed to exist on another plane. I wasn't threatened by other women, and Larry never asked me about other men. That was what excited me most about Larry: he could give me what I needed without demanding any more of me than I could give.

For two people unsure if they could ever love anyone more than they loved their work, and because I wasn't sure I could ever trust any man after what my bastard uncle did to me, my relationship with Larry was a perfectly blended, forget-your-cares cocktail: equal parts business and pleasure.

● ● ●

IN DECEMBER OF '95, when we'd been working together for eighteen years, Larry called and asked me to meet him at Miller's Pub after work.

Larry and I were regulars at Miller's. Before or after dinner somewhere else, we'd sit at the far end of the bar, away from the hard-drinking Loop lawyers and accountants, sharing our evening only with each other and James, the bartender who'd worked evenings at Miller's since the mid-Seventies, when Larry started drinking there. James put rounds in front of us until it was clear we'd had enough. At another place, we might've demanded another drink, just to prove a point. At Miller's, we stopped, figuring James knew best.

I assumed that our reason for meeting that night, to the extent we needed one, was the publication of a local-boy-made-good profile of Larry in the Peoria paper. The week before, I'd given the reporter a quote for the piece, saying that Larry could take a mediocre script and make a great radio commercial. The moment I'd given it, I knew the quote would read like little more than an agent promoting her client and herself, but what did I care? I wasn't chasing any business downstate, and Larry was as good as I'd said.

When I walked into Miller's, Larry wasn't at the bar. I caught James's eye with a wave, and he pointed me to the back corner of the restaurant. I found Larry in a booth decorated with mangy golden garland and yellowing plastic mistletoe. He leaned over a nearly finished drink that obviously wasn't his first of the night.

I took off my coat and tossed it onto the bench opposite Larry. "Looks like the party started without me."

The waitress must have followed me to the booth. She stood between us, showing her crooked-toothed smile to Larry. Larry pointed at me.

"Vodka tonic with a lime," I said.

"Two of those," Larry said.

"You got it," said the waitress.

"Is that the article?" I asked, taking my seat.

Larry picked up a folded section of a newspaper from under the small booth lamp and tossed it in front of me. The editors had used a headshot of Larry smiling like a troublemaking kid. The quote I'd given, in its entirety, was the last line of the first paragraph.

I skimmed down to Larry's discussion of his instrument and the care he took with his voice.

"'My voice wasn't my livelihood yet,'" I said, reading Larry's quote aloud, "'but I always protected it. For example, I smoked, but didn't inhale. I still don't. Sinatra smokes the same way.'"

I looked up and dropped the paper back in front of him. "I guess that makes you Sinatra, then."

Larry didn't say anything.

"More like Joey Bishop," I added.

He watched his ice melt. Except to find out what I was drinking, Larry hadn't looked at me. I had another crack at the ready, one about this not being much of a party, but I skipped it.

"What's the deal, Larry?"

He smiled then, the way people smile at a funeral, which probably explains my first guess as to what was wrong: I thought one of Larry's parents had died.

"We've had a good run, Elaine," he said.

Hearing those words, in that voice, chilled me.

"What do you mean?"

"I mean we've both done better than we could've imagined."

I'd had it with the slow build-up. "What the fuck are you getting at?"

"I'm going with another agent."

I snorted. "What?"

I'd heard the words—I wanted him to repeat them. But Larry just stared at his drink, and his words repeated themselves in the silence.

I leaned toward him, over the empty space on the table where my drink should have been.

"You've done national television spots for Ford, Aquafresh, and Old Spice," I said. "You're still the national radio voice of Hertz and Maalox. I made your voice the sound of quality in Chicago, which is why advertisers will pay twice the running rate to get it."

My eyes were locked on his face, but he was still looking down at his drink, as if he'd been expecting this reaction and was just waiting it out.

"Look at me, Larry," I said, sharply.

He raised his eyes just a little.

"Name another agent in Chicago who could build you a better book of local and national work and keep it growing."

He shook his head. "I can't."

"You're goddamn right, you can't."

I sat back, and the waitress put our drinks on the table. I took a swig of mine, still staring Larry down, feeling like a lawyer who'd just nailed her closing argument. Given the case I'd made—given what *I* had done for him—how could Larry work with anyone else?

"The agent works out of Los Angeles," he said.

My confidence began to leave me in a slow, steady leak.

"She says that with my reel—with my voice—she can get me film work, audio books. More work. The kind of work I haven't done before."

The kind of work I knew almost nothing about. The kind I couldn't get him if I tried.

"She wants to get me on camera, too."

This woman was flattering Larry with Hollywood promises. Larry was good-looking, but he wasn't on-camera material. Taking him out from behind the microphone and putting him in front of a camera was no better an idea than sending Eric Clapton onstage without a guitar— sure, the guy can sing a little, but that's not what anybody pays to see. How many times had she pulled this same move with Midwestern talent? Why couldn't Larry see it for what it was? I started to picture this L.A. agent—younger than me, with long, blonde hair and perky little tits, sitting in an office above a boulevard lined with palm trees, on the phone with Larry, selling him a version of himself that doesn't exist—and for the first time, I felt upset about another woman in Larry's life.

Larry and I had a signed contract. I could've kept him for radio and television if I wanted. But I wouldn't do it. The freedom to come and go as we pleased, to turn down an offer to meet for drinks or leave while the other was still sleeping, had been the crux of our relationship, and our personal and professional lives seemed impossible to untangle. In that moment, I worried less about Larry leaving my agency than I did about him leaving Chicago.

"Will you work out of L.A.?" The smallness of my voice frightened me.

"Some of the time," he said. "But most of my work is here, so I'll keep a place in Chicago."

My work is here.

My *work* is here.

I heard the remark both ways and felt doubly snubbed, first by the idea that Larry could so easily divorce his success from all I was still doing to help him achieve it, and then that I was nowhere to be found on Larry's short list of reasons to keep one foot in Chicago.

With some reason to believe that Larry wasn't moving to L.A. forever, I found the courage to leave the bar.

"I wish you a lot of luck," I said, grabbing my coat and swinging my legs out of the booth. "You'll need it."

I stood up and threw my coat over my arm.

"Elaine, let me take you home."

In his tone—even drunk, Larry is a master of tone—I heard the suggestion that I was being unreasonable. That pissed me off. I took a quick step toward him and, to this day, I would swear he leaned away from me, afraid.

"You've fucked me once already tonight, Larry."

● ● ●

THE NEXT DAY, I called everybody who owed me money for Larry's work and told them to pay up. When all of Larry's fees were in house, I had my comptroller cut his final check and put it in the mail.

"Any note?" the bean counter asked.

"No note."

Then I purged my office of everything with Larry's name on it. I boxed up tapes of the spots he'd recorded and copies of the contracts I'd signed on his behalf and put them into storage. I would've chucked it all in the trash, but I knew that business break-ups like the one Larry had put in motion could be messy, and that these records were my proof that I'd made Larry money and paid him fairly. I wasn't about to find myself in a lawsuit, trying to explain why I'd thrown away every shred of evidence of my and Larry's work together. I'm a businesswoman. Not a schoolgirl.

The purge extended to mementos of time spent with Larry— room-service receipts, matchbooks from 4 a.m. bars, a menu I'd stuffed into my purse after a dinner celebrating Larry's Aquafresh booking, and a brochure for a Virgin Islands vacation we'd talked about a hundred times but never booked. I even threw out a placemat autographed, in 1986 at Larry's drunken request, by Tony Bennett, who had descended upon Miller's Pub with his entourage when we were having a nightcap.

"Elaine," it read. "You're dynamite! And Larry ain't bad. Tony Bennett."

It's not that I was through with Larry. I wasn't. It's just that I was sure that things between us would never be as good as they'd been when we were working together. I didn't want to be reminded of that fact every time I opened a drawer.

I thought I'd tossed out everything until a few weeks later, when I was looking for an invoice and found a framed photograph of Larry and me. We were at a table for two against a backdrop of knotty-pine paneling. It took me a moment to recognize the back room of the Twin Anchors restaurant in Old Town. The photo had survived my disposal of all things Larry, hidden behind the yellow-green fronds of a potted plant I kept on the file cabinet next to my office door and never remembered to water.

Holding the frame in my hand, it occurred to me that I hadn't thrown away any pictures of Larry and me. This was probably the only one I'd ever had. A relationship like ours didn't lend itself to photo opps. We'd never been to a wedding or a charity gala together—we'd never set up a date with more than a day's notice. I wouldn't have had any photos of Larry and me if the Twin Anchors hadn't allowed a photographer to walk around taking pictures and Larry hadn't bought one to make him go away. The purge had made artifacts of our relationship scarce, which made this image seem more precious. And there were some things about Larry and me, I decided, that I did want reminding of—like the fact that we'd once posed for and purchased this picture to get rid of a photographer and back to our conversation.

The plant that had been hiding it died soon after of not-so-benign neglect, but the photo of Larry and me is still on top of that cabinet, kept mostly out of sight behind the wilting, browning leaves of my latest victim.

● ● ●

FOR MONTHS, THE only place I heard Larry's voice was on the radio. He had kept most of his old clients—Jewel Foods and Wendy's among them—but Hertz dropped him. His replacement was a guy who sounded a little like Larry but had only a pale shadow of Larry's vocal command. In Larry's hands, the Hertz work had been crisp and precise, like the driving of a champion road racer. The new guy was cruising wet city streets on bald tires. I wondered if some higher-ups in creative at the agency that handled the Hertz business had worried I might cut them off from Skyline's talent if they continued to work with Larry. That thought had me feeling like a big swinging dick in this business, a far cry from the quiet assistant I'd been when I started out, until I wrapped my head around its discouraging flipside: the agencies still working with Larry might have decided that, if they could have Larry Sellers, they could live without Elaine Vasner and her list.

In August of '96, cabbing home to my apartment after visiting a sick girlfriend in the hospital and dining out alone, I heard the first spot Larry did for a client he hadn't booked through me. The advertiser was Connolly Auto, a family-owned trio of dealerships known for bottom feeding: buying up cheap airtime on the big AM stations, making a low-end spot, and running it for years. The spot opened and closed, as all Connolly Auto spots did, with the dealer's jingle, which lifted and twisted a Cole Porter melody and rhymed "Connolly" with "quality." But this time, instead of some non-union, no-talent stooge, it was Larry sandwiched between the singing, his subtle vocal touches drowned out by a loud instrumental loop of the ridiculous jingle.

When the spot was over, I leaned my head against the cab window. This was not on-camera work in Hollywood. It was a bad local job I would never have allowed Larry to take. I knew there was no way Old Man Connolly had paid the rate I'd demanded for Larry. And while his voice may have been helping the Connolly Auto brand, the spot was poison to Larry's. Worst of all, everyone in the business would hear the spot eventually—Connolly's run-it-into-the-ground media strategy would make sure of that. I was still the top agent at Skyline—making almost as much money without Larry as I'd made with him—but hearing that spot gave me the feeling that everything I'd worked to build was being torn down around me.

* * *

A FEW WEEKS after hearing Larry's Connolly spot, I was in my office when the receptionist, Lisa, showed up at my door.

"Excuse me, Elaine?"

That she had gotten off her ass instead of picking up the phone at her desk told me something was wrong. "Yes?"

"I have a call for you," Lisa said. "It's Larry Sellers."

She almost whispered his name, as if she were scared to say it to me. I hadn't told her to screen Larry's calls. But there she was, standing just outside my doorway, asking for verbal permission to transfer Larry's call to my phone, a task she'd done without a second thought a hundred times before. I had the horrifying thought that, for months, without my noticing, everyone at Skyline Talent—even Lisa—had been seeing me as a jilted woman.

I turned her pity back on her. "Lisa," I said, shaking my head.

"Yes?"

"What are you doing? Go back to your desk and transfer the call."

"Okay."

Ten seconds later, my phone trilled, I answered, and I heard Larry's voice say my name. He didn't sound sheepish or ashamed or chastened. He sounded as he always had.

We met for a drink that night at Trader Vic's. We were both a little stiff at first, and the jokes Larry made to loosen things up fell flat. But soon the Mai Tais were doing their work, and we were more comfortable. Larry mentioned a play he'd seen at the Goodman, and we discovered we'd seen it the same night. We hadn't run into each other, though, and if Larry had seen me with my date, an ad guy a few years younger than me, he didn't cop to it. I asked after the bartenders and regulars at the places we used to drink together, places I mostly stayed away from now, and Larry inquired about my girlfriend, Nancy, the one I'd been visiting in the hospital the night I heard his Connolly Auto spot. I told him that Nancy's cancer seemed to be heading into remission. This bit of good news about a woman he'd never met brought a warm, genuine smile to Larry's face, and the brief glimpse into his big, soft heart gave me a lift.

We went upstairs to the Palmer House and got a room. I'd supposed we were too drunk to do any more than pass out, but once we were alone, we attacked each other, pulling off our still-buttoned clothes and clacking our teeth in the frenzy. I pushed Larry down onto the bed, put my hands on his chest, and ground him into me, expelling as I fucked him all of the anger and frustration and anxiety I'd accumulated in the past nine months. Even as I grunted and seethed my way to orgasm, I listened to every note Larry made, the sounds of feelings that words could only sell short.

I left him before the sun came up. I was meeting a new client and needed a shower and a change of clothes. As I sat in the back of the cab, I replayed the evening in my mind and realized that Larry hadn't tried to tell me everything was rosy with his new agent, and that I hadn't bragged about how well things were going at Skyline. And I'd left the Connolly Auto commercial unmentioned, like you would a big red pimple on the nose of an old woman. In fact, this date, for all it felt like old times, was different in that we never talked business. Not once.

A week later, Larry would spend a half-hour of our evening rendezvous recounting a voiceover session he had done in the old Capitol Records Building in Hollywood. He would describe, in detail, the acoustics and layout of the enormous studio and what he called the "Come Fly With Me vibe" of the place. I don't think we ever got together again without discussing the industry from one angle or another. But I remember believing, as the taxi covered the eight blocks from the Palmer House to my apartment in the gray darkness of the early morning after our reunion, that my relationship with Larry, which had always been business first, had changed in a way I hadn't imagined possible—that what was personal between us had finally trumped the professional.

● ● ●

FOR THE NEXT four years, Larry and I saw each other whenever he came to town. I dated other men if they asked and I was interested, but the bar for my interest was set pretty high. I turned down more than a few good dinner invitations because I preferred to wait and see if Larry called. More often than not, I spent those would-have-been date nights alone, but I didn't mind, because I knew Larry would be calling any day now, and if he didn't, I'd call him myself.

I was alone—in my office, long after close of business—when the questions came.

Why is it that Larry has never once, so far as I know, been jealous of another man in my life?

Does he believe that he'll always have me, no matter what?

Is he looking for another woman? A better woman?

If he meets her, will Larry leave me all of a sudden, over drinks, the way he left Skyline?

It was official: I wanted more from Larry, and I was ready (finally) to offer him more of myself (if he wanted more), to let him into the dark places he'd glimpsed (maybe) in the way we made love. I wasn't sure what had made me ready. Maybe it was my bastard uncle dying (alone, he rotted for days—serves him right) three years before. Or maybe it was my turning forty-eight and the end of the twentieth century. Whatever the explanation, I should have made some good-faith effort to answer the questions I'd asked myself.

Instead, I tried to make Larry jealous.

At a benefit for the American Cancer Society, I met Bill, a lawyer who had lost his wife seven years before to breast cancer. Bill was a good ten years older than me. His hair was thinning at the crown of his head and he had gone a little soft in the middle. But his suit looked like it cost more than Larry's entire wardrobe, and its perfect fit reinforced my impression that Bill, though not a scintillating personality, was comfortable in his own skin.

After two rounds of martinis picked up from passing trays, Bill asked me out with the same quiet confidence he'd shown when he started chatting me up.

"Why not?" I answered.

And when he asked where we could meet for a drink, I said, "How about Miller's Pub?"

Bill met me outside that night, and we walked into Miller's together. I looked for Larry at the end of the bar. He wasn't there.

That was fine. I didn't need him to be.

Bill and I took stools in the middle of the bar, just to the right side of the tap handles. James, in his white shirt and black vest, saw me right away, but instead of bringing me my usual and addressing me by name, he laid cocktail napkins in front of us and said, "How are we doing this evening?"

James was leaving it up to me to say whether or not we knew each other. His sticking to the bartender's code gave my date with Bill the feel of an affair, which it wasn't, but I was hoping Larry would see it just that way.

"We're dandy, James," I said. "How are you?"

"Can't complain," James answered, smiling politely. "What can I get you?"

"What do you say, Bill?" I said. "Martinis worked pretty well the first time."

Bill smiled and shrugged. "All right with me."

I looked at James, and he nodded.

"Two martinis," he said.

"With olives, please, James."

"You got it."

I sat with my body facing Bill, resting my right elbow on the bar. He made a couple of jokes—bad puns, really—and I laughed at each of them, leaning toward him and putting my hand on his thigh. When James checked on us and returned with two more rounds, I made sure he saw me having a good time.

Bill paid for the drinks and left a huge tip. I hoped the money became a nice detail when James followed the part of the bartender's code that demanded he tell Larry everything.

Bill and I left together. When we were halfway down the block, away from Miller's, I stopped and turned to him.

"Well," I said. "I should be getting home."

"Oh," he said, looking disappointed. "Of course."

"Thanks for the drinks," I said. "And the conversation."

"My pleasure."

After an awkward moment of watching Bill try to decide what to do next, I made his decision for him. I took a quick step toward him, put a hand gently on his face, kissed him quickly on the lips, and stepped away before he could wrap his arms around me.

"Good night, Bill."

"Good night," he said, stammering a little. Then, excitedly, he added, "Can I hail you a cab?"

"I'm fine," I said, yelling back to him over my shoulder. "Thanks."

I walked the damp sidewalks of Wabash Street in the direction of my apartment, leaning into a cold, northerly wind and bubbling with anticipation. I was certain that Larry would call the next day, or the day after, or the day after that. We would meet for drinks somewhere—not Miller's this time. We'd talk shop, like we always did, and I'd watch Larry repeatedly, silently talk himself out of asking any questions about the man I'd taken to our old place. And even with all we were leaving unsaid, I would guzzle down a feeling only Larry could give me: being with someone who really knew me. Then we'd get a room somewhere. And when the door had closed behind us, I would stand there in the dark—Larry would have to come to me. He would kiss and press and paw me, and we'd fall onto the bed. He might try to mention Bill then, but I'd shush him and urge him on and listen to him say how good it feels until we're finished, and I'm in his arms, and we both understand that we're back where we belong with no reason to ever leave again.

But Larry didn't call the next day. Not the next day, either. Bill called, though, on that third day, and asked me to dinner.

"Why not?" I said.

And I went and I drank until it wasn't so hard to laugh at wordplay that wasn't funny. There must have been ten good bars between the restaurant he picked and Miller's Pub, but when I suggested we have a nightcap there, Bill jumped at the chance—I think he thought that Miller's was becoming *our* place. Once again, we sat near the taps and James brought us martinis. By that point, I thought everything Bill said was hilarious, even though it wasn't, and we laughed until closing time. Before we parted on the street, Bill pulled me in for a long kiss. When I thought it might go on forever, I pushed him away and, smiling, I fanned myself with my hand, as if his cold, wet lips had burned me up with passion. Then I found a cab home, feeling certain that Larry would call the next day to reclaim me.

But he didn't.

I told myself that this was silly, that I should just call Larry myself and invite him out for a drink if I wanted to see him. But something inside me wouldn't let me do it. So I waited for Larry to call, and Bill called instead, and I agreed to see him again.

After dinner at a French bistro in Old Town, we cabbed downtown to Miller's.

"It's tradition, now," Bill joked.

When he had finished his drink, Bill went to the bathroom. I caught James' eye.

"Two more martinis?" he asked.

I shook my head. "Have you seen Larry?"

"No, I haven't."

Suddenly, I hated that goddamned poker face of his.

"Bullshit, James. He drinks here whenever he's in town. When's the last time you saw him?"

"I haven't seen Larry since the last time he was in here with you."

I smiled, then, and tried a different tack. "All right, James. I'll ask you this. If you *had* seen Larry, would you tell me?"

At that, James shifted his attention to a guy at the far end of the bar who may or may not have been calling for it, and our conversation was over.

With just a few moments before I had to bury myself again beneath the woman I'd let Bill believe I was, a woman who was falling for him and thought he was the funniest guy around, I considered the possibilities. James might be telling the truth, I thought. Maybe Larry hadn't been into Miller's. Maybe he hadn't called me because he was in L.A., auditioning for TV pilots or recording books on tape. Maybe he had no idea I was seeing anyone else. But what scared me was the good chance James was lying, that Larry had been coming into Miller's and, when James told him I'd been showing up with the same big-tipping, suit-wearing lawyer, Larry had thought about it and decided he didn't give a shit.

I managed to plaster a smile on my face when Bill returned, but I felt hollowed out by the idea that Larry had given me up without a fight, without even a phone call. It didn't matter to me that I couldn't be sure this was the case. That I believed it was possible told me all I needed to know. And every day that Larry didn't call would make that possibility look a little more like cold, hard truth.

Before last call, Bill led me out to the street and pressed his lips over mine.

"Come back to my place," he said.

I thought about the offer just long enough to remember that Larry hadn't given me any good answer to the only question I was still asking. Then I said, "Why not?"

● ● ●

OVER THE NEXT few months of Larry not calling, I learned some things about Bill, starting with just how sweet he was. From his colleagues, I learned that Bill had a reputation as a canny attorney, but I saw none of that slyness in his personal life. He was honest and straightforward in ways I'll never be.

In bed, Bill was competent, if unimaginative. He treated each session of lovemaking as a test he either passed or failed and made my orgasm the only report card. Bill passed most of the time, but just barely.

Something else I learned: Bill had even more money than he'd let on. In the late eighties, he'd won a class-action judgment against a big credit-card company. His take was fourteen million dollars. Since then, Bill had made wise investments—he was still working mostly because he still liked the work. Once he'd let me in on these little secrets, we started going to the city's best restaurants on weeknights I might otherwise have ordered takeout. At least once a month, Bill would fly in a chef from New York to make dinner for the two of us in his Randolph Street penthouse. When we'd been together six months—only Bill had been counting—he took me to Paris for four nights. We stayed at the George V and ate each meal in a restaurant recommended by a chef Bill knew personally. I felt like I was living someone else's life, but it was a nice life.

Bill mentioned Miller's Pub whenever we passed its garish, red neon sign—"That's where it all started," he would say—but we stopped going there, mostly because I stopped suggesting we go. I kept thinking I would run into Larry somewhere—if not in the best restaurants, then on the street or at the theatre or in a bar downtown. In Paris, I was certain I saw him drinking in a brasserie where Bill and I were having lunch. It wasn't him, of course, but I needed three long glances to be sure. Once the spell had been broken, I could see that the man at the bar was taller and thinner than Larry had ever been, and I wondered if my memory of him had become so distorted that the man I was missing—and living it up to spite—wasn't Larry, either.

In the summer of 2001, when Bill and I had been together eight months, he sailed us up and down the shoreline of Chicago's North Side while I mixed myself martinis and drank from a clear plastic cup. We were heading south past Belmont Harbor when Larry's voice came on the boat's built-in FM radio. I had helped Larry get his first commercial for Jewel Foods years ago. A creative director I knew had asked me to send over the demos of any artists I handled who might be right for the campaign he had described to me. The only demo I sent him was Larry's. Since then, Larry had done more than two hundred spots for Jewel. If you had played audio of Larry reading the phone book to the average radio listener in the Chicago metro, it would have been even money that she'd say, "Isn't that the Jewel guy?"

I knew everything about this piece of business. I knew the spot I was hearing on the boat, advertising weekend specials on berries and avocados, was a new one. And I knew that my creative-director pal recorded every new Jewel spot at Sweet Sound Chicago, a studio famous for its near-perfect acoustics and deep distrust of digital technology. Which meant that Larry hadn't been patched in remotely, from L.A. or anywhere else, to record this spot. Which also meant that he had definitely been back in Chicago in the past six weeks. And hadn't called me.

I decided right then that I'd never speak to Larry Sellers again. I would not call him, and if he called me, I would hang up. The decision had everything to do with my pride, which was wounded by a realization I hadn't allowed myself to have until I heard Larry's new spot: for months, my staying after work to audition unsolicited demos had been nothing more than an excuse to spend an extra hour near my phone, waiting for Larry to call.

For our one-year anniversary, Bill took me to Tokyo, and then Sydney, where he rented a boat and sailed us across the bay. Back in Chicago, though, the glamour of the lifestyle Bill provided began to wear off. I never would have guessed I could get so easily spoiled, given the hard-working neighborhood I came from, but even the best restaurants get old if the dinner company isn't interesting. Then Bill confided in me that he'd been drinking more than he'd like, and that, if it was all the same to me, he'd prefer to drink on weekends only. So we started eating earlier, I drank wine instead of liquor with dinner, and most of our evenings ended with the two of us in bed watching the local news, like a suburban couple too timid to venture out of the hotel suite and into the big city, content to have life reported to them while other people lived it.

After two years of balking at the idea, and despite my creeping boredom, I let the lease run out on my apartment, put most of my stuff in storage, and moved in with Bill. I had started out with Bill to make Larry jealous but stayed because he was a decent man, and I didn't see how life would improve if I were living alone with less money. And when I hung around after work to listen to demos, I wasn't waiting for Larry anymore. I was trying to kill an hour of an evening I knew would drag on until our ten o'clock bedtime.

Now, almost a decade into a twenty-first century that still feels like the time of somebody else's life, my contentment is an easy sell, except when it isn't. Like the afternoon Bill and I went to the movies and I heard Larry narrating one of the coming-attraction trailers. The film we saw was a tearjerker, but it wasn't so sad right away, so Bill found it strange that I was wiping my eyes during the opening credits.

We were standing at the curb a half-block from the theater, waiting for a taxi to appear, when he said, "You must have seen that ending coming."

"I'd read the reviews."

When Bill turned away to look again for a cab, I crossed my arms against the cold wind coming in off the lake and held myself as tightly as I could.

It's only after incidents like these that listening to the unsolicited demos becomes about Larry again, a contest between my desire to hear him say my name and my refusal to call him—which one will the vodka drown first? Pride floats in vodka, it turns out. The urge to call Larry dies first every time, and I go home to the palatial penthouse where nothing interesting, nothing fun, ever happens. But part of me believes that, one night, as I sit at my desk, listening to those hopeful, untalented voices, my pride will sink like a stone. That I will call Larry and, if he answers, I will ask if him to meet me for a drink. That I will try to reclaim even some small portion of the rich life we had until I decided—for reasons that Bill's abundant, unwanted love has shown to be idiotic—that my life with Larry wasn't enough.

• • •

BILL RETIRED FROM his practice in 2009. He teaches one day a week at DePaul's law school and spends the rest of his time at home, re-reading books he loved as a young man and watching television. He's pushing me to retire, too. He wants us to do all the traveling we can.

I wouldn't mind more travel. Besides, things are slower than they used to be at Skyline—the 2008 financial-system fuck-ups gummed up the advertising money machine—and I'm not naïve enough to believe we need my income. But how would I fill even a week of ten-hour days in that apartment with Bill? What the fuck would I do? I picture myself sneaking swigs of hard liquor while Bill's in the pisser and grinding my teeth as he reads aloud from *Gulliver's Travels*. So when he brings up retirement, I work the conversation around to our next scheduled trip. It's usually only a few minutes before Bill gets excited and disappears into his office to research the Buddhist temples in and around Bangkok, or the best sailing route between Sweden and Denmark. Then I finish my bottle of wine, go to sleep, and wake up groggy but grateful I have some place to go that isn't Bill's apartment.

* * *

ON A TUESDAY in late June 2010, I hear from an ad agency that one of my clients, a woman I've handled since the mid-1990s, has been selected as the voiceover talent for a new, multi-spot, national radio campaign promoting a major cruise line. I've helped this woman build a strong book of local business—she works a lot—but she has never had a national-campaign payday. Tonight, as the office empties out, it's my privilege to call her. She's cooking a pasta dinner for her kids—I can hear them yapping in the background—and when I tell her just how handsomely her hard work has paid off, she doesn't believe me at first. I have to ask her if she thinks I would joke about something like this. Then she screams and starts to cry, and it's all a little much, but I let her have her moment before telling her to settle down so I can give her the date and time of the first session. When the call is over, I open the window, light a cigarette, and try to enjoy a sense of accomplishment even as it fades into the grayness—it's a feeling, but I can only describe it as a color—that is the backdrop for everything I think and feel.

Nine padded envelopes—the day's unsolicited demos—are stacked in my inbox. I drain the last swallow of cold coffee from my mug and splash some vodka into it, just enough to loosen up the dark-roast dregs and carry them over my tongue. The taste isn't as bad as you might think. There'll be a coffee-vodka on the market soon, if there isn't already. You watch. With the dishes done, I pour more vodka, take an envelope from the stack, and start the first audition of the night.

The ritual is pretty mindless these days. A long silence from the CD player is usually my first clue a demo is over, and as I put in the next one, I can't recall what I've just heard because I haven't been listening. Instead, sitting in my chair, I've been mentally reviewing the fuck-you-pay-me calls I made that day and watching pigeons huddle in shadows on the roof across the alley.

But tonight, my ears are grabbed by the rich, resonant voice featured in the fourth demo I pop into the player.

"When you cross the threshold of Ulysses S. Grant's home in Galena, Illinois, you step into an era of warfare and wisdom, slavery and freedom, heartache and heroism."

I can see the speaker's lips and tongue moving before I see anything else. The enunciation is clear, crisp and without any frills. Each syllable carries everything it needs and nothing more. There are no jingles in this demo, no silly voices, no little jokes—just an *a cappella* medley of clips I imagine were recorded in a bedroom and stitched together on a computer.

"Purchasing a television from Arc Home Electronics means more than stereo sound and an HD picture. You get the satisfaction of spending your hard-earned dollar with a family-owned business that's served Chicagoans like you for more than sixty years."

The voice is that of a young man who sounds older than he is, a combination I like very much: older male voices are in high demand, and a young man can make money for his agency for a long, long time. The performances show range where it matters—in tempo, volume, and energy—and the whole thing is done in deadly earnest. The kid is playing it straight and pulling it off.

"Chicago Blackhawk hockey: Winning is everything."

Then I do something I almost never do: I play the demo again. And I'm not even halfway through it when I lean over to retrieve the last envelope I threw in the trash can and pull out the cover letter I hadn't bothered to unfold. The letter is as brief and straightforward as the demo. It reads, "Dear Skyline Talent, Please find my voiceover demo enclosed. I appreciate your consideration. Sincerely, Simon Davies."

A phone number is printed beneath the signature. I don't recognize the area code, which makes me suspicious about where this Simon Davies lives. I'm not about to sign a kid who has to drive in from the fucking sticks and can't find his way around the city. I check the envelope and see it has no return address. No postmark, either.

Simon Davies delivered his demo by hand. How fucking earnest is that?

I'm getting excited about this voice. But as the grayness in my mind begins to thin, I lose trust in my excitement. I worry that I'm only falling in love with the possibility that, after all these years, I *might* still have an ear tuned to money-making talent. So I put the demo in my top desk drawer and begin a one-week cooling-off period to make sure I'm not just hearing what I want to hear.

● ● ●

SEVEN DAYS LATER, July 4th has come and gone, I've hidden and killed three bottles of Grey Goose in Bill's apartment, and I've nearly forgotten the sound of Simon Davies' voice. I arrive at my office Tuesday morning intent on skewering my belief that I can sell this kid and his voice, even in a down market. I listen to the demo again, in the light and relative sobriety of the morning, and I decide I wasn't hearing things. Simon's demo is better than most of my clients' audition reels.

I tell the new receptionist—receptionists at Skyline last about as long as any plant on my file cabinet can live without water—to call him in for a meeting that afternoon. The timing is a test: if the kid can drop everything and make it to my office for a same-day meeting, chances are good he can do the same for a voiceover session. But the main purpose of the interview is to find out if I'm wasting my time—and risking my reputation—on a savant who can't make eye contact or a prima donna who thinks his talent makes the world go 'round. The earnestness of his demo package leaves me pretty sure Simon is no prima donna and worried he might be a weirdo. I want proof that he bathes. I want to know he can have a conversation without chitchatting about collecting locks of hair or eating his stool. Simon Davies gets two minutes to convince me I can send him on a job without the creative director calling to ask what the hell I was thinking.

He arrives early and I make him wait. It's twenty minutes after our scheduled appointment when I allow the receptionist to send him back to my office. When he shows up at my door, I glance at him over my reading glasses and wave him in.

"Give me a second," I say, returning my eyes to the paper in front of me.

"Sure," he says.

He stands just inside the door and casts his eyes quickly around the office. I move my lips, pretending to be reading a contract, but I'm actually inspecting Simon. He looks a little younger than I thought he would, but he's presentable. He's wearing khakis and a collared shirt, both a little wrinkled, but clean. His dry, brown hair is straight and weakly parted on the left side. He's a few feet away, and I can't smell him. So I decide to begin the interview.

I remove my glasses and let them hang from the cord around my neck. Without getting up, I say, "Hello, Simon."

"Hello," he says.

He maneuvers around the chair in front of my desk and shakes my outstretched hand. His handshake isn't as firm as I like, but he isn't slipping me a dead fish, either.

"Have a seat," I say, pointing to the chair in front of me.

"Thank you."

"Thanks for coming in."

"Thank you."

The way he says the words makes it sound like he's thanking me for thanking him.

"Thank you for having me, I mean."

"Of course."

I can tell already that Simon Davies isn't a sociopathic weirdo, but he isn't normal, either. He has trouble with small talk and seems to be doing something with his head—not quite a twitch, but a little shake—before he speaks. The movement causes—or maybe tries to cover—a split-second delay in his responses that a stopwatch couldn't capture but my ear can't miss. If I were a matchmaker sending Simon out on blind dates, I might still be worried. But I don't see that any of Simon's—I'll call them quirks—would annoy a creative director or her client, assuming he can deliver the goods in the sound booth. And his voice is as crisp, clear and resonant in person as it was on his demo.

"Shall we get down to business?"

"Sure," Simon says, trying a friendly smile.

I don't smile back. We're not there yet. "Have you been talking to any other agents?"

"No."

Not a savvy answer, but I'm not surprised.

"Do you have a cell phone?"

"Yes."

"Good. Let me lay out the ground rules for you, Simon."

Leaning forward, I narrow my eyes and turn my head just slightly, so that my left eye is closer to him than the right. This is a routine I have developed over the years to make one thing clear: none of what I'm about to say is a joke.

"I'll need you on call," I say, "like a surgeon, between 8 a.m. and 5 p.m., Monday through Friday. You're available unless you've told me forty-eight hours in advance that you're not. Can you agree to that?"

After another little headshake, Simon says, "Yes."

"If I call you with a job, I don't want to hear about your girlfriend or your boyfriend or your dying grandmother. I want to hear you say, 'Yes.' And saying 'yes' means that you'll be at the session in perfect voice, at least ten minutes before your call time. Can you agree to that?"

"Yes," he says. "I can."

I ask myself if I believe him, and I do. "Good."

I give him a quick, fake smile, thinking he will take it as a sign he can relax a little now. He doesn't seem at all relieved.

"Is this going about how you thought it would go?" I ask.

He does that head thing again.

"I had no idea how this would go," he says.

This makes me laugh out loud. "Good answer."

I decide I'm beginning to like Simon Davies but banish my next thought as soon as it occurs: the last artist I'd signed who possessed Simon's exceptional vocal skill—the talent to place each word in the listener's ear with a jeweler's gentle precision—was Larry Sellers.

"You'll be billed out at $150 an hour for non-union sessions and at scale for union radio and television work," I say. "Until we get you in the union, that is. Then we'll push for more than scale. No matter what your hourly is, we charge the agencies an additional fifteen percent, so Skyline's fee doesn't dip into yours. Our fifteen percent of any residuals comes out of your earnings."

"So, do I pay you?"

"No," I say, shaking my head. "I pay you. All your payments are made out to the agency. We take out your fee and deposit the rest into your bank account. Taxes are your responsibility. If you've got no money to pay them when they come due, don't come to me. The best advice I can give you is to think of every $150 as $100 and move the difference into an account you don't touch until tax time. Is this all making sense?"

"I think so," Simon says.

"Good."

He doesn't sound too sure, but I can't get myself interested in pinning down his misunderstanding. I'm on a roll.

I lift two thin, stapled documents from a stack of white paper striped with the edges of pink and yellow carbons and hand the documents to Simon.

"This is your contract," I say. "One copy is mine, the other is yours. It's a standard contract, the one all our new talent signs. Show it to a lawyer if you like, but if he knows anything about the voiceover business, he'll tell you it's more than fair."

Most of my new clients are so grateful to be with Skyline that they sign whatever I give them right away. But every once in a while I get one, like Simon, who can't ignore a piece of advice some well-meaning boss or grandfather gave him: *"Never sign anything without reading it first."*

Do these people actually believe that they understand what they're reading? That they can really pick out the places where they might be getting fucked? The advice should be, *"Never sign anything without going to law school first."* Then reading a contract might be worth the time it takes.

I give Simon a moment to review the contract and, while he does, I scan it myself. A few phrases of the language my attorney and I have crafted—"exclusive representation," "one tenth of all residual payments," "binding until such time that the AGENCY terminates"—come together as I drag my eyes across them. Contracts: what good are they, really? They can't hold together what's falling apart. Larry's contract didn't keep him with Skyline, and nothing else I'd done had kept him with me.

I decide Simon has had enough time. "Any questions?"

He wiggles his head and asks, "What is the length of this contract?"

The contract's duration is right there in the document—the Legal Eagle has missed it. But the question isn't a bad one, and I wonder if Simon has just a little more savvy than I've given him credit for.

"A year from now, we'd need to sit down, see if everyone is happy, and modify or renew the contract."

Then Simon takes a pen from the Mason jar on my desk, signs both copies of the contract on his right thigh, and hands them back to me.

"Very good," I say.

I sign and date both copies and hand one back to Simon, who rolls it into an uneven cylinder.

"I thought about putting some music behind your demo," I say, "but I think it's fine, for now, as it is. It'll be up on our website in a day or two. If it hasn't gotten you any work in three months, we'll have you record something else."

At the mention of three months without work, Simon begins to look a little sick.

Larry never liked waiting, either.

Every new client shows up in my office believing I'm the gatekeeper, that once they're in with me, they'll have all the work they can handle. I use that myth to get the contract signed, and then I start debunking it. I don't ruin the moment by outlining the stark reality that Simon would make more money waiting tables than he will as a first-year voiceover artist. But I start ratcheting down the expectations. I don't want to get a phone call from a kid who's left his steady job and is wondering why the gatekeeper hasn't let him through the gate.

"How does all that sound?"

I give Simon a smile—a real one, this time—to show him that, my three-month warning notwithstanding, I believe I'll find him some work. Eventually.

"Good," he says.

"Well," I say, "sounding good is our business."

It's a corny line I've used for years, but it seems to give Simon a thrill. I extend my hand to Simon, and he stands to take it.

"I'll be in touch, Simon."

"Okay," he says. "Thank you."

I put my glasses on and scan down my list of phone calls to make. When I look up again, Simon is still in my office, standing beside the door, staring at the dead plant on my file cabinet.

"What are you doing?" I ask.

"Is that Larry Sellers?"

My pulse picks up—and not in a good way—at the mention of Larry's name. I realize then that Simon isn't looking at the withered plant but at that goddamned photo of Larry and me, which is still where I left it years ago. The thought that I deserve the sick feeling in my gut—that I have nothing but my own weakness to blame—prompts me to pull the feeling close, as if burying my face in my regret will teach me a lesson I have always needed to learn.

I haven't answered Simon's first question when, still staring at the photograph, he asks another.

"Is he your client?"

"Not anymore."

"He left the agency?"

The disappointment in his voice annoys me. "Some years ago, yes." Then I start to worry that I've signed Larry's nephew or something. "How do you know Larry Sellers?"

"I don't," Simon says. "But I admire his work. Especially for Jewel Foods."

With that, I've had all of Simon's earnestness I can take.

"Goodbye, Simon."

He turns to me, and I give him a hard look that betrays none of my inner churning and sends a clear, unspoken message: *Get out.*

His head shakes a couple of times as he backs out of the office. Then he smiles and says, "Thanks again for your time."

And he's gone.

I spend the rest of the afternoon making the calls on my list, and I push even harder than usual to get my people paid *now*. The bullying I do probably costs me more money in the long run than I manage to collect over these couple of hours, but I don't give a shit. Getting what I want, down to the second and the cent, feels absolutely necessary.

A little after five, I hear people saying goodbye to each other down the hall, and a few women pass my office with their summer jackets over their arms and purses over their shoulders. When the low-level bustle of closing time goes silent, I pour myself a few fingers of vodka and drink it down. I pour another one. Then I pick a bubble-cushioned envelope off the top of the stack in my inbox. I slide my letter-opener into the narrow gap between the body of the envelope and its adhesive flap and drag the blade across the opening. Leaving the cover letter inside, I pull out a thin plastic case that protects an unmarked CD. I put the CD in my player and press play. A man clears his throat twice, on mic. Then he begins speaking over a recording of an actual radio commercial for the American Red Cross. Beneath the man's reed-thin tenor, I can hear Morgan Freeman doing the spot as it should be done. When this audition is over, I see that my vodka is gone and fix myself another, keeping the bottle tilted until the drops thrown up by my pour leap over the rim of my mug and dot the papers around it.

I'm in the middle of the day's seventh demo when my pride, having clung to driftwood for years, finally goes under. I pick up the phone and dial the number I still know by heart. With the first ring, my pride resurfaces, gasping for air, dredging up an anxiety for which I've never found the words until now: that Larry was always enough for me, and I was never enough for Larry. I listen to the second ring and the third, hoping to God he doesn't answer, but as the fourth ring purrs in my ear, I want nothing more than to hear the voice of Larry Sellers—that voice!—speaking only to me.

6

Simon

AT FIRST, THE waiting wasn't so bad. Getting an agent had taken only two weeks, and Elaine, the agent who signed me, had represented Larry Sellers. These were good reasons to wait for work with expectation it would arrive shortly.

Some people quit their day job when they get what they think is their big break. I didn't have a day job, but the day after I signed with Skyline Talent, I called Helen, the liturgical coordinator at St. Asella's.

"This is Simon Davies," I said.

"Who?"

I waggled. "Simon Davies. I was the lector the past two weeks?"

"Oh, yes," Helen says. "What can I do for you, Simon?"

"I'm calling to say that, unfortunately, I won't be able to continue lectoring at St. Asella's."

I did not say that I would never again so much as set foot in that decaying little church, but that's what I meant.

"You're going over to Old St. Stephen's, aren't you."

"No, no, that's not it. There's an illness in my family."

This was not a total lie. My mother's illness had killed her, and I told myself that if she were alive to hear some of what I was feeling in the fallout of the humiliating experience I'd had at St. Asella's the day before—not during mass, but after it—I might have found it within myself to overcome my embarrassment and hard feelings, stand up before the strangers and misfits of St. Asella's, and do what I had committed to do. But my mother was dead, and I couldn't find what I needed without her.

"Oh, I see," Helen said. "Well, I'm certainly sorry to hear that. I'll update the schedule and see if I can find a replacement for this Sunday."

Helen does not pry about the family illness and does not mention the six-month lectoring commitment I'd signed. Perhaps she'd learned the hard way that pressing a lector into service makes for bad liturgy.

"Thanks very much," I said. "I'm sorry for the inconvenience."

"That's all right. Bye now."

I flipped my phone closed, tossed it onto the couch, and almost immediately, began waiting again for the damn thing to ring.

● ● ●

THREE DAYS BEFORE—a Sunday, my second at St. Asella's—I was standing at the back of the church with the gospel book under my arm as people entered one or two at a time, in silence, through the three sets of wooden double doors to my left. As they found their way to seats that maximized the distance between themselves and their fellow parishioners, I wondered why any of these people bothered to come to this decrepit church. I had an easy answer to that question for the many among them who seemed, as I had been doomed to be before rebuilding my voice, isolated and odd: I assumed they had nowhere else to go, that they were taking refuge in the one place so desperate for bodies that they would never be turned away. The strangeness of these people—their exile from the world—stirred up a defensive revulsion.

That's not me, I told myself. *Not anymore.*

Then I saw a woman who was everything the misfits of St. Asella's were not. For one thing, she was beautiful. Her skin had been bronzed in the sun, and the curls in her deep brown hair gleamed when she passed through the beams of the sanctuary's overhead spot-lamps. A cotton dress met her body at its curves as she made her way past soot-covered, stained-glass windows toward the back of the church, hugging a silk shawl around her shoulders. And there was more to this woman than her beauty. People seemed drawn to her. They stood up in their pews and shuffled to the aisle to greet her with a hug or a handshake, or whisper a few words to her, before she moved on down the side aisle. An old woman with a four-footed cane—I recognized her from my first Sunday at St. Asella's—interrupted the slow progress that she and her doddering husband had been making toward a front pew to exchange pleasantries with her. What was most striking, though, as I watched the younger woman turn the corner around the last row of pews, was her projection of a confidence that seemed impossibly complete.

This was someone with a place in the world.

I had expected her to pass me on her way to wherever she was headed, but the woman stopped and stood immediately next to me on the church's back wall. The fine wrinkles around her eyes suggested that she was some number of years older than me—in her mid-thirties, maybe. The scent of her, carried on the air she'd moved on her walk, was floral but so subtle that it left me wondering if she was wearing any perfume at all.

I waggled—twice—and prepared to hand over the Book of Gospels. "I'm sorry," I said, "are you lectoring today?"

"No," she said, smiling. "That heavy book is all yours."

"Oh," I said. "Okay."

"I don't think we've met," she said, holding out her right hand in front of me. "Catherine Ferrán."

She pronounced the surname with an accent I supposed was Spanish and a meticulousness I could appreciate in any language.

"Simon Davies."

"Nice to meet you, Simon. Are you new?"

"Yes." I waggled and nodded. "Very."

"Well, welcome," Catherine said.

"Thank you. So, you're not a lector?"

Catherine shook her head. The organ lowed from the choir loft, as if she'd cued it. "I'm the cantor," she said. "I'll walk up right behind you."

There had been no cantor—no singing at all—during the first mirthless mass I'd attended at St. Asella's. As I processed toward the altar on that second Sunday, Catherine's singing at my back—clear-voiced and pleasant, giving no clear indications of professional training—was a dog whistle for the part of me that wanted a place in the world. It took all the restraint I could muster not to turn around, watch and listen as Catherine passed, and follow her wherever she went. Sweat pricked through the pores of my upper lip at the thought that Catherine might lump me in with the misfits and oddballs of St. Asella's. What I wanted was for

Catherine to see me as someone who would have a place in the world, and soon—not someone like *them*, but someone like *her*.

After mass, I stood within earshot beneath the sparse shade of a young ash tree while a rag-tag gathering of old, lonely men and strange women took their turns asking Catherine to recount her month-long trip to Morocco. She spoke to each one of them with patience and charm. After waiting his turn for about ten minutes, an old man stammered at Catherine, nervously worked the brim of a rumpled felt hat through his hands. I got the idea that Catherine was the only woman—maybe the only person—to whom this man would speak for some time.

The last person (besides me) waiting to chat with Catherine was an older woman. Her fine, curly gray hair was pressed flat where she'd slept on it. The skin around her eyes was red and swollen and her mouth was loosely pursed, as if the muscles that do the pursing were nearly exhausted.

Catherine, facing away from me, shook her head as she asked the older woman something—I didn't hear what. As her brittle, trebly voice scattered in the summer breeze, I could pick out only part of the older woman's response, a name: *Rose Marie.*

Then the two of them embraced in a way that flipped all of my assumptions on their head: the older woman was soothing *Catherine*, stroking her back and whispering consolations through her tired lips. When they pulled away, the older woman smiled and squeezed Catherine's hand. She rooted in her purse for a pen and scribbled something on the back of a tattered envelope. Returning the pen to her purse, she pulled out a tissue and gave it to Catherine. Then the older woman walked away, toward the parking lot on Franklin Street.

Catherine turned toward the crumbling stone of the church steps and blew her nose into the tissue. I saw then that she was crying.

Standing there, watching Catherine cry, felt wrong somehow. I decided to leave, but before I could, Catherine caught sight of me. I froze. She didn't seem surprised to see me.

Taking just one step toward her, I asked, "Are you all right?"

With her eyes on the steps, Catherine said, "Her name is Jeanne."

She balled the tissue into her fist. "She's lived with her sister, Rose Marie, for years, since Rose Marie's husband died. They go everywhere together. They take bus tours all over the Midwest. This was the first time I'd seen Jeanne without Rose Marie in months. So I asked, 'Where's Rose Marie?'"

Catherine sniffed, rolled her eyes skyward, and shook her head. Keeping my distance had begun to feel more rude than respectful, so I took another few steps toward her.

"And Jeanne tells me," Catherine continued, "that Rose Marie was diagnosed with cancer three weeks ago and given three months to live—maybe less. She's at home now. In horrific pain. And Jeanne says to me, 'I'm afraid to be alone.' And before I can say anything that helps"—Catherine looked at me, as if she owed me an explanation—"I just started crying." Then she stomped her right heel against the cement and said, "Somebody should have *told* me! I've been home for days. I could have done something for her by now!"

As I listened, wondering what to say, I recalled that in the moment I'd felt closest to Brittany, I hadn't needed to say anything at all. Given the sadness of Jeanne's story, I felt a little guilty at my excitement that Catherine was sharing it with me.

"I need to get my purse," she said.

What I heard was Catherine asking me to wait for her.

"Okay," I said.

Catherine hurried away down the gangway, leaving me alone in front of the church. Feeling the heat and my nerves, I moved back into the shade of the ash tree. I glanced over my shoulder at Bartlett Street and waggled. I watched the blurry shadows of the tree branches swaying and I waggled again. I had little idea what, if anything, I was going to say, but I wanted my voice at the ready.

When she walked out from behind one of the church's heavy oaken doors, Catherine was smiling. Her eyes were dry, and she was carrying herself with the confidence I'd noticed when I first laid eyes on her.

"Hi," she said, stepping carefully down the steps in her nude heels.

"Hello."

"I'm sorry about all that."

I shook my head and waggled. "You shouldn't be."

She nodded. "So, how are you?"

"I'm fine. Good."

"I'm glad to hear it," Catherine said.

With this bit of small talk, I could feel Catherine closing the door to the closeness we had shared a moment before. But I wasn't ready to go home yet.

"Are you going this way?" I said, pointing east, toward the lakefront.

"Yes," Catherine said.

Just like that, we were walking together. We crossed Franklin Street in the striped shadow of the El tracks. The shawl that had covered her shoulders during mass had slipped down around her waist. The only ring on either hand was a chunky piece of opaque, pale green plastic on an index finger.

"People really love you here," I said.

She laughed. "It's not like this every week. I've been gone a while."

"Are you glad to be back?"

Catherine tilted her head just slightly. "Mostly."

"It sounds like that woman you were talking to—"

"Jeanne."

"Jeanne," I repeated. "It sounds like she's having a rough time."

Catherine inhaled deeply through her nose. "Rose Marie is taking all the chemo and radiation the doctor will give her. Jeanne's worried the treatment will kill her before the cancer does." Catherine shook her head. "She must be terrified."

"My mother died of cancer," I blurted.

"Oh," Catherine said. "I'm sorry."

"She was diagnosed at stage four, so she didn't want any radiation or chemo," I said. "She just let the cancer do its work."

Catherine waited a beat. "Did you try to convince her to get treatment?"

I shook my head. "No."

I didn't tell Catherine that I'd wanted desperately to make an argument for treatment, an argument that would have required more nuance than my full range of nods, headshakes and gestures could have communicated. In the end, I'd made no argument. I'd just watched her die.

I missed my mother right then. I like to think that it's because I missed my mother that I decided, despite the fact that we'd just met and that she'd just been crying, that I'd ask Catherine to have lunch with me.

"Once more people at St. Asella's find out about Rose Marie's diagnosis," Catherine said, "Jeanne is going to have a lot of help. She won't cook or clean for weeks."

I smiled at what I'd assumed was a kind of joke—how could the people of St. Asella's help Jeanne when they were scarcely able to help themselves? But when I glanced at Catherine, I saw no sign that she was kidding around.

"How will people find out?" I asked.

Catherine shrugged. "I'll tell them."

We veered toward the curb, moving around the low, wrought-iron fence that defined the sidewalk eating area of a restaurant called Local Bistro. Enormous oval plates garnished with fresh fruit were heaped with pancakes drowning in syrup and French toast smeared with whipped cream. Potatoes, cubed and browned, surrounded omelets flecked with red and green peppers. Flatware clanked against ceramic, and a baby, only his chubby legs and blue ankle socks visible from beneath a stroller's sun canopy, squealed for his parents.

At an opening in the fence, I stopped and tossed my thumb in the direction of the door, turned to Catherine, waggling as I did, and asked, "Would you like to have lunch with me?"

What I meant was: *Show me your place in the world.*

Catherine's eyes grew with surprise. Then she dropped them and smiled.

"I can't," she said.

Flushing with embarrassment, I waggled in plain view. "No problem." I started walking east again. Then I added, "Maybe some other time."

In that moment, I had no intention of asking Catherine out again. Ever. I was simply trying to save face: Catherine would pretend to remain open to the idea of our having lunch together at some point in the future, and I'd wordlessly agree never to ask her to lunch again. But Catherine kept going.

"Simon, I'm newly divorced, and people at St. Asella's know it. You lector there. I'm the cantor. And I have no plans to get an annulment or anything like that. So," she said, "I can't see you. Socially."

She stared at me, waiting for me to affirm what she'd said.

Does she expect me to believe that our having lunch would get her thrown out of that desperate parish?

And what if it did? Why would Catherine let St. Asella's and its misfits stand in the way of anything she wanted in the world she inhabited every hour of the week but one?

She wouldn't, I decided. *No one would.* Which meant that Catherine wasn't interested in me and was going out of her way to ensure I knew nothing would change how she felt.

I should have been able to take this rejection in stride, but I made an adolescent's mistake: I allowed my hurt feelings to stir up memories of Brittany telling me we were finished. I started living both rejections at once, right there on the sidewalk. The shame of them heated the blood in my face and my stomach twisted with anxiety.

Sweating from the forehead, I waggled twice and said, "I think I understand."

Catherine nodded, smiling. "I knew you would."

I kept walking with Catherine because I didn't know what else to do. If I'd had a good excuse to leave, I would have taken as many waggles as I needed to say it. But I couldn't come up with one, so I kept putting one foot in front of the other.

Breaking the painful silence, Catherine picked up the conversation about where she'd left it, as if I'd never asked her to lunch. "Poor Jeanne," she said, shaking her head. "What an awful scene she's returning home to. Thank God she has St. Asella's. My father used to say that even when everything else in your life is coming apart, you can still count on community, if you're part of a good one. And St. Asella's is a good one, you know?"

I got the idea that Catherine was giving me a pep talk, including St.

Asella's and its community in a list of parting gifts I'd receive now that I'd been denied a place in her real world. With a little less pain in my gut and embarrassment clouding my head, I might have heard that Catherine's pep talk had been intended as much for herself as for me. But what I heard was her trying to lump me in with the misfits she tended. And what I did was take her little pep talk apart.

"I don't know if it's a good one," I said. "And I don't think community is good for much."

"What?"

"If anyone shows up at Jeanne's door with buckets and rags or a hot meal," I said, "community won't have anything to do with it. Any help she gets will come because of you."

Catherine shook her head and smiled, as if I simply didn't understand the way a community worked.

"Me and a lot of other people."

"No, I was there last week, when you weren't. I saw none of the community you're talking about. No one was hanging around on the sidewalk, chatting away. How many of the people you'll ask to help Jeanne know her already?"

Catherine moved her head back and forth, calculating.

"Not know *of* her," I said. "*Know* her. How many of them have been to her house? How many say anything more than hello when they see her?"

Catherine stared at me. She seemed surprised to find herself in an argument.

I shrugged without taking a waggle—I didn't need one. "They're strangers to each other," I said. "A parishioner at St. Asella's is no more likely to help me than anyone on the street would be. And the people who don't know Jeanne personally, but help her anyway, will do it because they know you."

"All right," Catherine said. "Simplest terms. Where would Jeanne have gone this morning if there were no St. Asella's?"

I shrugged again. "A coffee shop," I said. "Or a restaurant. Does it matter?" Then I said, "Maybe she would have stayed at home with her dying sister."

As soon as I'd said it, I knew I'd made a mistake. In trying to make a point about community at St. Asella's, I'd implied that Jeanne had been wrong to leave her sister, and the exhausting duties of caring for her, for even one hour. I meant every negative thing I'd said about St. Asella's, but I regretted having said anything at all about Jeanne. I should have told Catherine this. I did not.

I was taking the waggles I needed to say *I've got to go*, when Catherine said, "This is me."

We stood before seven stories of molded cement accented with green plate glass. On the other side of the double doors, an older African-American man wearing a dark jacket and tie sat behind a tall wooden desk in a marble foyer that led to a set of elevator doors. Even a kid from outside Peoria could see that this was an apartment building. I had walked Catherine home, another bitter consolation prize in a game I had lost badly.

Catherine turned to me with a practiced, professional air of courtesy. "Thank you, Simon," she said. "I'll hope to see you next Sunday."

That Catherine would invite me back to St. Asella's, after what I'd said about the place and its people, made me realize that my ranting about strangers and heaping judgment upon old women had only served to confirm for her that I was just another misfit. All hope of showing Catherine that I was someone like her, a person with a place in the world, was lost. I could've collapsed in a pile and wept.

She pulled the handle of the lobby's glass door and walked in without another word. She greeted the doorman, and his face lit up with a smile that lifted the ends of his black moustache. I watched Catherine wait for the elevator, her back to me. Then I noticed the doorman staring at me through the green glass. He wasn't smiling anymore.

• • •

AFTER A WEEK of waiting in vain for the memory of my bungled interaction with Catherine to fade, and for Elaine or Connor or anyone else to call me, hope was hard to come by. To make matters worse, having begged off of my lectoring commitment, I'd given up my best chance to prepare for the voiceover work I was waiting for. So I stayed in my apartment, the only place in the world where I felt I belonged, and waited. I'd left myself with little else to do.

Outside my living-room window, the Tuesday-afternoon-rush hour had begun. Cars and trucks on Bartlett Street accelerated through expiring yellow lights and ran brand-new reds as they made their way to and from the interstate. Office workers cutting out of work early—men in collared, bright plaid shirts and pleated pants, women in short-sleeve, silk blouses and flared slacks that covered all but the pointy toes of their high heels—crossed Bartlett and entered the tavern on the corner or continued on to a bus or a train or a parked car. Seeing so many people coming from somewhere and going somewhere else needled my envy and my shame. Surely these people were waiting for something big to happen in their lives, just as I was. But they were *doing* something while they waited.

In front of the sagging three-flat next door to mine, an elderly woman pushed a two-wheeled aluminum cart nearly filled with groceries packed in white plastic bags. The cart seemed to be doubling as a walker for the woman, who walked slowly and with a slight limp. What little downward pressure she could apply to the cart's handle was barely enough to keep its short, cylindrical front legs from scraping the sidewalk.

In about half a minute, the woman traveled two sidewalk squares—about ten feet. The nearest grocery I'd found—a Jewel Foods store—was six blocks away. At that pace, she must have been walking for the better part of an hour. Her cheeks were glazed with sweat, but the woman seemed calm and unconcerned, as if she had no doubt she'd get where she was going.

Her facial expression of patience and confidence helped me place the woman: she was from St. Asella's. I hadn't recognized her without a four-footed cane in her hand and her aged husband teetering at her side. I was not excited to see anyone from St. Asella's—I wanted no reminder of my disagreement with Catherine and of her distant, benevolent invitation to join the ranks of the misfits already in her charge—but if I had no choice but to see someone from the parish I'd left behind, I was glad it was this woman. Looking back from a short distance made safe by my certainty that I would never return there, I decided that, of all the people I had encountered at St. Asella's, and despite the fact that we'd never spoken to one another, I liked this woman best.

From behind my open blinds, I watched the woman pass in front of my apartment. She was at the foot of my building's cement front steps when a front leg of her cart caught the edge of a deep crack in the sidewalk. She staggered into a lame hop, keeping her feet beneath her, but her cart twisted and toppled with a metallic crash. A red, gelatinous sauce spilled out of a cracked glass jar. Lettuce lay limp on the sidewalk. Two oranges mimicked the traffic racing away from the highway until one fell into the gutter and the other came to a rest in front of the barred windows of the corner tavern.

The woman dropped her hands to her side and stared at the mess. Then she took two unsteady steps forward, bent gingerly at the waist and knees, and reached for a fallen plum.

I stepped into the nearest pair of shoes I could find and hurried out of my apartment. To be clear, that the woman was from St. Asella's had no bearing on my going out to help. Any halfway decent person would have found it impossible to stand by while the woman risked breaking her hip to pick up groceries.

By the time I'd run down my stairs to the sidewalk, the woman was slowly unfolding herself to upright, like a science-fiction radio-show alien emerging from a long journey in the tight confines of an egg-shaped pod. In her hand was the plum she had reached for. I slowed to a walk, for fear of scaring her. Taking a waggle, I leaned into her field of vision.

"Excuse me, ma'am?"

Both of her legs were shaking with destabilizing tremors, and she looked worried in a way she hadn't before, as if this accident had made her suddenly aware of a weakness she'd been ignoring.

"Would you mind if I helped you?" I asked.

Her graceful smile flickered. "Please," she said. "Thank you."

I righted the grocery cart to keep any other foodstuffs from falling out and put its handle in front of the woman to give her something to lean on. Then I retrieved a white plastic bag that had expelled all of its contents except one box of spaghetti.

"Do you still want everything?" I said, looking at the produce on the ground.

"Oh yes," she said. "Whatever we don't peel, we can wash."

I gathered every foodstuff I could find, even the orange in the gutter, its leathery skin covered in dust. I wiped it off on the front of my jeans before dropping it in the plastic bag.

Soon, only the broken jar was left. I picked the bigger fragments out of the sweet-and-sour sauce, stacked them curved-side down in the palm of my left hand, and dropped them in the trashcan on the corner. Wiping my hands on the tail of my t-shirt, I returned to the woman, who was still standing where I'd left her. She was steady on her feet, but she did not seem ready to start walking again. She leaned on the cart, taking deep breaths.

"Okay," she said. But she didn't make a move.

"Where do you live?" I asked.

With what appeared to be great effort, the woman raised her age-spotted hand off the cart's handle and pointed up the street. "Just around the corner."

"Okay." I waggled. "Would it be all right if I walked with you? I could push the cart, if you like."

She nodded. I took the cart handle, and she tucked her right hand into the crook of my left elbow.

To walk at the woman's pace, I moved in a kind of slow motion, rolling each step heel to toe over several seconds. I guessed it took two minutes for us to pass the tavern and reach the corner. In the presence of the elderly stranger, I felt different than I had just minutes before—not better, necessarily, but different. I had been living in my head, with no outside conversation, for almost a week, and until this woman put her hand on my arm to steady herself, I had not been touched by anyone since shaking hands with Elaine at the end of our meeting.

"This way," the woman said, giving my arm a weak tug.

We walked west on Huron Street, into the sun, which still hung above the residential towers at the end of the block. I lowered my eyes to the sidewalk, watching the woman's steps, matching mine to hers as best I could.

"You know," she said, "your replacement wasn't very good."

I had no idea what she was talking about. *My replacement?*

I'd begun to worry that the heat and stress of her outing had made her delirious when another explanation dawned on me: she'd recognized me from St. Asella's, and my "replacement" was whoever they'd found to lector at the noon mass two days before.

I let the remark pass without comment, hoping to end an uncomfortable line of conversation.

"I asked Catherine where you were," she said, "but she didn't know."

Did anyone at St. Asella's, I wondered, *experience even a moment's confusion without looking to Catherine for clarity?*

Holding up my end of the conversation seemed to offer the best chance of ending it quickly. I waggled and said, "There was an illness in my family."

"Oh," the woman said. "I'm sorry to hear it. Anyone you'd like me to pray for?"

Answering "yes" would have required me to flesh out my lie with additional detail, and the thought of this woman praying for my false intention made me grimace.

"I appreciate that," I said. "But my mother isn't sick anymore."

"Oh, good," the woman said. "Thank God for that."

We passed a gated parking lot bordered by a tall, chain-link fence topped with razor wire. As we approached a restaurant just west of the parking lot, patrons enjoying an early dinner in sidewalk seating glanced up at us. A couple of women older than me, but much younger than the woman on my arm—women about Catherine's age—stared and smiled at what must have looked to them like a Norman Rockwell tableau come to life. Without deciding to, I smiled in the chaste, unthreatening way I imagined a young man in such a scene would smile.

We walked into the shade of an arched green awning, its white-trimmed fringe rippling in the wind, and the woman came to a stop.

"Here we are," she said.

The doorman got out from behind his desk and opened the door.

"I was wondering when you'd be back," he said to her, smiling.

"I made it," she said.

"Yes, you did." He reached for the cart handle. "Thank you, sir, I'll take this from you."

"Sure," I said.

The doorman was twice as broad as me at the shoulders. His voice alone, a booming bass, was overpowering.

"I'll bring the groceries to your door, Mrs. Landry," he said. "Then I'll be back for you."

"Thank you, Thomas," she said.

"You're welcome."

Thomas wheeled the cart inside. Bearing the weight of the cart and its contents with just two fingers, he walked up four steps and disappeared down a hallway.

"Thank you, too," the woman—Mrs. Landry—said to me.

"It was no trouble."

We stood stock-still under the awning, my hands folded in front of me and one of hers still clinging to my arm.

"Will you be reading on Sunday?"

Mrs. Landry raised her eyes to meet mine. The strain made her neck and head tremble.

"We need you now more than ever."

All other things being equal, I would have gone back to lectoring at St. Asella's just because Mrs. Landry wanted me to. I would have stood in front of everyone and read for her alone. And at the words "we need you" I felt a flicker of excitement at the possibility of returning some sense of purpose to my days. But it would be weeks before I understood what Mrs. Landry meant when she said that I was needed now more than ever. I didn't ask her to explain, because no explanation would have changed my mind. I'd decided that returning to St. Asella's was tantamount to acknowledging that I was the misfit Catherine believed me to be. Under those circumstances, I was never going back to that church. And I didn't have the heart to lie to Mrs. Landry again.

"I don't think I'll be back," I said.

Mrs. Landry smiled patiently and nodded, then returned her head to a resting position that aimed her gaze at the limestone base of her building.

Thomas pushed the front door open and offered Mrs. Landry his elbow. "Here we go," he said.

Mrs. Landry removed her hand from my arm and placed the other on her doorman's.

"Thank you," she said to Thomas.

"Of course." Then, glancing over his shoulder at me, Thomas said, "Thank you, sir."

I waved to Mrs. Landry as I backed away, but she didn't see the gesture. She went inside without saying goodbye.

I started the short walk back to my apartment, walking quickly because I finally could. Without Mrs. Landry on my arm, none of the women dining on the sidewalk looked up at me as I passed.

Only when I was standing inside my living room again, wondering what the hell to do next, did I realize that Mrs. Landry had extended—and I'd refused—an open-hearted welcome of the kind my mother would have offered me if she were still alive.

7

Catherine Ferrán

"*TEN CUIDADO CON los ricos.*"

Be careful around the rich.

This was my father's warning to me, a caveat passed down to Eduardo Ferrán by generations of *campesinos*, his ancestors and mine. Coming of age in Franco's Spain only confirmed my father's suspicions of the wealthy. He carried these suspicions with him when, as a twenty-four-year-old man with a university education in engineering but very little English, he immigrated to the States in 1964.

When my father told me to take care around the rich, he meant that I should stay away from them. It is no accident, then, that the services I provide as an interior designer are available only to people my father would have considered rich. Every American-born daughter of an immigrant father resents and opposes his advice. *My concerns are not your concerns,* I recall thinking to myself as I rode to junior high school in the taxi my father drove to make our living. *Your problems are not my problems.* But my father's words about the wealthy have stayed with me. They have saved my one-woman business who-knows-how-many times. A daughter of an immigrant father lives in this kind of tension: even as she dismisses it, she worries that some of her father's advice might be wise and never really lets it go. She holds his might-be wisdom in a dark corner of heart, just in case.

My father's advice about the rich rises to my attention when, on a Thursday evening in June 2009, Daniel Shadid introduces himself to me at a charity gala in the cavernous Navy Pier ballroom. I've never met him before but already know all about him. Like me, he's a first-generation American on his father's side. Unlike me, he is of Lebanese descent and has made a fortune as an investment banker. He poured much of that fortune into Shadid.com, a suite of online number-crunching tools for day traders. After selling the site and its algorithms in late 2000, he retired with a net worth in the nine figures. He was thirty-nine.

Since then, Shadid has applied his substantial energy and influence to the protection of human rights and the pursuit of famous friends. He visited Burmese refugees in Thailand with Angelina Jolie and her retinue and accompanied George Clooney on a trip to Darfur. Shadid seems to want to *be* Clooney—he's always in a suit but rarely wears a tie, his olive skin is perpetually tanned, and he's allowed his hair to go salt-and-pepper. Shadid has never married, but his serial romances last for months, rather than days. My theory on that: Shadid stays with a woman long enough to look more like the serious philanthropist than the multi-millionaire playboy.

Why do I know so much about Daniel Shadid? Interior designers who make their living in Chicago cannot help but absorb every detail of his life. Shadid's equivalent of Clooney's Lake Como retreat (where Shadid has spent several long weekends) is the ever-growing number of luxury condominiums he owns in Chicago. Shadid serves elaborate dinners at his North Michigan Avenue penthouse and then, for their privacy and his, sees that each of his guests and his or her date is taken by town car to one of his properties. In the pictorials published in the trades each time one of his new living spaces is unveiled, I've noticed a few consistent elements. His taste leans toward the modern, as if each room were styled not for George Clooney, but for Hitchcock's Cary Grant. To better impress guests who pack light and don't stay long, Shadid and his architects plan for wet bars and saunas where anyone else would put closets. And while the rest of us search one-of-a-kind shows and foreign bazaars for pieces that fit our clients' limited budgets, Shadid's designers ponder the problem of how to feature—or, in some cases, employ as mere accents—fine and modern art from Shadid's personal collection. My clients who know him—or know people who know him—tell me that Shadid never boards a guest in the same condo twice, preferring to give Hollywood's most famous do-gooders a progressive tour of the guesthouse-*cum*-museum he has built out across the most luxurious buildings in Chicago.

In the course of our conversation, which begins as I wait for a glass of cava at the ballroom bar, Shadid extracts three pieces of information from me: that my profession is interior design, that I know of his ongoing guesthouse project, and that I'm attending the gala not with a date, but a friend. I suppose he also notices that I'm not wearing a wedding band. I removed it a little more than a month ago, the night I discovered from our April 2009 mobile-phone bill that Richard, my husband of more than eight years, had been sleeping with both his paralegal and his personal trainer. *("Ten cuidado con los ricos"—Ay, papá, tenías razón acerca de Ricardo.)* Even as I answer Shadid's question about how I like my River North neighborhood, my thumb swabs the underside of my naked ring finger.

The tickets to this gala were a last-minute gift from my best client, who was called to Copenhagen on business and did not want the two twenty-five hundred dollar meals she purchased with her donation going to waste. I do not have big money, like the people who bought their own way into this party, but any interior designer making a living in this city knows how to converse with rich people. This is the reason I offered the second gala ticket to my friend Nicola Hayes. Nicola runs her own interior-design firm, which, like mine, is small and successful in the sense that it employs only its owner but employs her well. Though we're both intent on making something big of our respective businesses, Nicola and I never compete for work.

"There's no need to compete," Nicola said to me once while we shared tapas and a pitcher of white sangria. "We'll divide the city. Half for you, half for me."

"How much of my half do I have right now?" I asked her.

"About one half of one percent."

And we laughed as we clinked our glasses.

While Shadid tries to place me in his extensive network by naming interior designers and asking if and how I know them, I see Nicola over his shoulder. Hiding the gesture with the sleight of hand of a person practiced in the art of sipping cocktails, Nicola opens her eyes wide, as if to ask, *"Do you believe what is happening to you right now?"*

"I'm close to closing on a penthouse space at Roosevelt and McCormick," Shadid says, reclaiming my visual attention.

"I know the building," I say.

"Have you seen the penthouse?" he asks.

"I haven't, no."

"It's stunning," he says. "Thirty-eight hundred square feet. Lake views in three directions."

"All but a few of the building's units have lake views, I think."

Shadid ignores my attempt to bring him back down to earth.

"I'm having the unit stripped and the walls knocked down," he says.

"I want a designer to help me reconceive the space. Perhaps you'd join me for the walkthrough?"

Shadid is the greatest patron of interior design in Chicago, but he almost never works with local designers. The pose he strikes—an elbow on the bar, one leg crossed in front of the other at the shin, the lip of his glass just inches from my own—reminds me that, at thirty-six years old, I am what passes for an age-appropriate object of the forty-eight-year-old Shadid's affections.

Ten cuidado con los ricos.

"Mr. Shadid—"

"Daniel."

"Daniel, I've read enough about you to know that you don't book your designers yourself. Whoever joins you on that walkthrough will be vetted by Claire Weber."

Claire Weber was one of the most successful independent interior designers in the city until she went in-house, full-time, with Shadid. Two of my best clients are former clients of Claire's.

"Who says you haven't been vetted already?"

"Well," I say, smiling politely, "I haven't had a call from Claire or one of her people."

"Don't be so sure that proves anything."

He thinks he is being clever and mysterious, but the idea that this entire conversation has been some kind of charade, that Shadid already knew the answer to every question he has asked me, is more alarming than anything else. Regardless, I give him my card and tell him that I'd be pleased to talk more about how I can help him as a designer. He puts the card in the pocket of his tuxedo jacket and tells me to expect a call.

The call does not come. Nine months later, the March 2010 issue of *Chicago* magazine runs a photo spread of Daniel Shadid's Roosevelt Road penthouse, which features panoramic views of the skyline and Lake Michigan, unobstructed sightlines into the bowl of Soldier Field and, on the wall of an otherwise unremarkable anteroom, a Willem de Kooning canvas only recently discovered by the artist's estate and purchased at auction by Shadid himself.

● ● ●

TO MARK THE beginning of my post-divorce life, I'll spend the month of June 2010 in Morocco: three weeks purchasing decorative pieces for clients in the open-air *souks* of Marrakech, Tangier and Casablanca, and a week of rest and relaxation at a spa in Essaouira. The truth, though, is that my new life is already underway. It started on May 1, 2009, the day I moved out of the condo I'd shared with Richard. About a week later, on a Sunday I was determined not to spend moping around my new apartment, my life began to take a shape I would never have expected for it.

In Chicago, a person with any interest in Catholicism can curate her experience of it by shopping around for a community of like-minded people. My decision to attend a Catholic mass for the first time in ten years had nothing to do with community. When I met Richard back in 1998, I decided to stop going through the motions at mass on Sunday mornings just to honor my father, who had been dead for four years by then. Instead, I'd spend Sundays doing things I actually *wanted* to do, like reading and working out and going to brunch with the man I was already imagining I would marry. With Richard out of my life, what I wanted was some reminder of my life before I met him, so the idea of going through the motions of the mass felt comforting. And as those motions would be basically the same at any Catholic church, I saw no reason why the parish nearest my apartment would not do.

When I walked through the doors of St. Asella's for the first time, I very nearly turned and walked out. The church was dark and humid, like the inside of a mausoleum, and the stained glass was covered in a dull film. There were only a few people in the church, sitting far apart from one another, as if they had reserved multiple rows for themselves. Worried that I might have misread the mass schedule, I looked for an usher, but no one was standing near the church doors. I decided that, having already made the short walk from my apartment, I'd try to say a few prayers.

I found a place in a pew near the back and knelt on the threadbare padded platform in front of me. But I didn't pray. I watched. Over the next ten minutes, about fifteen people came through the church doors. I guess I was half-expecting to see someone *like me*—a professional who lives in the neighborhood and happens to go to church, someone with some wounds in need of tending, maybe, or a nostalgia for tradition, but a life I would recognize. So far as I could tell from the messages they sent, consciously or not, with their dated hairstyles and ill-fitting clothes, none of the people in that church were anything like me. I recalled another lesson that my father had tried to teach me: "God sees differently," he'd say, the words drowning in the thickness of his accent. "Talent, money, nice clothes, a beautiful face—these things don't matter after all."

Kneeling in that depressing church, surrounded by strange, tasteless churchgoers, I decided that God and my father had been wrong about that one.

At noon, an organ started up in the choir loft and a heavy priest waddled down the center aisle. I remembered the opening song from childhood, but no one else was singing, so I didn't sing, either. On the altar, the priest started the mass with a blessing. The people in the pews mumbled their responses or made no response at all, and the priest went ahead with the prayer, expecting nothing of them and nothing of me. And as I settled into the ritual rhythms of sitting, standing, and sitting again, I began to enjoy the isolation, the sense of knowing no one there and no one knowing me. I enjoyed it so much that I came back to St. Asella's the following Sunday, and the Sunday after that, to enjoy it again. At the very beginning, my return to Catholicism was less of a move toward something than a weekly, hour-long retreat from the heartache and obligations of life as I knew it.

But after a few weeks, I began to feel like a scavenger feeding on the decay of what, according to the parish history published in the weekly bulletin I'd picked up, had once been an authentic community. St. Asella's was built by working people—immigrants, like my father, Italians, like my mother's parents—and I couldn't get past the sense that, by showing up on Sundays to stand, sit, kneel, and leave without saying a word to anyone, I dishonored the immigrants who'd poured their sweat and treasure into the construction of this church. Even if I could do no more than go through the motions, there were other motions to perform.

After the fourth Sunday mass I attended at St. Asella's, I climbed up the dark spiral stair case to the choir loft and asked the startled organist, a nerdy little man who squinted to keep the frames of his glasses from slipping off of his nose, if there had ever been a cantor at this church.

"Oh boy," he said, shaking his head. "Not for some time. Not for years!"

"I see," I said. "Well, I just thought I'd ask."

"Are you a singer?"

"No," I said. "But I can sing these songs. Church songs. It's possible I would be just slightly better than no singing at all."

"Well," he said, "you should talk to Helen."

"Helen?"

"She's the—I want to say scheduler, but that's not it." The organist looked away and lowered his head, searching his memory for Helen's title. He snapped his fingers. "Liturgical coordinator."

"Oh," I said. "Okay."

"She's probably on the altar, cleaning up. That's where she usually is after mass."

Stepping gingerly down the worn cement stairs of the choir loft, I considered trying to satisfy my sense of obligation to long-dead immigrants by dropping a few more dollars into the collection basket. But I kept walking, down the stairs and up a side aisle to the sanctuary, where I found Helen. She'd clothed her pear-shaped figure in a bulky wool sweater, hopelessly unfashionable jeans and white sneakers. She stood awkwardly on her toes as she extinguished a beeswax taper with a brass bell.

I introduced myself and offered to volunteer as a cantor.

"Are you willing to sign a six-month commitment?"

Commitment. Hadn't I been coming here to enjoy an hour with no commitments?

"I'm sorry," I said, shaking my head with confusion. "A commitment to what?"

"To cantor at the noon mass and give me three days' notice if you can't make it."

It was a moment before I was certain she wasn't kidding. I figured the commitment could be dissolved whenever I liked by my leaving St. Asella's and never coming back, so I agreed to sign it.

Helen led me into the sacristy and pulled a piece of paper from a drawer at the top of a freestanding maple cupboard. "What was your name again?"

"Catherine," I said. "With a C."

"Last name?"

"Ferrán." I spelled the name without waiting to be asked.

She slid the paper across the top of the cupboard and handed me the pen she had used to write my name. I scanned the paragraph-long, boilerplate commitment statement and signed the blank line beneath it. Helen added the date next to my signature.

Then Helen pulled out another copy of the commitment from the drawer, turned it over to the blank side, and wrote "Cantor Schedule."

"You'll be here next Sunday?" she asked.

"Yes."

She wrote the following Sunday's date, reprinted my name next to it, and, with two pushpins, posted the sheet on a bulletin board above the cupboard.

"Try to be here fifteen minutes before noon," she said. "I'll get the song list from Paul"—the organist's name, I would learn later—"and I'll put it on the lectern on the left side of the sanctuary. Take a book from any of the pews and bring it to the back. You'll process in just ahead of Fr. Dunne."

Helen picked up a purse by its shoulder strap and held it at her side. "You're welcome to leave your purse back here during mass. I do. Nobody has ever taken anything."

"Okay," I said.

Then, having trained me well enough, Helen left.

I had expected that the people of St. Asella's would not take much notice of the woman singing up near the altar. But they did. After the first mass I served as cantor, ten people—probably a quarter of the people in attendance—stopped me on the sidewalk in front of the church to shake my hand and thank me. The next week, people who thanked me asked my name and gave me theirs.

This is how it all started. If I had not volunteered to sing, I might never have met anyone from St. Asella's. I might have gotten whatever fix I needed and left after just a few more Sundays. I will recall this moment and wish that I had kept my silence and my seat near the back.

• • •

NOT EVERYONE I encountered at St. Asella's lived on the margins. I would meet an accountant, a legal-aid lawyer, a professor of anthropology, and a devoted young grandmother whose daughter and granddaughter lived in an apartment just down the hall from her own. But only the aged, the lonely and the grief-stricken deemed it appropriate—or necessary—to share their personal problems with me as we stood near a small crowd on a public sidewalk. An old man named Joseph told me I reminded him of his daughter, adding that he hadn't seen her in fourteen years. Jill, a single mother of three, confided in me that she had lost her job managing a diner on the North Side. And Doreen, a woman older than me but not as old as my mother would have been if she were still alive, leaned in to whisper about her heavy perimenopausal bleeding.

"It's happening now," she said, breathing the words into my face. "As we speak."

Carrying on even a simple hi-and-bye conversation in front of St. Asella's made me anxious, but I would listen to these confessions and try to respond with genuine sympathy. When I'd heard them all, I would hurry back to the sacristy, grab my purse, and head straight home to my apartment, congratulating myself for having given a few troubled people a chance to get their worries off their chests before I put those worries completely out of mind.

This went on for weeks before I realized that the people sharing their problems with me were actually asking for my help.

Before considering the burden I'd be taking on by making concrete efforts to help anyone at St. Asella's, I called Xabier, a friend who owned a Spanish restaurant in the South Loop. I had designed his interior for well below my usual rate—there aren't so many of us in Chicago with ties to Spain, so we stick together. I thought he might have something for Jill, the mother of three who'd lost her diner job.

"Are you looking for anyone right now?"

"Well," he said, "I just lost my back-of-house manager."

"I may have someone for you."

"Who?"

"A woman I know. Her name is Jill."

"Does she have restaurant experience?"

I decided that diner experience counted as restaurant experience. "Yes."

"Can you vouch for her?"

I don't even know her. "Of course."

"Send her over."

"Can she bring her kids?"

"To the interview? Sure, why not."

"Perfecto. Gracias, amor."

"Ciao, Catalina."

The following Sunday, I gave Jill a slip of paper with Xabi's name, the address of his restaurant, and the date and time of her interview.

She stared down at the paper and said, "I'll have to find a sitter."

"He said you can bring the kids to the interview, if you want."

She arched her eyebrows, surprised as much, I think, by Xabi's flexibility as by my having given any thought to her kids.

A week later, I was standing by the church doors, waiting for the opening procession to begin, when Jill surprised me with a cheek-to-cheek hug.

"I got the job," she said, pressing her head to mine.

"Congratulations," I offered.

"Thank you," Jill said, sniffling. "Thank you so much."

I thought of my father then. Jill and the parishioners of St. Asella's were my father's people: *los pobres en espíritu—the poor in spirit.* Maybe they, more than God, were the discovery he had in mind for me when he dragged me to mass all those years. Maybe they were the reason I could feel now the warmth of my father's presence as near to me as if he were still living.

● ● ●

FINDING JILL A job made me think that helping these people was easy.

Why hadn't my father given me any advice about arrogance and pride? It's possible that he had. It's possible I hadn't listened.

Jill had been working for Xabi only a week when I pulled Doreen aside after mass and asked if she was still experiencing bleeding.

Doreen nodded and said, "A lot."

"Do you have health insurance?"

She shook her head.

"Are you free any day this week?"

"Free for what?"

"I think we should visit a doctor."

Doreen pulled her chin toward her chest and looked up at me. "I don't like doctors."

"Doreen," I said, "you need to have this looked at. It's probably nothing, but it could be something serious."

She shook her head again.

"I'll pick you up," I said, "I'll drive you to the appointment, I'll read a magazine in the waiting room, and I'll take you home when you're done."

I watched Doreen examine my offer in her mind, looking for any sign of the bad intentions she might have learned to expect.

Then she said, "All right."

I rescheduled a Wednesday-morning client meeting and picked Doreen up in front of St. Asella's locked doors. She wasn't comfortable with my knowing where she lived, which was fine with me. I didn't want to know any more about Doreen than I needed to. We drove to the Near West Side location of a free women's health clinic recommended to me by a nurse in my gynecologist's office. I watched Doreen answer some basic health questions, listed in Spanish and then English, on a blue piece of paper clipped to a transparent, fuchsia-tinted board. I returned the questionnaire to the receptionist, and Doreen sat with her purse in her lap, stealing glances at the Latino women and children waiting to be seen by a doctor.

When the nurse called her name, Doreen didn't get up.

"Okay, Doreen," I said. "They're ready for you."

Doreen just stared at the short nurse in pink scrubs, who held open the door to the examination rooms with her round, ample behind and glared impatiently at the only woman in the waiting room she deemed likely to be named Doreen.

I leaned forward in my chair and put my hand on the back of Doreen's. "Would you like me to go in with you?"

"Take me back to the church."

"Doreen—"

"I don't want to be here," she said, raising her voice. "Take me back to church!"

I apologized to the nurse, who seemed totally unfazed by Doreen's display. In the time it took for me to drive back to St. Asella's and see Doreen out of the car, we did not speak.

If my father had still been living, I would have called him the moment Doreen got out of my car to give him a piece of advice: *Ten cuidado con los pobres. Derrocharán tus días miércoles.*

Be careful around the poor. They'll waste your Wednesdays.

• • •

ONCE I'D DECIDED to help the people of St. Asella's, it didn't take long for their needs to overwhelm me. For help, I turned first to the people I'd helped already.

I gave Joseph's phone number to Jill and asked her to call him once a week, just to chat.

"He and his daughter are out of touch," I told her. "He mentions it every time he sees me."

Jill stared dubiously at the piece of paper on which I'd written Joseph's number. "When should I call him?"

"Whenever you can."

"Does he know I'll be calling?"

"I'll let him know."

It was clear to me that Jill had little interest in taking even five minutes of her limited time with her kids to call a lonely old man she didn't know. But she shrugged and said, "Okay. I'll do it."

When Mrs. Landry, an older woman with a cane and a quiet, bright-shining personality, informed me that a young woman who attended St. Asella's—the granddaughter of "a dear, departed friend," Mrs. Landry said—was coming home from the hospital with a son born two months premature, I worked the sidewalk crowd after mass for commitments to deliver a freezable meal to the St. Asella's rectory, where Helen would keep it refrigerated until the new mother's boyfriend could pick it up. By the time I left St. Asella's that day, I had commitments for six meals. Jill said she would bring something from Xabi's restaurant. Doreen offered to bake a lasagna. Jeanne and Rose Marie, sisters in their seventies who had lived together since Rose Marie's husband died years ago, volunteered to make two meals a piece.

"Are you sure you can manage that?" I asked them.

"Of course!" Jeanne said. "We make dinner every night. We'll just make extra."

"There are two of us, honey," Rose Marie said to me. "I'll do the slicing, she'll do the dicing."

And then each woman let out a laugh that sounded like a recording of her sister's, trilling up the scale and back down again. I laughed with them.

The scheme depended on parishioners doing favors for people they barely knew, as repayment of a favor they had received or a down payment on one they believed they might need someday. But the investments that the people of St. Asella's made in one another delivered a return I hadn't expected. At some point—I did not notice until after it had passed—the help that they provided to one another ceased to be repayment or prepayment of any debt and became what we do at St. Asella's. It became *who we are.* Many St. Asella's parishioners believe in God in a way I never will. But by saying *yes* when we might otherwise say *no*, we give each other good reason to believe in community at St. Asella's.

And when I do something—even something small—for a person in the little community we've made, the doing of it feels nothing at all like going through the motions.

● ● ●

BECAUSE IT IS no one's business and, frankly, because I worry what people in my life will think of me when they find out, I go five months without telling anyone that I've started going to church again. When finally I do tell the person I trust most in the world, I am reminded why I have been keeping word of my churchgoing to myself.

Nicola and I both started our careers as unpaid interns at Cote D'or Designs, a well-regarded, luxury interior-design firm in Chicago. Nicola took my place when I left Cote D'or for my first paying job in the business, but we didn't meet until 2002, when a colleague introduced us at a gallery opening in River North. There, Nicola and I each discovered how badly we needed to share, with someone who understood it, the trying experience of interning at Cote D'or.

"Did you have to get lunch for Diane?" Nicola asked me.

"Every day," I said. "The raw plate."

"With a side of baked potato wedges."

"Of course."

"And *do not* forget the dipping sauce," Nicola continued. "The girl at Vegan Life knew me and my order, which was Diane's order. I had drilled the dipping-sauce thing into her mind. She always, always, *always* put dipping sauce in the bag. Then, one day, my usual Vegan Life girl was out sick or something, I was in a hurry, and I forgot to check the bag."

"No dipping sauce," I said.

"No dipping sauce."

"And Diane sent you back."

"She didn't have to," Nicola said. "The second she said, 'I don't see any dipping sauce,' I started running back to Vegan Life. In heels."

I laughed.

"Well, dipping sauce is 'made with real veggies,'" I said, quoting the chalkboard menu we had both seen so many times.

"That dipping sauce is the only thing keeping Diane vegan." Then, with her cocktail poised in front of her lips, Nicola added, "The day Vegan Life closes, look for Claudia at a pig roast."

When the opening was over, Nicola and I found our way to the nearest wine bar, where we kept telling our stories. After that, we started meeting for drinks whenever client work took one of us into the other's neighborhood. We became regulars at the various exhibitions and specialty-store openings around town and at monthly meetings of the Women in Small Business Council. I told Nicola about Richard's cheating before telling anyone else.

Nicola Hayes is more than my favorite plus-one. She is my closest friend.

So, when Nicola calls on a Wednesday and asks if I will take her second ticket to a Fall 2009 Humanities Festival session featuring Petra Blaisse, a Dutch designer we both admire, I accept before I ask for details.

"Just tell me when and where," I say.

"Fantastic!" Nicola says. "It's Sunday at one o'clock in the Art Institute ballroom."

"Sunday afternoon?"

"At one o'clock. Weird, I know. Don't worry—I'll have a drink if you will."

"That's so disappointing," I say.

"What is?"

"That it's happening on Sunday at one," I say. "I won't be able to go."

"Oh," Nicola says. "Okay."

And she isn't prying, or feeling spurned and petty; she is looking for a way to help when she asks, "What do you have to do?"

Because Nicola is my best friend, I respond without my usual caution.

"I have to go to church," I say.

"Oh."

And I hear, in that one syllable, the tone I have heard Nicola use to mask—from everyone but me—her distaste for a small room packed with oversized furniture or carpeting installed over a vintage hardwood floor.

I feel the need to explain myself.

"I started going after I left Richard," I say. "Just once a week. It isn't even a religious thing. I've met some people there who need help, and I'm trying to help them."

"What kind of help do they need?" Nicola asks.

"Finding jobs, getting to and from doctor's appointments, meals after surgeries," I said. "That kind of thing."

"And you, like, take them to the doctor?"

"It's not just me. Everyone who gets help pitches in to help someone else."

I wince at my description of the St. Asella's community, which makes me sound naïve and, by implying a *quid pro quo*, does no justice to the sweat equity the people of St. Asella's are investing in one another.

Nicola says, "Can't you skip it this week?"

I sigh. "I can't. A woman in the parish is recovering from pneumonia, and she lives alone, and I need to find some volunteers to make meals for her."

Relating this detail buoys me a little, as it shows my work at St. Asella's to be, at least in part, a case of women helping women in need. This is something that my friend Nicola can appreciate. But Nicola is focused on another detail entirely.

"What kind of church is this?"

I want to say Unitarian, but I recall that I have just used the word "parish" and guess that Nicola may already know the answer to her question.

"It's Catholic," I say, as if this fact is incidental.

"Really?"

She is disappointed.

I tell myself that Nicola's decision not to spare me her disappointment is a mark of our friendship, and that I should find her honesty encouraging. But I'm not encouraged.

"Like I said, Nic, it's not a religious thing. It could have been any church. It's just that I was raised Catholic, so that's the kind of church I went back to."

"But you'd left all that *behind*," Nicola says, as if I've suffered a relapse.

"All of what?"

"All of that Catholic stuff," she says. "The all-male oligarchy in the silly hats. The railing against the rights of women and gays and lesbians. And all those pedophile priests!"

"Nic," I said, "you know me. I hate those things."

"But you're associating yourself with them," she says.

"No, no," I say. "People at this church are helping each other and making a community where there wasn't one. The big Church—the men who make the rules—they have nothing to do with it."

"I think you're kidding yourself."

I've heard Nicola condescend before, but not to me. I'm not sure how to respond.

Then, with a heavy breath, Nicola says, "I'm sorry."

I brighten at the thought that Nicola is over this and that my going to church will be added to the short list of topics that we will never discuss again.

"I wish I'd done more when you left Rich."

"Oh," I say, trying to reassure her. "But you did so much!"

"Not enough, apparently."

This is when it registers that Nicola's apology is not for anything she has said, but for whatever failure of hers may have led to my seeking sanctuary in a chauvinistic, homophobic institution.

I know that if I agree to skip church and join her at the conference session on Sunday, the rift opening between my friend and me will be healed immediately. But I believe what I have said—that the little community we have made at St. Asella's is worth something, and that the Church at large does nothing more than give it occasion to come together once a week. And if there is concrete good for me to do at St. Asella's, and people—many of them women—are counting on me to do it, I don't see how I can walk away from them, even to please a friend.

"Thanks for the invitation," I say. "Let me know how Petra does, okay?"

"Sure," Nicola says.

Having thoroughly bewildered one another, we hang up.

The conversation stays with me for days, like a stomach virus. Over and over, I ask myself how well I understand my own involvement at St. Asella's. Is it as I have come to see it—a worldly woman's engagement with people living on the margins? Or might St. Asella's still be, as Nicola suggested, little more than a jilted ex-wife's hiding place?

A week later, when Petra Blaisse has come and gone, Nicola has not called me. I suppose that she has decided that, if I truly wanted to know how Petra's session was, I should have attended it.

Ten cuidado con los ricos.

That night, staring at the shadows thrown onto my bedroom ceiling by the street light, I recall a story my father told me as I sat with my arms crossed in the front seat of his taxi, having been overruled in my wish to skip church that Sunday. When he was a young man living in Zaragoza, he said, my father's friends were mostly like him: university-educated; believers in democracy, labor unions and free speech; young people reduced, in the oppression of Franco's Spain, to making small, anonymous donations to Catalán fringe groups and grumbling to one another in cafés. But among his friends, only my father practiced Catholicism, and they scolded him for what they called his participation in Franco's fascist regime by way of the Church that validated it.

"My response," my father told me, "was so consistent that, in time, my friends would recite it before I could speak it myself."

I remember my father waiting, as we idled at a red light, for me to ask about his usual response, and the rush I felt in refusing to play along.

"I would say to them, 'Franco has taken everything else. This, my faith, I will not give up for him.'"

I may have rolled my eyes. I was a terrible teenager.

"Even your friends will criticize you for being Catholic."

There was no bitterness in my father's words. He'd long ago accepted this reality as a condition of the life he chose.

Riding in that cab, I resolved, with a venom I was too cowardly to show my father, that: *My friends won't criticize me for being Catholic because I won't be Catholic.*

I wonder now if my father knew me better than I knew myself, or if he simply understood the inevitability of life's disappointments and guessed where I would turn when they touched me. My father may also have guessed—correctly, as it turns out—that by the time life was taking its toll on his only daughter, he'd be dead, and she would not have him to turn to.

Awake and alone, I wrestled with the possibility that my friends are less tolerant of me than my father's were of him, and the fact that my involvement with the people of St. Asella's has made me the kind of person I once vowed I'd never become. And the delayed karmic consequence of my having dismissed and disrespected my father arrives as a paralyzing fear that, having so recently lost my husband, I've also squandered my friendship with Nicola Hayes.

• • •

AT THE MARRAKECH airport, having already spent hundreds of dollars shipping home four ceramic vases and seven copper lanterns, I stand in line at the Royal Air Maroc ticket counter to check two cheap suitcases bulging with embroidered fabrics, hand-woven rugs and thuya woodcarvings. My feet, soft and supple after my second spa pedicure, nestle into the padded leather soles of new sandals. My toes, painted a deep, dark green, look like two turtle families, each sharing a brown, braided shell. I watch travelers and airport workers as they walk from one end of the terminal to the other, enjoying a range of motion in my neck made possible by a week of daily deep-tissue massage.

When I'm through security, I pass the time in a chair near an unattended departure gate, watching waves of heat rise from the tarmac. As the month-long celebration of my life after divorce comes to an end, I'm not looking forward to my return. Forty-two voicemails await me. None of them are from Nicola. (I've already checked.) I'll spend much of the next month carrying Moroccan handicrafts into the homes of my clients, and half of them, for reasons that having nothing to do with good interior design, will kindly ask me to carry them right out again. And, of course, there is St. Asella's. After a month of having more delicious food than I can sample laid out for me at every meal, I'll go back to coordinating lasagna deliveries for the indigent and infirm and hunting down new jobs for the jobless.

Ten cuidado con los pobres.

A small, private jet accelerates and takes off before my eyes. I wonder if Daniel Shadid feels a sense of relief when leaving Africa. I wonder if the feeling troubles him at all, or if he flies home with his mind and heart at peace, having done what he has come to do. For Daniel Shadid has been cleverer in arranging his life than I've been. Shadid keeps an ocean between himself and the people he's committed to help. In Chicago, Shadid's only duties to them are to attend thousand-dollar-a-plate dinners and bid on silent auctions. He's reserved his hometown as a playground.

Daniel Shadid has no St. Asella's.

• • •

THE WARMTH OF the welcome I receive from the people of St. Asella's takes me by surprise. Before mass, I am stopped every few steps by someone standing up at the end of a row to grasp my hands, ask about my trip and, at a low whisper, update me on her life. The bigger surprise, though, is how easily my own warmth rises to meet theirs. At the airport in Marrakech, I reduced the people of St. Asella's to their problems. But in the face of their inelegant kindness, the humanity of these people is harder to ignore, and it stirs my own. Before I have reached the back of church, I am convinced again that what I said to Nicola is still true: There is a community here, and it's worth something to all of its members. Even to me.

Mrs. Landry, with her husband standing unsteadily at her side, meets me at the mouth of the side aisle. She raises her hand to pat my arm, gently.

"It's good to see you," she says.

"It's nice to see you, too, Mrs. Landry."

"Did you meet the new lector?"

"I don't think so," I say, but what I've heard is *lectern*, and I look over my shoulder expecting to see a new podium at which I will do my singing.

"He's by the doors," Mrs. Landry says.

"Oh," I say, and when I see a young man in a sport coat standing by the church door with a big red book in his hand, I put her meaning together. "I'll introduce myself."

My return to St. Asella's is proving full of surprises. Perhaps the biggest surprise of all is that the new lector, Simon Davies, is *really good*. The quality of his voice and performance oblige me to listen to what I have been ignoring since I was a girl. And as I listen, I get an almost uncontrollable urge to laugh. The high level of quality Simon brings to the amateurish proceedings at St. Asella's is comically out of place. It's as if I am flipping through channels and happen across a network news anchor on cable access recapping a three-car parade with his customary gravity. As he reads to us, I get the sense that we are a tribe of two, Simon and me: we have some of the talent and appeal necessary to make one's way in the world, and yet, here we are, volunteering at shabby St. Asella's. I allow myself to imagine that Simon Davies will help me help the needy of St. Asella's find a foothold in the world. I go so far as to envision a day in which parishioners might go to Simon, instead of me, with their problems. By the time he completes the second reading, I have plans for him. But Simon has other plans for himself and for me.

On the sunlit sidewalk after mass, I am greeted by more people and made to summarize my trip to Morocco several times. It has been a month since I have had any contact with the people of St. Asella's, and I find that I am expecting tragic news—that someone has died or been injured in a car accident. At first, most of the news I hear is good. With her two sons in tow, Jill tells me that her daughter has been accepted into a magnet school that will give her the quality education that her neighborhood school could not. And lonely old Joseph, whom Jill has been calling once a week, is expecting a visit from his daughter, her first in years. Then I see Jeanne, of Jeanne and Rose Marie, the pair whom I have come to think of as our community's beloved aunts. The look on her face seems to send storm clouds in front of the sun.

"Are you all right, Jeanne?" I turn around and look for Rose Marie, but I do not see her. Only Simon Davies is still waiting. "Where's Rose Marie?"

Only when I turn back to Jeanne do I understand that Rose Marie isn't there, that Rose Marie is the reason Jeanne is so upset.

"She's dying," Jeanne says.

Jeanne tells me that Rose Marie went in to the emergency room with what the sisters believed to be a bad case of the stomach flu, or maybe appendicitis. It is late-stage pancreatic cancer. There is no drug to take, no operation that would do any good. Rose Marie is in pain. She is unable to keep food down. And she is dying.

"I'm so, so sorry, Jeanne," I say.

Jeanne nods and wipes her upper lip. Then she says, "I'm afraid to be alone."

Now *I* am crying—for Rose Marie and for Jeanne, but also—maybe mostly—for myself.

At my request, Jeanne pulls a scrap of paper and a pen from her purse and writes down her address.

"I'll make sure some meals get sent over," I say.

"That's very kind," Jeanne says. "Thank you."

Jeanne reaches back into her purse. I hear the muted jangle of a ring of keys. She hands me a tissue.

"Again, Jeanne," I say, "I'm so very sorry."

I wrap my arms gently around Jeanne in a last, desperate attempt to give her some comfort. And I feel Jeanne's hand patting my back.

When Jeanne whispers, "It'll be okay," I know she isn't talking about her own problems. Jeanne is comforting *me*.

This realization starts me crying again. But as we pull away from one another, I smile to let Jeanne know that I will be fine, and that I appreciate her kindness. She gives my hand a shake, then releases it and walks to the parking lot.

I turn toward the church doors to blow my nose and notice that Simon Davies is still standing there. I don't much care what he thinks of the scene he has witnessed. I am drenched with embarrassment. I cannot absorb any more.

I give Simon the outline of Jeanne's story, and he listens, still standing at a distance. He waits for me while I retrieve my purse from the sacristy, and when I return, we start walking in the direction of my apartment. I outline for Simon the ways in which the St. Asella's community will pitch in to help Jeanne—home-cooked meals and house cleaning and groceries. Focusing on the concrete, meaningful good that the St. Asella's community can do for Jeanne and Rose Marie distracts me from my inability to solve their problems and my own, and I begin to brighten. For a moment, I can see that this upsetting episode has given Simon an authentic and fully human introduction to the St. Asella's community. I stop short of asking Simon to pitch in to help Jeanne, though. I wait to see if he will offer to help.

What he offers is to take me to lunch.

He tries to be casual, but I know when a man is asking me out. And Simon's proposition changes things. What changes first is how I see him.

Something in the way Simon asks me to lunch—his earnestness, maybe, or the hopefulness he tries to conceal—shows me another similarity between us, one that I have not noticed before: Simon, too, is lonely. And though Simon may see me as an answer to his loneliness, I know that he is not the solution to mine. We are not a fit.

For one thing, I'm not ready, so soon after the divorce has been made official, to be going to lunch with men I barely know. For another, Simon is too young for me. But what disqualifies Simon from my dating pool is the very basis for the tribal affinity I felt between us—that Simon has a talent the world can use and chooses to use it at St. Asella's. Seen through the lens of romance, Simon's presence at St. Asella's is grossly unappealing.

My refusal of Simon's invitation to lunch is less than elegant.

"I can't," I say.

Simon's embarrassment is immediately visible. "No problem," he says. "Maybe some other time."

My stomach tightens. I can't have Simon believing I've left the door open for any romantic involvement. I need him to forget about me and buy into the role I've envisioned for him at St. Asella's. So I come up with an excuse I hope will spare Simon's feelings and give my refusal some finality.

"Simon, I'm newly divorced, and people at St. Asella's know it. You lector there. I'm the cantor." Then I say, "And I have no plans to get an annulment or anything like that. So I can't see you. Socially."

In the tense wrinkles above his eyebrows and the pink rising in his cheeks, I see that Simon takes my refusal as an insult.

"I think I understand," he says.

He continues to walk with me, and I return to the conversation we were having before Simon knocked it off course.

"What an awful scene Jeanne is returning home to," I say. "Thank God she has St. Asella's."

I go on about the value of community, comforting myself with heartwarming thoughts of Jeanne's fellow parishioners shouldering some share of her enormous burden. I'm prepping Simon to hear the pitch I have already decided to make at a later date, when Simon's asking me to lunch is just a mildly embarrassing memory.

"I don't think community is good for much," Simon says.

"What?"

"If anyone shows up at Jeanne's door with buckets and rags or a hot meal," Simon says, "community won't have anything to do with it. Any help she gets will come because of you."

Trying to disagree with more grace than I showed in turning him down, I smile, drop my eyes to the sidewalk and say, "Me and a lot of other people."

"No, I was there last week, when you weren't. I saw none of the community you're talking about. No one was hanging around the sidewalk, chatting away. How many of the people you're going to ask to help Jeanne know her already?" Simon asks. "Not know of her. *Know* her. How many of them have been to her house? How many say anything more than hello when they see her?"

He shrugs.

"They're strangers to each other," he says. "The people who don't know Jeanne personally, but help her anyway, will do it because they know you."

The arrogance and petulance of Simon's attack—not on the value of community at St. Asella's, but on its *existence*—irritates me. It's just like a young, white, American man to think he can explain something he knows nothing about to the woman who made it. Worse, Simon is stirring up my bad feelings about Nicola. I've replayed our last phone conversation time and again, discovering in each reimagining some clever retort I wish I'd made to my friend's refusal to see any value in my work at St. Asella's. And I see in my confrontation with Simon a chance to win where I lost with Nicola.

"All right," I say. "Simplest terms. Where would Jeanne have gone this morning if there were no St. Asella's?"

The question seems to confuse Simon. "A coffee shop," he says. "Or a restaurant. Does it matter?" Then he says, "Maybe she would have stayed at home with her dying sister."

In the way Simon hits the word *dying*, I hear him implying that Jeanne abandoned Rose Marie to her suffering when she left the house for an hour. Whether or not he really believes what he has suggested—and I doubt he does—I can see in Simon's twisted lips and hanging head that he knows he has forfeited the high ground from which he was staring down his nose at St. Asella's.

A minute later, we're standing in front of my building. I say goodbye and, from Simon's former position on the high ground, add that I hope I'll see him next Sunday.

As victories go, it isn't much of one. But as I walk to the elevator, I allow myself to believe that, if I had pushed back just a little harder in my conversation with Nicola, or challenged her with just the right question, I might have won that argument, too.

● ● ●

THE NEXT DAY, Monday, I try to organize a meal-drop for Jeanne. I start with Helen, hoping that she will agree to let us use the rectory freezer to store any meals provided by any volunteers who cannot drop them off at Jeanne's.

"Hello, Helen," I say. "It's Catherine Ferrán."

"How are you?"

"I'm fine," I say, "but I'm calling with sad news."

"Oh?"

"You know Rose Marie?" I realize then that I do not know Rose Marie's last name. "Of Jeanne and Rose Marie?"

"Oh, yes," Helen says. "Cancer. Just dreadful."

"You know already," I say, unable to hide my surprise.

"Before you came around, Catherine, *I* was the woman who knew things around here, and there are still a few things I find out about before you do."

I laugh at this, mostly because I am glad that, for once, word of a community member in hard times has spread without my spreading it.

"How did you hear?" I ask.

"Jeanne called a few weeks ago and asked me to put Rose Marie's name on the prayer list."

"Wait. Jeanne called a few weeks ago?"

"Yeah," Helen says.

Not once has it occurred to me that Rose Marie was given her diagnosis more than a few days before.

"Okay," I say. "So, who should I tell that I'd like to bring dinner for Jeanne one night this week?"

"You just told her."

"You're running the meal planning, then."

Helen laughs. "No, honey. You are."

"There's nothing set up for her?"

"Just the dinner you promised."

"I found out *yesterday* that Rose Marie was sick! What has Jeanne been doing for food?"

"I don't know," Helen says. "Cooking it herself, I guess."

I recall Rose Marie's line about the sisters splitting the duties of slicing and dicing and imagine the terrifying aloneness, after all those years of making dinner as a twosome, that Jeanne has experienced each time she opened a can of soup and poured it into a cold saucepan while Rose Marie slept fitfully in her sickbed.

"I don't understand," I say. "Why didn't you set something up for Jeanne if you've known about Rose Marie's diagnosis for three weeks?"

"That's your department," Helen says, sharpening her tone. "Not mine."

"I was in Africa!"

"That's right! And I was *here*, doing my job, which covers pretty much everything else that needs doing around here!"

I am speechless. In the brief silence, I try to absorb the facts: for three weeks, Jeanne has been caring for her dying sister and, because I was away, no one at St. Asella's has done a damn thing but add her sister's name to a prayer list.

I hear the echo of Simon Davies telling me that the community at St. Asella's is no community at all, just a cult of loyalty to—or dependence on—one woman. But I tell myself he isn't right. I tell myself that people in a community have roles. Part of my role is to organize volunteers to cook meals for people who need them. And Helen, if she wishes, is free to limit her role to writing names on prayer lists.

"All right," I say. "If I find any volunteers, can they store the meals in the rectory freezer for a few days if need be?"

Helen lets out a sigh that reverberates in the speaker of my mobile phone. "Before we go any further, Catherine," she says, "let me apologize. I didn't mean to snap at you."

"It's fine, Helen," I say, clipping the words.

"It hasn't been a good morning around here."

Suddenly, Helen does not sound like herself. She sounds as if *she* is the one who has received the cancer diagnosis.

"How so?"

"The Archdiocese called," she says. "They've named nine parishes they're closing in three months to cut costs. St. Asella's is on the list."

Speechless again. But it isn't Helen who has silenced me this time. It is Nicola. The big, institutional Church—the same body I told Nicola had nothing to do with what we were doing at St. Asella's—is shuttering the parish. In the judgment of the Archdiocese of Chicago, whatever community we may have created at St. Asella's is not worth preserving. On this point, Nicola Hayes and the hierarchy of the Roman Catholic Church are in complete agreement.

● ● ●

JILL AGREES WITHOUT hesitation to make and drop off chicken soup for Jeanne. Doreen donates another lasagna. Though both Jill and Doreen know Jeanne and Rose Marie well enough to say hello, neither has heard the news of Rose Marie's illness.

"Did Fr. Dunne read her name from the prayer list?" I asked Jill.

"He might have," she said. "I guess I haven't been listening that closely."

As it turns out, *no one* I call knows Rose Marie has cancer. And this casts doubt, from an entirely different direction, on the legitimacy of community at St. Asella's. It seems that, once she called Helen, Jeanne didn't tell anyone else at St. Asella's—her parish for decades—that her sister was dying. She just waited for me to return.

I make a pot of vegetarian chili and ladle it into ten, two-serving plastic containers. I pick up Doreen's lasagna and deliver it, along with my chili, to Jeanne's apartment. The donated food is more than enough to feed Jeanne through Sunday, when I should be able to find additional volunteers. But my doubts about the community at St. Asella's erode the sense of purpose that attended my past efforts to help its troubled members. Now, in this, too, I'm just going through the motions.

I tell no one that St. Asella's is closing—because Helen has asked me to, but also because there's nothing to do about it. I know enough about Catholicism to know the Church, like Franco's Spain, is no democracy. There will be no referendum or real debate. The rest of St. Asella's may as well hear this news when they're together. The most any of them can do is commiserate. But I will not need their commiseration. For me, the closing will be a relief. I'll see out my obligations, maybe exchange phone numbers with a few more members and, if they call to request my help, I'll do what I can. But I know already that without Sunday gatherings to span the chasm that separates my world from theirs, they won't ask me for anything.

The sense of obligation that gets me out of bed on Sunday morning is not enough to make me hurry, so I arrive at St. Asella's later than usual. When I walk through the main doors, Helen is standing in front of them. We exchange rueful smiles.

"Waiting to see who'll be here when the news breaks?" I ask her.

She shakes her head. "Recruiting a lector, if I can. Simon Davies called up and quit. Just the beginning of our dismantling, I guess."

I tell myself that Simon's quitting is nothing more than another display of immaturity, but I can't quite fight off the idea that after just a few weeks here, Simon sees St. Asella's more clearly than I did after more than a year.

At the start of his homily, Fr. Dunne makes the announcement that only Helen and I know is coming.

"My friends," he says, "I received a call this week from the office of the Cardinal. I was told that the Archdiocese plans to close our parish in three months."

In the pews, there are none of the courtroom-scene gasps and tittering I have been expecting. The parishioners are silent, except for one among them—an older woman I hear but cannot see—who cries out, "Oh, no!"

She seems to be asking, *Now this, too?*

After mass, the sidewalk crowd hums with the nervous energy of residents displaced by an apartment fire. The realists are asking one another where they'll go to mass once St. Asella's doors are closed. Predictably, many make arguments for the parish next closest to their own home. Urging others to travel further, they tout the preaching abilities of priests they've only heard about and the architectural beauty of churches they've never entered. When they ask me what parish I'll choose, I say, "I really don't know," and I ask them to cook a meal for Jeanne. I don't tell them the truth: that I have decided that my dalliance with Catholicism ends with my obligation here. The last mass at St. Asella's will be my last mass. My father's wisdom worked for him. It isn't working for me.

A few parishioners cannot accept the closing.

"Can we fight this?" Doreen asks me. She appears as dulled and weakened by terror as she was the time I took her to the clinic.

"We can try."

She nods, waiting for me to say something more. I shrug and shake my head. After a few moments of silence, she leaves.

I begin my walk home. When I reach the stretch of sidewalk from which I made my impassioned defense of the St. Asella's community before Simon, my face reddens at the humiliating thought that he'd seen right through a lie I hadn't even realized I was telling.

• • •

I AM WAITING for a client in the small, unattended lobby of her building the following Tuesday, the thirteenth of July, when my phone rings.

When I answer it, a woman's voice says, "Catherine Ferrán, please."

Despite my women-in-small-business pride, I feel a little embarrassed to be answering my own phone.

"This is she," I say.

"This is Claire Weber, calling on behalf of Daniel Shadid."

I'm not sure if Claire realizes she's speaking to the person she has asked for, or if she's on auto-pilot and answering a question I haven't asked: *Can I tell her who's calling?*

"Hello, Claire."

"Hello, Catherine."

I move to the glass façade of the lobby. I am *not* letting this call drop. "How can I help you?"

"I'm calling because Mr. Shadid—"

I briefly indulge my fantasy that the great Claire Weber hates herself for selling her agency and taking a cushy, in-house job that requires her—publicly, at least—to refer to her boss as "Mr. Shadid."

"—has acquired a new property, and he would like me to consider you for the project."

"Oh," I say. "I'm flattered."

In her long pause, Claire lets me know that I should be.

"Mr. Shadid has not yet closed on the property, but I have been granted access for a two-hour walkthrough this Sunday at noon. You will have the first hour to assess the space. In the second hour, you will share with me your initial impressions and recommendations. You're available to meet this Sunday?"

The conflict in the timing is as evident to me as it was when Nicola invited me to the conference session. I understand that taking this meeting with Claire will mean missing mass at St. Asella's. And this time, the decision is easy. Life is too short to keep going through the motions.

What I say to Claire Weber is, "I will be there."

● ● ●

SHADID'S LATEST ACQUISITION is a penthouse just east of the Magnificent Mile. At 4,200 square feet over two floors, it's the largest of his guesthouses for the famous and famously philanthropic.

I meet Claire Weber in the marble-floored lobby, and she leads me past a small army of doormen to a private elevator. Standing with one foot inside the elevator car, she swipes a fob in front of a black pad and presses the button next to the letter *P* on the control panel.

"You have an hour," Claire says, stepping out of the car.

"Okay," I say.

As the doors close and the elevator begins its forty-eight-floor ascent, I take a deep breath and try to forget how important the next hour is for my career. I tell myself that the same design principles that have served me so well in smaller units and in less impressive buildings will stand me in good stead in Daniel Shadid's new penthouse. But I cannot make myself believe that's true.

The elevator slows to a stop, and the doors open into the penthouse. I enter a long, narrow hallway with gently bending walls and walk toward the daylight reflected in the finish on the mahogany floor at the far end. When I reach the edge of the wall, I peer around it into the unit's great room. That the room is lined on three sides with floor-to-ceiling windows makes it seem somehow infinite. I take in the westward view. Looking out over the sprawling Chicago suburbs, I'd swear that I see the curve of the earth.

Daniel Shadid has found a space that might impress George Clooney.

Before I allow myself to consider recommendations, I walk the entire floor plan. The penthouse is fully built out but unfurnished. The walls have been painted a matte eggshell white. I count three bedrooms, each with a master bath. I open every closet to assess its space's potential as a humidor or a sauna or a sky-high, climate-controlled wine cellar. Off the largest bedroom is a vast, south-facing terrace. A glass door slides easily on its clean, lubricated track, and the air rushing out of the unit takes my breath with it. The terrace has a wrought-iron railing taller than my waist, but I approach it with caution. I've never been this high above the earth in open air before. Like a child, the first thing I do is look for my apartment building, but it's obscured by the reflective-glass façade of a boutique hotel one block north and another block east of it. My eyes pan right, and I recognize, in a gap between two skyscrapers, the green copper patina of the St. Asella's spire. My sense of obligation rises but doesn't put up much of a fight. By the time I'm standing inside the silence of the penthouse again, re-taming strands of hair the wind has pulled from bobby pins, I'm thinking only of the task I have less than an hour to complete.

There is a phenomenon in which a person who reaches the highest echelon of her field experiences insights that eluded her at its lower levels. In the hour I spend alone in the space, my talent somehow expands to encompass the penthouse and envision it as a conceptual whole. The penthouse is Gibraltar—the narrow entrance to the deep blue of the Mediterranean seascape, the gateway to my father's Spain, Shadid's Lebanon, and the Morocco of my travels. I see a distressed North African tapestry cut into four strips and hung horizontally on a wide white wall, posing an organic contrast to the cool modernity of the aluminum frames of the floor-to-ceiling windows. In each bedroom, I'll demand a subtle seascape—a color photograph or a rendering in oil—recasting the blue sky that surrounds the penthouse as the Mediterranean itself. For the great room, I'll commission a long table of reclaimed cedar, rough-hewn but carefully constructed to allow for the easy addition and subtraction of leaves. And on the wall of the largest bedroom, a once-in-a-lifetime moment for Shadid's most honored guests and a secret tribute to my father and the Spain he loved: a Picasso from Shadid's private collection.

I recommend the Gibraltar concept and its manifold manifestations to Claire Weber with complete conviction. She listens, but doesn't comment. Her silence doesn't rattle me.

We finish in the largest bedroom. When I mention the Picasso, Claire says, "Mr. Shadid has only one Picasso canvas in his collection. It was recently installed in another unit."

Her tone suggests that discussion of the Picasso is closed. I am not having this.

"Then I recommend that he have it uninstalled and put here," I say. "Or that he buy another one."

The corner of Claire Weber's closed mouth lifts just slightly as she regards me. It's as if she is seeing me for the first time.

She looks at her watch. Then she pulls her smartphone from a bag that certainly cost a few times my monthly rent and begins typing.

"Mr. Shadid will be expecting you for lunch in fifteen minutes," she says. "There is a car waiting downstairs."

This is the first mention of any meeting with Shadid.

"Is this part of the interview?" I say.

"He'll ask questions about your concept, if that's what you mean," she says, still typing.

I begin to worry I am being played, that the opportunity to recommend a concept for this penthouse was Shadid's way of getting me to lunch under circumstances I would readily accept. When we met in the Navy Pier ballroom—I gave him my business card, I recall—I left almost no other avenue open to him. It takes some nerve to believe it possible that Daniel Shadid, with so many women at his disposal, would go to all this trouble to have lunch with me, but once I get the idea that there is even a small possibility I've wasted the best concept of my career on a playboy's ruse, I cannot shake it.

"How did I get this opportunity?"

"I called," Claire says, walking out of the bedroom. "You answered."

"That's not what I mean." I follow her into the hallway. "You could have had any designer for this job. And we've never met. How did you get my name?"

We are on the stairs leading up to the main floor of the penthouse when Claire turns to me. "Mr. Shadid doesn't work with the latest hot designer. He makes the next hot designer. I scout for him. I read blogs. I visit spaces. I ask colleagues about talent. And I talk to my former clients, two of whom are now your clients. They recommended you."

"Oh."

"Satisfied?"

"Yes. Thank you."

But I have one itch left to scratch, and when we reach the narrow front entryway—the straits of the Gibraltar I have imagined—I ask one final question.

"Are you considering anyone else for this work?"

Claire does not turn around when she says, "Not anymore."

By the time the elevator doors open, I can see how my lunch with Daniel Shadid will go. I'll outline the Gibraltar concept, answer any questions he has about it, and hear his suggestions. I'll do these things with the confidence of a designer who already has the job. But at the first reasonable opportunity, I'll steer the conversation to Shadid's work in Africa, giving him every chance to impress me with his stories of traveling with movie stars, meeting with tribal leaders, and making measurable improvements in the lives of people half a world away. Then, without mentioning St. Asella's by name, I'll tell him that I've spent the past year volunteering and now want to work on a larger scale, to contribute to structural and systemic changes that will change people's lives. I'll ask him how I can best support his humanitarian efforts. I'll work my way into Daniel Shadid's exclusive world of auctions and galas and celebrities, a world in which frozen lasagna is no currency.

But even if I never rub elbows with the world's richest do-gooders, this lunch will be the beginning of yet another new life. I'll leave St. Asella's behind and search for my father in my work instead of among his people. I'll find some way, through Shadid, to shore up small communities that can make use of my time, talent and treasure without depending on me to hold them together. Starting today, the only problems I carry home with me are my own.

And the moment my meeting with Daniel Shadid is over—the first minute I am alone—I will call my friend Nicola Hayes to tell her all about it.

She will be so happy for me.

8

Simon

IT HAD BEEN two days since I'd picked up Mrs. Landry's spilled groceries and ushered her back to her apartment. In that time, I'd started showering in the middle of the night. I didn't know what time, exactly, only that it was dark outside. When I showered and slept didn't seem to matter under the weight of my unshakeable anxiety that, spending all this time alone, with no voiceover scripts to rehearse and no Sunday readings to prepare, my vocal folds were beginning to atrophy again.

How could I know, I asked myself, more than eighteen years later, how many days or weeks into my silence it had ceased to be a matter of choice? So I started talking, just to talk, saying whatever was on my mind. And some of what I heard myself saying—one-sided conversations with my departed mother, for example—scared the hell out of me.

I decided I needed to speak face to face—and soon—with someone I know. And the only person in Chicago I really knew was Connor.

Even if there had been no Larry Sellers and no Skyline Talent, I'd have moved to Chicago because Connor was there. I needed to be around him because his success was the stick by which I measured my own. I was pulling for him to succeed in comedy. At the same time, I hated the thought that he'd realize his dream more fully than I would mine. Success could only be a good thing if each of us enjoyed his own version, and in equal measure.

When we were kids, I'd fight Connor to a stalemate of my own making. Without warning, I'd tackle him to the ground, straddle him, and punch his upper arms while he bucked and scratched and clawed at me. I was two years older than him and bigger than he was. I could have stayed astride him for as long as I liked. But at some point in every fight, I allowed him to flip me onto my back, sit on my chest, and punch my shoulders. I resisted a little, to make him believe he was in a real fight. And when I'd taken the same pounding I had doled out—when we were even—I'd throw him off of me, get to my feet, and walk away. *Fair and square,* I'd think.

When I was fifteen and he was thirteen, Connor flipped me without my help, and when I tried to heave him off and end the fight, I couldn't. He did what I'd taught him to do: punched me until we were even. Then he stood up and walked away, without apology, just as I'd always done. Even as I lay there, on my back, stung by the sudden loss of my dominance, I was proud of him.

After that, I stopped tackling Connor and, to his credit, he never started one of those fights. But my wish to be even with him didn't stop with the fights. It kept up throughout our teenage years, throughout my silence. Knowingly or not, our mother perpetuated it. If she kissed one of us on the head, she tracked down the other in his bedroom or the side yard and kissed him, too. She would spend the same amount of time, to the minute, helping Connor with his homework that she'd spent talking me through mine. Until the year she left my father, she made the same dinner—hot dogs and homemade macaroni and cheese—on Connor's birthday and mine, and once, she even showed us receipts to prove she'd spent the same amount of money on our gifts. I don't know whether my mother created these rules or just played by them. But even after she died, I still wanted nothing more than for Connor to have the same share of what he wanted that I had of what I wanted—not one bit more, or less.

It was July 15th. I'd been living in Chicago for six weeks, and Connor still had not returned my call. In the midst of my long wait for voice-over work, I wasn't looking forward to measuring my success against my brother's because I knew I'd come up short again. And it was hard for me to admit that I was totally dependent on Connor for the company I sorely needed, while he didn't seem to need me for anything. But I knew I'd get no greater share of what I wanted in the world if I kept spending every day in my apartment, talking to myself.

So I typed out a text message: *I'd like 2 c u soon. Let me know when u r free.*

I sent the message and watched the pixilated animation of an envelope fly over the horizon line on my phone's tiny screen, mindful that I'd fixed nothing of what ailed me. I'd only given myself something else to wait for.

• • •

I WAS LYING awake in bed that same Thursday, a couple of hours later, when I heard what I thought was the motor of my window-unit air conditioner rattling at a different speed. Only when the sound stopped and started again did I look to my bedside table and notice my phone vibrating slowly toward my radio. I picked it up, expecting to see Connor's name on the display. I saw Elaine's name instead.

The adrenaline hit was my first in days. My heart pounded and my windpipe tightened up—I took five waggles to loosen it as I hurried into the living room. I assumed she was calling to recommend changes to my demo or confirm some contractual detail. That she was calling me at all contradicted my suspicion, which had been growing over the past few days, that I'd never hear from Elaine Vasner again.

Standing in front of my desk in a t-shirt and boxer shorts, I flipped open my phone and said, "This is Simon."

"How are you, Simon?"

"I'm good, Elaine." I took another waggle. "How are you?"

"I'm fine," she said. "Did I wake you up?"

It sounded less like a question than an accusation.

"No," I said.

"You have morning voice, Simon," Elaine said. "I can hear it. But you answered when I called. That's all that matters to me, assuming you weren't screaming yourself hoarse at some bar last night."

I waggled again. "I wasn't."

"Good. You've been booked for a job."

"What?"

Elaine pushed past my shock, which she must have been expecting.

"A creative director I've worked with for years called me looking for a new voice, a young man who doesn't sound like a kid. I think the words she used were 'credible' and 'precise.' Anyway, I sent her a copy of your demo, and she called back the next day to say that now, when she reads the part, she can only hear it in your voice."

I needed two waggles to say, "Wow."

"Wow is right," Elaine said. "It's a radio spot for Red Bull and it'll run in seven markets—New York, L.A., Chicago, Houston, Atlanta, San Francisco, and Las Vegas."

My gut tightened with pleasure. I had assumed my first job, if I ever got one, would be a local commercial. This was a national spot.

"The agency is Burnett. They're recording on Monday at 1 p.m. I'm assuming you can do it."

"I can do it."

"Good," Elaine said. "You're booked for an hour and a half, but they think it'll only take an hour. Have you ever been in a recording studio before?"

I hesitated, trying to decide whether or not the truth was the wrong answer. Then I told the truth. "No."

"I didn't think so," Elaine said. "Let's go over a few things. The moment you walk into that sound booth, put your headphones on. Without them, you can't hear the director, and you can't hear yourself the way you need to."

"Okay."

"If the script is multiple pages, spread the first few across your stand. Don't spoil any takes moving paper."

"Okay."

"There'll be a circular screen in front of the mic. It's there to keep your *P*s from popping. Start with your mouth about four inches away from the screen. If they want you closer to it, or further away, they'll tell you. And make sure you're not leaning forward. Stand up straight and get comfortable. You'll be on your feet for at least an hour."

I waggled. "Right." I thought about reaching for a pen and paper on the desk a few feet away, but I didn't move. I was afraid I would miss something.

"Some newbies see a microphone and start babbling," Elaine said. "Don't speak until somebody tells you to. They'll ask you to do a run-through so they can adjust the levels. And when you do the run-through, do it the way you'd do a take that counts. That's the only way to get the levels right for the keepers. Are you following?"

"Yes."

"When they have their levels," Elaine said, "the director will ask you how your foldback is. You don't know what foldback is."

"No." By then, I was admitting my ignorance greedily. I'd never been so certain I was getting good advice.

"Foldback is the sound of your own voice in your headphones," Elaine said. "It might be too loud. It might not be loud enough. They'll work with you to find a level comfortable for you. You need to hear yourself, but too loud is no good. You need to protect your hearing. Your ears are more important in this business than you might think."

"Okay."

"When your foldback is set, it'll be time for the first take," she said. "From there, you do what you do. And give the director what she wants, even if you think it sounds wrong, even if you think it's a bad idea. When you're in studio on somebody else's dime, it isn't your opinion that matters. Got it?"

"Got it."

"All right," Elaine said. "The session is at Kinzie Street Studios. That's on Kinzie Street."

"Okay."

"That was a joke, Simon."

I hadn't realized. "I know."

Elaine made a noise, something between a snort and a sigh. "The agency sent me the script," she said. "I'll e-mail it over to you. I'll send the address of the studio, too."

"Thank you."

"This is a good job, Simon," Elaine said.

I waggled. "Yes."

"It's the kind of job that can pay some bills and get you another job. Make sure you nail it."

Something cold in Elaine's voice made me blink. "I will."

"Good. Look for my e-mail."

"I will."

"Have a nice day," Elaine said, taking—as another joke, maybe—the falsely polite tone of a customer-service representative.

"Thanks again, Elaine."

I flipped my phone shut and leapt into the air, pulling my knees up as high as I could, and pogoed up again as soon as I landed.

My wait for work was over.

I fell onto the couch, breathing out low moans of happiness through the broad smile on my face, exhausted by the adrenaline and by my private show of exuberance. I may have let myself enjoy the moment for a couple of minutes before my compulsion to prepare got the better of me. I walked to my desk, opened my laptop, and pressed the Send and Receive button above my e-mail inbox. There were no new messages.

Then my phone, still in my hand, pulsed twice, and the display indicated the delivery of a text message. I opened the phone. The message was from Connor.

"Free tuesday," it read. *"Meet u at the lakefront if u want."*

In the time it had taken him to respond to my desperate request, my ambivalence about seeing Connor had evaporated. I *wanted* to see him. I wanted to measure myself against him. I wanted Connor to know that, in a race in which a tie was a victory for me and a devastating loss for him, I was gaining ground.

• • •

I STILL REMEMBER the incident that convinced me—for what seemed, at the time, to be once and for all—that I would never wring from my life even a fraction of what Connor would achieve in his.

I was sitting on a tree stump outside Leyton High on a warm, windy September afternoon, waiting for the short, pencil-yellow bus that would pick up Connor and me. Maybe ten feet away, Ken Hyde and Miro Kowalski—freshmen, like Connor—were sitting on the grass in front of my brother, giving him the audience he needed to burn off the energy and ideas he'd pent up during the school day.

"You guys have Mr. Remacher?" Connor asked them.

"For science," Ken said.

"Me, too," Miro added.

Connor hiked up the waist of his jeans to his bottom ribs, curved into a slouch, and took long, loping steps across the grass, recreating with high fidelity Mr. Remacher's strange carriage.

Ken and Miro laughed hard.

"That's perfect," Ken said.

"What about Ms. Gorski?" Connor asked.

"The gym teacher?" Miro asked Ken.

Ken nodded without taking his eyes off of Connor.

Connor pressed his palms flat against his lower back, over his kidneys, with his fingers spread wide and their tips pointing straight down his legs. Then he hung his head forward and flattened his lips. "Ladies," Connor said, voicing the "l" from the back of his mouth, "if you *do* not get moving, you will have no time to shower and the boys will smell your *stinky feets*." He clapped twice. "Let's *go!*"

As Ken and Miro laughed, I smiled to myself. Just a couple of weeks into the school year, Connor had Ms. Gorski's Polish accent, in all its thickness, down pat.

"Do Mr. Lucas!"

Connor shot Ken a look. In a decision that coincided roughly with his starting high school, my brother had begun denying all requests, at home and in public, for routines and impressions he had once done the moment he was asked.

"I'm not a trained monkey," he'd say. And when he was feeling particularly justified in his refusal, he'd add, "I'm not doing any of this for you, anyway. I do it for me."

Ken and Miro knew Connor's stance on command performances—Connor had turned them down before. But, perhaps having already decided to imitate Mr. Lucas, Connor glanced in all directions for any sign of the loud, little man who taught my history class, and then became him.

"We're running out of time," Connor's Mr. Lucas said, "so I'm going to go Pentangelo here. Mr. Pentangelo, which president made the call to drop the first atomic bomb on Japan?"

"Roosevelt," said Connor's Pentangelo.

"No!" answered Connor's Mr. Lucas. "No! No! Pentangelo! I went to you because we were short on time! We needed the right answer, Pentangelo! Now the period is almost over and your classmates are under the impression that Franklin Delano Roosevelt green-lit the first atomic bomb! The man was rotting in his grave, Pentangelo! *Truman*, Pentangelo! Truman dropped the bomb!"

Midway through the routine, Ken and Miro had fallen onto their backs, laughing with the abandon of much younger boys, but Connor saw it through to the finish, showing no mercy as his still new friends gasped for air between paroxysms of delight.

I was more awed than amused. I had witnessed Mr. Lucas' memorable dressing down of Giuseppe Pentangelo, one of the best students in my junior class, and knew for a fact that Connor hadn't been there to see it. I guessed he had heard it through the open door of his own history class, which met in the classroom across from Mr. Lucas' during the same period, but that didn't explain how Connor had so completely captured the physical reality of the exchange. He had even stood over Ken and Miro in the same way Mr. Lucas had loomed over the sheepish Pentangelo. Somehow, my television-obsessed little brother had mastered a radio listener's trick: He had seen Mr. Lucas with his ears.

Ken and Miro lay on their backs for a minute or so after Connor relented. As they caught their breath, the boys spouted laughs that deteriorated into sighs of exhaustion. Miro was the first to sit up again.

"Who is that?" he asked.

Ken propped himself up on his locked arms, and each one of us followed the path of Miro's gaze with his own.

"That's Candace Andersen," Ken said.

That a freshman such as Ken Hyde knew the name and face of a junior after only a few weeks at school would have been surprising if the junior had been anyone other than Candace Andersen.

Candace was an academic star who didn't flaunt her intelligence—she did her homework at home and rarely discussed grades. She was kind and well liked. And beautiful. That afternoon, she was sitting on the concrete base of the school's flagpole with an open paperback in hand, her brown hair moussed into a thick bouquet of curls flecked with golden blond.

By coincidences of class schedule, classroom layout, and alphabetical order, my assigned seat in Mr. Lucas' history class was next to Candace's, and I had occupied the desk behind hers in Mrs. Vallort's English class the year before. We didn't know each other well—I couldn't speak, so no one knew me well—but when we passed in the hallway or arrived at class, Candace would say hello. I'd respond with a polite, close-lipped smile intended to hide the following truths: that Candace Andersen enthralled me, that whenever I imagined speaking again, I imagined my first words would be "Hi" and "Candace," and that once, in a moment of the hopeful delirium that was an occasional symptom of my solitude, I'd envisioned Candace inviting me on a walk after school. I imagined her telling me that she knew how I felt about her, that she felt the same way about me, and that I could hide all I wanted from everyone else but didn't have to hide myself from her anymore. And we would kiss long enough for me to forget that I didn't know how to kiss, long enough for me to learn how, maybe. Then Candace would pull her lips from mine, smile, and kiss me again.

"Dude," Miro said to Connor, keeping his vocal volume low, "you should do those impressions for her."

As she waited for her ride home, Candace crossed her long legs beneath her pleated skirt, keeping her eyes locked on her book. Connor squinted at Candace, seeming to contemplate Miro's challenge. Then Connor started out across the small, green patch of lawn between himself and Candace.

Over his shoulder, he said, "Don't let the bus leave without me."

I think he was talking to me.

Miro and Ken looked at each other, their eyes open wide with anticipation.

"Oh shit!" Ken whispered to Miro, smiling.

The boys were surely imagining themselves, as I was imagining myself, in Connor's shoes. From a short but safe distance, and from the far side of a wide gulf of charm and talent, the three of us experienced the nervous thrill of recklessly approaching an uncommonly pretty girl.

As he neared her, Connor circled in front of Candace and waved. Candace hadn't met Connor, so far as I knew, but she smiled and said hello. The afternoon wind was gusting, and the rush of it in my ears had the effect of static in a weak radio signal, clipping some words and drowning others. But I did hear Connor say our last name.

And I heard the gorgeous ring of Candace's voice when she said, "Simon's brother?"

Connor claimed me minimally, with a nod, hedging his bet as to whether his being my brother was a good or bad thing in Candace's eyes. Then, as the wind kicked up again, Candace must have said her own name, because Connor stepped up to her and shook her hand. Something in the way he did that made her laugh.

That Connor could make Candace laugh with a handshake threatened me so deeply that I couldn't help but look away. For a few moments, I watched the wind thrash the slender branches of a hulking willow. Then I heard Candace laugh again, and my eyes followed the sound. Candace had closed her book, and Connor was doing Mr. Remacher's walk. When he finished, Candace tucked her book between her thigh and the concrete, freeing her hands to applaud Connor with false formality. Connor took a profound bow. And Candace laughed again.

Then Connor became Ms. Gorski. Over the gusts, I made out "stinky feets" and "let's go!" Candace threw her head back, raising her smiling face to the sky.

"She's loving it," Miro said.

Connor skipped his bow and went straight into his Mr. Lucas. He paced and pointed to the invisible Pentangelo, then became him just long enough to give the damning wrong answer.

"No!" Connor shouted. "No, Pentangelo!"

As Connor gesticulated above the invisible Pentangelo, Candace, who'd had a ringside seat for the original Lucas-Pentangelo exchange, watched my brother with her smiling mouth agape.

When the scene was finished, she didn't laugh, and she didn't applaud. Staring at Connor and shaking her head, Candace Andersen said, "Unbelievable!"

She went on praising Connor in lilting words I couldn't make out. Like me, Candace had found my brother's performance even more amazing than it was amusing.

Connor kept his eyes on Candace, guzzling from the fire hose of her admiration without spilling a drop. When she was finished speaking, he held up his index finger, as if to say, I've got one more. And he just stood there. He slouched, but he didn't move a muscle and he didn't say a word. He stared off toward the state highway that marked the eastern border of the campus. He dropped his eyes to his feet, put his hands in his pockets, and swayed back and forth, slowly.

I strained to hear over the weakening breeze, waiting for Connor to speak in one of his thousand voices, but he said nothing.

"I give up," Candace said, shaking her head. "Who is it?"

Connor shrugged and lifted his palms. I recognized that gesture. It was one of mine. He was asking her, *pretty please*, to guess.

Candace sat rigidly on the concrete block. "I really don't know."

"Seriously?" Connor shouted, himself again. He sounded annoyed, even hurt.

"Who was it?"

"You couldn't tell that was Simon?"

Candace stared at Connor for a moment. Then she turned her face and squinted into the afternoon sun. It was at least a second before I realized she was looking at me. My face went red, and I stared into the distance, just as Connor had done in his impression of me.

"I'm only kidding," I heard Connor say.

Candace said something I didn't hear.

"Really," Connor insisted, "it was a joke."

Out of the corner of my eye, I saw that Candace had picked up her book again. Then, with her customary kindness, Candace said, "I'll see you around, Connor."

Connor held up his hands in protest for a moment before dropping them. "All right," he said. "See you around."

She hadn't stuck up for me, really—not with the same fervor with which she'd praised Connor the moment before. But Candace hadn't enjoyed—hadn't *allowed herself* to enjoy—a laugh at my expense. Now, more than ten years after the incident, I know that Candace's refusal to laugh had more to do with her bedrock decency than anything else. But that day, wallowing neck deep in my silent self-loathing, I could only understand her non-laugh and the squinting glance that followed it to mean that Candace Andersen, the girl of my daydreams, pitied me.

Having sent their champion into the arena, Miro and Ken absorbed some of the embarrassment Connor had suffered and the humiliation he had doled out. Ken repeatedly zipped and unzipped the small pocket of his backpack while Miro uprooted individual blades of grass and tore them apart between his finger and thumbnails. For my part, as Connor made his way back across the lawn with his head down, I envisioned sprinting at him, pouncing on him like a predator, and beating him bloody, but I did no such thing. I knew that Connor was probably obsessing over the one laugh he'd gone for and failed to get, that he would replay his impression of me for days, dissecting it for flaws in character and timing, discounting the praise he'd received for his Mr. Lucas impression. The punishment Connor would inflict on himself was sure to be worse than any beating I could have meted out. So I left him untouched. That was my revenge.

I've since wondered if any of Connor's suffering over the next few days was rooted in some feeling that having done that impression of me, for Candace and right before my eyes, was wrong. My guess is that comedy, except insofar as doing it well was a kind of moral imperative, was not a matter of conscience for Connor, but I can't be sure. The fact that he didn't apologize to me doesn't settle things one way or another. Except for the meaningless apologies our mother had forced us to make, Connor and I had never apologized to one another. Every fight, every petty tattle, every humiliation that one of us perpetrated against the other was flung without comment onto the smoldering pile of wrongs we had done one another over the years. This was how it was between my brother and me: we went on with things, to the next right or the next wrong. I never thought to ask Connor why the men in our family didn't apologize to each other. I assumed he'd learned this unspoken maxim the same way I had: by watching our father.

The bus arrived as the sun began to sink beneath the leafy tops of the tall oaks west of campus. As Connor and I were driven home, sitting as far apart from one another as was possible, I found myself admiring him even before my shame had cooled. Someone just out for laughs, or to impress a pretty girl, might have been satisfied with Candace's astonished response to the impression of Mr. Lucas and quit while he was ahead. But for Connor, even the big stage that an audience with Candace Andersen provided was little more than a workshop. In his own mind, Connor wasn't performing. He was preparing for bigger performances to come. And in his ruthless determination to understand, by the time his golden opportunity arrived, what was funny and what wasn't and why, Connor was willing to make his mute older brother the butt of a joke, even as I watched. Slouched against the vinyl backrest of a bus bench, lost in my silence, I imagined what seemed impossible—a world in which I had a voice like the voices on the radio—and understood that, even if the impossible came true, I stood no chance of pulling even with someone as ambitious and cutthroat as my brother.

●　●　●

FIFTEEN MINUTES AFTER Elaine and I hung up, a new message appeared in my e-mail inbox. The subject line read, "FW: Red Bull Comedy Tour Radio – The Pitch Man."

The embedded chain of correspondence between Elaine and someone from the ad agency consisted mainly of logistic and administrative information—the date, time and location of the session, my hourly rate, and my union status. At the end of one of her notes, the ad-agency representative, who did not seem to be the creative director Elaine had known for years, wrote, "PLEASE make sure your client arrives at the session ON TIME, which is to say a few minutes BEFORE the session's official start time."

Elaine seemed to take exception to this request.

"Thank you for the lesson in punctuality and professionalism," she wrote in reply. "My client will be at the session on time. While we're on the topic of punctuality, let me remind you that I expect my client to be paid on time. If I don't have a check IN HAND by the agreed upon date, your boss will get at least one phone call from me the first day payment is overdue, and every day after, until payment is received in full. Which is to say I'll have MY FOOT UP YOUR ASS if the check is late. Understood?"

I made mental notes to get to the session a half-hour early and never cross Elaine.

I double-clicked the attached file—my first real script! And from the moment I began to scan page one, I realized it was not at all what I had been expecting.

The script called for three different voice actors to engage in a kind of conversation. In my role as the Pitch Man, I was to relate the following details: This fall, comedians David Cross and Patton Oswalt would co-headline the Red Bull No Bull Comedy Tour—seven shows in seven cities. Tickets in each city would go on sale Tuesday, September 4th, at 10 a.m. Tickets were limited, so listeners were advised to act quickly.

Delivered without interruption, my lines would not have taken twenty seconds of airtime. But the script called for Cross and Oswalt—playing versions of themselves—to interrupt the Pitch Man with derision of the corporate sponsor and direction about the Pitch Man's "energy."

"Only Red Bull," the Pitch Man would say, "could bring two comedians of this caliber to the same stage on the same night in seven American cities."

"Yeah," Oswalt would interject. "I think democracy in Iran is next on Red Bull's list."

"Tickets are limited, so act fast!" the Pitch Man would say. Then, addressing Oswalt and Cross, he would ask, "How was that?"

Cross and Oswalt were to deliver a simple answer—"Great!"—in unison.

And the bracketed direction beside their answer read, "[EVERYONE BUT THE PITCH MAN CAN HEAR THAT CROSS AND OSWALT ARE BEING SARCASTIC.]"

This script was a *parody* of the straight-announcement voiceover work I'd admired and studied all my life. And the Pitch Man, a square and hapless stereotype of my heroes, wasn't in on the joke.

My disappointment didn't stop there. That the script featured famous professional comedians made it seem like a piece of Connor's New York dream misdelivered to me in Chicago. But this was not the only way that this job seemed better suited to Connor than it was to me: the Pitch Man wasn't just a voice, and he wasn't some version of myself. If he were any part of me, the Pitch Man would *never* have asked the comedians' opinion of his work—he understood radio commercials better than they did. No, the Pitch Man was someone else entirely. He was a *character*, which made him more Connor's than mine.

Despite myself, I entertained a scenario in which Connor went to the recording session in my place. He would introduce himself as Simon Davies to people who had never seen my face. He'd enter the sound booth and bring the Pitch Man to life as a character in a voice that was imperceptibly different from my own. And for his trouble, Connor would get the chance to work—in the same commercial if not the same studio—with two big-time comedians. The creative director and the client would be pleased, Elaine would be pleased, and so long as Connor went in my place for any future sessions run by that creative director, no one would be the wiser.

But these were merely the public aspects of the scenario. Its horrors would play out in private. I saw myself sitting on my couch, alone during the session's appointed hour, writhing in the knowledge that I'd handed Connor a job he had neither chased nor earned and given up my first chance—maybe my only chance—to be a voiceover artist.

Then I imagined hearing Connor's voice, in place of mine, on the radio.

At this thought, I made the only decision I could live with. I'd play the Pitch Man myself, and do it the only way I could: the way that Connor would have done it. From the blind of my silence, I'd watched my brother become thousands of people who were not himself. I *knew* what he would make of this Pitch Man, and that was all I needed to know. If the creative director was already hearing the Pitch Man's voice as mine, I could gamble that my own pale rendition of the flesh-and-blood character Connor would've created would be good enough for her.

Over the next few days, between rehearsals, I was hounded by the thought that my living some part of Connor's dream, and appropriating his talent, sullied not only this job, but the year of spasm-inducing work I'd put into rebuilding my voice. Each time the thought nipped at my heels, I answered it with the lesson my brother taught me on the front lawn of our high school: *Don't let anyone, not even your brother, keep you from getting what you want.*

I, too, could be cutthroat.

To run neck-and-neck with Connor after a lifetime spent so far behind him, I'd take anything of his that I needed.

9

Connor Davies

IN JUNE OF '08, when I visited my father and Simon at home for the first time in a year and a half, I got two surprises. The first: Simon could talk. The second: when Simon spoke, I heard my voice.

"Are you doing that on purpose?" I asked him.

He looked confused. "Doing what?"

"Are you imitating me?"

"No, Connor," Simon said, smiling. "That's just how it comes out." He did that robotic head-tremor thing and added, "This is the only voice I've got."

I'd assumed at first that Simon, while teaching himself to talk again, had developed a talent for doing impressions. I'll admit to feeling some relief when he said that he had only the one voice, even if it was mine. That Simon sounded like me didn't matter much, anyway. I could do a lot more with my voice than he would ever be able to.

We had this little chat standing in the kitchen of the house we'd grown up in. Simon was still in his busboy's uniform—black button-down shirt, black pleated pants, scuffed black leather shoes. His hair, weighed down with sweat and oil, was pressed close to his head.

Simon could speak all right, but had no clue how to make conversation. I felt like I was improvising a scene with a frightened, level-one student. Just for something to say, I asked Simon what he was most looking forward to, now that he had a voice again.

Simon dropped his eyes to the dirty linoleum floor, looking sheepish and a little reluctant to answer. Then his lips crept into half a smile.

"I don't know," he said. He did another headshake. "Meeting a girl, I guess."

I laughed. "Just one?"

I'd meant to suggest that, with so many women out there, Simon might not want to limit himself to one. What had made me laugh, though, was the idea that any woman worth having would have Simon.

Simon didn't laugh, but he smiled smugly, as if suddenly having a voice or not having one for so long had clued him in to some insight I would never have.

"I only want one," he said.

As my brother stood there, enjoying his one-girl-one-guy fantasy and overestimating his wisdom, I formed an opinion I still held in the summer of 2010 when Simon moved up to Chicago: I liked Simon better when he couldn't talk.

• • •

A COUPLE OF weeks after he moved to Chicago, Simon called my phone, and I didn't answer. In a voicemail, Simon told me that Brittany—the girl he'd found and convinced to stick around for a while—was finished with him. In the playback of my brother's voice, I recognized myself again, but this time, the person I heard was me at my weakest and my worst. I heard myself the way I was the night I slept with Brittany.

When I went down to Carbondale to visit Simon, I was on a streak. Since finding out that *Saturday Night Live* had hired a Chicago actor who wasn't me, I'd been doing an improv or sketch set wherever I could get one, paid or not, every night, and taking home a girl from the show's audience. I made sure to get her first name and to remember it, no matter how drunk I was. If I was awake when she left my bed, I'd say her name and say goodbye. In those four months, I took only one night off from comedy—the night I spent at Simon's place in Carbondale. But that wasn't the night I broke my streak of sleeping with women I hardly knew.

A little more than a week later, I was in the back of a bar on Belmont Avenue in Chicago, getting paid in booze to improvise with a bunch of stiffs I'd met in a commercial-acting class. I started drinking before the show, hoping that the white noise of a liquor buzz might drown out the question I kept asking myself: *If this is the best show you can get tonight, how good are you, really?*

As I stood onstage at the start of the set, I did what I'd done a few times before at these off-off-everywhere sideshows: I picked one woman out of the audience and played for her only. I would never let on what I was doing. I didn't make eyes at the woman from the stage or ask her for a word we could use to start a scene. But from the moment I chose her, no one else in the audience mattered to me. Everyone else could go on whispering and checking their fucking phones for all I cared.

The woman I picked that night, from a crowd of about fifteen people, was sitting with three girlfriends. She had straight brown hair parted down the middle and enormous brown eyes. Her thin black t-shirt was fitted to her. She was fucking beautiful—that's what I noticed first—but my first *thought* about her was, *She is smart.* Something in her eyes made me sure of it.

Then I did my thing. I created characters on the spot, made scenes out of the directionless babble of the stiffs, and set them up to make and take the laugh lines. In improv, you only look as good as the people onstage with you. By the end of our set, the people onstage with me looked okay. Only someone who had done what I did that night—who had spread himself wide open to hold a scene together—would have thought I looked any better.

When the lights and music came up, the woman I had been playing for was standing alone. Her friends were crowded around Sammy, the guy who'd invited me to join his group onstage that night.

I went up and introduced myself to her.

"What's your name?" I asked.

"Erika."

Remember that, I thought. "Can I get you a drink, Erika?"

"Got one," she said, raising a nearly empty pint glass. "Thanks."

I took a swallow of bourbon, nodding, and reset my feet. "You know Sammy?"

Erika glanced at Sammy. "Uh, not really. I'm a friend of his cousin's."

"Oh, cool. Sammy's a good guy."

And a terrible improviser, I thought.

"So, what did you think of the show?" I asked.

"What did *you* think of it?"

"Honestly?"

Erika shrugged, as if to say she didn't care if I answered honestly or not.

"Not great," I said.

She nodded. It looked like she was trying not to smile.

"We missed more opportunities than we took," I went on, sliding into the kind of clichés that pro athletes doled out to reporters after a tough loss.

"Huh," she said. "Why do you think that is?"

"Well—" I glanced away, trying to find a polite way to say that my fellow improvisers—Sammy included—were brutal.

"Because your head wasn't in it, maybe?" she asked.

I felt like I'd been slapped. "What do you mean?"

"You winked at me. In the middle of a scene."

"No, I didn't."

"Yes. You did. Then you winked again and waved to me."

I didn't remember doing any winking or waving, but I was pretty well drunk by the middle of the set and drunker still by the end. Drinking during a show isn't an issue, in and of itself, so long as I deliver onstage. But if I had winked at Erika and waved to her in the middle of a scene, nobody—not even Sammy—had committed any worse crime against improv that night than I had.

Just then I had a thought I'd never considered: that doing improv every night was not making me better, but ruining me.

"You're better than this," Erika said.

Somehow, I was sure she meant I was better than this bar, the winking, the drinking—all of it. I wanted that to be true.

Then she handed me a piece of paper. It had a phone number on it.

"I wrote it down after you winked at me. The second time."

Then Erika picked up her purse and rejoined her friends.

My streak broke that night. I went home alone. And the next day, I called Erika.

I knew she wasn't in comedy. I would have seen her before, if she had been. But as it turned out, Erika was in the business: she's a voiceover artist. I was watching her nap on my couch on a Sunday afternoon, a few weeks into what I consider the first real relationship I've ever had, when I realized that I was living Simon's dream—*I only want one*, he'd said. This thought and the guilty feeling that followed it were just the opening acts, though. The headliner was a *holy fuck* realization that left me feeling unsafe, as if I'd found my apartment door wide open and its locks drilled out: if I fell in love with Erika—and I was headed that way—what I'd done to Simon could be done to me.

• • •

ERIKA AND I had been together almost three months when I got a text message from Simon: *I'd like 2 c u soon,* it said. *Let me know when u r free.*

My first thought was that he knew.

Maybe Brittany had confessed what she and I had done that night in Carbondale. Or maybe Simon had just pieced together that Brittany and I had been flirting. That I was gone when he woke up. That she broke up with him soon after. However it'd happened, I knew the chances were good that Simon had found me out. And now he wanted to see me.

I hadn't mentioned anything about Erika to Simon. Hell, I hadn't said shit to Simon since Carbondale. So far as I knew, Simon had no idea that Erika existed. But I *had* let it slip to Erika that I had a brother. Then I spilled that he'd moved to Chicago and wanted to be a voiceover artist. Since finding out about Simon, Erika had been asking me when we could meet my brother for a drink. I'd put her off each time, using a put-in rehearsal or show as an excuse. But she kept asking. I knew if Erika and I stayed together, I wouldn't be able to keep the two of them apart forever. She'd made Simon—I'd coughed up his name, too—another mystery to draw out of me.

Erika had made it clear she wanted to know everything about me. If a part of my past I didn't want to discuss came up, Erika pushed me to tell her more. "No secrets," she'd say. She seemed to believe that the stuff I didn't want to talk about would cement us together if I shared it and tear us apart if I didn't. I'd shared a few nuggets—about my mom dying and my dad's drinking—and Erika had never used anything against me. She made a dangerous game as safe as it could be. But this secret—that I'd slept with my speech-impaired older brother's first and only girlfriend—was different.

You're better than this. That's what Erika had had said to me the night we met. I *wanted* to be better in every way Erika could have meant, and I believed that as long as she and I were together, I could be every bit as good as she thought I was. So here's what had me so skittish: that if she found out what I'd done to poor, sorry Simon, Erika would decide that she'd been wrong about me—that, really, I wasn't much good at all.

I never wanted Erika to find out, but the worst-case scenario was her finding out from someone other than me. If I got cornered into telling her myself, I could spin it as a confession I'd made to bring us closer. But if she heard this story first from *Simon*, of all people, she'd leave me—maybe not right away, but she would leave. I was sure of it. And given our history, why wouldn't Simon try to get even by ruining things between Erika and me? I obsessed over this unhappy ending because it was pretty much what I deserved.

I didn't want to see Simon. I needed no reminder of who I was at my worst. But if he and Erika were going to meet one way or another, I needed to know what he knew. So I agreed to meet him the following Tuesday, a day I knew Erika would be in the suburbs helping her father clean up his landscaping for the summer. If Simon didn't know what I'd done, I wasn't about to tell him. But if he did, I'd have to tell Erika about Brittany and me. The only question would be when.

Fucking Simon. My whole life, he'd been the worst kind of audience: the kind that watched but never laughed. And now his voice—*my* voice—made Simon a threat to the best thing I had going.

● ● ●

SIMON AND I would fight when we were growing up.

Sometimes, he would just tackle me out of the blue. Other times, I would more or less start the fight with something I said. Simon would be moping in his room, listening to his radio, and I would barge in and start talking in my Simon Voice. Deep and mush-mouthed, the Simon Voice made my brother out to be a slow, dull ogre. I was doing a caricature of Simon, not a character. I knew the difference before I understood the words. But given that the kid was a mute, imitating him in any voice at all gave him plenty of reason to get pissed off.

"I like radio," I'd say in the Simon Voice. "Radio is the best."

On his good days, Simon would ignore me.

"Ooooooo, this kid is annoying," I'd say, speaking as Simon and referring to myself. "I wish he'd just let me listen to my little radio! He thinks he's so funny with his voices. And all his talkety-talk!"

Simon would only take so much mockery in my cartoonish impression of the voice he didn't have. The low limit of his patience for this routine gave me something to respect about him.

When he'd knocked me onto my back, Simon would press my cheek into the carpet with one hand and pummel my shoulder with the other. And I fought back, hard. I arched my back to break his pin, like I'd seen pro wrestlers do on TV, and drove my knees up and back, into his spine. I dug my nails into the hand on my face and whacked at his locked elbow with my balled-up fist. There was something in this combat that bound us together. I remember having this thought while he was punching me, and I was gouging him: *This says we mean something to each other. Brothers fight. Simon and I are brothers.*

The moment I got the upper hand, I'd hit Simon as hard as I could until he threw me. After a while, I figured out that the way Simon fought—giving me a beating, and then taking one from me—was part of his sick fixation on making everything even-steven. I came to hate Simon's fucking fake draws. I didn't want to be even with him in anything. So I fought to win. Every time.

If she was home, our mother would charge in and break up our fights, grabbing by the arm whoever was on top and pulling him off. Then she'd stand us up, face to face.

"Apologize to your brother," she'd say to me.

"Sorry," I would say.

Then she'd look at Simon. "Apologize."

Simon would fist-bump his chest, the gesture we'd all agreed, somewhere along the line, meant he was sorry.

But neither of us actually meant these apologies. We were already imagining our next floor battle, not payback and not a preemptive strike, just *what we did* with no more thought than we'd give to chewing our afterschool cookies.

Once, when I was about thirteen, I flipped Simon off of me before he was ready. He fell hard and hit his head on the leg of his desk chair. I punched at Simon's face with both fists, landing only a few blows between his forearms before our mother pulled me off and slapped me across the face. That fight—right through the slap—was the best moment of my life to that point. I had *won*. Even our mother could see it.

After my big win, neither of us threw a punch for years. We were still shitty to each other, though. I'd whistle "The Sound of Silence" at him, and he'd shake his head, mocking me, while I sat with our father watching ballgames that bored me. Most of the time, we left each other alone. I let Simon check his progress or lack of it against mine in any way he wasn't too ashamed to do it, while I paid almost no attention to his small successes and failures. By ignoring him, I was sending Simon a message: that he would never be as good as me in any category worth a damn.

In other words, by refusing Simon's fights, I kept winning.

Winning by not fighting was easy when things were going my way. When things were going badly, though, I'd feed my raw need to win the old-fashioned way. The night Simon introduced me to Brittany, I was taking every win I could. Even the wins that were losses.

● ● ●

ERIKA WAS NOT the only good fortune I'd had since returning from Carbondale.

Raam Kersati was the big dog on the Chicago improv scene and, at a few years north of forty, its elder statesman, too. When I started taking improv classes back in 2006, I'd doubted that Raam was as good as everyone said he was—*If he's still in Chicago,* I thought, *how good can he be?* Then I saw Raam's two-man show at the Improviso Theatre. Sixty minutes. A single scene. Every word improvised. Not one word wasted. Buzzed on bourbon and nearly exhausted from laughing, I wanted to buy Raam a drink and apologize for even *thinking* he was anything less than one of the best improvisers in the business. I kept just enough of my head to leave Raam the hell alone.

Four years later, a month before I visited Simon in Carbondale, I was doing a late-night set at Improviso for the twenty-or-so improv geeks and Cub fans sticking around until last call to watch me and a few other unknowns make shit up. Raam stepped onstage unannounced. I thought he was going to put a stop to our set right up until the moment he joined it.

I'd never been better than I was in the scenes I did with Raam. His characters were so real. He made it easy to find the true, which made it easy to find the funny. Raam was the kind of improviser who made everyone around him better without looking any worse himself. Standing next to Raam when the lights came up, feeling shockwaves of applause from a crowd that seemed to have doubled, I believed for just a moment that, even if I never made it to New York, I'd done something in comedy worth doing.

I'd heard the rumor that Raam had turned down several offers—including one, more than ten years before, from *Saturday Night Live*—because they'd refused to guarantee him creative control. At Improviso, Raam had all the control he wanted, so he played in primetime: a two-person show that sold out the 10 p.m. slot every Thursday. Raam's show had been on hiatus since his most recent scene partner, a woman named Sandra Keefe, moved to Los Angeles with a role in a Judd Apatow film. For Sandra's replacement, Raam had his pick of every improviser in Chicago.

He called me first, and I was ready.

To prepare for our opening, we improvised six fifty-minute scenes in a tiny room with no audience, learning each other's tendencies, strengths, and weaknesses. Then, on a Thursday night, billed as Raam and Connor, we opened to a sold-out crowd at Improviso. The reviews were raves, and the work was more satisfying than any I'd had. After years of drifting from bar to bar, performing for liquor, I'd landed in the best improv show in Chicago. I was a long way from *Saturday Night Live*, but I could see it from where I was standing on Raam Kersati's shoulders.

Raam and I were still doing afternoon sets to a hundred empty seats twice a week, creating characters no one would see and laugh lines no one would hear to make sure we killed every time we worked in front of an audience. It was one of these practice sessions that had pushed my meeting with Simon to a morning hour, before decent bars were serving. My neighborhood was long on dry cleaners and short on coffee shops, so I told Simon to meet me at the lakefront, just south of the nine-hole golf course at the north end of Lincoln Park, a half-mile from my apartment.

I'd settled on an outdoor meeting place without checking the weather forecast. It was July, and predictions made more than a day or two out aren't worth much in Chicago, anyway. But when I left my apartment late Tuesday morning, the sun was out and the temperature was perfect for a guy wearing a t-shirt and jeans. I imagined that, having lived my whole life in the Midwest, I'd developed a sixth sense that enabled me to predict weather conditions days in advance.

At Irving Park Road, I looked west for a bus that would get me to Lake Shore Drive before I could cover the three city blocks to the lakefront on foot. I saw no bus, but I did see dark gray clouds, their front edge forming a sharp line against the blue sky. *Some sixth fucking sense,* I thought. The wind and rain were on their way.

I walked across the softball fields to the tiered cement platforms—they looked like bleachers for giants—that passed for beach on this part of the shoreline. Simon wasn't there. I checked my phone. He hadn't called or texted. I sat down on the top platform and took in the blue expanse of Lake Michigan. Then I turned and faced the park. I didn't like the idea of Simon seeing me before I saw him.

I spotted Simon when he was still a long way off, walking alone across the softball fields with his head down. He may have been staring at the grass and clover in front of his feet, or just lowering his eyes out of the sunlight. I'd learned my brother's body language when it was the only language he had outside of a few made-up signs, but nothing in his posture or the steady pace of his steps gave me any clue about what Simon was meeting me to do or say. All the same, I couldn't shake the idea that he was ready to take from me what I'd taken from him.

I crossed the bike path and waited for Simon on the grass.

When he saw me, about twenty yards off, Simon raised his hand. I returned his wave. When he got closer, I put out my hand.

"How are you, brother?" I asked.

Simon shook my hand a little too firmly, like a guy trying to prove a point about his hand strength, as if *hand strength* would decide everything.

Then he did his little headshake and said, "I'm all right. How are you?"

"Fine."

Simon nodded.

I gave him an opening to say whatever it was he had come here to say, hoping we could get into it quickly. But Simon said nothing. So I opened a hand toward the cement platform like it was the couch in my apartment.

"Have a seat," I said.

We crossed the bike path and sat down, facing the water.

"I've never been here before," he said.

"Lincoln Park?"

Simon shook his head. "To the lake."

"This is your first time seeing Lake Michigan?"

"Yeah."

It was a reminder of how small my brother's world had been when he couldn't speak. That smallness lingered like a hangover. Simon had been living in Chicago for six weeks, and I guessed he'd spent most of his time in his apartment.

We sat there another minute, looking out over the water.

"It's beautiful," he said.

And it was. But by then, I didn't give a shit about beauty. I wanted to know why Simon had asked to see me. Just asking the question, though, was too blunt an approach, even for me, so I pussyfooted in that direction.

"So how are things, Simon?"

He shrugged and wiggled his head. "Not bad," he said. "Considering."

That word—*considering*—made me nervous. Considering what? Considering that he was still finding his way around a new city, or that his brother had fucked his girlfriend while he slept in the next room? After years of knowing what was on Simon's mind without his saying a word, I couldn't read him. It was as if his ability to speak was hiding his thoughts and feelings in a way his silence never had.

"So what have you been up to?" I asked. "Since you moved to the city."

"Well," Simon said, "I made a voiceover demo."

"That's good."

I waited for a follow-up that didn't come. *Is this some kind of fucking interview?* I wondered. *Am I going to have to yank every thought out of him?*

"So how'd it turn out?" I asked.

"Pretty well," Simon said, nodding.

He looked so pleased with his little achievement that I wanted to laugh. I managed to swallow that urge.

"Did you send the demo out?"

He wiggled his head. "To a few agencies, yeah."

I nodded, leaving space for him to say something else. He didn't.

"Have you heard anything?" I asked, letting a little of exasperation into my voice.

"Yeah," he said. "I have an agent now."

"No shit," I said, glad to be getting somewhere, finally. "What agency?"

"Skyline Talent," Simon said, watching me.

What Simon probably saw was his younger brother looking impressed and anxious all at once. Skyline Talent was a top agency in Chicago. Actors who did their commercial work through Skyline did well. How did I know for sure? Skyline was *Erika's* agency. It's not like actors hang out at their agencies all the time, but it skeeved me out that Erika and Simon had a point of connection I couldn't control.

"That's a good agency," I said.

Simon twisted his lips to the far side of his face and looked out over the lake again. He seemed to be fighting back a smile.

"They're doing pretty well for me so far," he said.

"You got a gig already?"

He nodded. "I did a session yesterday."

"That's fantastic," I said.

"So are you the voice of Chicago Auto Wreckers now? Will I be passed out on the couch and hear your voice coming out of my TV at three in the morning?"

He shook his head. "It's a radio spot. For Red Bull. Seven markets."

As he sat there watching me, waiting again for me to react to news of his success, I realized what our meeting was about: Simon was here to tell me how well he was doing and to see my face when he told me. It was his twisted even-steven thing. Nothing more. He didn't have a clue about what had happened with Brittany and me that night.

Right then, I could have lay back onto the concrete with my arms flung over my head and laughed with relief. But I didn't. Instead, I made an honest attempt to give my brother some of what I thought he'd come for.

"I'm really happy for you, Simon," I said. "Saying you want to get into voiceover is a long way from making a demo, sending it out, getting an agent, and getting work. Doing all that took balls. I'm proud of you."

As I spoke, I watched Simon's eyes narrow and his mouth untwist from its smile. My guess was that he thought I was fucking with him.

"I mean it," I added, as earnestly as I could.

"Thanks," he said, flatly.

I didn't understand Simon's reaction, but I was too happy to bother figuring it out. My life with Erika was what mattered, and for the moment, it was safe.

A flash lit up the sky, which had gone from clear blue to a pale gray. Thunder followed a second or two later. Behind us, wind was thrashing the trees that lined Lake Shore Drive and carrying a white food wrapper over the softball fields.

"We're about to get soaked," I said.

It was a weather prediction even *I* could get right, and as soon as I'd made it, the rain started coming down, and hard. Simon and I stood up and looked around. A cluster of tall oaks was the only cover nearby, and they made better lightning bait than shelter.

Sidestepping in its direction, I shouted to Simon, "There's a field-house between the softball fields and the golf course."

Simon nodded and wiped his wet hair out of his eyes.

I started to run, and Simon followed. We stayed on the concrete bike path at first, dodging the already overflowing puddles. Then a man, a jogger headed in our direction, was nearly blown down onto the concrete barrier's second level by a gust of wind. He caught his balance at the last moment and, when he headed inland, Simon and I did, too.

We cut across the softball fields, the green of the outfield almost fluorescent against the gray light all around it. It had been a long time since I'd run anywhere, and even longer since Simon and I were crossing a wide-open stretch of land together, running as fast as we could. What carried my feet over and into the mud puddles was my sudden confidence that a mistake I'd made more than three months before would not undo every good thing that had happened since.

We cut through a row of young trees between the softball fields and the golf course, and I saw the fieldhouse. I called for Simon's attention and pointed it out. A few seconds later, he passed me. Now that he knew where we were going, Simon was trying to get there first. I let him: I didn't need this win. Simon could have it.

I ran through the water spilling in sheets from the eaves of the old fieldhouse and came to a stop in the narrow, covered courtyard between its two wings. Simon was doubled over with his head down and his hands on his knees, breathing heavily and spitting frothy saliva from his mouth. I pulled off my t-shirt and wrung it out. Vapor rose from my bare arms in the cool, humid air. I wiped some of the water from my eyes with my hands and peeked up and out from under the eaves. It was still raining, but not quite as hard as it had been, and the western sky, behind the storm front, was a bright, milky white. Catching my breath, I watched the rain spill over the fields and had a moment of good feeling, the kind usually killed by any reminder that my comedy hadn't taken me to New York yet. But this moment seemed to spread out in time and even in space, wrapping itself around the fieldhouse and the softball fields and the oak trees. Erika seemed to have done the impossible: carved out a place for some happiness alongside my ambition.

Then I felt Simon's eyes on me. He was standing a few yards away, his waterlogged t-shirt stretched unevenly across his bony shoulders, giving me the cold, hard look I remembered from the days I'd invaded his bedroom to mock him. But I wasn't making fun of him as we stood in the fieldhouse. I wasn't saying anything.

"What about you?" he asked.

"What do you mean?"

There were a couple of headshakes before he said, "How're things going with your comedy?"

I had almost forgotten this part. Simon's success and failure couldn't be measured on their own terms. He needed to hold them up next to mine.

"Things are going pretty well, I guess," I said. "I'm in a two-man show at the Improviso Theatre. It's a good gig. I'm glad to have it."

That was all I wanted to say. But Simon wasn't finished with me.

"Have you done a show yet?"

With Simon back in his measuring mode, I found I could read him again. And what I read was him asking, *How real is this gig?*

"We opened a month ago," I said.

"How are the houses?"

Is anyone making any money on this show?

"Good." I stopped short of saying the houses were sold out. Offering that detail felt like taking Simon's bait.

"Nice," Simon said, nodding. "When is the show?"

"Thursdays at 10."

That's primetime, I thought, but I kept my mouth shut.

"Where is it, again?"

This question was Simon's way of telling me he'd never heard of the Improviso.

"The Improviso Theatre," I said, enunciating the words clearly. I nearly added, *Did I stutter?*

"What's the name of the show?"

I smiled. Simon knew that I'd been in shows with terrible titles like "Cirrhosis, Where Art Thou?" and "Cubs and Bulls and Bears: Oh My!" He might have been banking on the answer to this question undercutting everything else I'd said. I had long admired Raam Kersati's righteous hatred of goofball comedy shit like silly names for shows, but I'd never appreciated it as fully as I did in this moment.

"Raam and Connor," I said.

"Raam?"

"It's a guy's name. Raam. And Connor. That's the name of the show."

Simon smiled then, too. The expression looked genuine to me, as if the part of him that wanted good things for both of us had fought through to his face.

"You're a marquee name," he said.

"It's a very small marquee."

Simon laughed, startling me. His voice was my baritone, but Simon's laugh—a high-pitched, clipped eruption—was all his own. I wasn't used to the sound, but I liked it. I wondered if I would've spent less energy antagonizing my brother and more trying to entertain him if Simon, in his muteness all those years ago, had found some way to laugh.

The smile faded, though. Now that Simon had his voice and an agent and a national radio commercial on his reel, tying with me wasn't good enough. He wanted to win now, just as I always had. He needed to see that I was jealous of him, or threatened by him. That's how he'd know he was winning. By the time we'd made it to the fieldhouse, Simon must have realized that, though the point tallies were as close as they had ever been, he'd lost this round of the fight he'd started years before. And it wasn't my success in comedy that had decided things, really. It was my happiness—my ability to be happy for him—that told Simon he was losing. Thanks to Erika, I'd defended my title exactly how I liked to: without throwing a punch.

When you win that way, you don't rub it in. I gave Simon what privacy I could without stepping out into the rain, which was still coming down in a steady, soaking drizzle. I walked in front of the east wing of the fieldhouse, staying under the building's long eaves. With my back to my brother, I twisted my t-shirt into a thick cord, wringing the water out of its fibers. Then I unfurled the shirt and slapped it against the wall, leaving a wet mark on the masonry.

"Any of this stuff getting you any closer to *Saturday Night Live*?"

Simon was standing at the mouth of the courtyard, looking at me and leaning forward a little, demanding an answer with his body.

That kicked up an anger I hadn't felt in years, the kind you reserve for the people who know where you're weak and aim for that spot. It was one thing for Simon to ask me how my comedy career was going so he could run the numbers on his own worth. It was another for him to dare me to admit I wasn't where I wanted to be, just moments after giving him a glimpse—I *know* he saw it—of the happiness I'd finally found.

I could have let it go. I could have left. Nothing Simon had said had changed anything about my life with Erika or my show with Raam or my chances of getting a shot at *SNL*. I didn't need to say another damn word to him. But Simon had ignited my desire to win the old-fashioned way.

"Raam got an offer from *SNL* years ago," I said, "and he turned it down."

Simon shrugged.

"They're scouting talent for the season after next," I said. "They'll see me in this show."

"When?" Simon asked. What he meant was, *What makes you so sure?*

"I don't control when," I said. "What the fuck do you know about it? Do you know when you'll get another voiceover job? Or *if*?"

That shut him the fuck up, but I kept going.

"No," I said. "You don't."

As we stood there, I swear I was glad that I was the guy who'd fucked Simon's girlfriend. That's what told me it was time to leave.

"I'm going," I said.

I started out into the rain without cutting the distance between Simon and me. We'd started with a handshake, but finishing with one would have come too close to an apology neither one of us would be making.

"Thanks for meeting me," Simon said.

I stopped and turned around to look at Simon, and when I saw his face, I laughed because I could see that he was being sincere. After saying all of that hurtful shit, Simon was thanking me for the chance to say it.

I turned my back on him and shouted over my shoulder, "Good luck, Simon."

Coming out of my mouth, they sounded like the last words you might say to someone you were finished with. That was no accident. But the mindfucking thing is, I *did* wish good things for Simon, even then. I didn't want them to arrive that day or that year, not after all his shit-talking, but I still wanted his life to work out, eventually. I guess I was becoming the better person Erika already believed I was.

The rain stopped as I approached Lake Shore Drive. When I came out from under the viaduct, the sun broke through the clouds in shafts of light. With a damp shirt over my bare shoulder, I walked home to the apartment I was sharing with the woman I loved.

• • •

AS THE DRINKING went on that night in Carbondale last April, Simon got quiet. He sat in his folding chair, sipping his beer, his closed mouth spread out in a smile. Occasionally, he'd do a few headshakes and answer a direct question, but most of the talking he did was done with nods and shrugs. Maybe I should have found his return to silence and gestures comforting, but I didn't. I found it irritating.

If he can talk, I thought, *he should say something, instead of making me carry the conversation with his girlfriend at his own goddamn apartment.*

I shot him a couple of looks, but he missed them. He stared with smiling eyes at the rods of the porch railing or the ratty evergreen branches poking through it. It would've been one thing if Simon were just enjoying being drunk. But I got the idea that Simon was letting his happiness fill him in a way that left Brittany and me on the outside, watching. If I'd been happier myself, and less drunk, I might have decided that Simon hadn't experienced enough happy moments to know they should be aimed outward. Instead, I wound myself up into believing that Simon might as well have been jerking off in front of me while, not knowing what else to do, I tried to make his girlfriend laugh.

Eventually, Simon stood up and gave us a wave that meant, *Good night.*

"It's not even midnight," I said. I wasn't trying to get him to stay. I was trying to make him feel bad for leaving.

Simon shrugged.

"He can't manage his stutter very well when he drinks," Brittany said. "You've probably noticed he hasn't said much in a while."

"Oh."

That took the edge off my anger, but didn't erase it. It wasn't Simon's silence that had bothered me. It was the way he'd indulged himself in it.

Simon took a step toward me and extended his hand. I shook it without getting up. "G'night, brother."

He gave me a nod that meant, *Thanks for coming.*

I felt like a fucking chump for having driven all the way from Chicago for this.

Brittany stood up, knocking her folding chair back against the railing. "I'm going, too," she said. "There are some sheets, a blanket and a pillow on the couch for you. Stay up as long as you like. Bourbon's in the kitchen."

"Thanks."

She took my hand and pulled it until I stood up. I wobbled onto one foot before righting myself.

"It was great to finally meet you," she said.

Then she gave me a hug, pushing her breasts into my chest and standing on the tips of her toes to put her cheek against my ear. For the first time in a long time, I had spent my evening talking to a woman I wouldn't be taking to bed, and the feel of her in my arms gave me a taste of what I'd be missing.

Brittany went inside, and Simon gave me one more goodnight wave. I waved back, lazily. He closed the porch doors, leaving me to my whiskey and the early-spring night silence of his neighborhood.

I had a couple more drinks. Around two in the morning, I put my sticky glass in the kitchen sink and took a long piss. Then I spread the sheet out on the couch, got under the blanket, and rolled onto my right side, facing the television. As I lay there, I enjoyed a little fantasy, something to fill in for the orgasm I wasn't having. I was on a New York stage playing some character—a garden gnome, I think—opposite an actress playing a schoolgirl. The words I heard in my head made no sense strung together, but we were getting big laughs from the audience. Even when they were silent, I could feel them smiling. Before the nonsense scene was over, I was asleep.

The first thing I saw when I opened my eyes was Brittany standing over me in the darkness. Her hair hung forward, shrouding her face. She was naked from the waist down.

"What the fuck are you doing?" I whispered.

She pressed her hand to my mouth firmly.

She shook her head. *Don't talk.*

Then, gently, she dragged her hand over my lips, down my chin and my chest to my belt buckle.

When she had my pants undone, she pulled off her top, revealing her taut torso in the weak streetlight coming through the picture window behind the couch. She took my hands and put them on her chest. I was still drunk but knew what I was doing. I mashed her tiny breasts together and took the nipples between my fingers. That was all it took to get hard. I threw off the sheet and pulled down my pants. She unwrapped a condom and rolled it down over the shaft. Then I grabbed Brittany by the hips, pulled her onto me, and found my way inside her.

All evening, I had resented Simon's happiness. In my own silent moments of self-indulgence, I'd imagined his contentment dissolving into the tears I'd sometimes found on his face when I'd barged into his childhood bedroom. But I don't think I would have fucked Simon's girlfriend if I hadn't allowed myself to believe for a split second that Simon, in his insane desperation to make things even between us, had begged her to do this.

● ● ●

I WASN'T SURE how long we'd been onstage that last Thursday in July, but it must have been long enough. I could feel Raam guiding our scene toward an ending.

Then, because he's a fucking pro and generous as hell, Raam gave me one more perfect set-up, and I laid down the royal flush of improvised callbacks: fully in character, in the flow of the story we had invented on the spot, I closed the scene with the very same audience-suggested word we'd used to start it.

The lights went down. The music came up. And once the stage lights were blazing again, Raam and I were greeted with whooping so loud it barreled over the raucous applause and rang my eardrums.

But delivering the closing laugh line wasn't my biggest achievement in a show I still consider one of my best ever. For the time that Raam and I were in scene, I lost myself so completely in my characters that I managed to forget two staff writers from *Saturday Night Live* were sitting in the audience.

Marcus Reiser, the artistic director at Improviso, had called me the day before.

"*SNL* is coming to see the show," he said. "Tomorrow night."

My heart rate jumped, but I couldn't piece together the details.

"I don't get it," I asked. "I thought they were fully cast."

"One of the featured players said something in the press about the show not being funny, and they let him go."

"Oh."

"They're sending teams all over to find a replacement. Two guys are coming to Improviso."

"To see me." Something in me needed to hear him say it.

"Well, they're not coming to see Raam," Marcus said. "They're finished going round and round with him. Which reminds me, don't mention any of this to Raam."

"I don't understand. Raam doesn't want to be on *SNL*."

"Jesus, I know that," Marcus said. "I'm worried he'll get pissed that the industry—and *SNL* in particular—is treating his show like a farm team."

Marcus had a lot to gain from the big boys' raiding his club for talent. Stories of unknowns being discovered drew students into the training program that was Improviso's cash cow. But I didn't like the idea of putting Raam in a bad spot. Marcus must have guessed this.

"Don't worry about Raam," he said. "If he says anything to you, tell him to see me. Just do the show like you've been doing it. Go out there and kill."

"Okay," I said.

And that's what we did.

Between bows, I shielded my eyes from the stage lights and scanned the crowd—a sellout, despite the thunderstorms that had lashed Chicago that afternoon and evening—for two people who looked like *SNL* writers. Call it stereotype or playing the percentages, but I assumed they would be white, male, and in their thirties. About half the audience fit that description, though, and I couldn't make out any of the people sitting in the booths at the back of the room. So I stopped looking for the writers and looked for Erika. I spotted her standing between the seats and the bar, clapping for us. Her open, loving smile warmed me in a way that even the audience's extended appreciation did not. Then Raam thanked the audience again, applauded its members like an athlete thanking the home crowd, and took a final bow.

I followed him to the back of the stage, under the frame of the short stage door he opened, and into the narrow passage that led to the club's tiny green room. Raam surprised me by stopping in the passageway and turning to face me.

"Good show," he said, wiping sweat from his forehead with the sleeve of his shirt.

"You, too. Thanks for that last line."

He waved me off. "All I did was set it up."

"Yeah, well, we both know that's the hard part."

"We know." Still catching his breath, he leaned back against the plywood wall of the passageway. "But the morons who run Saturday *Night Live* might not."

I should have known that nothing that happened at Improviso could be kept from Raam. The club was *his*—it belonged to him more than it belonged to Marcus or the owner. I started to explain, but Raam interrupted me.

"You knew they'd be here?" he asked.

I thought he was going to tell me I should have told him, that hiding this kind of thing was a crime against improv as Raam practiced the art.

"I knew, yeah, but—"

"It doesn't matter," he said, waving me off again. "It doesn't. What matters is that I had no fucking idea whether you knew they were here or not. You made your characters, and you stuck to them. You didn't sell out the scene for cheap laughs. You were no different out there tonight than you are when we do this in an empty room."

To this day, I'm not sure I've been paid a better compliment.

"You won't get *SNL* this time," Raam said, unrolling his shirtsleeve from a cuff at the elbow. "They saw me three times before they made an offer. They saw Sandra"—the woman I'd replaced in Raam's show— "twice, and she decided to take a film job rather than wait around for Lorne Michaels to tap her. But you'll get an offer eventually. You have TV good looks, and your comedy is plenty good enough."

"Look," I said, "I know what you think of the show—"

"Those are *my* hang-ups. If you want the job, I hope you get it. Until then—"

Raam popped me on the shoulder and headed toward the green room.

"—let's keep doing what we're doing." Shouting over the hum of the crowd on the other side of the wall, he said, "I think people like it."

In the green room, I toweled off my face, changed into a dry shirt, and grabbed my backpack. Improviso audiences hung around to drink after the show, and performers were expected to mingle. "People want access to the talent," Marcus had told me. "It's part of what they're paying for."

Raam was exempt from the mingling rule. He exited through a back door and took the El home to his partner. That left only me to field meaningless, over-the-top praise from drunks and improv-scene hangers-on and to look like I was fishing for compliments by standing around near

the bar. Most nights, I just did my time: twenty minutes or two bourbons, whichever came first. But that night, given how well the show had
gone and that Erika was there, I figured it was worth spending an extra
ten minutes at Improviso to see if the *SNL* writers had anything to say
to me.

When I came out from backstage, the seats around the cocktail tables were empty, but the bar was packed seven- or eight-deep. Waiting
at the edge of the stage with a bourbon for me was Andre Rebrov. Andre
was a native of Chicago's Ukrainian Village—there were traces of his
parents' accents in his *R*s—and a solid, experienced improviser. I'd sat
in with his team at Improviso a couple of times, and he'd been a regular
in the audience at Raam's Thursday-night shows for years. Andre was a
schmoozer. He dove into the gossip and politics of the comedy scene in
a way I did not. He talked about who was fucking who, who Second City
was scouting, and which improv team you'd never heard of was lighting
up the small stages. But as after-show mingling went, drinking with Andre was easy time. I was glad to see him.

"Hey, Dre," I said, stepping off the stage.

"Good show, my friend," he said, handing me the glass.

"Thanks. And thanks for the drink."

"Thank Donna. I told her it was for you, and she gave it to me."

I assumed that Donna was the bartender. Andre always knew the
bartender's name.

"I'm going to remember that trick the next time I see this show and
don't feel like paying for a drink," he said.

I stared at the mass of people around the bar as if it were an outdoor
pool on a cold, cloudy morning. Even the possibility of meeting the *SNL*
writers wasn't enough to make me want to dive in. Andre must have read
the distaste on my face.

"It's not that bad," he said.

"It's close."

"I'll put it another way," he said. "You don't have a choice."

Andre was right about that.

"It's not like you have to hear their life stories," he said. "Just get to the edge of the crowd. We'll keep talking. And Marcus won't have anything to say about it."

We slipped past a few people on the outskirts and stood on the railing of the shallow ramp that led up to the club's small lobby. It was as good a place as any I could have hoped to stake out. The people on the perimeter of the bar crowd were standing with their backs to us, and the *SNL* writers would have to walk right past me when they left, if they hadn't left already.

I spotted Erika sitting at the bar. She said something to Donna that made the bartender laugh while pouring two drinks at once. Erika and Donna had never met, so far as I knew, but a stranger might have guessed they had known each other for years. I already understood, of course, that Erika had an uncommon power to put people at ease. What surprised me was that she had any of that power in reserve after expending whatever energy it took, day after day, to make me so comfortable with her. I wondered if I had reached the point at which I was doing most of that work myself. Maybe it wasn't work for either of us anymore.

"The show got off to an interesting start," Andre said.

"How do you mean?"

"With you kicking a guy in the audience."

I had forgotten about this. When Raam and I came out to start the show, a lanky guy in the front row, wearing long cargo shorts and a baggy white t-shirt, was splayed out in his chair, cooling the heel of a big, blindingly white hi-top shoe on the stage. In my book, this is a pretty serious violation. The audience should stay the fuck off the stage. I'd had to compromise that principle working in the back rooms of bars, where people cut across stages that weren't really stages to get to the bathroom, but I wasn't about to let some guy rest his foot on the Improviso stage while Raam and I tried to create the most important scene of my life out of a single word. As Raam described the format of the show to the audience, I glared at the guy. He noticed me glaring and stared right back, but he didn't move. So I stepped to the front of the stage and kicked the guy in the sole. He put his feet on the floor then, and I smiled down on him with false friendliness.

"Not my usual opening move," I said.

"It was a risk," Andre said, but his smile told me he had found the risk delicious. "You might have lost the audience before you started."

I saw no point in regretting the move after the fact. If I'd lost the audience, Raam and I had won them back. I tried to shrug off the entire line of questioning. "I heard a few people laugh when I did it."

"Maybe," Andre said. "But no one thought you were joking."

I felt two quick taps on my shoulder and turned to find two women standing behind me. The taller one wore a Cubs t-shirt tied up tightly at her back, exposing a tan, flat stomach. Her shorter friend stood next to her, smiling. Her teeth were whitened to a faintly blue hue, and her big breasts bowed the thin vertical pinstripes on her Cubs baby tee.

"Great show tonight," the taller woman said.

"Yeah, you were awesome," her friend said.

They looked me up and down as if they wanted to take me backstage and take turns blowing me. The men I guessed were their boyfriends, muscle-bound guys with bent-brim Cubs caps pulled low over their eyes, were standing right behind them, watching me. This was the kind of dead-end flirting and bit-part, psychodrama playacting that Improviso's mingling policy threw me into.

"I'm really glad you enjoyed yourselves," I said, hoping that they could hear I didn't mean it. "Were you guys at the game today?"

I made a point of including their boyfriends in the question. I wanted them to see that I knew what the fuck was going on here and that I wanted no part of it.

"We were supposed to," the shorter girl said, "but it was rained out." She frowned like a child.

"Yeah," the taller girl said. "But we hung around the park for a while. And drank a lot." She shrugged as if to say, *So there's that.*

"And we've been out ever since!" shorter girl said.

Then both women raised their arms above their heads and hollered, "Woooo!"

With a wide, river-rat smile, the taller woman's boyfriend slipped his

T-bone of a hand under her long, rain-tangled blonde hair and massaged the back of her neck.

"That's great," I said. "Well, thanks for coming."

"Yeah!" the taller woman said. "Awesome show!"

I raised my glass to them and turned back to Andre with my eyes wide.

"Yeah," he said, hiding his lips with his glass. In that word, I heard Andre's agreement with everything there was no need to say.

Andre took a sip of his drink and swallowed. "So. I heard from Denny Fabris."

"Oh, yeah?" Denny had been one of the top young improvisers in Chicago before he moved out to Los Angeles. "How's he doing out there?"

"He's great," Andre said. "Lots of hiking."

This was code, and I understood it. Andre was telling me that Denny had become yet another ambitious improviser who had moved to Los Angeles for career reasons and now, when he chatted with old pals back in Chicago, talked mainly about his outdoorsy hobbies and the fantastic weather that made them possible. Because these transplanted comedians didn't mention work, we assumed they hadn't found any worth mentioning.

"I like Denny," I said. "I hope something shakes out for him."

"I don't give a shit," Andre said bitterly. "He can keep hiking in the sunshine."

That made me laugh.

Then, over Andre's shoulder, I saw the guy whose shoe I had kicked. He was moving toward us, and his eyes were locked on me.

"Shit."

"What?" Andre said.

It occurred to me then that a paying customer could use his "access to the talent" for something other than conversation. As the guy bore down on me, with a buddy as tall as he was, but thicker, right behind him, I had only one thought: *I'm about to get my ass kicked in front of the writers from* Saturday Night Live.

When he was right behind Andre, the guy in the hi-tops said, "Hey, man."

"Hey," I said.

"I just wanna say great show—"

"Thanks," I said, bracing myself.

"—and I'm sorry about having my foot up there, man. That was some bullshit, right there."

The guy dropped his eyes and shook his head, laughing at himself, and I felt myself smile.

"No problem," I said.

The guy swung his hand up and back, but not to slap me. I put my hand out and he took it, curling his four fingers around mine and giving our fists one sharp bounce.

"We cool?" he asked.

"Oh, yeah," I said. "Definitely."

"Alright. We're gonna roll out. We'll catch you again."

"Yeah," I said. "Thanks for coming out."

I watched the two of them walk up the ramp to the front doors. The bouncers stiffened as they passed.

"That could have gone very differently," Andre said.

"Yeah."

I sought out the reassuring sight of Erika sitting at the bar. But before they could find her, my eyes landed on another face coming toward me through the crowd.

Simon's.

It had been nine days since we'd met at the lakefront. In that time, I'd more or less put Simon out of my mind. But seeing him at Improviso, uninvited, with Erika just across the room, ripped off the scabs that had formed over my worry and paranoia. Nine days was more than enough time for Simon to find out or piece together what Brittany and I had done. And this was the only place he knew to find me.

As Simon made his way through the small groups clustered around the bar, I tried to act as if I had nothing to worry about. But when Simon had maneuvered into earshot, the first thing I said was, "What are you doing here?"

These were not the words of someone with no worries—not the way I said them, at least. Until he followed my eyes to the guy standing next to him, Andre seemed to think I was putting the question to him.

Simon took several headshakes. "What do you mean? I came to see the show."

"I didn't know you were coming," I said, trying to recover.

Simon shook his head again. "I didn't want to make you nervous or anything."

My first reaction was to laugh at the idea that, with two writers who held my career in their hands sitting in the audience, knowing that Simon, too, was in the crowd could have made me nervous. But it would have. Standing next to Simon, I was more anxious than I'd been at any point that night.

"Andre," I said, "this is my brother Simon."

Andre squared his shoulders to Simon's and shook his hand. Simon shook hands the way our father did, without looking the other man in the eye.

"Are you in from out of town?" Andre asked him.

"I live here now," Simon said.

"Excellent," Andre said. "What did you think of the show?"

Inhaling, Simon nodded and shifted his eyes from Andre to me, and back again. Then he did a headshake and said, "It was really, really good."

"They're fucking incredible, aren't they?" Andre said.

"Yeah," Simon said. "They are."

I believed that Simon had meant what he said—that the show was really good. But when given little choice but to agree with Andre's exaggerated praise, I heard my brother's resentment creeping in at the edges.

None of us seemed to know what to say next. Andre and I sipped our drinks. Simon didn't have one, which made things even more awkward. I would have offered to get him one for a chance to get away, but I recalled Brittany telling me that drinking fed his stutter, and anyway, I didn't want Simon here long enough to finish a drink. But Simon just stood there, glancing at the people drinking and laughing around him. I got the idea he was waiting for Andre to leave so that he could say what he really wanted to.

I tried again to catch sight of Erika—this time, to reassure myself that a thick crowd still separated her from Simon. But someone else, a woman with thick, magenta-streaked hair, was sitting in Erika's place.

"Is he gone?"

Erika put her hand on the back of my upper arm and gave it a gentle stroke.

"Is who gone?" I asked her.

"The guy you kicked."

"Oh," I said. "Yeah, he's gone."

"I thought he was going to start something," she said.

"So did I."

"I would've had his back," Andre said, putting his hand on my shoulder.

"Thanks, Andre," Erika said, smiling at him. "And what does that look like? You having Connor's back?"

"In this case, it would have consisted mainly of me getting my ass kicked, I think."

"Well," I said, getting ready to bolt, "we should really get—"

Erika stuck her hand out in front of Simon and said, "I'm Erika."

Simon took Erika's hand in his and, I noticed, he had no trouble meeting her eyes. "Simon," he said. "Nice to meet you."

She would tell me later that it was not his face, or even his name, but his voice—so much like mine—that gave Simon away.

"Your brother?" Erika asked me.

"Yeah," I said.

Erika gave me a shove, my punishment for not introducing her to Simon the moment I knew he was here. "It's so great to finally meet you, Simon," she said. "I've been asking Connor about you for weeks."

Simon smiled, but said nothing. I was a little surprised that my brother had enough sense to play along with the idea that this meeting, with the girlfriend I'd never mentioned to him, was a long time in coming.

I rested my hand on the small of Erika's back. "Are you ready to go?" I was willing to miss my chance to meet the *SNL* writers to ensure that Erika's conversation with Simon was a short one.

The look Erika gave me made it clear that she found my question rude. "No, I'm not, " she answered. Then she turned to my brother. "Simon, what do you say we find a booth and talk some shop?"

Simon looked confused. "What kind of shop?"

"You're a voiceover artist, right?"

I could have kicked myself for sharing that detail with her.

Simon did a headshake and said, "Yes."

"So am I! Who are you with?"

"Skyline Talent."

"Me, too! Are you with Todd?"

"No," Simon said. "Elaine."

"The queen bee herself! Impressive. I'm with Todd. He's okay. You can tell me if Elaine is any better. I kind of hope she's not. No offense."

Another smile spread slowly across Simon's face, as if he could not believe his luck.

I started after them and said to Andre, "I'll catch you later."

Erika spun around and pressed her hand against my chest. "Where do you think you're going?"

"With you guys," I said.

"No, no," she said. "No comedy boys allowed."

"Very funny."

"I mean it," she said. "You stay here. Come on, Simon."

I think she thought she was doing me a favor, leaving me out in the open for the *SNL* writers to find me. Erika was the only person I'd told they were coming. But she was also teaching me a lesson: that I shouldn't have kept Simon from her for so long. She headed toward the back of the club, and Simon followed her. My brother and my girlfriend were about to have a conversation I could neither hear nor control, and Simon would have every opportunity—if he knew—to tell Erika what I'd done with his girlfriend while he slept.

"Fuck." I said, letting my backpack fall to my feet.

"What?" Andre asked.

"Nothing," I said. "It's just that I kind of wanted to get out of here, and now I'm going to be here a while."

"You can't leave yet," Andre said.

I assumed Andre was referring to the mingling policy. "I probably could. I've done my twenty minutes."

"They still might come by."

"Who?"

Andre forced out a fake laugh. "Please. Do you think I don't know what's happening here?"

I understood then that Andre knew the *other* secret I was keeping. He'd been banking on my chance to meet the *SNL* writers becoming his chance, too. And he wasn't alone. If Andre knew that the *SNL* writers were here, so did most of the other comedy nerds crowded around the bar. Suddenly, my need for the *SNL* writers to validate what I'd done onstage was about more than my career in New York: it was a matter of saving face in Chicago.

Now I have *to stay,* I thought.

With hard feelings hanging in the air between us, Andre and I stopped talking. I located Erika and Simon. They were sitting on the same side of a booth, and each of them was drinking a cocktail. Both of these things struck me as strange, but I could see Erika's face, and she was talking and smiling between the sips she took through her stirring straw. If Simon knew about Brittany and me, he hadn't told Erika yet.

"Do you think they're gone already?" Andre asked.

"Who knows."

Andre and I watched the bar crowd thin out for what must have been another twenty minutes. That's how long it took me to decide that the only thing left to do was to walk out on the *SNL* writers before it was completely obvious to everyone that they had walked out on me. I was about to tell Andre I was leaving when I heard someone shout my name.

I turned to find Marcus Reiser hurrying down the ramp that led from the lobby. His hair was clumped into thin, sweaty strands, exposing the liver-spotted skin of his scalp.

"Hey, Marcus," I said.

"They didn't make it."

I made myself say something. "You're shitting me."

Marcus shook his head. "They were supposed to fly in this afternoon, but the storms here grounded them. They tried for a later flight and couldn't get on it. They never left LaGuardia."

I stood there, nodding, with my jaw clenched. There was nothing more to say.

"We'll get them here," Marcus said. "Soon."

Marcus and I both knew that he couldn't get the *SNL* writers here. They would come when they were sent again. *If* they were sent again. No sooner.

He excused himself and walked away.

I never give a shit who is in the audience. I'd improvise in an empty room just for a chance to do it the right way. But when I learned that the *SNL* writers hadn't seen me perform, what I thought was, *Everything I made tonight was wasted.*

"Fucking unbelievable," Andre said, shaking his head.

All I could think to do was lay eyes on Erika. I stepped back, finding a sightline past a tall guy who had moved between us. When I saw Erika, she looked worried. And Simon was talking a mile a minute.

What the fuck is he saying? I wondered.

Then, while I watched without either of them knowing, Simon put down his empty glass, reached his hand slowly toward Erika's face, and leaned in to kiss her.

I plowed through a cluster of people I should have gone around and toppled a cocktail table, shattering two glasses on the ground. As I neared the booth, Erika swatted at Simon's reaching hand and said, "What are you doing?"

I grabbed Simon under the arms and pulled him out of the booth.

Erika yelped and called after me, but I didn't listen.

Backpedaling, I dragged Simon past two more booths to the club's fire door and pressed my ass against its push-bar handle. When I had him in the alley, I threw him to the ground. He broke the fall with his right hand—I saw the wrist bend—and rolled once before landing in the thistle growing against a tall wooden fence.

After what he'd done, and all that hadn't happened for me that night, I was craving an old-fashioned win. I wanted to kneel on Simon's chest and punch him in the mouth. But I had already won, in the oldest of old-fashioned ways, the game that Simon, whether or not he knew what I'd done in Carbondale, had restarted that night: I had fucked his girl-friend in his own apartment, and Simon hadn't even touched his lips to Erika's.

Game over.

I was finished with Simon. I yanked on the handle of the fire door. It was locked. So I headed for the long, narrow gangway that led out to Clark Street.

I was still in the alley, passing under the bright light of a security lamp, when I heard footsteps on the loose asphalt behind me. What he threw was no sucker punch. Simon let me see it was coming. I ducked, but not far enough, and it landed at the hinge of my jaw.

When I looked up, dabbing at the blood oozing from the skin of my ear, Simon was heaving air through his nose, and every sinew in his neck was pulled taut. He was having what my father used to call a fit. With his stutter choking him, Simon held up his fists just below his shoulders, leaving his face exposed.

Simon wanted me to hit him back. He wanted everything to be equal between us. More than anything, he wanted us to fight because fighting would say that we mean something to each other.

Brothers fight. Simon and I are brothers.

While he stood there, waiting for me to make us brothers again, I looked Simon in the eyes until I was certain he could see that I under-stood *exactly* what he was asking me to do.

Then I walked away.

Walking toward Clark Street in the darkness of the gangway, I imag-ined that Simon was where I had left him, his bawling smothered by a silence he couldn't break.

And that was fine with me.

10

Simon

WHEN MY PHONE lit up the Monday after I saw Connor perform at Improviso, and I saw it was Elaine, I figured she was calling to fire me.

I had already played out two plausible scenarios. In the first, Connor has outed me to Erika in the aftermath of our melee, calling me "a fucking stutterer" or something of that ilk, and Erika, disgusted with me, has notified Skyline Talent of the career-killing disability I'd hidden from everyone.

In the second, Erika has informed Elaine that she met another voice-over artist represented by the agency and that he had behaved inappropriately toward her. Elaine was running a business. She wouldn't care to hear me explain that I'd gotten carried away after Erika and I swapped our stories of signing with Skyline and after sharing, with a woman who knew how to listen and seemed to value every detail I divulged, my account of my mother's grace and courage in the face of cancer. If she believed my behavior posed a risk to her agency, Elaine Vasner would cut me loose without a second thought. Elaine didn't need me. There were other voices out there.

Staring at the vibrating phone in my hand, I experienced a calming sense that I was living a moment I had known would come to pass. I had believed since my first meeting with her that Elaine would eventually decide—just as Brittany had—that I lacked something. That I was not enough.

I flipped open the phone and waggled. "Hello, Elaine."

"Hi, Simon."

No small talk. "What can I do for you?"

I heard Elaine's desk chair creak, and she let out a breath I hadn't realized she'd been holding. "I got a very strange call about an hour ago."

I almost said, *From Erika.* "You did."

"Yeah. From Leo Burnett's New York office. To book you for a job."

What?

I waggled. "What?"

"Apparently, they handle the advertising for a soccer team. The New York Red Bulls. They want you for a radio campaign."

Elaine had always given me the impression that, in her business, she had seen it all. Now, she sounded as mystified as I was.

"I don't even know how they heard you," she said. "I asked the kid on the phone—somebody's intern—but he was no help."

She snorted and, in her disdain for the intern, Elaine was recognizable as herself again.

"I'd be surprised if they were on the web auditioning Chicago voices," she added.

"Why?" I asked.

"There's no need," she said. "New York is lousy with talent."

She meant voiceover talent, but my first thought was of Connor. "It must be."

"Red Bull is the soccer team's sponsor," Elaine continued, thinking aloud. "Maybe Burnett's New York office has final approval on all Red Bull creative, and someone there heard your Comedy Tour spot."

"Could be."

I had no idea. I was still getting my head around the idea I wasn't being fired.

"Anyway," Elaine said, "they want you in New York at the end of this week."

"They want me to *go* there?"

"That's what I asked the intern," Elaine said. "He assured me they do."

I'd assumed the ad people would record me remotely, relaying their direction over the phone to an engineer in a Chicago studio. The idea of traveling to do voiceover had never occurred to me. Then again, traveling, in my mind, was something other people did. I'd never even been on an airplane before.

"You'll fly out Thursday afternoon," Elaine continued. "You'll stay the night in a hotel and do the session Friday morning at eleven sharp. They'll fly you back Friday night if you want, or Saturday or Sunday if you want to spend some time in New York."

"Did they send a script?" I asked.

"No."

"Did they describe it at all?"

I wanted to rehearse, of course, but what I really wanted was to hear that the job was straight announcing work: say the name of the team, deliver the names of its star players as if they were heroes of Greek epics, read the website address and the phone number, and say the team name again. This kind of work was all vocal technique, and I could do it as well as anyone. On the other hand, if the spot called for character work, I'd need to imagine how Connor would do it just to fake my way through the session. After what I'd done at Improviso, appropriating anything from Connor, even if only for work that was rightly mine, seemed more complicated. We weren't kids trying to get Candace Andersen's attention anymore. We were adults with much more to lose.

"The intern didn't say anything about the script," Elaine said. "But I'll forward whatever comes through, Simon, don't worry. Get back to me by tomorrow about how you want to handle your return flight."

"I will."

"This is a gift, Simon. You're good, but you can't earn this kind of thing."

I nodded and waggled. "I know."

She sighed, as if to say that dealing with me was exhausting. "Congratulations, Simon."

I heard a smile in her voice.

"You, too, Elaine."

I flipped the phone shut. I realized then that I had envisioned this sequence—a call from New York, a job that could launch a career—many times, but I had always imagined it happening for Connor. New York was the landscape of my brother's dreams.

And the landscape of Brittany's *life*! She was there, navigating crowded sidewalks and climbing the stairs of old walk-up buildings in pursuit of musty, valuable books. I had fantasized, of course, about seeing Brittany again and showing her, somehow, that I was more than she'd thought

I was. Now, my voiceover work, work that Brittany may never have believed I'd get, was taking me right to her.

But making it to New York wasn't my fantasy; it was Connor's. And he was living in Chicago in a relationship with a woman who was a voiceover artist.

Nothing was happening the way it was supposed to.

That day, I gave up on my quest to match Connor's success. Life, in its messiness, would dole out parity on its own terms, or not at all.

● ● ●

BICYCLISTS SLIPPED THROUGH narrow gaps between cars, and people on the sidewalk moved at speed, as if they'd heard that rain were about to pour down from the cloudless sky over Manhattan.

Traffic, though, was at a standstill. The man driving my taxi slammed his open palm on the steering wheel and gesticulated at the congestion before him, muttering something in a language I didn't understand. A block ahead of us, an enormous green truck with spinning yellow lights on top of its cab backed into the intersection. The vehicle's standard, metronomic warning beeps were barely audible over the low roar of idling engines and drowned out completely by car horns bleated in vain.

A policeman wearing sunglasses and a short-brimmed hat with a badge on the crown strolled into view between lanes, his hands tucked into the armpits of his bulletproof vest. As he moved, he shouted, "We got a water-main break! Street is closed! We're going to be here for a few minutes, so be patient!"

The policeman's message was met with a chorus of honks, which he answered with a sarcastic smile as he moved up the street.

The taxi driver, seeming to suffer from a traffic-induced claustrophobia, looked in every direction for a way out. Through the rear window and the scratched, tempered plastic that separated him from me, the driver saw that cars half a block behind us were turning off the closed street onto an open one. I counted five cars between the cab and its only escape valve. We were stuck.

"You go now," the driver said.

The doors unlocked. I turned around in time to see him stop the meter.

"You go," he repeated, shooing me out of the cab.

"But we're not at the hotel."

"Two blocks east. You go."

He glanced down at the driver's side door, and the lid of the trunk released with a thud.

I had a vague recollection that cab drivers weren't allowed to eject their passengers without good reason, but I had no way to hold the driver accountable. So I got my wallet out.

"Can I have a receipt, please?"

With an upper lip curled in against yellow teeth, the driver tore a piece of paper from a pad and thrust his hand through an opening in the transparent barrier between us. I handed over twenty-eight dollars, only twenty cents over the fare. The driver didn't complain.

I opened the door on the sidewalk side and stepped onto hot pavement. The air was clogged with an invisible cloud of exhaust disgorged by the trapped cars. Breathing shallowly, my own lips curled in a version of the snarl I'd seen on the driver's face, I pulled my bag from the trunk and closed the lid harder than necessary.

The taxi's taillights flickered, and its engine dropped into gear. I worried that the driver was about to crush my legs against the bumper of the car behind me as punishment for my display of displeasure. But as I dashed onto the sidewalk with my bag in hand, the driver pulled *forward* to within a few inches of the car in front of him. Then he threw the car into reverse and popped his back wheel up and over the curb. I jumped back as his bumper caught and toppled a metal box that, when upright, dispensed free copies of *The Onion*. With the two right tires on the sidewalk and the two left in the gutter, the driver steered his cab back toward the side street that other cars had been using to make their escape. A woman in a skirt and high heels, carrying a briefcase over her shoulder, screamed and hurried down the stairs of a garden-level convenience store. Seeing the woman take cover, a man wearing headphones glanced over his shoulder and jumped ass-first onto the sill of a restaurant's open front window.

He shouted, "What the *fuck*, man?"

People honked and yelled at the yellow sedan, but the taxi driver kept backing up until his rear wheels reached the far side of the open street, where he cut off a car making a legal right turn. The commotion caught the attention of the cop who'd made the water-main announcement. He pinched the walkie-talkie on his left breast and tucked his chin to it as the driver, his tires squealing, accelerated through the sharpest turn his vehicle was capable of making and sped out of my sight.

I stood there, waiting for someone to meet my eye and ask, *Can you believe that?* But the drivers quickly re-fixed their attention on the water-main break up ahead, and the woman and man who'd shared my experience of being nearly mowed down by the cab walked on without saying a word. Someone coming around the corner at that moment would've had no idea that, half a minute before, pedestrians had been dodging a car on the sidewalk.

I circled the intersection two blocks east three times before I found my hotel. The budget chain's logo, usually emblazoned prominently in green script, was subtly set in steel against the building's gray stone base, as if the home office had made an ill-considered attempt to capture for the chain's Manhattan franchise the underground appeal of a nightclub that had no sign.

The hotel lobby was furnished only with a few tall potted plants and four modern, cubic armchairs arranged around a narrow glass table. At reception, I was told that my room was still being cleaned.

"Oh." I waggled and asked, "When will it be ready?"

The desk clerk, a short woman who spoke in kind, quiet tones and an English gently accented with the sounds and rhythms of her first language—Spanish, maybe—clicked a few keys on her keyboard and narrowed her eyes at the monitor in front of her.

"Ummmm, I can't say for certain. It could be another two hours. Or more."

"Or more?" It was already late afternoon.

"I do apologize for the inconvenience," the woman said, sliding audibly into a rehearsed customer-service spiel triggered by my suggestion of impatience. "If you like, I can hold your bag for you."

I looked at my duffel, which contained my laptop, clothes, and what liquid toiletries were in bottles small enough to avoid seizure during the screening to which I'd submitted at O'Hare International. I was reluctant to give up the bag—traveling alone to a strange city and seeing my shampoo and deodorant confiscated at the airport had awakened an attachment to my possessions—but my shoulder and forearm were tired from lugging it, and the idea of waiting idly and indefinitely in a hotel lobby, as I'd done so many days in my Chicago apartment, made me feel ill in the gut and the head. I hoisted the bag onto the counter. The woman wrapped a tag around one of the straps, tore off a ticket with the number forty-three on it, and handed the ticket to me.

"Thanks," I said, without meaning it.

"You're welcome, sir. And again, I'm sorry for the inconvenience."

● ● ●

OUT ON THE sidewalk, I pressed my back up against the hotel's stone façade to keep out of the way of people who, unlike me, had somewhere to go and knew where they were going. My unease with my aimlessness was exacerbated by the unshakable feeling that I didn't belong in New York, and Connor did. I was still consumed by the possibility that the script I'd be handed the next day—a script no one had bothered to send me yet—would make me an impostor in my own shot at the big time by calling for a character that only Connor could create. Having traveled this far, what choice would I have but to guess what character Connor would have made and deliver a counterfeit?

I walked south at a brisk pace of a person doing more than killing time. Only a few blocks away from the hotel, I started scanning for some internationally familiar landmark—the Empire State building, maybe, or Madison Square Garden—but I recognized nothing.

At Canal Street, I turned onto a stretch of sidewalk narrowed by wheeled racks of scarves and t-shirts and carts of handbags and sunglasses. Between the merchandise stalls were a few small restaurants, ranging from a by-the-slice pizzeria to a candlelit bistro with a menu displayed in a wood-framed glass box beside the door. And at the curb, in front of every store and restaurant and currency exchange, was garbage. Limp heads of lettuce spilled out the mouth of an untied bag, and twisted drywall struts jutted out from plastic cans unevenly dusted with plaster powder. A man in a filthy white apron carried a trash bag up four steps from the lower level of a deli, crossed the flow of foot traffic, and dropped the bag at the curb. In the humid air, I caught the odor of decay mixed with a sweetness, like the aroma of overripe fruit.

I turned off of Canal onto a quieter street lined on both sides with what appeared to me to be apartment buildings, none more than seven or eight stories tall. The buildings' first floors—some at sidewalk level, others a short flight of stairs above it—were salons and clothing boutiques and coffeehouses. With fewer pedestrians around, I felt less desperate for purpose and relaxed a little. I slowed down to read proclamations, handwritten on chalkboard easels, of the arrival of fall fashions and Pacific Island coffee blends. I had nearly reached the end of the block when I noticed a small brass plaque clouded with patina and fitted into a brick pillar in front of a four-story brownstone. The embossing read, "The Manhattan Museum of Radio Arts."

Instantly, I was certain that I had found a place in New York—maybe the only place—in which I belonged more rightly than Connor did.

At the top of the front steps, I tried the door. It was locked. To the right of the door was a box with four black, rectangular buttons, and I pressed my thumb against the button labeled "MMRA."

The anticipation of a human voice in a doorbell speaker can silence a big city. As I stood waggling before a hexagonal array of aluminum vents, no ambient noise registered with me.

Then: a young man's voice. "Yes?"

"Hi," I said. "I'd like to tour the museum?"

"Sorry," the voice said. "We close in fifteen minutes."

I took a short, desperate step toward a microphone I couldn't see. "I'll be quick."

A pause, then a click. "Do you have a membership?"

"No."

"It's a fifteen dollar donation," the voice said. "For fifteen minutes."

"That's fine." I would have paid twice that rate.

There was another silence, during which, I imagined, the young man tried to come up with some other way of dissuading me from patronizing the museum so close to its closing time.

He must have come up short.

The lock of the brownstone's door hummed to life, and I entered a foyer. Electric candles in a fixture threw a ghostly, flickering light. Near the first door on the right was a burnished copy of the brass plaque I had seen on the pillar outside. I took another waggle and opened the door into a long room lit by small, halogen bulbs suspended from copper wires. Exhibits were installed at regular intervals along the all-white walls. The only other person in the room was the embodiment of the voice in the speaker.

The kid looked a few years younger than Connor. He stood slouched behind a white desk with a ring of keys in his hand, dressed in dark jeans, an unzipped black hoodie and a black t-shirt one size too small.

Without looking at me, the attendant said, "Fifteen dollars."

I took a ten and a five out of my wallet and laid the bills on the counter.

The attendant picked up the bills and thwacked down in their place a plastic device about the size of my cell phone. Then he reached down below the counter and tossed a set of headphones with foam earpieces—the kind of headphones I had been offered on the airplane—next to the device.

I picked up the headphones and the device and said, "Thanks."

"We close in fourteen minutes."

I made my way over creaking floorboards to the tiny museum's far corner, mostly to put some distance between the attendant and myself. The exhibit occupying that corner was titled "The Battle of the Century," and it featured a printed reproduction of a photograph of two men wearing high-waisted shorts and standing toe-to-toe in a boxing ring bathed in light. The caption read, "In 1921, Jack Dempsey and Georges

Carpentier fought for the Heavyweight Championship of the World and changed radio forever. Press 094 to hear more."

I plugged the headphones into the device the attendant had given me, put the headphones over my ears, and pressed zero, nine, and four on the keypad.

What I heard was a minute-long audio segment about Dempsey's defeat of Carpentier and the hundreds of thousands of Americans—many of them New Yorkers—who gathered around their radios to hear it on Hoboken's WJY. Sound effects—the transistor whine of an old radio set tuning in a signal, a bell announcing the start of a new round, a cheering crowd—rose and fell behind the voice of a female narrator, enhancing her performance, which was, to my ear, straight-announcement work of the highest quality.

"No single event," the narrator said of the Dempsey fight, "was more important to radio's transition from a point-to-point communication system with primarily military applications to a method of reaching and entertaining the masses."

The narration faded neatly into a crackling, hissing re-creation of the ringside broadcaster's climactic call.

"Seven, eight, nine . . . ten! It's a knockout! Jack Dempsey is the winner and still world champion!"

By the time the segment was over, the archival image of Dempsey and Carpentier seemed less authentic—and less significant—than the vivid sensations and three-dimensional images the audio had conjured in me. I hadn't visited many museums in my life, but I guessed that this was one of the few in which what you observed mattered less than what you heard. I took this as yet another indication that I had found somewhere in this city I belonged and, with my back to the attendant, I smiled.

The next exhibit, entitled "The General," was a bronze bust of David Sarnoff, founder of the National Broadcasting Company and chairman of the Radio Corporation of America. I was calling up the accompanying audio program when my eye caught the title of the next exhibit over: "The First Commercials."

With an hour to spend in the museum, I might have heard out

the Sarnoff piece. With fourteen minutes—*More like twelve, now,* I thought—I abandoned the paean to executive genius for a piece that seemed more likely to speak to me.

The visuals of the first-commercials exhibit were limited—an illustration of a radio tower bearing the call letters WEAF, with white semi-circles rippling out from the antenna, and a blown up black-and-white photo of a studio cluttered with nests of wires and ancient analog equipment. I scanned the images in the time it took me to enter 0, 9 and 6 into the audio guide, and then gave my full attention to the voice of the narrator.

"In 1922," she began—it was the same woman who had done the Dempsey narration—"the Queensboro Realty Company paid one hundred dollars to New York station WEAF for the rights to ten minutes of airtime. They used that time to broadcast a scripted monologue about novelist Nathaniel Hawthorne. But the executives of the Queensboro Realty Company weren't peddling books. They were selling a bucolic ideal of home life in a community far away from the congestion and pollution of the city, and they were using Hawthorne's writing to do it. The monologue's sole purpose was to attract potential renters to a new apartment complex in Jackson Heights. The name of the complex? Hawthorne Court."

There was nothing wry or ironic in the narrator's delivery, but I couldn't help but laugh. It was hard to imagine anyone being taken in by such a hokey, dishonest ploy. I remembered enough of the *The Scarlet Letter* to know I wouldn't want Hester Prynne's neighbors living next door to me. Even harder to accept was the idea that anyone would've given ten minutes of attention to one commercial.

Almost as if she'd heard me think it, the narrator addressed the latter objection.

"In the New York radio market of the early 1920s," she said, "Queensboro Realty's one hundred dollars bought something close to a captive audience. There were few stations to tune in and no television sets to turn on. And in an age before standard sixty-second spots and clearly defined commercial breaks, it was difficult for listeners to discern where programming ended and advertising began. Commercials were read by the same men who read the news and made social commentary, and the only hint of a transition from regular programming to a sponsor's content was the sound of paper being shuffled. In the blurring of these lines, advertisers saw an opportunity they were willing to pay for, and commercial radio was born."

The narrator gave way to a second voice, and I recognized its timbre and range immediately. The voice belonged to the same man who had re-created the call of Jack Dempsey's knockout of Carpentier, but the ringside patter was nowhere to be heard. In its place was the polished diction of a man who would have been considered fit, in the 1920s, to broadcast from the bully pulpit of a New York City radio studio. In just a few syllables, that vocal style—the amplitude of its dynamics, a phlegmy rattle in its lower register, and the vaguely English way in which vowels erased the consonants that followed them—filled out the details of a man's life. Old money. Boarding-school education. A receding hairline that offended his vanity. A one-pack-a-day smoking habit. Unlike the narrator, whose talent was for the straight announcement I hoped to make my bread and butter, the man in command of this second voice—who could bring to life a boxing play-by-play man one minute and a blue-blooded radio host the next—was a character creator. Like Connor.

"It is fifty-eight years," the radio host said, "since Nathaniel Hawthorne, the greatest of American fictionalists, passed away. To honor his memory, the Queensboro Corporation, creator and operator of the tenant-owned system of apartment homes at Jackson Heights, New York City, has named the latest group of high-grade dwellings Hawthorne Court."

A second excerpt from the ad began as the first faded out, and a third selection faded in over the end of the second. In this way, the commercial was condensed into what might have been ninety seconds but felt much longer. Even a gifted creator of characters couldn't make this script live and breathe in the twenty-first century. That said, if I'd been offered a chance to endure the unabridged commercial, I probably would have given it my last ten minutes in the museum, observing some version of the principle my father followed when he watched a one-sided White Sox loss to the final disheartening out.

Mindful that my time was running short, I scanned a paragraph beneath a headshot of New York actor Joan Alexander, the definitive voice of Lois Lane on the long-running serial *The Adventures of Superman*, and quickly reviewed a collage of newspaper headlines recounting the panic caused by Orson Welles' production of *War of the Worlds*. An installation dubbed "The Death of Radio" displayed a timeline of cultural moments—the invention of television, the introduction of dashboard cassette players, the first MTV telecast, and the arrival of the iPod—at which the demise of radio had been prophesied. I needed no commentary to be reminded of what I already knew: radio survives. It's the cockroach of media.

The next exhibit I saw stopped me cold. Printed in blue type across the top of a freestanding, linoleum-coated slab was its title: "Harrison Walz: The Voiceover Artist."

I had never heard of Harrison Walz. A single-paragraph biography informed me that he was a commercial announcer in the 1930s and '40s for WOR in New York. A black-and-white photo showed Walz in a suit jacket and tie, wearing wooden headphones over thin hair slicked straight back, standing with script in hand before a large microphone branded with his station's call letters, his countenance frozen in mid-utterance of a long vowel—an *a* or an *i*—his eyes smiling, his free arm raised and bent gracefully at the elbow as if he were conducting a symphony.

Beneath the photograph was a quotation attributed to Walz himself: "I am not an announcer."

In the Walz exhibit, I heard a negative echo of my identity as a voiceover artist who only wanted to announce. Why would Walz, billed as *the* voiceover artist, deny that he was an announcer? I turned to the narrator—my colleague, as I had come to think of her—for answers.

"Harrison Walz," the narrator said, "did one voice—his own—and he employed it on behalf of the sponsors of the biggest radio dramas and comedies of his time. In the late 1940s, if you'd asked a New Yorker if he knew Harrison Walz, chances were good she would have said,

'Oh, sure. The radio announcer.' Walz was credited as an announcer at the beginning and end of some of the highest-rated broadcasts in radio history.

"But in an interview he gave to *The New Yorker* in 1953, Walz bristled at the term. 'I am not an announcer,' he declared, in what the columnist described as Walz's 'signature, clear-as-a-bell baritone.' Walz went on to explain that 'an announcer simply vocalizes the text put in front of him, and if he's any good, he vocalizes well. I do something more. If there is any heart in a sponsor's script, any humanity at all in the words, I make it the centerpiece of my performance. And the audience can *feel* the humanity coming through the radio, even if my voice sounds the same as it always has.'

"For hundreds of Walz's contemporaries in stations across the country," the narrator continued, "simply announcing the text put in front of them was good enough to earn a living. And surely Harrison Walz was handed commercial scripts so shallow or coarsely consumerist that he could find no humanity in them. But by digging deep and finding something human in so many of the scripts he performed, Harrison Walz created and played many more characters than the famous radio actors with whom he shared a studio. He made the craft of commercial voiceover an art form, one that many voice professionals would claim to practice, but few truly understand."

The audio ebbed into silence. I stood before the exhibit, afraid to move. I had dreamed throughout my long silence of becoming what I thought of as the best kind of voiceover artist: a highly skilled straight announcer. Now, near the end of my accidental pilgrimage to this one-room tribute to radio's survival, I'd heard emphatic testimony from one of the Great Voices that announcement and voiceover artistry were entirely distinct, that a straight announcer was no voiceover artist at all.

Worse, I knew deep down that Walz was right. What had made Larry Sellers my hero was the way his voice made me *feel* when I heard it. Until that moment, though, I hadn't been conscious that I'd been hearing anything more than the richness and precision of his delivery. They didn't have names, they didn't have silly voices, but Larry Sellers had been finding and creating characters—human beings behind the words—for as long as I'd been listening to him. Larry Sellers was a voiceover artist, just as Harrison Walz had been.

I yearned for the seconds-ago past in which my legitimacy as a voiceover artist seemed to hinge on the kind of script I'd be handed for the New York Red Bulls session. Now I could see that I was already an impostor: I wasn't really a voiceover artist. And in that moment, I was certain I never would be. I believed I had as much chance of creating a character on my own as I did of growing six inches taller.

Even the Manhattan Museum of Radio Arts was a place where Connor belonged and I did not.

I felt a tap on my shoulder and turned to find the attendant standing behind me.

"We're closed."

I nodded. "Yeah."

"I need the docent."

I pulled off the headphones and handed them over, along with the audio device. The attendant unclipped a karabiner from his belt loop and pinched a key between his thumb and forefinger. Then he gave me a look that said, *Get out.*

I started walking. The attendant followed. Nearing the door, I noticed an exhibit I'd missed on my way in. A triangle of warm, yellow light shone up from behind an old wooden radio cabinet, illuminating the exhibit's title—"The Voices"—and a dedication: "In honor of the on-air personalities of New York radio."

The installation had the collective, anonymous feel of a memorial marking a mass grave, and I understood that hastily buried among the newsreaders and traffic reporters were the practitioners of straight announcement, the soullessly technical virtuosos who had recorded hundreds of commercial scripts without finding even one character lying moribund on the page and reviving her.

● ● ●

WHEN I FINALLY got into my hotel room, I didn't open up my laptop to see if the script for the next day's session had been sent to me. I dropped my bag in a corner and left the laptop zipped inside it.

I drew the curtains, blacking out the city lights that were beginning to outdo what little daylight remained. I stood on the heel of one shoe and lifted my foot out of it; the other shoe I wrenched off with my hands. I undid my belt, pulled down my pants, and stepped out of them. When I was out of my t-shirt, too, I stood still alongside the queen-size bed, feeling my sweat evaporate into the cool, stale air. I threw all but one of the bed's pillows onto the floor, gathered the comforter, blanket and sheets into my hand, and yanked them back. I hadn't eaten since leaving Chicago, but I wasn't hungry. I wasn't tired, either. The sensation of rushing into bed without any thought of going to sleep was familiar—I'd done this many times—but this time was different. I had a voice now, and I'd bet everything on it.

I sat down at the head of the bed, peeled off my socks, and swung my bare feet onto the bed sheet, which felt cool but rough to the touch. Then I reached over to the bedside bureau, picked up the clock radio, and turned it on. Scanning through the stations, I studied every character-driven commercial I could find, trying desperately to make myself— overnight—into a voiceover artist.

A real one, this time.

11

Lily Eisenberg

I CHECK THE calendar on my phone: yes, today is Friday, August 6th, and yes, I told everyone on my team that we'd record voiceover from 10 to 11 a.m. at Steel Cut Studios. I'm staring at the fucking calendar event I sent out. For the life of me, I don't see any good reason why we are twenty minutes into the session and the talent I *flew to New York for one hour of work* isn't here yet.

Simon Davies' tardiness doesn't seem to matter much to my client, Kevin Earley. He's standing with his back to me, waving his arms around and talking at the sound engineer and my intern. An audience of any size makes Earley louder and more annoying.

"So I find the guy who looks like the level head in the group—"

Earley's dress shirt, starched to the stiffness of cardboard, lets out a muted crack as he rests his hand on the shoulder of an invisible man.

"—and I say, 'Look, man. You gotta get your boys outta here or we're gonna have problems.' And the guy gives me a look—the real fuckin' stink-eye—and he says, 'You'd better get *your* boys outta here, because *my* guys ain't leaving.' Now we got fuckin' problems."

We *do* have problems. We have this studio for only forty more minutes, and we haven't recorded a thing.

Earley's audience—one man and a weasel of a kid—is slouched into opposite corners of an overstuffed, black leather couch. The man is Derrion, the engineer Steel Cut has provided for the session. The enormous hood of his oversized dark blue sweatshirt rumples down over his shoulders, and he is chewing on the knotted end of a drawstring. Derrion's calm, unchanging expression is that of a man getting paid whether he is running a soundboard or pretending to care about some crazy white guy's story. On the other corner of the couch is Michael, the intern I've been stuck with for two weeks. He is somebody's nephew. His only credentials are having muddled through four years of prep school and two semesters of pass-fail classes at Brown. The official reason Michael is assigned to me is that he wants to be a copywriter, like me, but when I opened our first meeting by saying, "So you want to be a copywriter," Michael responded, "Not really."

"Oh." I thought I might have stumbled onto an argument for pawning him off on someone else. "What do you want to be?"

"A creative director," he said.

"Really."

He nodded. "I'm an idea guy."

So far as I can tell, the Idea Guy has no idea that I hate him. I have not been trying to hide this. Perhaps Michael has failed to notice the white-hot loathing in my eyes because, when he looks at me at all, he stares at my tits like a hungry toddler.

To Kevin Earley, though, Michael pays unblinking, worshipful attention. He is completely taken with the down-market, white-ethnic version of manhood Earley is selling.

"By now," Earley says, "my buddy is in another guy's face. They're nose to nose. And nobody is stepping in to stop it. We're crowding around, itching for somebody to throw the first—"

A tone from the intercom interrupts Earley's story.

"Simon Davies is here for Lily," the receptionist says.

"Thank God." I stand up. "Michael, would you bring Simon back, please?"

"Whoa!" Earley says. "I'm just getting to the good part."

"I'm sure Derrion can't wait to hear it," I say.

Earley points his hand at Michael, who has not moved. "The kid might learn something."

"We've got half an hour to get this spot."

"And whose fault is that, Lily?" Earley asks. "I didn't pick the talent. You did."

I transfer my hard stare from Earley—you can only give a client so much grief—to my intern. And what does Michael do? He looks at Earley, all but asking my client to overrule me.

"Better do what she says, kid," Earley says.

In his tone, I hear what Earley doesn't say: *You know how these bitches can get.*

With an eye roll he probably thinks is subtle, Michael gets up and walks around the far side of the mixing console to the control-room door. I watch him, daring him to challenge me again, but the weasel just pouts.

When Michael is out of the room, Earley slides his hands into the pockets of his pleated pants, takes a few steps toward me, and says, "You're taking all this pretty seriously, wouldn't you say, Lily?"

I don't answer. I don't even shrug my shoulders. Derrion tries to escape into the kaleidoscopic screensaver playing on the monitor in front of his empty seat at the soundboard.

Then, at a low volume meant to signal that he is speaking some profound truth, Earley says, "Let me put it another way. If you think this spot is going to sell New York Red Bulls tickets, you're the only one." He shakes his head and swipes his hand through the air. "Not true. My idiot boss agrees with you. But what the fuck does he know? He likes soccer."

This is Kevin Earley in a nutshell: doing work he doesn't believe in, for a man he doesn't respect, in a sport he sees as a waste of time and money. From the day I started working with him, Earley has made no bones about wanting to get out of professional soccer and into professional baseball, and not any-way, any-how. Earley wants an in-house marketing job with the Yankees.

"The biggest brand in sports," he says, referring to the Yanks.

He's right about that much.

I'd never tell him so, but I want out of soccer and into baseball as badly as Earley does. Unlike Earley, though, I *love* soccer. I started playing on traveling teams as a ten-year-old and played all the way through college. I became who I am running alongside girls—and, later, women—matching them step for step, my thick, kinky ponytail bouncing with every footfall and my pale blue eyes glued to their hips. (A player can't fake you out with her hips. Hips don't lie.) As we ran and shoved and clawed at each other, I shouted in their ears, making them believe with the breath I wasted on words that I still had another gear if I needed it. I was never much into scoring goals. I threw my body in front of hard heads and cleated feet to win the ball and, if I felt like she needed it, I'd use my shoulders and spikes to teach a striker a lesson. Whenever

I walked off the field a winner, I would hear the catty, stage-whispered comments—losing brings out the worst in people—about the central defender with the bleeding knees.

What a bitch. She'll make some guy miserable some day.

What makes you think she likes guys?

I let them say what they wanted. My answer was up on the scoreboard.

When I was seventeen, playing in a weekend tournament outside Baltimore, I answered a whisper coming from inside me. I went to the hotel room of a girl I had bodied for position and kicked in the ankles for ninety minutes that afternoon. I watched her undress. And I kissed every bruise I'd given her.

Kevin Earley grew up playing football. The American kind. More than once, I've heard him slander soccer as "a sport for pussies." Whenever he says that, I make a silent bet that I've already had more pussy than Kevin Earley will ever get.

I'm not sure Earley has even read the script we are about to record. It's the first script I've had total creative control of, a side benefit of the general opinion at my ad agency that the soccer side of the enormous Red Bull account is where creatives go to die. Assuming the Red Bulls buy decent airtime for it, this spot will sell tickets. I know it will. But selling Red Bulls tickets is a distant second on my list of priorities for this spot. I need it to do something else entirely. I need it to sell *me*.

The control-room door opens. Michael walks in and heads straight for his place on the couch as the thick, insulated door closes slowly on its noiseless hinges. I'm about to ask Michael where Simon Davies is when a young man catches the closing door and pushes it open again.

"Simon?" I ask, taking a step toward him.

He nods oddly and says, "Yes."

"Lily Eisenberg," I say, shaking his hand.

"Nice to meet you."

Simon smiles and I smile back, but my smile is fake. I'm pissed he's late.

"This is Derrion, our engineer."

"Hello," Simon says.

"How you feel?" Derrion says.

"Lounging on the couch over there is Michael Hendershot," I say. "He's interning at the agency."

"Hi again."

Michael lets out a little laugh, letting all of us know what he thinks of Simon's quaint, Midwestern greeting.

"And this is Kevin Earley. He's with the New York Red Bulls."

"How's it going," Earley mutters, sounding bored already. He shakes Simon's hand without turning to face him.

"Pretty well," Simon says. "How are you?"

"Peachy."

Finally getting the vibe of the room, Simon doesn't say anything else. He seems stiff and nervous and looks to be working on more than a few sleepless nights. That he is jittery *and* overtired *and* late should piss me off even more, but Simon's tardiness has begun to work in his favor. I'm mostly relieved that there's still time enough for Simon to give me the one perfect take I need to take my last good shot at getting into baseball.

"We're about twenty-five minutes behind," I say, "so we should get started."

"Wait," Simon says. He looks as if I've just told him there's no Santa Claus. "My agent told me II o'clock. I thought I was early."

"The session started at ten. It *ends* at eleven."

"But my agent told me eleven. I'm sure of it."

I am just about to tell Simon that we don't have time for a whodunit when I remember who called Simon's agent to book him.

"Michael, what time did you tell Simon's agent he should be here?"

"I don't remember."

"Yes," I insist, "you do."

"Look," he says, "I might've adjusted for Chicago time."

My eyes squint as I try to decipher what the hell he might mean. "Chicago is an hour *behind* New York. The time you gave him was an hour ahead."

"I guess I only think in hours ahead of Eastern Time," he says with a shrug. "My family vacations in Europe."

"You're not looking too good here, kid," Earley says.

"We don't have time for this," I say, picking up the thin stack of paper in front of me. "Kevin, Simon—I apologize for the confusion."

"No problem," Simon mumbles.

"Like I told you," my client says. "Late, early—" He shrugs and shakes his head. "Nothing we do here makes a lick of difference."

I don't agree, but I don't argue. What can I say that won't invite Earley to tell us all—again—that we are wasting our time and effort?

"Here's the script, Simon," I say. "Take a minute to read it over."

"Great," Simon says, taking the sheet of paper from me. "Thanks."

With a grunt, Derrion throws his bulk forward, stands up, and settles into his seat in front of the recording console. I pass out copies of the script to the others, even Michael. While Simon studies up, I skim the sentences I hammered on for days, over thirty drafts.

It took twenty drafts to come out from behind my favorite parts of soccer: the dirt, bruises and blood that separated winners from losers. As a player, I'd lived for the vicious, spikes-up tackles and the elbows thrown into throats when a corner kick takes flight. But the Red Bulls spot couldn't be about these things. It needed to capture the feel of the live event from a *fan's* point of view, not a player's. And to see the game as a fan does, I had to get in touch with my feelings for the game. Just that phrase—"my feelings for the game"—makes me want to puke. I'm not impressed with feelings and people who indulge them. What impresses me is doing what needs doing, despite how you feel. I like people who play hurt, keep the pain to themselves, and make their opponent feel it, too. That's more than a way to play soccer. It's a way of life. *My* way.

By the twenty-fifth draft, though, I'd made it off the field and into the seats. I imagined a clear evening with the perfect temperature and low humidity. I described the elegant rising and setting of a goal kick and tried to capture with my words the exhilaration of watching two players run at full speed, chasing the ball into open space. To write these things, I had to stand naked before my love of the game—not as a player, but as a fan. I felt more defenseless—vulnerable might be the better word— than I ever had standing naked in front of a woman. I didn't like that feeling. I promised myself that the moment the script was approved, I could leave all those feelings on the page, where they belong. Then they would be some voiceover guy's problem. Not mine.

The script is a single paragraph, seven and a half lines that time out to forty-nine seconds in my slow, monotonous reading, leaving at least ten seconds for the swappable tags that advertise the dates and times of upcoming games. The narrative follows the arc of a live New York Red Bulls experience, from the stadium gates' opening to a last-second victory for the home team, and its imagery—a field of perfectly manicured grass, a white ball soaring to seemingly impossible heights—lends to soccer the reverence that radio commercials usually reserve for national parks and for baseball.

This is no accident. It's the angle I'm playing.

Kevin Earley has worked every connection he has to land a job with the Yankees. He's bought dinners for guys who know somebody in the front office to increase the chances that the next time the Yankees need somebody in marketing, they'll call him. I don't schmooze. It's not me. For the past three years, though, every time the Yankees have needed somebody below director level in marketing, they've called me first. The offers weren't official—nobody in the Yankees' HR department has my résumé on file—but they were real. I know, because the woman who made the offers is my sister, Terri Schorr.

And if Kevin Earley knew all this, he'd despise me even more than he does.

● ● ●

NINE YEARS OLDER than me, Terri was already a giant in sports marketing when I was still at Ithaca College. She was the youngest Director of Marketing in the long history of the New York Yankees franchise, and the first woman to hold that position. She's won more Sports Marketer of the Year awards, from more organizations, than anyone but my mother cares to count. Terri's glass statues and brass plaques occupy almost every inch of the credenza in my mother's dining room. Except for an eleven-by-seventeen portrait of Terri with her perfect family—her husband Jeff, a Wall Street lawyer, and my three gorgeous nieces—an entire wall of my mother's living room has been dedicated to framed trade-magazine covers that feature Terri. "My cover girl," my mother calls her, as she shows off the glossy photos to neighbors and friends. Behind Terri in each one of those cover shots are the overlaid N and Y recognized the world over. The Yankees *are* the biggest brand in sports, and nobody outside the team's baseball operations plays a bigger role in building it than Terri Schorr does.

Does my sister's success with the Yankees look like the answer to all my problems? It's not. It *is* the problem.

Terri knows I can write. She's told me so. I never send her my work, but my mother nags me for it, and I send it to her, knowing full well that it will end up in an envelope in Terri's mailbox at Yankee Stadium. The only thing my mother wants more than to see me married—"To a man or a woman," she told me once, "I'm not particular"—is for me to join my sister in the Yankees' marketing department. She's no baseball fan, my mother, but to her way of thinking, Terri could ensure I'd never want for work.

"Jobs at advertising agencies don't last," my mother says, parroting a truism she heard on some reality show. "If you were with Terri and the Yankees, I'd never have to worry about you!"

She's not wrong about working at an ad agency. By and large, when your client is gone, you're gone, too. What my mother forgets, though, is how much she loves to worry, and what she doesn't understand is that I can never work for the Yankees. In my own mind, Terri's accomplishments haven't opened any doors. They've closed entire city blocks. To get where I want to go, I have to take the long way around.

Three times Terri has asked me about working for the Yankees. Each time, she has done it the right way. Privately. Respectfully. When I say *Thanks, but no thanks,* she doesn't push or pressure me. She doesn't even ask for an explanation.

"You should take your career where *you* want to take it," she says.

And I believe that Terri means what she says. But I've never been able to convince myself that, when Terri made these offers to me, she believed I was the best person for the job. I can't shake the idea that she is such a big fucking deal—so big she doesn't really need the Yankees anymore—that she can burn some political capital getting her kid sister a job, with no better reason than giving her mother some peace of mind. No, I can never work for the Yankees. If *I* can't be sure I'd be getting the job on my merits, why would anyone else believe I've earned it?

My sister's success is the reason I have turned down Kevin Earley's dream job three times to keep promoting a soccer team named for a cocktail mixer. It's the reason I use my maternal grandmother's maiden name—Eisenberg—on my business card. It's why I've kept my sister's identity a secret from my colleagues and sworn her to keeping my professional whereabouts from hers. Terri's success with the Yankees is also the reason why, after a lifetime of rooting for Jeter and Posada and Rivera and anyone else who wore the navy blue pinstripes, I've written a soccer spot with the specific intention of catching the ear of New York's other baseball team: the Mets. When it airs, I'll send a recording of the Red Bulls commercial to the Mets' director of marketing. My best hope is that he'll listen to the spot and decide, with envy that burns him up inside, *That should've been ours.*

I figured I could take a year to turn my "Take Me Out to the Soccer Match" idea into a campaign and send each major piece of it to the higher-ups in Mets' marketing, gradually moving my résumé to the top of the list of people to call the next time the department has an open position to fill. As it turns out, I won't have the chance to do things slowly.

Four days ago—Monday morning, August 2nd—my group creative director, Allison, sat me down and delivered what she thought was good news.

"You've done a nice job on the soccer slice of the Red Bull business, Lily," Allison said. "I read the radio spot you wrote. It's good."

"Thank you."

"I want to give you a shot at the big time. I'm moving you to the energy-drink side of the account."

I said nothing.

"We're prepping a new campaign. I need TV spots—nationals—and if I like what you write, you'll work with that director—what's his name, the guy who did that movie with the cars and the robots? Anyway, you'll spend two weeks in L.A. as the writer on his set. It's the closest most of us ever get to living the Hollywood dream."

I knew better than to protest. I'd seen many creatives fight the move from one piece of this business to another. The arguments went nowhere. On Allison's team, you went where you were told, or you left the agency.

"You don't look too excited," Allison said.

"Oh, I am," I lied. "It's just that we're doing some cool things on the soccer side now. We've finally found our footing, you know?"

"I know," she said. "That's why I can afford to move you off of it."

I nodded and faked a smile.

"Finish the spot you're working on," she said, as if my commercial were just something to be crossed off a list. "We'll talk again next week." Allison stood up and stuck her hand out in front of me. "Congratulations, Lily."

Standing and shaking Allison's hand, I felt more like I was being laid off than accepting a promotion. A move to the energy-drink side of the Red Bull business would be fantastic news for someone who wants to make a career of copywriting, no matter the industry. For someone looking to get into baseball—for me—the move is a disaster. Red Bull is an energy drink, sure, but not the sporty kind. It's a party beverage for a young demo with little interest in ballgames. If soccer is a detour on the route I've mapped out, the energy-drink business is a black-ice skid into a ravine. There's even more riding on my soccer spot now than there was when I wrote it. My first shot at parlaying my work for the New York Red Bulls into a job with the New York Mets is the only shot I'll get.

And my ace in the hole is Simon Davies.

Walking slowly back to my cubicle after my meeting with Allison, I heard a snippet of a recorded voice through an open office door. What caught my ear first was the vocal integrity of each spoken word. I was standing a good fifteen feet away from the speakers—they weren't even pointing in my direction—and every syllable kept its shape and edges over the distance. Other people have voices like light bulbs: bright but diffuse. This voice had the focus of a laser beam. But what kept me listening outside a colleague's door was nothing mechanical. In the words he spoke, I could hear the young man's reverence for his work. His approach, which seemed almost religious, sparked a sense of mystery I hadn't experienced since I was a girl sitting in temple on Rosh Hashanah. Right then, I knew I had to have this voice for my spot. No other voice gave it a better chance of working for me and for the Mets.

I rapped my knuckles on the doorframe and ducked my head into the office of Bill Albert, a doughy, balding senior copywriter staffed to another small sliver of the Red Bull account: The Red Bull No Bull Comedy Tour.

"Who is that?" I asked, pointing in the direction of his desktop speakers.

Bill stared at me through his thick, wire-frame glasses, as if he were translating my question into another language he understood better. By the time he finished, the voice I'd heard had given way to another.

"David Cross?"

"No."

"Patton Oswalt."

"No. It's nobody famous, I don't think. The other voice."

Then he leaned forward, took his portable laptop mouse in hand, and squinted at the tiny screen as he scrolled.

"Simon Davies," Bill said.

"Is he out of New York?"

Still reading the screen, Bill pinched his face and bared his teeth like a burrowing rodent. "Chicago," he said.

With the tiny budget I had for this commercial, flying in talent for the session should have been out of the question, but I poured almost as much creativity into the finances as I'd lavished on the script. I called the recording studio and told them we wouldn't need two hours, that one would do it. I used my credit-card frequent-flyer miles to book the round-trip flight. I'd pay for his hotel room and meals out of pocket.

If I was only getting one shot, I was taking it with Simon Davies.

• • •

NOW, I REGRET cutting the session in half. I want to give Simon as much time as he needs to ease into that reverential state of mind, but I have only twenty-five minutes left.

While Simon pores over the script as if I've asked him to perform it from memory, Kevin Earley finishes his story for Michael, detailing the damage done to people and property in a fight we are to believe began with one hothead on the other side of the standoff finally throwing a punch and ended with Earley and his buddies kicking ass with fists and pool cues.

I have given Simon all the time I can spare.

"Any questions I can answer?" I ask him. "Before we get started?"

Simon glances at Earley and appears to clear his throat without making any noise.

"Would you say there is any character in this script?" Simon asks.

My first thought is that I've been insulted. "Excuse me?"

Simon tries again. "Would you say the script is about a person? A human being?"

From the couch, Michael looks at me as if to ask, *Is this guy for real?*

"It's about soccer," I say. "Plain and simple."

Simon nods like a man admitting he's asked for more than he deserves. "Okay."

Then Earley takes a step toward Simon and says, "Let me take the pressure off you, guy. None of this matters. At all." The red jewel of Earley's large class ring glints in the studio light as he jabs a right hand at the sound booth. "You're going to go in there, say some words, and then I'm going to go have a drink, all right?"

Everything Earley says is directed at Simon, but the person he's trying to bully is me.

There's only one feeling I've never had any trouble expressing: anger. And my anger sharpens the words I use to tell off my client.

"Why don't you just *pretend* you give a shit, Kevin." Then I add, "Here's an idea. Pretend you work for the Yankees."

Something in the way I say this leaves little doubt that I think pretending is the only way Kevin Earley will ever experience his dream job.

In a split second, the consequences of my outburst play out in my head. Earley will yell and scream and pull the plug on the session. He will call my creative director and complain. I will be fired. I will be left with no job, no references, and no spot to send to the Mets. I've scarcely had the chance to think these things when I realize I don't have everything right. Earley is livid—I can see it in his eyes—but he isn't yelling. He's wearing a smile as wide as the Hudson.

In that moment, I understand with heart-sinking certainty that I've handed Kevin Earley something—I'm not sure exactly what—but it's something he's been lying in wait for.

"It's funny you should mention the Yankees."

Still smiling, Earley walks to the backside of the recording console so that all of us can see his face. He's in complete control of the room. I can do nothing but watch.

"You know how many seats there are in the new Yankee Stadium, kid?" he says, twisting at the hips to face Michael.

Michael is nervously sliding his thumbnail between his two front teeth. He shrugs. "Forty thousand?"

"Fifty-thousand, two-hundred ninety-one," Earley answers. "It's fucking huge. And from at least a few thousand of those seats, the game is basically unwatchable. A bad angle or obstructed view or both. Yankees' ticket prices are the highest in baseball, in a shitty economy, and more than half the home games are against losing, no-profile teams. Despite *all* that," he says, clearing invisible smoke from the air in front of his eyes, "the Yankees led the American League in attendance last year. You know how they did it?"

The question isn't rhetorical. Earley is waiting for an answer.

"I don't know, man," Derrion says, sitting on his little rolling chair. "Yankee tickets sell themselves."

"Bullshit," Earley says. "Not for a weekday game against Minnesota, they don't."

He looks around at each of us—Michael, Simon, then me—waiting for someone else to venture a guess. No one says anything.

"People who know sports marketing know how the Yankees fill their seats, even against bad teams. The Yankees have Terri Schorr."

I want to throw up. I don't know how Earley found out—by stalking Terri online, maybe, or over lunch with someone in the Yankees front office who knew our family growing up—and I have no idea how long he's been waiting to tear off my mask.

"Terri Schorr is the best woman in sports marketing."

The way Earley hits *woman* makes me want to scream. Earley and men like him aren't good enough to carry my sister's briefcase.

Then Earley looks at me and pays my sister a compliment: "She could sell out a Red Bulls game."

And you can't, Lily. Earley doesn't say the words, but everyone in the control room hears them.

"I'd kill to work with Terri Schorr," Earley says, still looking at me. "I've been trying to get a meeting with her or her boss for years. But where am I?" He raises his palms and looks around with disgust at the analog soundboard, the unfashionable recessed lighting and worn carpet. "I'm stuck in fucking soccer. With Terri's little sister."

Michael's eyes dart to me. "But your last name is Eisenberg."

I'm not sure Michael knows my *first* name. I've never heard him use it. Later, when I can think straight, I'll find it interesting that the surname that pegs me as a Jew was right on the tip of his tongue.

Simon is sweating from the forehead and the upper lip, and his jaw muscles are flexing beneath the skin. He wants out of here, I can see that, but I can only let him go as far as the sound booth. I don't remember the last time I needed rescuing, but I need Simon to save me now.

"We should get started, Simon," I say.

Simon clears his throat again—audibly, this time. "Okay," he says.

The two syllables sound clipped, as if he can't quite get enough air.

I worry that Earley will try to stop Simon—*Stick around, guy, there's more to tell!*—but he lets him leave for the sound booth. Earley picks up an open folding chair, carries it past Michael, and plops it down, back-wards, between my seat and Derrion's. He straddles the chair's built-in cushion and props his forearms on the aluminum backrest, like a kid trying to act cool in a Molly Ringwald movie, or a copy of a copy of James Dean. I'm sure Earley has used the same stance when he sits down next to a woman in a low-cut shirt and offers to buy a round of drinks for her and her girlfriends. As he stares at me, daring me meet his eye, all I can feel is his menace.

The moment Simon puts on his headphones, I am in his ear.

"When you're ready, Simon, do a read-through so Derrion can get some levels."

Simon nods, then he nods again, and only then does it hit me that he isn't nodding. He is loosening up his neck, maybe, or indulging a tic he cannot control any longer. He starts to read. His voice is raspy and tight, as if the air in his lungs isn't air at all, but hot tobacco smoke. I steal a glance at Derrion. His hand is on the mouse, but it isn't moving. He is staring through the glass, wincing at Simon.

"Why don't you give us another one," I say to Simon.

Simon rolls his head around and around, as if he's trying to induce vertigo, and then he speaks. In the first sentence, he interrupts himself twice to swallow.

"All the times you heard me say I wanted to work for the Yankees," Earley says.

His blood is up, but his volume is down. I'm the only audience Earley needs now.

"I must have sounded pathetic," Earley says, goosing the word pathetic with a hiss.

Simon is looking at me through the glass, his eyebrows arched, as if he's waiting for me to say that his last reading was good enough and he can go home now. I decide against another read-through. I gamble that, for Simon, rehearsals are meaningless because they can't generate the pressure of a real take.

"Okay, Simon, we're going do to one for real now," I say, pressing the mic button. "Do you need water or anything?"

Or hot tea? Or whiskey? Anything to let out the voice I heard in Bill Albert's office.

Simon shakes his head. He isn't speaking unless he has to.

"Okay, then."

"Take one," Derrion says.

"When you're ready, Simon."

Simon begins another anaphylactic non-performance of my script, and Earley picks up his monologue where he left it.

"I asked myself why you never put me in touch with your sister," he says. "At first, I figured you thought I wasn't good enough—not good enough for the Yankees, not good enough for Terri." A laugh escapes from his nose. "Now I know different."

"Let's try another take, Simon," I say.

"Take two," Derrion says.

Simon sounds as if he's being garroted from behind. He does neck rolls between each throttled sentence.

"This isn't about what you think of me," Earley says. "It's all about what your sister thinks of you."

"Stop it, Kevin," I say, quietly. "Please." Then, over the mic, I say, "We're ready for another one, Simon. Try to relax, okay?"

"Take three," Derrion says.

Simon begins again. I close my eyes and listen to the asphyxiation of my commercial and my career.

"Your sister doesn't think *you're* good enough for the Yankees," Earley says.

I say nothing.

"If she did, you wouldn't be fucking around in this minor-league sport. You'd be in the big leagues already!"

When I open my eyes, Simon Davies is staring at me, helpless.

Save me.

"It's a good thing you never mentioned me to your sister," Earley says. "I don't want your stink on me."

I stand up suddenly, sending my wheeled chair into the wall of hard drives and tape decks behind me.

"Yo," Derrion says.

He is scolding me for my carelessness with his equipment, but I don't apologize. I jerk open the control-room door.

"That's it," Earley yells after me. "Run out of here! Prove your sister right!"

I cover the fifteen feet to the sound-booth door with quick, choppy steps, fighting back the oncoming wetness in my eyes. I try to get angry—*Fuck Kevin Earley, fuck the Red Bulls, fuck that fucking intern*—but when the anger comes, it's useless. Empty.

As air rushes past the open sound-booth door and into the hallway, Simon whips his head around. He looks like a terrified child.

"Come out here, Simon," I say, holding the door open. "Please."

Simon takes off his headphones and carefully hangs them over the top edge of the music stand. I get the idea he is certain he is being fired. I *would* fire him if I could replace him in the next fifteen minutes, but I can't. My options are Simon or nothing.

I let the door close and we stand face to face in the weird, soundproof silence of the hallway.

"Look," I say to Simon. "When I told you the script was just about soccer, I lied. It's about me. I imagined myself as a fan in the stands, I saw the game I've played all my life, and I wrote down everything there is to love about it. The *love* in it"—I mean the script, but I point at the sound booth—"is mine. I'm the human being in the script."

I could go on. I could tell him that the language is borrowed from baseball and why that matters, that this spot is my only chance at the dream I've been chasing for years, that if this commercial doesn't happen, the detour I've taken around my sister's success will become something else—a permanent rerouting away from the life I want and my opportunity to measure up, on my own terms, to the great Terri Schorr. But I don't say any of these things.

What I do say is vague and incomplete, but the moment I say it is the closest I've come to standing naked in front of a strange man. "I need this to work."

Simon's eyes stay locked on mine, but his rigid neck relaxes. He drops his chin just slightly and lifts it, then makes the same pair of movements two more times—a perfectly normal nodding of the head.

"Me, too," he says.

They're just two words, but he got them out, and they give me the feeling that Simon understands me.

"Okay," I say.

Simon nods—normally, again—and turns to the door. With his hand on the stained balsa wood, he rotates his head slowly through his neck's full range of motion. Then he pushes the door open and disappears into the booth. The ritualism of Simon's movement is chilling. Standing alone in the hallway, I'm confronted again with the possibility that I have rented damaged goods.

When I return to the control room, Earley is on his feet and holding court again.

"You get ahold of your sister?" he asks me. "Is she stopping by to save your ass?"

I ignore Earley and meet Derrion's eye. "Do another take."

Derrion's silence and stillness are his way of asking me why anyone would waste the time and server space recording another unusable take from Mr. Tourette's in there. I stare down at my script, pretending not to understand Derrion's question. Eventually, he spins around in his four-wheeled chair to face the console, clicks his mouse twice, and holds down the mic button at his station.

"Take four," he says.

When Simon opens his mouth, the voice that fills the control room has the same tone and tenor as the voice I heard coming from Bill Albert's office, but it isn't Simon's voice. It's *mine*. Simon has become the fan I imagined when I wrote this spot and the person I hope it will make me. In his humble, hopeful delivery of the words, I hear my own aspirations. And as he begins his rich rendition of the second to last sentence of my script, I pull my eyes away from Simon—my ears and my heart he won't let go—and find that everyone in the control room—even Michael, even Earley—is absorbed in his performance.

Simon Davies has saved my ass. We have saved each other.

12

Brittany Case

I knew that Simon would call some day. I didn't know if he would be mad, heartbroken or just confused, but I knew he'd call. So when his number came up on my phone that Saturday morning, I wasn't surprised. I was relieved. What needed to happen was happening.

I started trying to disentangle myself from Simon long before I actually broke up with him. I worked slowly, at first, snipping the strings between us with cold shoulders and sharp words. Then life handed me a machete and I swung it. Simon's brother, Connor, came to visit us in Carbondale, and I slept with him. That act gave me the emotional wiggle-room I needed to rent an apartment, sight unseen, in Brooklyn, and to tell Simon I'd be moving on without him.

It wasn't until after repaying the money I'd borrowed from Simon that I realized I wasn't as free as I thought. Cheating on Simon had kept me tethered to him. Walking to work, or sitting on my couch with a book and a mug of chai, I would lose minutes wondering how and when—to my mind, these were the only unknowns—Simon would find out what had happened. Would Connor drop it on him during an argument? Or would Simon, poring over the last days of our relationship, looking for any explanation for our break-up but the simplest one—that I couldn't love him anymore—stumble upon some telling detail? A missing condom in the box under our bed, maybe, or a sleep memory of the smell of sex on a night we didn't have it? It might have been better for both of us, in the long run, if I'd admitted everything while breaking up with him. But I hadn't—I hadn't seen the need—and I was afraid that calling up Simon any time after that, just to tell him I'd slept with his brother, would make me the kind of crazy ex-girlfriend I'd always detested. Simon would have to find out without my help, and when he did, he'd call me. And I believed that when I'd let him say whatever he had to say about my sleeping with Connor, the last thread between Simon and me would be cut.

But when Simon called, he didn't mention his brother. He asked me to meet him for coffee.

Simon doesn't have the guile to set up an ambush.

He doesn't know, I thought. *Fuck.*

I didn't want to meet Simon for coffee. I had no interest in giving him the chance to prove to either one of us that he's over me, and if there was something he wished he'd said the day I told him we were finished, I didn't want to hear it. But I took the gamble that I'd find some way, short of telling him about Connor and me, to make this coffee chat our last meeting.

He offered to come to Brooklyn, but I said I'd meet him in Manhattan. Part of what I liked about Brooklyn is that it seemed impossible that Simon could exist there. I told him to meet me at a Starbucks just over the bridge from my apartment.

When I arrived, Simon was already at a table for two. He stood up when he saw me. I went straight for the coffee line.

"Do you need anything?" I said.

Seeing his head shake before he spoke, I felt a slight twinge, the same sensation I'd experienced when I was cleaning out my grandfather's closet after his funeral and caught a whiff of his living scent.

"No," Simon said, pointing to the paper cup sleeved in cardboard on the table in front of him. "I'm good."

When my iced coffee was ready, I walked quickly to the table and sat down across from Simon, keeping my sunglasses on. When we were together, Simon had been able to intuit—not always, but often—what I was feeling just by looking at me. I never liked that.

"How are you?" Simon asked.

"I'm fine," I said. "How are you?"

"Pretty good."

He seemed pretty good. He had showered and mussed his hair around with some kind of product, which I knew he did only in advance of what he called, in his sickeningly precious, provincial way, "special occasions." He was skinnier than I remembered but, then again, I was skinnier, too. Living on very little money was easier to do cohabiting in

Carbondale than it was living alone in Brooklyn. I guessed the same was true of living alone in Chicago. And I was certain that Simon was living alone. His hair and good posture couldn't hide his hangdog loneliness.

"So you're here for work?" I asked.

"Yeah," he said. "An agency flew me in for a voiceover session."

"They *flew* you in!" I said. "Impressive."

I couldn't let that slide. *Flew me in?* As if they would have made him take the bus from Chicago?

Simon closed his eyes and nodded, embarrassed by his grandstanding and, I'm sure, a little hurt by my calling him on it.

"How'd it go?" I asked.

"Not bad," he said. "Getting through security was a little—"

"I meant the job, Simon."

"Oh," he said, embarrassed again, but trying not to be. "It got off to a rough start. But we got there. Eventually."

By then, I understood that part of the reason Simon had invited me out was to show me that he had dragged himself up from mute to voiceover artist, just like he'd said he would. I saw a chance to cross off one more item on the list of things Simon might resurface to ask of me.

"You really made it happen, Simon," I said. "Congratulations."

"It's just one job."

"I'm sure you'll get other jobs."

I believed that, too. Sitting across from him in New York, I had the disturbing feeling that Simon could be my equal in something other than our fathers having fucked us around.

"How's the rare books business?" he asked, smiling kindly.

"Good."

"Had any sales?"

"A few, yeah."

"That's great!"

He waited for me to elaborate, but I did not.

"So it's going well," he said.

"Yeah."

"That's great," Simon said again. "I'm happy for you."

"Thanks."

The truth was, I had sold zero books. I hadn't even built an inventory. For months, I'd been scouring estate sales and collection liquidations and coming away empty-handed. Long-time dealers with brick-and-mortar storefronts on the Upper East Side and climate-controlled storerooms in the Bronx appraised the collections, bought up the bargains for themselves, and overpriced what they left behind, shutting out the small-time competition. I was not in the rare-books business yet—I was working at the enormous Barnes and Noble on Court Street—but I was not about to let the narrative of this get-together become: *Simon is living his dream, and Brittany isn't.* The lie wasn't all about pride, though. I was making sure that Simon wouldn't decide I needed help and try to help me.

"Are you still volunteering?" Simon asked. "With the babies?"

Jesus, I thought. *This again.*

While we were together, Simon had started a couple of times to discuss his concern that my feelings for him were too much like my feelings for the inconsolable, unviable infants I held every week as a NICU volunteer. I'd never allowed him to finish that thought. Now, I recognized that Simon's question about the babies was his roundabout way of asking about my feelings for him.

"I don't do that anymore."

"Why not?"

"It finally dawned on me that those babies aren't my responsibility."

I stared at him from behind my sunglasses until he dropped his eyes to the cup in his hands.

Then Simon shook some of the tension from his neck, looked up at me, and did something he'd never done before.

"How are things with your father?" he said.

"My *father?*"

"Yeah."

It had been a stated rule of our relationship that Simon was not to mention my father, under any circumstances. Except to say that my father could rot in prison and *then* in hell for all I cared, I'd discussed him with Simon only once. In that conversation—it was more of a monologue, really; once I got going, Simon didn't say anything—I was as honest as I'd ever been with anyone, even my mother, about how badly my father's stealing from me and lying to me had fucked me up, which made it the best and worst conversation I'd ever had. I was wiping my eyes with the heel of my hands when I said, "I don't want to talk about this any more. Don't ever bring it up."

And while we were together, Simon never said a word to me about my father.

Which means that Simon knew the risk he was taking when he asked after my father that Saturday afternoon. There was nothing to stop me from standing up and storming out. He must have realized by then that I was scorching the earth between us and decided he had nothing to lose.

On any other day, I would have told Simon to fuck off. That day, I couldn't.

"I got a letter from him," I said.

Simon needed two of his headshakes. "You did?"

I nodded. "Yesterday."

Another headshake. "What did it say?"

The letter was still in my purse, where I'd stuffed it the moment that reading it became too much for me, but I remembered everything I'd seen.

"He described a typical day," I said. "He gets up, he showers, he eats. He trades sob stories in the prison yard. The guards pace back and forth in front of the fence, half-listening to them. Then he eats again and does some reading. Then dinner. Then bed."

Simon didn't say anything. I kept going.

"He told me my mom is divorcing him. I've been on her to do it for years, and I guess she's finally going through with it—unless he's just lying for sympathy."

I was angry with myself for saying these things—for saying anything at all about my father—but I took some pleasure in how well Simon was listening. No one had been listening much to me lately.

"He's getting out a few months early, apparently," I said. "For good behavior."

Simon let the silence billow up and around us. Then he said, "What does he want?"

I smiled at how well Simon understood a man he'd never met. My father always wants something.

"Forgiveness," I said.

"How do you know he wants forgiveness?"

"He asked me for it," I said. "He used the word."

Simon looked away, seeming to weigh what he was learning about my father against what he already knew. "Did he apologize?"

I shook my head. "No."

"Has he ever apologized?"

"No."

The confused expression on his face told me that Simon was asking himself a question I'd already answered for myself: *How can he expect to be forgiven if he doesn't apologize first?*

I hoped my father would apologize some day. When he did, I'd know that I'd broken him. Whether he apologized or not, I would deny my father everything he hadn't managed to steal from me.

"I'm sorry, Brittany."

These profoundly unhelpful words meant that Simon wouldn't try to fix something he never could.

Here's the thing: Simon had me then. If he'd kept pulling away, if he'd said, "Well, I've got to go," I would've invited Simon to Brooklyn and, after a few drinks, into my bed. That's the sickness you deal with as the daughter of a father like mine. A man with more cunning than Simon had—a man more like my father—would've had me for one more night, at least.

But what Simon did was try to pull me closer.

"When was the last time you had a conversation like this?" he said.

I leaned away, repulsed. "Don't."

"I mean it. Have you ever had a conversation like this with anyone else?"

"Conversation isn't the end-all, Simon."

"Yes!" he said, as if I'd finally realized something he'd known all along. "It's the means to an end! *We* are the end!"

Just like that, I was sick of him again. I wasn't sure I'd done enough to make this my last conversation with Simon, but I couldn't take another minute of it.

"Goodbye, Simon."

The legs of my chair groaned as they skidded back across the ceramic tiles. I picked up my purse and walked out, leaving my coffee on the table.

I was halfway to the subway station when Simon shouted in my ear.

"You know why you always leave?"

"Jesus!" I said, startled.

"Because leaving is easy." Simon took three headshakes. "Being with someone is hard. Some people can't even do it. You *can* do it, though—with me, you can—but you won't, because it makes you vulnerable. And it's just so *easy* to stand up and leave."

I was too self-conscious to stop walking. We were that couple you see having an argument on the street, giving every passerby a two-second glimpse into the dysfunction of a relationship, and I didn't want to be any kind of couple with Simon.

"Leaving you wasn't easy," I said.

"It wasn't? You came into my living room, told me you were leaving, and left."

I said nothing.

"You can't lie to me," he said. "I know you."

I came to a sudden halt and shoved Simon in the chest. "You *know* me! You don't know me like you think you do! I stayed with you *months* longer than I should have. I *couldn't* leave you. I was so sure the next guy would make me even worse than I was."

People streamed past us in both directions. I was crying by then, and Simon's eyes were wet. Neither thing stopped what I'd started.

"Then that baby died in my arms. And I couldn't let go of her. After twenty minutes, the nurses had to pry her out of my arms. The feeling of holding that body and being afraid to let it go was awful, Simon, and what made it so awful was how *familiar* it was. So I did something I knew would make it impossible for me to be with you. The night your brother came to visit, I fucked him. While you were asleep."

Simon shook his head and opened his mouth, but no words came out.

"I knew what I was doing," I said. "I knew what your brother meant to you. And when it was over, as hateful as I felt, I had what I needed to leave you. I had something that would make a lie of everything we did if we stayed together."

I made a sound—one of those sad, not-a-laugh laughs—and wiped my nose.

"Leaving you wasn't easy, Simon. It was really fucking hard."

I heard in that statement an authority I'd lacked just moments before. *Leaving you wasn't easy.*

I'd paid my last debt to the past tense. I'd finished the work of leaving Simon.

Simon looked at me as if I were a stranger. I guess he was seeing the whole of me as I was. Without another word—his stutter may have made it impossible for him to say anything—Simon walked away. He didn't look back. I watched him out of the corner of my eye to be sure.

When he disappeared around a corner, I took off my sunglasses and dabbed my eyes with a tissue. Then I returned the mirrored lenses to my face and hurried to the subway with my head down, hoping to escape the notice of everyone around me. By the time the train made its first stop in Brooklyn, I was okay—better than okay, even.

I was finally free of Simon Davies.

13

Simon

I SPENT $150 of my own money—half of what I'd earned in New York—to move up my return flight to the first one out of LaGuardia on Sunday morning, the day after I saw Brittany. I was on the ground at O'Hare at 8 a.m. and in my apartment on Bartlett Street before nine.

I opened the door to three days of trapped August heat. The smell of the apartment recalled my least favorite duty as a busboy: running food waste out to a full dumpster on a humid day. The heat and the smell and three days away opened my eyes to the way I'd been living. The place was a mess. There were two open garbage bags near the back door, dishes unevenly stacked in a sink holding inches of fetid water, three plates smeared with ketchup on the table next to the couch. I took out the trash, washed the dishes, and scrubbed the kitchen sink, bathtub and toilet. Then I threw open a couple of windows, imagining that, on a Sunday morning, a Lake Michigan breeze might not carry a cloud of diesel exhaust into the living room.

The chemical lemon scents and the sight of dirty water swirling down drains gave me energy and motivation to keep cleaning—I'd surveyed the dust and grit on my floors and the funky-smelling pile of bedding on my mattress—but I was out of time. The plan I'd made required that I be early.

I took a quick shower and dressed in my least wrinkled pants and a white, button-down shirt that smelled clean, at least. I hung my blue blazer on the knob of the front door. Then I found my lector's workbook buried under unopened mail on my desk. With the windows open and the ancient air conditioner humming ineffectually in my bedroom, I sat on the couch to prepare the day's readings. I was going back to St. Asella's, if anyone there would have me.

• • •

I'D EXPERIENCED NEITHER spiritual awakening nor any burgeoning of my little faith. My decision to return to St. Asella's was an extension of the lesson that had saved my voiceover career from expiring before it began.

I'd been drowning in the quicksand of my stutter when Lily Eisenberg, the director of the New York Red Bulls session, called me out of the sound booth to tell me that the character in her script was Lily herself. I'd listened to Lily's client rave on about her sister's success with the New York Yankees, so I understood why this spot was important to her. Instead of dismissing Lily's compulsion to chase her more obviously talented sibling as having nothing to do with me and Connor, I found a way to accept that the brokenness in Lily was the brokenness in me, and I professed our likeness in the voice of a character that became as much my creation as hers. What saved me that day was my willingness to see my own brokenness in Lily and her character. Arrogant as he was, Connor had always possessed this humility before his characters. Living in constant fear of banishment to a life on the margins, I had never felt secure enough—before a character or anyone else—to embrace my frailty.

Until Lily.

After the session, I was already out on the sidewalk, heading for Washington Street, when Lily opened the front door of Steel Cut Studios and called my name.

When I turned, she ran toward me.

"What's wrong?" I shouted.

I thought there might've been some technical glitch. I certainly could have done another good take, knowing what I knew then.

But Lily didn't answer. No, she kept running until she'd nearly knocked me over with a hug that pressed the air out of my lungs.

● ● ●

IT WAS LATE on Saturday, the same day I met with Brittany, before I made any connection between the characters in Lily's script and the people of St. Asella's. I was back in my Manhattan hotel room, lying on the bed's slippery comforter. With the tall drapes drawn against the sunshine of a world in which my mother was gone and everything between Connor and me had been ruined by our betrayals of one another, I wallowed in silent repetition of the self-pitying question dredged up in the tumult of Brittany's making her final break with me: *where, if anywhere, do I belong?*

Not in New York. That much was obvious. And a review of my life in Chicago confirmed that I felt unwelcome in almost every place I'd been: at Skyline Talent, because of what I'd done to Erika and my fear that my stutter would be discovered; at Improviso, because it was Connor's stage and because, without any knowledge of the act I could have been avenging, I'd tried to kiss his girlfriend there; at St. Asella's, on account of the churlish, childish rant I'd directed at Catherine when she tried to lump me in with the parish's misfits.

It was my mental articulation of the word "misfits" that drew the through line from voiceover to my disregard for the people of St. Asella's. Though still mourning my mother, I'd failed to see my own grief in Jeanne's. I'd ignored the reality that I was *already* as lonely and desperate as the old man who waited patiently after mass, with hat in hand, for a brief exchange of small talk with Catherine. And by telling myself that lectoring was nothing more than a way to prepare for the voiceover work I hoped would come, I'd glossed over the fact that, like so many St. Asella's parishioners, I showed up at St. Asella's on Sunday mornings because I had nowhere else to go. I hadn't treated the people of St. Asella's with the same respect I'd paid to the human being in Lily's script: I'd refused to admit that what was broken in them was broken in me.

I, too, was a misfit.

Who else but a misfit must ask himself, again and again, where he belongs?

And like me, weren't the people of St. Asella's more than their brokenness? Didn't they have something to offer? Those who couldn't sing or play the organ or mend the altar cloth offered their presence and their prayers, contributions made precious by the scarcity from which they came. Meanwhile, I had cheapened my own offering of talent by with-holding everything else. Determined to stand apart from the misfits of St. Asella's, I'd hidden everything but my voice from them.

Only then did I see that my oddness offered a chance at belonging.

In the stillness of my drape-darkened hotel room, I decided to step out from behind the same self-protecting pride that had prevented me from bringing characters to life on my own, in the hopes of making some human connection in the last place I'd thought to try.

● ● ●

I WAS SITTING on my couch, shrouded in the still stifling heat of my apartment the Sunday morning I returned from New York, when I realized that the two scripture passages I was rehearsing, one from the Book of Isaiah and another from Paul's letter to the Colossians, shared a common theme: forgiveness. In the very next moment, my hurt feel-ings rose like a gag, and I flung the workbook into the partially drawn blinds over my front windows. The rush I felt as the book's binding cracked the aluminum blades out of shape and thudded against the window dissipated as the flapping, fluttering mess of cheap paper fell to the floor.

I sat on the couch for several minutes, contemplating in the Sun-day-morning city silence how empty my day would be if I gave up the plan I'd made and stayed home, instead. Then I stood up, stooped to pick up the workbook, and resumed my rehearsal. I wasn't ready to forgive Brittany, Connor, or my father. But I wanted to be the person who found the human element in those messages of forgiveness and read them aloud, with precision and rhythm, to the people of St. Asella's.

Of course, the odds that I would get that opportunity were very poor. It had been weeks since I called Helen to renege on my lectoring commitment. Even with a volunteer base as thin as that of St. Asella's, surely she'd found and trained someone to serve in my place by now. My preparation of the readings was, at a minimum, an act of good faith. It was part of my plan to find Helen before mass and ask her to reinstate me as a lector, if only one who filled in occasionally. On the off chance she needed me to read that afternoon, I wanted to be ready.

Should my service as a lector not be required, my plan called for me to take a place in a pew toward the back and attend mass as any other parishioner or visitor would. Even this contingency was fraught, however. Repeatedly, I imagined Catherine noticing me on her walk from the sacristy to the back of the church before mass and asking me, quietly but firmly, to leave. My decision to open myself to the people of St. Asella's guaranteed nothing. They'd have to open themselves to me, too, and I had already given their leader several good reasons to close the oaken doors in my face.

I entered St. Asella's forty-five minutes before mass was scheduled to begin. Just as I'd hoped, Helen was the only one there. I walked up a side aisle—taking the center aisle felt presumptuous—watching Helen light candles in tall stands on either side of the altar while the cool air of the empty church whirred in my ears. As I neared the sanctuary, I noticed that Helen, whom I'd never seen in anything other than dowdy blouses and blue jeans, was wearing a red skirt that revealed a few inches of white pantyhose above brown, slip-on flats. Her blue and maroon paisley blazer, at least a size too small, had enough padding in the shoulders to adequately protect a football player. Coming around the first row, I got a look at her face. She'd applied something dark around her eyes—eyeliner or eye shadow, maybe both—and her thin lips were flattered by a tasteful application of carmine lipstick.

Standing at the edge of the sanctuary, I took two waggles and said, "Excuse me, Helen?"

When she recognized me, Helen frowned. "What can I do for you?"

She spoke at a volume she might have used if she'd seen me half a block away. I recalled this same tendency in the corps of women who'd volunteered in my boyhood parish. They were no more capable of reverence in the empty sanctuary than they were in their own living rooms. Whispers and reverence were for those of us who hadn't sewn the vestments, cleaned the tabernacle, vacuumed the sanctuary carpet and polished the wood of the altar.

I stepped into the sanctuary to close the distance between us and take away at least one reason for Helen to raise her voice. "I'm glad I caught you," I said. "I wanted to let you know that I'm available to lector again. Whenever you might need me."

Helen drew a lick of flame inside the mouth of the brass lighter she was holding and returned a thin, smoking taper in its place. She turned to face me but did not descend even one step from the literal high ground of the altar.

"Let me ask you something," she said. "Was there really a family illness?"

I was about to tell Helen that I didn't understand her question when I recalled that "family illness" was the pretext I'd used to get out of my lectoring commitment.

I took another waggle and said, "Not really. No."

Helen smirked and shook her head. Her disdain was intended for me, but it also seemed to contain her assessment of a working life that required repeated dealings with lying, excuse-peddling adults.

"That's what I thought," she said.

I took this to be Helen's ruling against my petition to be reinstated as a lector. I was turning around, deliberating whether to find a seat in the back or head straight for the door, when Helen spoke up again.

"You left me in a real lurch. I spent the better part of two weeks trying to find someone in this parish willing and able to lector. But the only reader I've got right now called me ten minutes ago with a vicious summer cold."

With her painted lips sucked into the hollow of her open mouth, Helen looked to the back doors and shook her head again. Then she sighed without relaxing a muscle.

"I've got *nobody*," she said. "Except you."

I lowered my eyes and nodded to show that I understood the circumstances under which I was being taken back. "I rehearsed," I said, "so I'm ready."

"I know you are," Helen said, as if my readiness made having to take me back more irritating. She turned and stepped down carefully from the altar's riser in the direction of the open sacristy door. Still facing away from me, she shouted, "The big book is in the lectern."

I crossed the sanctuary in front of the altar and retrieved the gospel book from the lectern's single interior shelf. As I walked down the side aisle to the back of the empty church, I experienced some of the clarity of thought that accompanies a sense of purpose—I had a job to do now, and I knew how to do it—but I was under no illusion that doing two readings in front of this congregation would make me a part of it. If anything, Helen's resentment made me feel even more unwelcome.

I'd been standing alongside the church doors for only a moment when the six middle-aged Filipina ladies entered. Even for women so devout, they were arriving very early. Like Helen, the ladies were dressed more formally than usual. The shortest of them, who was also the most beautiful, wore a colorful silk blouse, its band collar closed at the neck with a wide, padded button. The angled platforms of her high-heeled shoes gave her another two inches in height, and a subtle shade of red marked the location of high cheekbones all but buried in her round, pleasant face.

The ladies were still making their way to the first pews on the church's right side when an old man—the same one I'd seen talking to Catherine after mass, I thought—walked through the door and removed his hat. He wore a brown suit with wide, notched lapels. The pink and orange diagonal stripes of his tie, which was wide like his lapels, were discolored below the knot by a dark blotch—coffee or soup spilled long ago, I guessed. As the man passed me on his way to the near side aisle, my nose detected camphor and body odor. I fought off my revulsion with a reminder that my loneliness and awkwardness were not so different from the old man's. As he shuffled up the aisle, I forced myself to see my brokenness in his.

The early arrivals continued at a slow trickle, but almost without interruption. Everyone was dressed, stains and dated fashions notwithstanding, in his or her Sunday best. I wondered if this was the feast day of a minor saint important here and nowhere else—perhaps St. Asella herself—or the anniversary of Fr. Dunne's ordination. Or perhaps Fr.

Dunne had dedicated a recent homily to that old summer stand-by of the priest who is out of ideas: chiding churchgoers for their inappropriately casual warm-weather clothing. All I knew for sure was that something had changed. Given how static and stale St. Asella's and its people had seemed to me, any change at all was unsettling.

By twenty minutes to twelve, the church was already half full—as full as I'd ever seen it—and people were still coming through the main doors. But none of them was the person I wanted to see most: Mrs. Landry. There was little for us to say to each other, but I wanted Mrs. Landry to witness that I'd returned, as she'd asked me to, and that I was finally able to accept some of the fellowship she'd offered me when I walked her home. I worried that, in the nearly four weeks since last I'd seen her, Mrs. Landry or her husband had suffered some grave illness or serious fall. Even standing on the outside of it, I understood that the St. Asella's community would be greatly diminished without her. Her tenacious grace seemed irreplaceable.

Ten minutes later, Catherine appeared at the front of the church. She wore a gray dress with a belt that accentuated her hourglass figure, and a stylish necklace of amber pieces strung in a cascade. As she passed through the sanctuary, I waggled twice and waited for her to start down the usual route of her Sunday-morning parade of mutual appreciation. But the appreciation never materialized. Though crowding in the front pews had pushed people to the very edge of the side aisle, only one woman reached out to grasp Catherine's hand. Catherine took the hand for a second and released it without slowing her progress toward the back of the church.

There was a dignified reserve in Catherine's perfect posture and the stillness of her head. She looked older than I remembered. The word "handsome" came to mind. I wondered if what I perceived to be changes in Catherine were actually changes in me.

When she turned the corner around the last pew, Catherine's closed lips spread into a smile. She seemed entirely unsurprised to see me.

"Hello, Simon," she said.

"Good morning."

We stood there with our backs to the wall, saying nothing. It was not an awkward silence so much as an ordinary one, as if I had not been absent from St. Asella's for weeks, as if our last conversation had been all politeness and pleasantries, as if dozens of people were not still streaming through the church doors and packing into pews, dressed for a wedding or a funeral.

After almost a minute, I waggled, turned to Catherine, and asked, "What's going on here today?"

She studied my face for a moment. "Didn't Mrs. Landry tell you?"

"I haven't seen her yet."

My answer seemed to confuse Catherine, but she didn't voice her confusion. "The Archdiocese is sending a representative today," she said. "Monsignor someone-or-other."

"Why?"

Catherine shook her head and raised her eyes to the distant ceiling. She was smiling, but seemed mildly put out.

"Sorry," I said. "Too many questions."

"No, no," she said, "it isn't you. It's this place. No one tells anyone anything." She turned to me. "St. Asella's is closing. The Archdiocese is shutting it down."

"Wait, what?"

"A diocesan official is visiting every parish on the closings list to explain the decision," she said. "The people of the parish are taking this mass as their chance to show the Cardinal that St. Asella's should be kept open."

"That's why it's so crowded."

"Yes."

"How did you do it?" I asked Catherine.

"Do what?"

"How did you get all these people here?"

"I didn't," Catherine said. "Mrs. Landry did. *She* called *me.*"

I felt stung that neither Mrs. Landry, nor anyone else, had called me. Then I remembered that, as we stood in front of her condo building, Mrs. Landry had personally invited me to return to St. Asella's, and I'd turned her down.

"So, Mrs. Landry knew the monsignor was coming before you did?"

I looked to the church doors again, expecting to see the four-footed platform of Mrs. Landry's cane crossing the threshold, but saw no sign of her.

Where is she?

Keeping her eyes forward, Catherine reassumed the reserve she'd displayed coming down the side aisle. "I haven't been coming to mass," she said. "I wouldn't have known about any of this if Mrs. Landry hadn't told me."

"Why haven't you been coming to mass?"

"It just isn't for me."

Her sharp tone made it clear that I shouldn't press the issue any further. Of the many changes I encountered at St. Asella's that day, this was the most disorienting: Catherine and I were *both* standing outside the community that she had given so much of herself to create, and I was the only one of us who wanted in.

Two altar boys in yellowed, ill-fitting albs hurried down the near side aisle with their heads down and their hair in their eyes. As they slipped past people scanning hopelessly for an open seat in the pews, the boys looked embarrassed, as if they were wearing Halloween costumes their mothers had chosen for them. When they reached the back of the church, the altar boys leaned against the wall alongside a wooden box labeled "Offerings for the Poor" and tried to disappear.

Fr. Dunne stepped into the sanctuary and turned back to the sacristy door to watch the aged monsignor follow him out. The monsignor was dressed just like Fr. Dunne except for a black cassock, the hem of which was visible beneath his green vestments. Slowing his usual frenetic pace to match that of the older man, Fr. Dunne led his distinguished concelebrant to the side aisle. The monsignor smiled and drew small, tasteful crosses in the air with his hand as he passed people seated in the pews. The action looked less like a blessing than it did the glad-handing of a politician.

"Do you think any of this will keep them from closing the place?" I asked Catherine.

"No," she said.

As gently as I could, I asked, "Then why did you come back?"

"Because Mrs. Landry asked me to, I guess. It was one last thing I could do." Then she looked at me. "Why did *you* come?"

I took a waggle without hiding it. "I didn't do things right the first time. I'm trying again."

Catherine nodded and, in her kindness, she didn't say what we both understood: that my first chance with the people of St. Asella's would be my only chance. We were witnessing the last, heaving gasp of a community that would not survive the closing of its parish. Those with cars, bus passes, or the time, energy and ability to walk a few extra blocks would find another parish. But their misfitting would follow these people wherever they went, and few would warm to their brokenness. They'd be outsiders in their adopted parishes, even more so than at St. Asella's. I wondered how many of them would lose forever the meager human connections they'd found at church.

As Fr. Dunne and the monsignor reached the back pew, the altar boys reluctantly took their position in the center aisle at the head of the still unformed procession.

"Well," Catherine said over a sigh, "here we go."

She moved toward the center aisle, giving the two priests a wide berth as they made their approach. I was supposed to be standing right in front of Catherine, and I knew it, but did not step forward. This mass was a death knell for St. Asella's, and the best I could do, as an outsider, was delay its tolling.

A bass note from the organ rumbled in my chest. A piercing treble chord followed. The congregation came to its feet. The altar boys started up the aisle. Even as Catherine, then Fr. Dunne, and then the monsignor turned to ask with their eyes what the hell I thought I was doing, I stayed on the wall, staring into the crowd of heads bowed over hymnals.

I'd stalled for only a few uncomfortable moments when the soft, cool skin of an open hand slid into my sweaty palm. Mrs. Landry was standing just inside the church doors, her smiling face raised with great effort on the end of her curved spine. Her husband stood behind her, shifting his weight from one foot to the other. And as she squeezed the meat of my hand with her arthritic fingers, accepting me into a community that was hers as much as anyone's, I mourned the passing of St. Asella's and marveled again at Mrs. Landry, who was broken in so many ways she did not try to hide yet utterly undefeated by her brokenness.

14

Larry Sellers

I'M ALONE, READING a magazine article in the waiting room of Don Biel's studio, when I feel a tickle high in my chest. I can't go into the session with a tickle. That's asking for trouble. I try to cough it away gently, but the dainty throat-clearing just makes the tickle worse, so I take a deep, crackling breath and cough hard, sending a wad of wet-cement phlegm into my mouth. That puts an end to the tickle, but the cough doesn't stop. Spasms sputter against my pursed lips, making it almost impossible to get air.

I barrel into the too-small bathroom, close the door, and spit the yellow mess—Sinatra would have called it "a clam"—into the rust-stained porcelain sink. Then I force in a breath and let loose with a coughing fit that sounds more like retching. As my gut clenches and my eyes water behind my bifocals, I worry that the ad people and their clients have come out of the elevator and are standing in front of the studio's unoccupied reception desk, alarmed and disgusted by the noises coming from the bathroom.

When the coughing is over, I stand with my hands on either side of the sink, drawing shallow breaths. I look in the mirror for specific things: globs in my goatee, sweat on my brow, any sign of blood in my nostrils. This is no time for how-did-it-come-to-this soul searching. I have work to do. And thank God for that.

I remove my glasses and rinse my face with a handful of cold water. I take a few paper towels from a stack on the toilet tank and press them to my forehead, cheeks and mouth. Then I return the nose pads of my glasses to the red divots they've pressed into my skin and apply a snappy tug to the lapels of my mustard-colored sport coat. The coat is an old one. I haven't been able to button it in years. But it still fits in the shoulders. Checking it in the mirror for any mucus I might have missed, I recall what Elaine Vasner said about the jacket the first time I wore it out: "Nice coat, Larry. Does it come in catsup, too?"

I take one more deep breath through my nose, just to be sure the coughing won't start up again, and open the bathroom door, scaring the shit out of a skinny, straight-haired kid standing at the front desk. It's the noise of the bathroom door opening that scares him at first, but he seems to jump again when he sees me. I wipe my hand over my mouth to make doubly sure that no flotsam from my coughing fit is glistening around it.

The kid is dressed conservatively for an advertising type. Wearing a long-sleeve collared shirt and navy blue slacks, he looks more like a kid heading off to Catholic school. But what the hell do I know about how young ad people are dressing this month? Maybe the schoolboy look is in.

"Are you with Ogilvy & Mather?" I ask.

The kid shakes his head. "No."

"Oh. Then who are you with?"

The kid shakes his head back and forth, as if considering whether or not to tell me the truth. Then he says, "Skyline Talent."

My old agency.

Elaine's agency.

Immediately, I am sure I have fucked everything up—that I jotted down the wrong day or the wrong time or the wrong studio—and that sorting out the confusion will discredit me in front of Don Biel, my only remaining connection to good voiceover work. What terrifies me, though, is my irrational but unshakable certainty that Elaine Vasner has sent this kid to edge me out of the voiceover business, once and for all.

"My name is Simon Davies," the kid says.

I couldn't give two shits what his name is. "You're booked for a session?"

"Yes."

"For Sears."

"Yes."

"At eleven?"

The kid nods.

"You're sure."

"Pretty sure."

I stand there, nodding at him. Then I pick up the September 2010 issue of *Sound Mixing* magazine and reclaim my seat in the studio's waiting area without another word. I'm in no position to chase the grim reaper out of here, but I'll be damned before I show him in.

● ● ●

WHEN I TOLD Elaine I was leaving Skyline—leaving Chicago, leaving her—to work in Los Angeles, she sneered and said, "Good luck out there, Larry. You'll need it."

She was dead right about that, as it turned out. I didn't have much luck in Hollywood. Casting directors kept telling me I didn't have the right look, and would you believe that two guys—just two!—had all but cornered the market for male-voiced movie trailers? I tried so many different combinations of guttural tones and tempos to deliver the phrase "In a world . . . ." I never did find a combo that won me much work.

Once her anger at my leaving had blown over, Elaine and I started seeing each other socially again when I was in Chicago for the commercial sessions that kept me solvent. But the word "social" doesn't quite capture the nature of our relationship. It had the *look* of something social. We met for drinks, and the sex, when we had it, was dynamite. Elaine knew what she wanted in bed and made sure she got it. Then she would make it all about me, and, well, I've made love to women more beautiful than Elaine, but no woman has ever made love to me so well as Elaine did. All that said, I could have had (and did have) cocktails and sex with other women. The real pleasure of seeing Elaine had more to do with business than romance. We talked about things—the best microphones, the worst scripts, the feel of the words in the mouth, vocal warm-ups, the merits of a dry run, how to handle bad directors, ad-agency radio budgets, the going rate for residuals—that none of our other dates would have understood or cared about. By the time she was no longer my agent, though, Elaine didn't see our get-togethers as business meetings, and I knew it. But I didn't do a damn thing about it.

While I was still out in L.A., chasing work and women who weren't Elaine, she started seeing a wealthy guy. James, the Miller's Pub bartender who had mixed hundreds of cocktails for Elaine and me over the years, told me that this new guy—a lawyer, if I remember right—was crazy about her. I couldn't bring myself to stand in the way of Elaine's relationship, not when what I really wanted was work and, on the days I didn't have it, some shoptalk and a nightcap and maybe a roll in the hay. I thought Elaine might call to tell me she'd found somebody, or that she was marrying this guy, but she never did. I didn't call her, either. Without a word, we went from seeing each other a few times a month for twenty-three years to not speaking for ten. And counting.

Just a couple of months ago, though—around the Fourth of July—I was sitting at my kitchen table with a drink in one hand and a cigarette in the other, holding its smoky heat deep in my lungs and ignoring the droning of the TV in the other room, when the phone rang. I leaned over to see the caller ID and stared, like the confused old drunk I was getting to be, at blocky, digital letters that read, "SKYLINE TALENT."

I was unable to move until the ringing stopped. I checked ten times that night for a message, but nobody left one, and without a message, I couldn't even be sure it was Elaine who'd placed the call. So I poured another drink, and then another, telling myself that Elaine and I were still better off leaving not quite well enough alone.

● ● ●

SIMON DAVIES IS sitting with his hands in his lap. And that's all he's doing.

Read a magazine, kid. Act like this isn't your first session, for Christ's sake.

It occurs to me then that this may be his very first session, and the thought that I am losing my place in this business to a rookie gives me another reason to hate him. But the cold spite I harbor for Simon Davies is nothing compared to my fresh, throbbing regret that I ever left Elaine and her agency.

The day I moved back to Chicago after six years of scuffling in L.A. was my best chance to tell Elaine what a fool I had been and beg her to take me back at Skyline. But I didn't call Elaine. She was with the new guy by then, and we weren't talking. Besides, I had other ways of getting work.

I asked Don Biel, who'd produced the demo I sent to Elaine back in '77, to cut together a reel of my greatest hits. The title I gave it—"Larry Sellers: The Voice"— borrowed Sinatra's crown and put it on my over-sized head. I figured that Ol' Blue Eyes wouldn't mind Ol' Mustard Coat helping himself in a time of need. Once the big Chicago agencies heard the reel, work started pouring in again, and I did something Elaine would never have allowed me do: I took every job I could get.

Elaine had built my career by making my voice a premium product. She set a high price for my services and increased demand by limiting supply. In other words, she forced me to turn down work.

"I don't see why I shouldn't do this one," I'd say, referring to a job offer made by an agency perfectly willing to pay my exorbitant hourly rate plus Elaine's ten percent.

"You just did a national campaign for another one of their clients," Elaine would say. "They'll start to think of you as their house guy, and then they'll feel entitled to get you at a discount."

"But it's good work," I would protest. "I want to do it."

"Think Nancy Reagan, Larry. Just say no."

With no agent representing me, I fielded every job offer directly, and because I wanted to work more than I wanted to make top dollar, I said yes. To everything. If it got me in a studio with a chance to make copy walk and talk, I took it. For three years, I worked at least three days a week, doing commercials, industrials, educational narrations, even *pro bono* public service announcements. If I wasn't recording, I was resting my pipes for the next session. My packed schedule kept the screw top on the vodka bottle. In those three years, I came the closest I've ever come to being happy.

The problem was this: I had it wrong, and Elaine had it right. My rate, which used to be two times scale, plus ten percent, started coming down in late 2004. That didn't bother me at the time, as I had more than enough volume to make up for the pay cut, and the work meant more to me than the money, anyway. Then the work started drying up. It went down to two days a week. Then one day. Then three weeks without a phone call.

Then, in February 2005, I lost Jewel Foods, a gig that had been my bread and butter for twenty years.

Therese Riggins, the long-time director of the Jewel account over at DDB Needham and a smart, tough woman—like Elaine—leveled with me.

"You've saturated the market, Larry," she said. "Your voice can't mean Jewel Foods if it means every other brand, too."

I was silent, beginning the grueling task of accepting that I'd done this damage to myself. I'd worked my way out of work.

"Do you do any other voices?" Therese asked.

"No. I don't."

"Well," she said. "I don't know what else to say. You'll have to wait this out."

What I did instead of wait was quit the union. Once off the books with SAG/AFTRA, I could start taking the non-union voiceover work that paid like shit but was plentiful in Chicago. And when word got out I was available for non-union sessions, I feasted. The little agencies handling their tiny budgets loved the idea of getting Larry Sellers for their voice projects. But the sheen of my novelty dulled with the non-union crowd in less than a year. Even in the minds of these small-time ad guys, I wasn't the voice of Maalox or Hertz or even Jewel Foods anymore. I was the guy who did spots for strip clubs in the south suburbs and "Call now!" bumpers for ambulance-chasing lawyers. I was nothing special.

Only then did I seriously consider calling Elaine and asking for help. But I couldn't persuade myself it would do any good. I'd rotted out my career so completely that even Elaine Vasner, even if she were willing, could work no magic with it.

· · ·

THESE DAYS, BEGINNING my thirty-fourth year in what's supposed to be an older man's business, work is infrequent. I might have a session every couple of months for a six-month stretch, then wait another six months for the next one. And if the person hiring me isn't a burnt-out copywriter on a nostalgia trip, I know I have Don Biel to thank for the job. Don still engineers most of the sessions that take place in his little studio, which he built and wired with his own hands. If a young creative director mentions between takes that she's looking for talent she hasn't heard before, or says she's having a hard time finding the right male voice for a campaign, Don gives her my name and writes down the address of the website he had his son build for me. I assume that my getting this Sears job—the job I *believed* I was here to do before encountering this angel of death Simon Davies—was a result of Don's unpaid work on my behalf, which means that my fucking up the particulars of this session may do more than get me blacklisted at Ogilvy. It might make it impossible, even if he still wants to, for Don Biel to recommend me to any of the agencies that keep his studio lights on.

The thought of walking out of here without Don in my corner makes me sick to my stomach. I used to complain to Elaine that the long stretches without work—and by "long," I meant a few days—were killing me. It was whiny exaggeration then. Now, it's closer to the truth.

● ● ●

I GLANCE UP from a *Sound Mixing* how-to on equalizing the dynamics of spoken-word performances and catch Simon Davies watching me. I imagine he's wondering if he'll ever be as old and as fat as I am. What else could he be thinking? He still isn't *doing* anything. I don't like Simon Davies. Not a lick. And as I find myself with no agent and little else left to lose, I decide to go at him at a bit.

"Are you nervous?"

My delivery—knowing, with a hint of accusation—is exquisite, and the question cuts through the room's close, stuffy silence.

The kid squirms in his seat. "A little."

"You look nervous."

I let the statement hang there, and I hope the kid is wrestling with a deep-seated fear that he isn't cut out for this line of work. My heart races as I imagine a chain of events that begins with the kid standing up and walking out, leaving Don and the Ogilvy people with a studio booked and no talent to record. *The Voice to the rescue!*

"Actually," the kid says, "I'm worried there's been some mistake."

"What kind of mistake?"

He shrugs. "Like I got the time of my session wrong. Or the day, maybe."

More hope! It might be *the kid* who is mistaken, not me!

I lean forward in my chair and peer at him. "What ad agency booked you?"

"Ogilvy & Mather."

"And they said the Biel Studio?"

"That's what my agent told me."

I thwack the trade rag against my thigh and sit back. "What makes you think you've got any of that wrong?"

"Well," the kid says, and then he gestures to me with an open, upturned hand. "*You're* here."

"You think I'm here to do voiceover."

His face goes pale. "Aren't you?"

I laugh blackly and shake my head. "You don't get it, kid. I could be with Ogilvy. I might be an in-house marketing guy with Sears. I might be an accountant here to see the guy who owns the studio. I could be *anybody*. So don't assume that my reasons for being here are your reasons. Don't assume *anything*. How the fuck would *you* know," I say, raising the volume of my voice as I descend in its range, "why I'm here?"

The kid looks like he might cry, and I'm feeling pretty good about that, when he points his hand at me again.

"You're Larry Sellers."

I've had cab drivers and contractors, the kind of guys who spend all day listening to the radio, recognize my voice and call out a brand. To them, I'm "the Hertz guy" or "the Wendy's guy" or "the guy from the titty-bar commercial." But never in my career—not once—have I been recognized *by name* by a stranger. That Simon Davies knows my name warms my dread. Who else but Elaine could have told him about me? And why had she sent him here if not to finish off the career I've been poisoning since I left her?

I swallow hard without moving my head even a little. "How do you know who I am?"

"I know your voice," the kid says. "And your work. Wendy's. Jewel Foods."

"How do you know my *name*?"

"My mom gave me an article about you when I was a kid. I've been listening to you ever since." The kid smiles to himself as he lowers his gaze to the floor. "I used to wave at my mom to shush her when the Jewel commercials came on."

Before I realize I'm speaking aloud, I say, "I always enjoyed those spots."

"I could *hear* that you enjoyed them," Simon says, looking me squarely in the eye. "Those Jewel commercials are a voiceover artist making something out of nothing."

"Well," I say, "the scripts did have a natural rhythm to them."

Simon shakes his head. "Nobody but you would have found it. The rest of us would have been reading a grocery list."

There is silence then, and I cannot interrupt it. I have the feeling you get in dreams: that things can happen to you but you are powerless to make anything happen.

Staring at the hands in his lap, Simon says, "I was convinced I could hear it in your voice when you *weren't* enjoying yourself."

I understand him instantly. "Maalox."

Now, it's Simon's turn to be astounded.

"They were trying to scare people," I say. "Heartburn on your wedding day, acid stomach in your big meeting, all that shit. I only did those spots for the work. I've always been a Rolaids man, anyway."

Simon laughs at this, and I would swear that in his laugh I hear the kid he was when I recorded those spots, performances I've never had occasion to discuss with anyone but Elaine.

It occurs to me that *this* is the camaraderie I long for when I am not working, the same easy harmony I had in mind when I'd ask Elaine to meet me for drinks: a give-and-take between people who appreciate the business of voiceover for the art it can be. The only better company is the kind that can only be found in the sound booth, when I give over my voice to the character I create. But there's no telling when I'll get to share in that company again. Simon is the one who is supposed to be at this session—not me. And unlike Simon, I no longer have Elaine's help in getting work.

"Do you work with Elaine Vasner directly?"

Simon nods.

"How is she?"

"I don't really know. I've only met her once. And when she calls, we only talk business."

That last word hurts in a way that makes me smile.

"Well," I say, sitting back in my chair, "you're lucky to have her. She's the very best there is."

I have said all I can bear to say on the subject of Elaine. My eyes drop to the magazine I am still holding open in my hand.

"She has a picture of the two of you," Simon says.

"She does?"

"In her office. It's mostly hidden by a plant, but it's there."

Simon's intention in bringing up this photo is clear: he is trying to be kind. And I experience his kindness as if it were a gulp of warm tea settling into my empty stomach.

Don Biel enters the waiting area, which means the session is about to begin. I haven't identified the misunderstandings that brought Simon Davies and me here to do the same job, but I'm done investigating. I know what I need to know. Simon Davies is no grim reaper, no angel of death sent to dispatch me from my professional life. He is here for the same reason I am: to work. And as I push myself to my feet to greet Don, I decide that if anyone is to take my place, it might as well be Simon Davies.

Don heads straight for me and puts his hand out. "How are you, Larry?"

"I'm fine, Don. Thanks. How's business?"

Don spreads his feet wide on carpet he installed on his hands and knees. "Okay," he says. "Not like it was, but we're not in trouble, either. How about on your end?"

"Slower than I'd like."

"Anything short of four sessions a day is slower than you'd like, Larry."

"You're right about that."

My antennae are up for any indication that Don is angry with me or pitying me—any sign at all that he believes I've missed a session he worked one of his own clients to get me—but I pick up nothing negative from him. Don, as usual, is all business, and nothing could be a greater comfort to me.

Don turns to Simon, who is standing directly in front of his seat.

"Simon?"

"Yes."

"Don Biel. Welcome to the Biel Studio."

"Same to you," Simon says, shaking Don's hand. "I mean, thanks."

The three of us stand in uneasy silence for a moment. To help us out of it, I turn to Don and say, "I assume you're here for Simon."

"I'm here for both of you, actually."

I narrow my eyes and shake my head, buying time for comprehension that doesn't come.

"The script calls for two voices," Don says. "The agency is recording you together to cut costs."

"The two of us in the booth?" I ask. "At the same time?"

"That's the idea."

Two microphones. Two voiceover artists. Two characters. A collaboration between a young up-and-comer and a gifted professional in the autumn of his years. The spot is a *duet*—just like Sinatra used to do.

As my fears of being finished in voiceover recede, if only for the moment, I see an opportunity: Simon and I will meet on days we have no work. We will eat up the hours talking character and craft and telling stories about the business. And maybe, just maybe, Simon will lead me back to Elaine, and she will take back the only part of me still worth having.

15

Simon

ON SEPTEMBER 27th, a Monday, my phone rang, crawling with each vibration toward the edge of an oily white tabletop at the hole-in-the-wall Italian sandwich shop on the same block as my apartment.

With a mouth chock-full of beef and gravy-soaked bread, Larry Sellers mumbled, "Is it work?"

I nodded, trying to chew, swallow and waggle at the same time.

"Elaine?"

I nodded again.

Larry sent the sodden food mass down his gullet. "Pick it up."

Holding the slender, gray clamshell in my hand, I glanced at Larry. "Should I—"

"Don't mention me. Answer it, for Christ's sake!"

Elaine informed me that I'd booked my first TV voiceover job, a thirty-second spot commissioned by a Chicago restaurateur who was opening a second location of his storied steakhouse in a new Peoria casino. Larry pulled a pen out of his shirt pocket and handed it to me. I scribbled the session details on a napkin.

When I hung up, Larry clapped his hands together.

"Ha-*ha!*" he said, as if he'd discovered something. Lowering his face to the sandwich, he said, "You're on your way, kid."

● ● ●

THE STEAKHOUSE PROPRIETOR attended the recording session, and he didn't spend it making phone calls or checking e-mail. He stood behind the soundboard in a short-sleeved silk shirt that hung over his enormous gut, listening to every take, and once he had figured out where the mic button was, he bypassed his helpless marketing guy and made his comments directly to me.

"A little slow," he said after an early take. He rolled his index finger in a tight circle, jangling the two gold chains on his wrist. "Pick up the pace a bit."

A few takes later, when I had the pacing down, he said, "That one's about a seven. We need a perfect ten."

I didn't even hear the next take. I was imagining the cathartic release of telling this guy to stick to a business he understood and leave the voiceover to me.

"That was another seven." The restaurateur pointed at his marketing guy. "Phil could give me a seven."

I glanced at Phil, looking for help or commiseration, but the beaten down copywriter, whose name was atop the script spread across my stand, had neither for me.

I did another take.

"Three sevens," the restaurant owner said. "Good if we're at the casino. Not so good here."

I laughed joylessly.

"You don't sound like you mean it, kid," he said. "I want to hear the steaks crackling in the pan."

Then get some goddamn sound effects, I thought.

"I want to see the meat on the plate."

People will see the meat. It's goddamn television.

He pulled his finger off of the mic button and barked something at Phil, who cowered under the much bigger man's scowl.

I wanted to make a show of slowly removing the headphones, dropping them on the floor, and walking out. But I made myself stay and somehow managed, through the fog of my superiority and my sourness, to recognize that what the restaurateur was asking for—spoken words that ignited all the senses—was precisely what I should have been demanding of my performance. Wasn't I just as critical of spots I heard on the radio? Didn't I want the same perfection the restaurateur wanted? Couldn't I see at least this much of myself in the steak man's beady eyes?

Why must even the most valuable lessons be learned over and over again?

I funneled the steak man's commitment, pride and attention to detail—everything but his Chicago accent—into my delivery. This version of the restaurateur—the man's vision of himself—was the character in this script. Who else would he have allowed poor Phil to write? Three takes later, the steakhouse king was standing with his arms folded across the topside of his belly, smiling broadly and savoring the perfect ten he'd been waiting to hear.

Back in the control room, I wished him luck with the restaurant and mentioned, for something to say, that I had grown up about ten miles from the site of the new casino. Shaking my right hand, the steak man put his left on my shoulder and invited me to come in for dinner—"On the house," he said—once the place had opened. He told Phil to take down my name and number.

"You still got any family down there?" the steak man asked.

My first thought was that I didn't, but I did. "My dad lives down there."

"Bring him in," he said, massaging the muscle at the base of my neck with his meat hook of a hand. "We'll give you guys the VIP treatment. And I'll come by the table and tell your old man he's eating free on account of your pipes." The steak man let out a wheezy laugh. "What father wouldn't be pleased as piss with that?"

● ● ●

TWO MONTHS LATER, when a call came in on a Monday night from the area code that covered Peoria and a hundred tiny towns downstate, I figured it was someone from the steakhouse following up on the boss's order to invite the kid from the commercial to come in for a meal.

I shuffled through excuses—the fact that I didn't have a car, a new job working nights, a recent commitment to veganism—as to why I could not accept the steak man's offer to host my father and me for dinner. Between the third ring and the fourth, I diagnosed my father with liver cancer.

That won't be a lie forever.

Then I flipped open the phone, said hello, and heard my father's voice.

"S— S— Simon?"

I needed three waggles to say, "Yeah."

"It— it— it's your dad."

A tobacco-smoke rasp eroded each syllable. He was shouting over a warbling din, and I could hear in his stutter that he'd been drinking for a while already.

"Yeah, Dad."

"I— I— I've been s— s— seeing your c— commercial on TV. S— saw it again t— tonight."

I had done only one television commercial. They must have been running the steakhouse spot around Peoria.

"Th— thought it was y— your brother at first. But he— he told me it was y— y— you."

Hearing my father stutter reminded me of the unrelenting threat that my own stutter posed to my livelihood and tapped a childish, unjust vein of my anger at the man: the stutter that dogged me was *his* fault.

My anger found its way out as annoyance. "You've got the television on pretty loud there, Dad."

"N— nothin' I— I— I can do about that."

"What do you mean?"

"People in here want to h— h— hear the g— g— game."

I had envisioned my father at home, sitting in his easy chair, with a few crumpled beer cans on the snack tray to his right. But I understood then that he was calling from the only other place I had known him to drink and watch sports. My father was at the Four Corners.

"I— I w— w— wanted to tell you," he said, "that w— when your comm— commercial comes on, I— I turn around and let the wh— wh— whole bar know that that's my s— s— son's v— voice. And I tell 'em wh— which son I mean."

The picture he painted was pathetic: a stuttering drunk shouting out to a barroom of indifferent patrons that the voice they were trying to ignore was his son's. None of them—except maybe the man who had mocked my stutter, and the guy who had tended bar that day, if they were still alive and drinking—could have understood why my father said what he said when that steakhouse commercial came on.

"Whoa, w— w— will you l— look at this!" my father yelled. "T— t— t— touchdown!"

I thought I heard someone else shout my father's name, and then a chorus of laughter. My father breathed a tired chuckle into the phone.

I imagined him sitting at the end of the bar, a fool and a mascot for men who weren't drinking alone, and the surly bartender opening and closing his empty hand in the direction of the phone, telling him to wrap up the call. At the thought of people laughing at my stuttering father in that bar, and his drunken attempt to laugh along with them, I felt my seven-year-old self flailing to prevent something that happened twenty years before.

"Dad," I said. "I need you to pay up and go home."

"W— w— what d— do you mean? It— it's only the f— f— first quarter."

"You can catch the rest of the game at home. Just get out of there."

"Y— you know, I— I— I was th— thinking it would be g— g— good if y— you came down."

"What?"

"F— f— for a v— visit."

"Jesus, Dad." I dropped my forehead into my fingers and started kneading it. "Fine. I'll come down. Will you pay up and go home now?"

"N— no need to p— p— pay up. I've got cr— cr— credit."

"Then just go, Dad. Please."

"All r— right. I— I— I'm going. S— s— see you, s— son."

I stayed on the line, as if I might be able to hear his boot heels hit the floor, his truck engine whine as he reversed out of his parking spot, and the front door of our house open and close again behind him. What I heard instead were the click and rustle of an old phone changing hands, and my father saying, "Here's your d— damn ph— ph— phone back."

Then there was the hollow—plastic crash of a receiver being smashed into its cradle. Then nothing. And despite my promise to come home and his promise to leave the bar right away, I could only believe that my father was still on his barstool, and that he would be there every night,

trying to right a twenty-year-old wrong no more within his power to rem-
edy than his stutter was.

● ● ●

THE TWO TAXIS outside the train station in Peoria that Saturday
night were station wagons. Adhesive decals had been sloppily applied
to their passenger doors, and cardboard-backed livery licenses were
wedged between dashboard and windshield. Two drivers, both older
men, wore heavy insulated coats and woolen caps to keep out the December cold as they stood between the vehicles, smoking and chatting
in low, familiar tones.

They noticed me at the same time. The thinner of the two, whose
skin hung from his face as if it were slowly melting in the heat of his
cigarette, exhaled two lungfuls of smoke and asked, "Can I help you?"

With my duffle bag in hand and my coat collar up against the whip-
ping wind, I asked him if he knew Leyton.

"Sure, I know it," the thin man said.

"How much to get there?"

"To the town square?"

"A few miles west of it."

"Twenty dollars."

"That sounds all right," I said.

The thin man turned to his buddy. "You take this one."

The heavier man nodded and flicked his cigarette to the opposite
curb. "I guess it's my turn."

He opened the glass hatch of his station wagon, and I threw my bag
inside. When he started up the engine, the radio came on, and I caught
part of a rant against President Obama's proposed budget before the
driver silenced the outrage with a quick spin of the volume knob and
made his engine our soundtrack.

We were out of Peoria and onto the county road in just a few minutes.
I stared out my window into the thick darkness. I'd become accustomed
to the orange-tinted haze that Chicago threw up against the night and

forgotten what real darkness looked like. In the damp chill of that night, the blackness weighed me down like a lead blanket.

As the taxi pulled into the sideyard, the headlights drew across my father's pickup, which was parked near the back door. Saliva thickened in my mouth and throat.

He's here.

I paid my fare and grabbed my bag. The taxi made a three-point turn on the weed-pocked lawn and accelerated in the direction of the county road.

The blue-gray light of a television flickered behind the drawn curtains in the living room. No other lights in the house were on. Right then, I regretted keeping my end of the bargain I'd made with my father the week before and found myself missing the Chicago apartment that had been, to that point, just a place to wait for work. I supposed that my missing it this way meant that my apartment had become a kind of home.

Even in the moonless darkness, I found my way to the track beaten and packed by years of daily walks—most of them my mother's—from the back door to the mailbox. The toe of my shoe clipped an empty aluminum can, and I envisioned my father finishing a beer in his truck and rebelling pointlessly against the no-littering rule of a woman who left him once by moving out and again by dying.

The door was unlocked. I pushed it open and stepped into the kitchen. With the lights off, it was the smells I noticed first. Some of them were odors of stagnation and rot not dissimilar to those in my own apartment when I returned from New York. But behind and beneath these were more subtle scents, a potpourri that could not be duplicated outside this house. The wood-paneled walls were still slowly releasing the pine cleanser they had absorbed during my mother's weekly cleanings. Petrochemicals leached out of the thick, waffled soles of my father's Caterpillar-issue steel-toe boots, which he shed at the back door each day after work. I even caught a hint of my mother's inexpensive, drug-store perfume, which Connor and I had bought her every year for Mother's Day and she'd dabbed on her neck and wrists on special occasions. When

I recognized the signature scent of a woman who'd been dead for years, I leapt to no conclusions about the supernatural or even the power of memory. I imagined my father, already drunk as he searched for socks to wear to the Four Corners, finding a bottle of my mother's perfume at the bottom of a drawer, holding it up in front of his eyes, and pinching the bulb of the atomizer to cover the stench he'd made and remind himself of all he has lost.

I was no taller and no heavier than I'd been when I left home two and a half years ago, but the kitchen and everything in it were smaller than I remembered. This place and its objects—the chairs at the table, the Formica table itself—loomed large in my recollection as the set for so many of the scenes that had defined my life.

And the man who'd played opposite me in those scenes was sitting in front of the television on the other side of the wall. I shoved my shaking hands into my pockets and took three slow waggles, trying to fortify my voice against the fear, nerves and bad memories that would beat down the gates before my stutter. Then I walked to the open doorway and leaned my head into the living room.

The person I found sitting in my father's chair was not my father. It was Connor.

We said nothing at first. I'd played out so many versions of our next meeting—another fistfight, a cold-shoulder shutout, everything but a tearful embrace—that I didn't know which version to enact when the moment came.

"What are you doing here?" Connor asked.

I needed a waggle. I took two. "Dad asked me to come down."

Connor nodded. Then he returned his attention to the old television set my father had bought when we were kids. "Me, too."

My first thought at hearing that my father had asked both of his sons to come home was that he must be sick, that the cancer I'd invented for him had found its mark.

"Do you think there's something wrong with him?" I asked.

Connor kept his eyes on a televised boxing match. "No more than usual."

"But he asked us both to come down here."

I was hard-pressed to recall another time my father had invited the two of us anywhere. He'd always wanted Connor to himself.

Connor's curiosity won his attention away from the TV. "When did he call you?"

"Monday night."

"Did you tell him you were coming?"

"Yeah," I said. "But I didn't tell him when until this morning. I left a message on the machine."

"He called me yesterday," Connor said. "Friday. I'm pretty sure he was calling from the bar. He asked me to come down to see him, and I told him I'd be there the next day. But when I showed up this afternoon, he was wasn't expecting me at all."

Connor let his eyes drift back to the boxing match.

"There's no master plan here," he said. "Just a lonely drunk making phone calls and forgetting them."

"Where is he?" I asked.

"You get one guess."

"The bar."

"Bingo."

I waggled again. "But the truck is here."

Annoyed at having to clear up more of my confusion, Connor adjusted his position in the soiled nest of upholstered foam.

"He disappeared into his room around five," Connor said, "and he came out with his hair slicked back and announced we were going down to the Four Corners. He doesn't have any food in this place, so I figured I might as well go. We sat at the bar for a while. I ate a couple of cheese sandwiches and had a few bourbons, and we watched the start of a football game. After a couple of hours of overhearing the assholes at the other end of the bar give each other advice about how to get out of paying child support, I was ready to leave. I paid our tab, but when I stood up to go, he told me he was staying. He asked me to stay, too, but I don't think he really wanted me to."

Connor let this statement sit for a moment, as if he was still trying to get his head around the idea that our father would rather drink alone at the bar than at home with the son who had traveled 175 miles to see him. My most recent phone conversation with my father had given me a way to understand that choice. He was splitting the evening. He had spent the first part of it with Connor. Now that he was good and drunk, he'd spend the rest of it with the malignant memory of the last time he was at the Four Corners with me.

"Anyway," Connor continued, "there was no fucking way I was spending all night in that bar, watching him get shitfaced. I told him I'd take the truck home and swing by to pick him up a little before closing time."

He drew a short, horizontal arc in the air with his finger, inviting me to look around the dark living room.

"So here I am," he said. "Waiting."

With our immediate questions answered, the conversation petered out, and in the silence that followed, Connor and I resumed our long, cold war. I went to the back door for my duffel bag and carried it through the living room without even glancing in his direction. We were on our own again.

The door to my old bedroom was closed, just as it always had been when I was home. I'd been so insistent that people knock on this door before entering that I very nearly rapped the particleboard myself before twisting the brass-yellow plastic handle.

I dropped my bag inside the door and flipped the light switch. One of the bulbs in the frosted-glass fixture on the ceiling still worked. The doorless closet on the far wall was empty but for a few hangers on the untreated wooden rod. The mattress and box spring were stripped of sheets and blankets. The drawers of my dresser were closed. I opened one of them, and then another. They were empty, too. Except for a thick, even layer of dust on the surfaces, everything was exactly as I had left it the day I moved out. It seemed that my father hadn't opened my bedroom door since I closed it almost three years before.

I walked around to the other side of my bed and picked up the radio that had been my only portal to the world of beautiful voices. To commemorate my move to Carbondale, I'd purchased a new, digital clock radio—the same radio now atop my bedside table in Chicago. I had taken some pride in leaving behind the talisman I'd clutched in my speechless isolation. But as I held the plastic box of wires and circuits for the first time since leaving home without it, I realized that its significance to me had changed entirely. This radio was no longer my only way in to a big city of recording studios I would never see. I was *living* in Radioland, and *my voice* was being heard on radios like this one. I was no longer on the outside, listening in, but on the inside, speaking out.

But I was not speaking out in the sense of saying something brave or important—not on the radio and not in life. Not often enough, anyway. Just minutes before, with Connor, I'd allowed myself to fall silent while a moment of truth passed into oblivion. Even standing in the house in which I'd reclaimed it, I had been unwilling to use my voice to upend the unlivable status quo of things between my brother and me.

With my old radio in my hands, I could see that my relationship with Connor awaited a transfiguration that only my voice could provide. I'd have to forgive my brother for Brittany. I'd have to say so—and mean it.

I understood, too, that I should be the first of us to forgive the other. It was my father, with his pride in the face of my silence, who'd taught his sons not to apologize. But it was I, with my refusal to pardon my father, who had taught Connor not to forgive. And the first step in my forgiving Connor wasn't an apology from him, but an apology from me.

Forehead sweating, I walked back into the living room and stood within Connor's line of sight to the television. He didn't look at me. With the side of his index finger across his upper lip and the rest of his hand forming a canopy over his mouth, he watched a prize fight that was clearly boring him.

"Connor," I said. "I want to say—"

What I would have given, in that moment, for a printed script. I had the voice I needed, but no fluency in the language of apology.

"—I'm very sorry for what happened at the comedy club."

No good. No responsibility.

"I mean," I said, waggling freely while my brother ignored me, "I'm sorry for what I did. To Erika. And to you."

Connor made no response.

"There's no excuse for it," I said.

And then I almost did something that would have turned my apology into an attack. I nearly said, *What I did is about the worst thing a guy can do to his brother.*

"I apologize," I said instead. "And if you give me the chance, I'll apologize to Erika. I want to, I mean. I owe her that."

Keeping his eyes on the television, Connor lifted his lips above his hand just long enough to say, "Forget it."

Forget it.

Forgetting was not forgiveness. Connor was doing what we'd always done: ignoring the wrong that one of us has done the other and moving on to do the next one. I couldn't blame him. I was the one who'd taught him not to forgive.

I rallied myself with the idea that Connor's failure to forgive me changed nothing, that what mattered more—what would change things—was my forgiving Connor.

I took two long, loose waggles. Then I said, "I saw Brittany."

Connor's didn't move a muscle, but his cheeks darkened to a red made violet in the blue light of the televised boxing ring.

I took another waggle. "She told me what happened."

I had used that phrase—"what happened"—on purpose, offering Connor the passivity and unaccountability I'd refused myself.

Connor picked up the remote from the snack tray to the right of my father's chair and turned off the television. The tube sizzled with static electricity and cast a dull gray light that faded slowly.

I didn't know if Connor was getting ready to say something, or if the act of turning off the television and plunging us into darkness was his answer. Then I heard the voice that sounded so much like mine but was not.

"Erika told me a hundred times that I should be the one to tell you," he said. "But I couldn't even *imagine* telling you."

Connor seemed confounded that his imagination, the source of his great virtuosity, could fail him. But I understood that Connor had been unable to envision a confession that didn't also require him to say he was sorry, and apologizing to me had proven impossible for him to imagine.

What astonished me is that Connor had found a way to tell Erika what he and Brittany had done. In his position, I'm not sure I ever would have.

"But now that you know," Connor continued, "and now that I know how you found out—"

He stopped there.

Then he said, "Erika was right."

I figured that this admission, permeated with audible regret, was as close as Connor would come to making an apology. And close was close enough.

I was still searching for the right words to use in accepting Connor's near apology when he said, "I'm sorry, Simon."

In a darkness that made a radio—no faces, just voices—of my father's living room, I could hear that Connor meant what he was saying.

I rushed through the three waggles I needed, conscious that each second I delayed increased my brother's uncertainty in unfamiliar territory.

"It's okay," I said.

But I immediately worried that "okay" didn't go far enough, so I uttered the foreign-feeling phrase: "I forgive you."

"Erika said you would." Two sharp exhalations—Connor's rueful laughing at himself—whistled in his nose. "She was right about that, too."

It was done. I'd apologized to Connor. He'd apologized to me. And I had forgiven him.

There was no sense that the earth had shifted on its axis. Even in an unlit room, in the house in which Connor and I had grown up, our exchange of apologies and my granting of forgiveness felt more transactional than transcendent. At best, it seemed that Connor and I had found a tool to use in the superficial upkeep of a relationship that remained in disrepair.

In the silence, I put unspoken words to my anxiety: *Why don't I feel any different?*

The image, when it came, seemed to deepen the room's darkness. Covering the ground around the crumbling foundation and rotting structure of my relationship with Connor, piled in waist-high mounds like discarded shingles, were the uncountable, still-unaccounted-for wrongs—punches and lies and public humiliations—we'd inflicted on one another over the years. Each of us had apologized, but only for the two most devastating injuries among so many sustained.

"What is it?" Connor asked.

I waggled. "There's so much more to apologize for."

Working backward chronologically, I picked the time I stood in a fieldhouse near Lake Michigan, with rain pouring down all around us, and discounted Connor's success in Chicago by reminding him that none of it had won him any work in New York. Having made one apology and accepted another, I could scarcely wait to apologize again.

I took a waggle and found I needed another one. Then another. Then another. An attempt to force out a word ended in a silent dry heave. I let my jaw hang loose and started a series of deep, slow rotations, waiting for any sign that my stutter was weakening, but its stranglehold only tightened.

"Look at me, Simon."

Through tears of strain, my eyes distinguished the outline of Connor's head and torso as he leaned forward in my father's recliner.

"We're even."

And with those two words, my brother gave me all the apology, forgiveness, and validation I'd ever wanted from him.

● ● ●

IT WAS A little before one in the morning when I steered my father's truck into Leyton's town square. The restaurant where I had worked as a busboy was closed for the night, its windows dark and the parking spaces in front of it empty. At the center of the square, a limestone obelisk, monument to the war dead who'd attended Leyton High, reflected feebly the light of a single flood lamp.

I parked across the street from a vacant storefront that had been a candy store when I was a kid and stepped out of the truck. The wind blew unbridled across the surrounding farmland. I hunched my shoulders up toward my ears.

I passed the unlit window displays of the stationery store and hardware store. The stationer's featured an array of hardback journals, scrapbooking kits, and letterpress greeting cards on a three-tiered landscape of red and green satin, each item carefully arranged on a dusting of artificial snow. The hardware-store owners had pinned their hopes for foot traffic on a narrow plot of matted artificial grass and the merchandise—two rakes, three spades, and a snow shovel—hanging from brackets on whitewashed pegboard.

Two trucks and a car were parked in front of the Four Corners. The hood of the nearer truck reflected the red light of the neon sign in one of the bar's high windows. My mind raced through fantasies I'd nursed since I was a kid—that I'd walk into the bar with the baseball bat we kept in our shed and club the man who had taunted my father and me; that I'd throw an angry cottonmouth into the man's lap as payback for his asking if I were part snake; that I'd stand between the tables and bar, staring in brave, stony silence at anyone who dared to speak to me until one or more of the patrons picked me up by the shirt collar and threw me into the street. Even as I neared thirty years of age, these unlived reprisals were still immediate enough to make me sweat. I took three waggles and reminded myself that things were different than they'd been when I was seven. Now, I could speak for myself.

I pulled open the door and walked in. A couple of guys sat near the back with their arms crossed on the table and their heads over their cocktail glasses. They couldn't have been the men my father and I had encountered the last time I was here. They looked closer to my age than my father's. A woman stared down into the fluorescent glow of the jukebox while a tall young man leaned unsteadily to whisper in her ear, repeatedly bumping the side of her head with the brim of his ball cap.

My father was sitting alone. Years of evenings spent hunched on a barstool seemed to have made him squat, and the hair at the back of his head was grayer and greasier than I remembered. So thick was the air of isolation around my father that I wondered if the bartender—another man I didn't recognize—was rewashing perfectly clean pint glasses at the far end of the bar to avoid standing anywhere near him.

I took a few steps toward the bar. I wanted to see my father's face. His lips were thin, and his mouth hung open as he stared up at the television. I watched his eyelids close slowly—I thought he might be falling asleep—but they opened up again at the same sluggish pace. The man I'd fought for years in silence had been worn down by time, liquor, and a loneliness that was, at least in part, of my making.

I pulled out the stool next to my father's and sat down, fixing my gaze on the TV. He turned his head to look at me and, from the corner of my eye, I watched him try to decide if I was real. Then my father returned his attention to the television and waited for me to tell him why I'd come here and what I wanted from him. But I didn't say anything. I kept my seat on the stool next to his, and we watched two football teams from universities out west play to an outcome that didn't matter to either of us. That we did these things at the Four Corners made them a reconciliation of the only kind my father and I could have achieved: the kind that didn't require either of us to say a word.

Acknowledgments

The Queensboro Realty Company did, in fact, pay for airtime on New York City's WEAF to advertise the Hawthorne Court development. Brief excerpts of the original radio broadcast appear in this book. Matthew Lasar's article, published at arstechnica.com in April 2010 under the title "AT&T's forgotten plot to hijack the US airwaves," and Elizabeth McLeod's piece, published in 1998 under the title "From Hawthorne to Hard-Sell," gave me valuable insight into the Hawthorne Court broadcast and its impact on radio.

Thomas H. White's scholarly paper, published in January 2000 and titled "'Battle of the Century:' The WJY Story," increased the breadth and depth of my understanding of Jack Dempsey's fight with Georges Carpentier. White's quotation of the broadcast's climactic call is paraphrased in this book. I also reviewed one of White's sources, an article titled "Voice-Broadcasting the Stirring Progress of 'The Battle of the Century,'" originally published in a June 1921 issue of a magazine called *The Wireless Age*. Both White's piece and the *Wireless Age* story have been republished at earlyradiohistory.us.

My appreciation for long-form improvisational comedy crystallized the night I saw T.J. Jagodowski and David Pasquesi invent credible (and hilarious) characters and scenes in front of an audience. Since that night, I have had the privilege and pleasure of taking in dozens of wildly funny characters and scenes created onstage by my brother, Pat Reidy, who made crucial contributions to the brief renderings of improvisation in this book, all of which were drafted and revised without a live audience. T.J., David, and Pat do instantly and in front of thousands what I can scarcely manage to achieve on the page with privacy and endless opportunities to edit. My hat is off to them.

Writers don't turn blank pages into novels and manuscripts into books without a lot of help. Thanks to: Jac Jemc and Beau Golwitzer, who kindly read and commented on early drafts; Gretchen Kalwinski, whose thoughtful editing proved the springiest of springboards for the novel's improvement; Jacob Knabb, Naomi Huffman, Catherine Eves, Alban Fischer, Ben Tanzer, Victor David Giron, and everyone at Curbside Splendor; my friends and colleagues at closerlook; my teachers and mentors, who know who they are; Robert Duffer, Mike Sacks, Ryan Bartelmay, Rene Ryan, Kevin Leahy, Patricia McNair, Nami Mun, Claire Zulkey, Steve Delahoyde, Mark Bazer, Liz Mason, Ryan Mason, the Trap Door Theatre Company, and Constance A. Dunn.

Finally, my deepest gratitude goes to my family and friends; to my parents, brothers and sister for their love and support; to Donovan and Dawson for loving one another as brothers; and to Tiffany, who gave me much of the time I took to write this novel and enriched my art with her own.

Dave Reidy's fiction has appeared in *Granta* and other journals. His first book, a collection of short stories about performers called *Captive Audience*, was named an Indie Next Notable Book by the American Booksellers Association. Reidy works at closerlook, inc., where he is the VP of Creative. He lives in Chicago, Illinois.

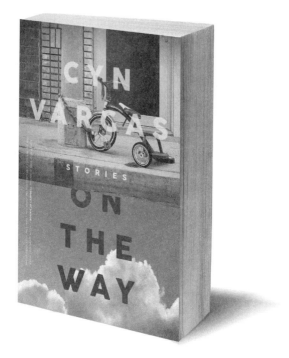

ON THE WAY

STORIES BY CYN VARGAS

"In these fresh, sensual stories, Vargas bravely explores family, friendship and irreconcilable loss, and she will break your heart nicely." —**BONNIE JO CAMPBELL**

Cyn Vargas's debut collection explores the whims and follies of the human heart. When an American woman disappears in Guatemala, her daughter refuses to accept she's gone; a divorced DMV employee falls in love during a driving lesson; a young woman shares a well-kept family secret with the one person who it might hurt the most; a bad haircut is the last straw in a crumbling marriage. In these stories, characters grasp at love and beg to belong—often at the expense of their own happiness.

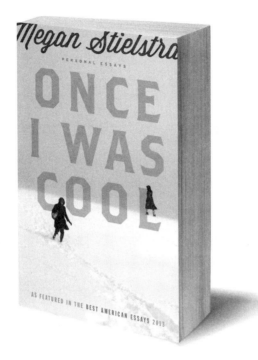

ONCE I WAS COOL
ESSAYS BY MEGAN STIELSTRA

"Stielstra is a masterful essayist. From the first page to the last, she demonstrates a graceful understanding of the power of storytelling." —ROXANE GAY

In these insightful, compassionate, gutsy, and heartbreaking personal essays, Stielstra explores the messy, maddening beauty of adulthood with wit, intelligence, and biting humor. The essays in *Once I Was Cool* tackle topics ranging from beating postpartum depression by stalking her neighbor, to a surprise run-in with an old lover while on ecstasy, to blowing her mortgage on a condo she bought because of Jane's Addiction. Or, said another way, they tackle life in all of its quotidian richness.